CW0032800£

ACKNOWLEDGMENTS

So many thank yous for today: where do I start?

My mum, thank you, Mum. You have read every chapter of the Stanton series as I have written them and love my story, I love you. To my beautiful friend Vicki. Vicki, you are my friend, my confidant and my most valuable critic, your incessant question "why" makes me always strive to be better. Thank you so much for everything you do. To Amanda, you were one of my first readers that contacted me through my Facebook page. There are no words to express how much I appreciate everything that you do for me and how much I value your friendship. You are one of the most thoughtful people I know. Thank you. To Rachel, you were a reviewer from the other side of the world that contacted me after reading Stanton to see if I needed help, and it turns out I did. You have become an amazing caring friend and along with Amanda you make me laugh every day. Thank you.

To the awesome girls from the Tee Swan's Troops gang, a bunch of girls who have banded together to support me with my writing and shout Stanton from the rooftops to anyone who will listen. Never in a million years did I think that writing a book or three would lead me to such beautiful caring women and I can't thank you enough for all that you do. To my beta readers, Jodie, Brooke, Rachel, Nicole, Sharon, Anne, Carly, Ainslie, Charlotte and Renee: thank you.

To the awesome bloggers and reviewers who have supported me. Authors like me would not have a career if it wasn't for the huge amount of work you all put into your pages and blogs. Thank you for your support, advice and for the new friendships I am making along the way.

And last but not least, my wonderful family. My three children and husband are the ones who have had to sacrifice the most for my passion...my time. Thank you, thank you, thank you. I love you all so very much and I could not have done this without your support.

I did it.

GRATITUDE

The quality of being thankful;
readiness to show appreciation for, and to return kindness.

DEDICATION

I would like to dedicate this book to the alphabet.
For those twenty-six letters have changed my life.
Within those twenty-six letters, I found myself
and live my dream.
Next time you say the alphabet remember its power.
I do every day.

COMPLETELY

I am completely in love with you.
I completely trust you.
But can you keep me safe?

CHAPTER 1

Natasha

Seven days earlier

LIGHT BULB MOMENTS

In what state does the subconscious mind need to be for one to be able to experience an awakening like this?

Is it the conscious mind? Does it need to be openly receptive to the information it had before? And why now? Why does this make sense only now? Why does it seem *so* real that it can't possibly be true?

I knew Joshua Stanton was wealthy. The houses, the lifestyle, the security.

Why the hell am I sitting here dumbstruck, peering out of the car like a child in a chocolate factory movie?

My name is Natasha Marx, I have thirty million dollars in my bank account.

I am in love with a billionaire.
And my life will never be the same.

The car slowly pulls into the driveway and tall black metal gates block the entrance. We are at the Kamala house in Thailand. The driver enters a code into the pin pad, and I watch them slowly open. My stomach drops at the sight of the huge stone fence surrounding the property and Joshua picks up my hand and kisses it as he smirks at my bewildered face.

"This is it? This is your house?" I ask. "Yes." He smiles softly.

Holy crap. The large lawn is at street level, but I can see it drops off to a cliff at the back of the property, and cobblestones line the driveway which winds its way through the tropical oasis. I can't see what's ahead and I crane my neck as excitement fills me. We drive past a waterfall, through the gardens to a circular bay.

"This is your house?" I repeat again as I frown. The main house is in front of us with driveways to the other houses on the property veering off to the side.

He leans over and kisses me gently as if sensing my inner freak-out mode. The car comes to a stop and parks in the covered area and other cars pull in behind us. My eyes explore the opulence surrounding me.

"Holy shit!" Abbie yells and I smile as I nod my head in agreement.

"Is this a house?" Bridget gasps. My God, I did not expect this. I expected a holiday shack on the hill, this is over the top frigging...I don't even know what...ridiculously extravagant money. Five men in traditional Thai dress come out of the house to the left, stand in a line and then simultaneously put their hands together, as if to pray, and bow.

"*Sawatdee Krap*" Joshua smiles as he and the boys bow their heads in reply. Oh shit, I didn't know about the bowing head and my eyes flick around to the others and I quickly bow my head to try not to be rude.

"*Sawatdee Krap*, Joshua," they all say and then burst into conversation.

Joshua and Cameron instantly reply in fluent Thai. Joshua then turns and pulls me by the hand to the front of the men.

"This is Natasha." He smiles as he picks up my hand and kisses it. They all smile and laugh at something he has said and then bow their head at me again. What...he can speak Thai? Oh jeez, I'm so punching above my weight here. Joshua smiles warmly. "Boys, can you show the girls to their house?" He grabs my hand and pulls me up the steps towards the house through two oversized carved timber doors.

"Oh my God!" I hear the girls scream excitedly as they disappear up the path to go next door and I shake my head in disbelief as Joshua pulls me into the house.

"Joshua," I whisper as I stop dead in my tracks.

"Welcome to our home, my precious girl." He bends and kisses me gently.

I'm overwhelmed, this is bullshit. High carved timber cathedral ceilings adorn the large room, the walls are rendered in a cream color, and dark timber floors are throughout. A wall of glass looks out to sea over the massive infinity pool and the backyards of the four properties are fenced individually for privacy. An island in the middle of the pool has a circular cabana, a thatched roof and lounge chairs are surrounding a fire pit. My eyes flick to Joshua. This is a visual sensation if ever I saw one.

"Are you serious?" I raise my eyebrows in question.

"Do you like it?" he asks.

I frown. "Ahuh," I whisper as I put my hands on top of my

head. I walk through the room and around to the left to an extravagant kitchen with every luxury appliance known to man. In front of it is a sixteen-seat dining table.

"How have you been happy to stay stuck in my tiny dump for the last month?" I frown. "This kitchen and dining area is the size of my whole apartment." I shake my head in disbelief.

He pulls me into an embrace. "I love your apartment. I feel more at home there than I do in my own home," he whispers into my forehead. "Money doesn't make you happy, Natasha, I know that firsthand."

We continue up the hall and through another set of double doors and my stomach drops. Dear God. A huge all white bedroom with a massive four poster bed in the center, fine white mosquito netting adorning it, and with yet another glass wall looking out to sea.

I burst out laughing. "This is the fucking bedroom?" I gasp. "Are you serious?"

He smiles broadly. "Look around while I go and get our bags." He leaves and I walk over to the window and put my hand on the glass as I stare out to sea. This place is unbelievable. Over to the left is another set of doors. I investigate and my eyes widen again. A white marble bathroom with a ridiculously large white stone bath sits in the center with a triple shower to the right. Bloody hell, Joshua Stanton, you are a mind fuck. I walk back out to the bedroom and run my hand up the beautiful thick timber of the post on the bed and stare up at the delicate netting. This is the most beautiful place I have ever been in. Stupid crazy rich. My eyes roam over to the bedside table and my heart stops...tears instantly fill my eyes. One lone white photo frame sits on the side table, a photo of Joshua and me. A selfie that he took of us on the beach one day all those years ago. We look so young. I am laughing at the camera and he is kissing my cheek. We look so happy...so in love. I have never seen this photo before, and I instantly pick it up as a lump of emotion forms in my throat. I turn to see Joshua standing in the doorway watching me silently.

"I love you," I whisper.

He nods as his eyes search mine.

"I'm so sorry," I whisper. How could I have put him through all this nonsense?

He nods again, unwilling to speak. "I'm here now." I smile softly.

He nods again.

"I'm not leaving again, I promise you," I whisper.

He drops the bags and rushes to me, burying his head into my shoulder and I smile. I've died and gone to heaven. I am in the most beautiful place on earth with the most beautiful man on earth. And he loves me, he's always loved me.

"The wait is going to be worth it, baby." I smile into the top of his head. "I am going to make you so happy." I start to shower his forehead with kisses.

He pulls back to look at me with darkened eyes. "Good." He smirks.

I smile broadly. "Good?' I question.

He smiles and nods again. "Because I am about ten minutes away from blowing in your mouth, my beautiful slut."

I laugh out loud and run into the bathroom. "You will have to catch me first," I squeal.

"One-way ticket," he growls as he runs into the bathroom and tackles me so that I fall onto the huge mat on the floor.

"You're going to pound town."

. . .

The flicker of the flames shadows my face as I stare into the fire. It's 10 pm and we are sitting outside on the lounge chairs surrounding the fire pit. Joshua showed me around this afternoon. This place is beyond heavenly. We went to the beach for a swim and his chef has just cooked us an amazing dinner. The others have headed off out on the town for a night of partying. I could think of nothing worse. How times change, I smile to myself. I am seated on one end of the long sofa with my feet up on the ottoman and Joshua has his head on my lap and is fast asleep. He's exhausted. He didn't sleep last night because of the break-in at my apartment.

I run my fingers continually over the top of his head and down his arm as I sit deep in thought watching the flames flicker. Who broke into my apartment? And what was the significance of my vibrator? I know I should believe that it's Coby Allender, but I don't. I think that was just a stupid coincidence that he mentioned it. It has something to do with Joshua, but what? My mind goes back to when it was taken, when was that? I rub my forehead as I think. It was when he came back to Australia and we were breaking up, not long after the hit on him. What was that hit about anyway? Was it an attempted hit or just a scare tactic? Somebody is trying to scare us. You don't steal a vibrator in a robbery and then return it unless you are specifically trying to scare the shit out of someone. It worked. I had the first nightmare I have had in weeks last night.

I run my hands over the top of Joshua's head as he sleeps on my lap. He's different here. The security has been dismissed. Max is staying in the last house on the block with the other guards and he has chosen not to go out tonight, although Joshua wouldn't have cared if he had wanted to. It's weird having all this privacy. My mind goes to Margaret and the horrible secret I am keeping. What a nightmare that situation is. Now that I know how Joshua has felt about me all along, I am riddled with guilt. He doesn't deserve to be deceived by the two people he cares about the most. I'm as bad as Margaret and I make myself sick. I've made the decision to tell him as soon as we get back to LA. It's going to be hard, but I have to do it because this guilt is eating me alive.

Joshua stirs, slowly wakes and sleepily smiles up at me. The honesty in his eyes cuts through me like a knife.

"Time for bed?" I smile softly.

He nods as he slowly stands. "Bedtime, Presh," he murmurs huskily as he grabs my hand and leads me to our bedroom. "I will be asleep before I hit the pillow," he sighs.

"Same," I murmur, but my mind is far from a restful sleep. I'm preoccupied with betrayal and paternity and vibrator stealing thieves and wondering if the man I love more than life itself will ever forgive me for keeping this secret and deceiving him.

It's our second morning in Kamala, the boys are in the gym at the end house and the girls and I are making breakfast. Actually, let me rephrase that. *I* am making Spanish Omelette while the lazy girls watch. Abbie is lying on the kitchen bench and Didge is sitting on a stool at the kitchen island. Apparently, they went to a karaoke bar last night and embarrassed themselves. What a surprise.

"I saw you on the dance floor, Bridget. Don't try and deny it." Abbie raises her eyebrows in question.

I look up from the frying pan. "Saw what?" I ask.

"Ben and Bridget had a moment." "Did not!" Bridget snaps.

I frown as I continue to flip the omelette. "Do you like him, Didge? You can tell me you know, I don't care."

Bridget bites her bottom lip as she thinks and shrugs her shoulders. "Not really," she mutters under her breath.

"Oh, please." Abbie rolls her eyes. "You are so into him."

"He's just a nice guy that's all. I like spending time with him but it's not romantically charged."

"Oh my fuck, did you just say it's not romantically charged?" Abbie frowns in horror.

I smile broadly and Bridget shakes her head as she smirks. "It's sexually charged, imbecile, not romantically charged."

Abbie scoffs. "If you are waiting for an attraction to be romantically charged you are going to be waiting for a lifetime. Shit doesn't happen like that."

"Does too." Bridget widens her eyes at Abbie to accentuate her point.

I nod as I agree. "It does, Abbie. With nice guys it happens." I start to lay out the cutlery and hand the bottle of juice to Bridget who starts to fill the glasses on the table.

"Blah, blah, blah, nice guys are boring. I want a bad boy to bend me over and I want sexually charged. Bang the romance shit you two go on about," Abbie replies.

"Nice guys bend you over," I mutter.

"Really?" Joshua coos from his spot at the doorway. I throw him a smirk. How long has he been standing there listening?

"You are a nice guy and yes, I am bent over regularly." My eyes hold his and he smiles sexily. He walks around behind me and kisses my temple as he wraps his arms around me.

"Stop it. You're all sweaty." I swish him away.

"You like sweat," he whispers darkly

"Eww, yuk, stop it,"

Bridget frowns. "You two are gross," she adds.

Joshua picks up an apple and takes a bite. "My house." His eyes dare her to reply.

She whips him with the tea towel and shakes her head.

"I'm taking a shower." Joshua kisses me gently on the lips and disappears out of the room.

My eyes flick to the two girls as their eyes meet. "What?" I ask.

"You two are really happy." Bridget shakes her head in disbelief. "I never thought I would see the day."

I smile warmly and nod. "Yes, we are." I have never been more in love with my beautiful man. Here he is how I imagined he would be if we hadn't had to put up with all of the crap in our lives. We are in a love bubble, one I don't want to pop.

"Who would have ever thought you would fall in love with a guy who is this rich?"

Abbie mutters as she takes a sip of her juice. "This whole resort thing going on here." She gestures around the room at our surroundings with her glass. "Could be half yours."

"It's Joshua's," I frown.

Her eyes hold mine. "Semantics."

"Anyway, so what happened last night?" I turn my attention back to Bridget to change the subject.

"Ben and I were dancing," she answers.

"Yes." I take a sip of my juice.

"And then the song changed so we were slow-dancing."

"Ahuh." I turn and start to butter the toast. "Then what?"

She goes silent and my eyes flick up to her from my buttering toast duties to see Ben standing at the door. Oh shit, did he hear us?

"Breakfast will be about five minutes, Ben." I smile.

Ben's eyes hold Bridget's, and she smiles softly at him. Oh, she does like him. I have seen that look before.

"Ok, thanks," he answers in his husky South African accent.

"Shall we go and wait on the deck?" Bridget smiles up at him.

He nods and smiles back gently. Oh, he likes her too. This is so frigging cute, and I feel my heart flutter a little as they leave the room.

Abbie gets up and walks over next to me. "This is stupid, how can she date Joshua's bodyguard?" she whispers.

I frown. "What do you mean?" I ask.

"Think about it. Every time Joshua needs him to go out at night, Bridget is going to want him to go out with her."

I frown as I start to dish out the omelette. "Not necessarily."

"Oh bullshit," she snaps. "Get a reality check."

"Just shut up and dish out the food, Abbs and keep that opinion to yourself. Don't say anything to Didge. She can like who she wants. I like Ben," I reply.

"Get this. She kissed him last night on the lips on the dance-floor and then he broke away."

I frown. "What...tongue kiss?"

"No, like a peck. But there was probably more that I missed."

"And he pulled away?" I frown.

"Yep, totally." She nods. "But then he was looking at her all doe-eyed all night, like he wanted more to happen but he didn't make a move."

"Hmm, I will ask Josh about it later," I whisper as Adrian walks into the room.

"Morning, ladies." He smiles.

I smile broadly at someone who is fast-tracking his way to being one of my favorite people. "Morning, Mr. Murphy, how was the gym?" I ask as Cameron walks in and takes a seat at the table.

"Yeah, okay." He flicks on the coffee machine.

"Go ask him now," Abbie whispers over the bean grinder.

"Shhh," I whisper. "Abbie, you are so punishing."

"That's why you love me," she replies.

Joshua returns from his shower and the seven of us all take a seat. I place the large Spanish Omelette in the middle of the table with the fruit and toast I have prepared, and everybody starts to dig in. Joshua is sitting opposite me.

"What's on the agenda today?" I ask.

Joshua swallows his food. "I thought we would go down and get you a motorbike license."

I look at him in horror across the table. "Why?" I answer.

"So we can go riding together," he states matter-of-factly.

I screw up my face. "Ah, no, not happening. I could think of nothing worse."

Joshua smirks. "What now? Why wouldn't you want to ride a motorbike?"

"Because I hate them and these roads here are frigging dangerous. I don't normally like to get killed on vacation," I mutter as I bite into my toast.

Abbie, Bridget and Adrian smile.

"Wouldn't you rather die doing something you love?" Joshua frowns.

"Exactly." I point my fork at him, and he smirks as he takes another bite of his food.

"How would you want to die then?" He raises his eyebrows.

I shrug. "So, doing something I love right?" I question.

He nods as he continues eating.

I think for a moment. "I would like to die in my sleep or eating a Big Mac."

Joshua screws up his face in disgust.

"I would like to die getting a head job," Cameron interjects.

"What a way to go." He shovels more food into his mouth. Ben laughs and Adrian rolls his eyes.

"I would like to die in Paris," Bridget says, smiling. "Underneath the Eiffel Tower."

Ben smiles warmly at Bridget and I drop my head to hide my smile at their interaction.

"What about you, Josh, where would be your favorite place to die?" I ask.

"Next to you," he replies quietly. I smile broadly and take his hand in mine over the table as I melt. The rest of the table breaks into moans of disgust at his gushy reply.

"What about you, Murph? Where would be your favorite place to die?" Joshua asks.

He shrugs and takes a sip of his coffee. "I don't know. I don't think I have a favorite place." He frowns. "Maybe here."

"Don't you dare fucking die in my house." Joshua shakes his head in disgust.

"That could be arranged you know," Cameron says matter of factly. "Ben and I could knock you off in your sleep." He drinks his coffee.

Adrian fakes a smile at Cameron.

"Can I get a motorbike license, Josh?" Abbie asks.

"Yes, of course. All three of you girls can. It will be fun and then we can ride around the island today." He smiles.

My stomach drops in fear. This is going to end badly. I just know it.

Turns out I was right. I told them to listen to me. After taking three hours to get my motorbike license Joshua was so appalled at my lack of prowess he wouldn't let me drive one anyway. So, I spent the afternoon on the back of his bike while everyone else had their own. We did have fun exploring the island, what a beautiful place it is...and the food is magnificent.

It's now 6 pm. We have stopped at Kamala beach and have been tubing for the last hour. Tubing. Being towed behind a boat on a huge inflatable tube, now this is what I call enjoyment. I keep falling off and have to be dragged into the boat by the poor workers. Joshua has even pushed me off a few times. It's every man for himself on this thing. The boys are doing everything in their power to push each other off at full speed. My stomach is sore from laughing, and I can't remember having this much fun. The boat drivers are getting in on it and doing zig zags in the water to try and throw us off. Abbie's bikini top even came off, much to Cameron's delight. The boat slowly pulls in and we swim slowly to shore.

"Hold onto my back, Presh," Joshua whispers as he goes under water.

"I can swim Joshua," I splutter.

His eyes dance mischievously in the water.

"I know." He smiles as he grabs me and pulls me onto his back, and the others all continue to swim into the shore. He grabs my legs and wraps them around his body.

"Let's fuck," he whispers over his shoulder.

I laugh out loud. "Let's not." I pick up a handful of water and splash him in the face.

"Did you just splash me?" he asks, affronted.

"No, it was a wave," I squeal as I start to make a dash for the shore.

Joshua grabs my ankle and pulls me back to him and dunks me hard.

I squeal with laughter as he continues to drown me. "I see nothing's changed." I giggle.

"What do you mean?" He laughs as he chases me through the water.

I cough and splutter as I laugh. "You used to try and drown me back in the day, remember? You are still a behemoth."

He raises his eyebrows as he smiles broadly. "Behemoth, hey? I think I need to fill that smart mouth of yours with my dick to shut it up." He splashes me in the face.

"This doesn't happen in my romance novels." I laugh as I splutter and go under, his warm arms then go around me and instantly I can feel his arousal. The mood instantly changes, and we are both brought to silence.

"Is this more like your romance novels?" he asks as his lips drop to my neck and his hips grind into mine.

I nod and kiss him gently on the lips. "Yes"

He smiles broadly. "Nice try, Marx." He dunks me hard again and swims to the shore.

"Watch out for sharks," he yells over his shoulder. Oh, of all the nerve.

"You are going to cop it later, Stanton," I yell after him. "Promises, promises," he replies as he swims off in the distance.

It is true, this doesn't happen in my romance novels...and you know what? This is life exactly how I want it.

"Shit, look at the bruises on your body," Cameron gasps. I look down at myself. We are on Adrian's pool deck. Adrian is in a deckchair on the right and then Joshua, me, Bridget and Abbie are lying on towels and Cameron is on a deckchair on the other side to the left. I'm not sure where Ben is.

"I know, all Joshua's fault pushing me off that tube of death yesterday." I smile with my eyes closed and my face tilted to the sun.

Joshua leans up on his elbow to inspect the bruises on the insides of my arms. "It looks like fingerprints." He frowns.

Cameron sits up and takes a closer look. "Yeah, that would be where they were pulling her back onto the boat."

"Oh right," Joshua answers. "Look at your hipbones, for Pete's sake."

I smile again with my eyes closed. "I didn't even feel it. Hey, take a photo on my phone so I can send it to Mum." I hand Joshua my phone and he starts to take photos of the bruising.

"I think I can safely say I won the tubing challenge, Presh." He gives me a smirk and a wink.

"Haha, so funny," I mutter. "Name the photo 'Joshua's trophies'."

He smiles broadly and texts it over.

"How did you do last night, Cam?" Joshua asks as he lies back down next to me.

"No good," Cameron replies with his eyes closed. What are they talking about? Oh right, they are talking about hooking up.

"Do you like Thai girls, Cam?" I ask.

"Ahuh." he answers, still with his eyes closed.

"What is it you specifically like about them?" Abbie asks as she raises the back of her forearm over her face to shield it from the sun.

"I don't know, the natural thing," he replies.

"Natural?" Bridget repeats.

"Yeah, you know, the carpet matches the curtains."

"The carpet matches the curtains." I giggle as I decipher that mentally.

Abbie screws up her face in disgust.

Joshua smiles and starts to slowly rub my oil sunscreen into my hipbones. He discreetly pulls me closer. I smirk, he loves my hipbones.

"Oh, dear God, Cameron, please tell me you don't date girls who have a carpet?" Adrian murmurs as he screws his face up in disgust.

Cameron smiles with his eyes closed. "Yeah, I can work with a sixties vibe," he replies.

"Oh gross," Bridget sighs.

"Yuk. I definitely don't work with carpet," Abbie groans. "In fact, sixties vibe carpet is a deal breaker."

"Yeah, especially shag pile." Bridget giggles and I laugh.

"How about you, Tash, does the carpet match the curtains?" Cameron asks as he leans up on his elbow to see my face.

"Fuck off," Joshua snaps. "Get your filthy mind off Natasha's carpet."

I giggle. "I'm right here, you know."

"Market research," Cameron mutters as he lies back.

"Not on the fucking market," Joshua snaps. Adrian laughs as his phone starts to vibrate.

He answers. "Murphy." He listens and then stands up in a rush, and we all fall silent.

"Don't you fucking dare!" he sneers. Joshua sits up immediately at the tone of Adrian's voice. Who the hell is on the other end of the phone? The girls and I glance at each other and frown.

"Don't bother," he snaps. "I'm not listening." He narrows his eyes in contempt as he shakes his head in anger.

"Don't call me, don't email me and stay the hell out of my life, Nicholas. We are done." He listens again. "Too little, too late." He hangs up the phone and throws it on the deckchair with such force that it bounces and flies straight into the pool.

Cameron immediately dives in after it and Adrian storms inside. Joshua's eyes meet mine.

I wait five minutes to see how the boys handle this. They all lie still and start to chatter as if nothing happened and nobody is going after him. Men are hopeless. I tentatively stand and walk inside where I find Adrian lying on his bed. I slowly lie down behind him and cuddle his back.

"Tash." He shakes his head as his anger steals his ability to speak.

"I don't want to say anything. I just want to lie with you," I reply quietly.

He lies silent and still while I troll my brain for the right thing to say. What did Nicholas say to upset him this much? He was only with him for a month...who am I kidding? I was only with Joshua for a month when we first got together, and I have been fucked over ever since. A lot of love can happen in a month.

"I want to go home," Adrian sighs.

I nod. "Okay," I answer. "We can go early. We are due to go in three days anyway."

Adrian shakes his head sadly as he rolls onto his back and puts his arm under my head. I gently kiss his chest.

"It will be ok, Adrian," I whisper. I know how a broken heart feels... it's lonely.

"I want to go home," he replies.

I nod and squeeze him that little bit harder. "Do you live near Josh?"

"No. I want to go to my parents' house," he replies.

My heart drops and my eyes close. I know both his parents are dead.

"I want to be depressed at my mother's house and have her fuss over me and make me fattening food and my father to tell me that Nicholas didn't deserve me in the first place. But no. They had to die, didn't they?"

He's angry that they died. It's a natural progression in the grieving process. I am still angry with my father for leaving me. I can't even imagine the pain of losing both parents at the same time.

"They would be here if they could, honey, you know that. It was a terrible accident, Adrian. They didn't want to die," I whisper as I kiss his chest again. He pulls me closer but doesn't answer. We lie still for another 15 minutes both lost in our own thoughts. Joshua walks in and sits at the end of the bed and grabs Adrian's foot.

"Want a drink? I'm making cocktails," he asks Adrian as he twists his foot.

"No," he replies flatly as he yanks his foot from his grip.

"Want to beat up Cam?" Joshua asks as he raises his eyebrows in question.

Adrian smirks. "Possibly," he replies.

"Get up and stop carrying on. If you want him back, go and fucking get him." Joshua stands and holds Adrian's gaze for a moment and then leaves the room. I smile at Adrian.

"Jeez, he has so much empathy," I smirk.

Adrian shakes his head. "That was Joshua being empathetic. Cameron is the soft one." I smile. My man is probably the worse communicator in the human world with me. It never once occurred to me that he is like that with everyone. And I didn't ever imagine that Cameron would be a soft-hearted communicator. I really am learning something new every day about these complicated men that have come into my life.

CHAPTER 2

I LIE in a post orgasmic state in Joshua's arms with my head on his chest. A deep level of contentment fills me that I have very quickly become accustomed to. Our love making this morning was tender and gentle. The deep connection we have now is incredible. I woke to find that he already had my body half there. He is the master of arousal and the fact that he doesn't bother to wait until I wake just amps me up even more. Gently he runs his lips back and forth over my forehead as he thinks. Our hands are linked on his chest.

"We go home in two days." I smile as I kiss his chest.

"Hmm," he answers vaguely.

I look up at him. "Can we stay a while longer? I love it here," I ask. "In fact, I think I want to live here permanently."

"I wish. No," he replies. "Would be nice though."

"Mmm," I reply sadly.

"Adrian needs to get back to work. I'm worried about him," he murmurs.

I smile as I pick up his hand and kiss the back of it. "That was some pep talk you gave him yesterday."

"What do you mean?" he frowns.

"'Get your ass out of bed', you sounded like his drill sergeant. It sure didn't sound like you were worried about him." I smile sympathetically for poor Adrian.

He rolls his eyes. "What would you want me to say? Oh, you poor thing, your life is over. Go and listen to a self-help tape."

I giggle. "Self-help tape?" I repeat. "Have you ever listened to self-help tapes, Joshua?"

He narrows his eyes and rolls over me as he holds my hands above my head. "The only self-help tape I listen to is how to fuck my girl into next week without ripping her apart," he whispers.

I laugh out loud as I roll to try to escape his grip. "I have never heard of that audio adaptation. What's it called?"

He bends and bites my neck hard as he holds me down and I laugh out loud as I try to escape.

"*Pound Town 101*." He growls into my neck as he bites me hard again.

I laugh out loud as I squeal and struggle.

He nods as he smiles wickedly. "Second disk is called, *Bend her over without breaking her*."

I squeal with laughter again as I continue to fight him. "Shut up and fuck me, Marx," he whispers darkly. "You are about to cop it."

It's our last day in Kamala. Our plane is flying us away from this heaven on earth tomorrow at 2 pm and into my new life. I'm nervous. Nervous about the life I am going to live. I feel confident that everything is going to work out between us, and I trust him completely. I smile. I trust him completely. I know in my heart of hearts that he wouldn't do anything to jeopardize our future together now. It was the best thing of all him finding my diaries. He knows now how deeply he is loved. The girls walk into the kitchen where I am making toast. The boys are in the gym.

"So, I have made a decision," Bridget whispers nervously as she looks around.

I frown. "About what?"

She looks around nervously again.

Abbie rolls her eyes. "No one can hear you in here, you idiot," Abbie snaps.

I smile and shake my head at Abbie who has obviously been forced to listen to this decision-making process more than once.

"I like Ben," Bridget whispers.

I smile broadly. "You do?" I ask as I raise my eyebrows. She nods nervously. "And I think he likes me."

I nod and pull her into an embrace. "I think he likes you, too, Didge. He would be stupid if he didn't." I smile.

She pulls out of my grip. "Did Josh say anything to you? I mean about him liking me?"

I shake my head. "No and he wouldn't tell me anyway even if he knew. You know Josh isn't a gossip," I reply.

"Anyway, blah, blah, blah," Abbie replies. "What are you going to do about it is the question." She takes a seat at the table and pours herself some orange juice as she waits for the reply.

Bridget's eyes meet mine and she shrugs. "Not sure."

I take a sip of my coffee. "You should just wait to see if something happens," I reply.

"I've been doing that, and nothing has happened. I was

thinking that even if he did like me, he couldn't really make the first move because he is Joshua's bodyguard, and I am a relative. So technically it would be unprofessional for him to make the first move."

"Oh God, not this again," Abbie groans. "Just fucking go out there and kiss him."

Bridget and I exchange deadpan looks.

"I'm telling you, make the first move," Abbie repeats.

We are interrupted by Joshua and Cameron who walk in and take a seat. They are laughing about something that has just been said. Joshua's eyes meet mine and I melt. How have I fallen so far for this beautiful man? I smile warmly and he holds his arm out for me to come over to him, which of course I do. He kisses me gently as I bend over him.

"How is my beautiful slut this morning?" he smiles gently.

Cameron chokes on his juice. "Oh fuck off, did you just call her a beautiful slut?"

I widen my eyes at Joshua to silence him and he slaps me on the behind as I walk back around to my seat.

"No. Stop eavesdropping, big ears," Joshua snaps as he picks up his toast. Adrian and Ben walk in and take a seat.

"Tash, do you and the girls want Ben and me to take you shopping for the day?" Adrian asks.

"Ohh yes," the girls immediately purr.

My eyes flick to Joshua. "No thanks, you girls go. I want to stay here. You know I hate shopping."

Joshua continues to butter his toast, deep in thought. "Josh, what are we doing today?" I ask.

His eyes meet Cameron's and then mine. "I'm working today Presh, sorry. I have to get a file to LA this afternoon."

I screw up my face, dejected. "Cam, what are you doing today? Do you want to come find a book store with me?" I ask hopefully. I know Cameron is an avid reader and that may entice him to come with me.

His eyes meet Adrian's and then Joshua's. "Umm, I have a date today, Tash," he replies.

I pout in my rejection. "I will just stay here alone and read my book then," I sigh.

"No, you will go with the girls and Ben and Murph," Joshua states matter of factly.

"I don't want to go shopping," I mutter as I take a bite of my toast.

"Suck it up, Cinderella, it will be fun." Adrian smiles as he grabs my hand over the table. "We leave in an hour."

The thing about shopping trips from hell is that they are just that...a living hell. It has been 10,000 degrees today and we have walked to every corner of every shop known to man while sweating our asses off. Ben and I have never exchanged more eye rolls in our lives. Adrian is on shopping crack, he has literally been the tour guide from hell. We have had four coffee stops and then a lunch stop in a restaurant. He dragged us to look at scenery and, in the end, even the girls were begging to get off this acid shopping trip. We arrived home and everyone went to rest. Joshua was nowhere to be found so I changed into my bikini and went for a swim and now I'm lying on a pool deckchair. One of the kitchen staff appears with a frozen margarita.

"Natasha, for you." She passes the drink to me as she smiles gently.

I bow my head in thanks. She is lovely. All of Joshua's staff are just plain lovely. This late afternoon is turning out better than I had expected and I smile as I take a sip of the divine cocktail. It is just on dark and the properties have fallen silent with everyone preparing for their night out. The staff all start to emerge from the house to light the candles and fire. I feel a kiss on my shoulder from behind, where did he come from?

"Hi baby." I smile as I run my hand over his stubble.

"Hi Presh." He bends and kisses me tenderly, his tongue gently swiping through my lips. Mmm, I like that kiss, I know that kiss. "How was shopping?" he asks.

I shake my head and sip my drink. "Chinese torture chamber times ten. You are coming to hell with me next time," I mutter into my drink.

He smiles broadly and takes a seat next to me on the reclining deck chair.

"Did you get the file off?" I ask.

"I did." He nods and smiles sexily as his eyes hold mine.

I can't help it, I mirror his stupid grin. "What?" I question.

"Just you." He smiles.

"What about me?" I question.

"I'm in love with you." His eyes hold mine and I feel myself melt a little. He picks up my hand and kisses the back of it. "I thought we would have dinner alone before we meet the others out tonight, is that okay?"

"Josh, I don't even want to go out. I just want to be alone with you in this beautiful place and drink margaritas all night with the man I'm enamored with."

He smiles shyly. "That's a good answer," he replies.

"Where do you want to have dinner?" I ask.

"Here, they are preparing now." He takes my drink from me and takes a sip and nods in approval at the taste.

"Are the others joining us?" I ask.

"Hope not," he answers as he raises an eyebrow.

"Me too." I take my drink back from him and smirk. He

stands and dives in the pool and swims a few laps while I watch him. The staff brings out another two margaritas...a girl could get used to this life...big time. It's silent and peaceful, just the two of us in this heavenly pocket of paradise, the glow from the candles and fire flickering on the water as the gentle breeze dusts our skin. Joshua emerges from the pool and disappears into the house and I lie back and close my eyes.

I wake to the gentle dusting of kisses up my arm.

"Are you ready for dinner?" He smiles with a look in his eye that I have never seen before.

"I am, just let me go and get changed."

"No." He shakes his head. "I want you dressed in that."

I look down at myself. "Joshua, I am in a white bikini and a sarong. I am not dressed for dinner." My hair is frizzy from the pool and I have no makeup on. I must look like shit. "I will just be a minute."

He smiles warmly and puts my shoes down onto the ground. "You look perfect, you are always perfect."

"You're very gushy today, Stanton."

I smirk. He smiles broadly. "Am I?"

I nod and raise my eyebrows. "I like it. Keep going and you just might get lucky tonight."

He smirks darkly. "Really? Is that all it takes?"

I smile as I lean in and kiss him. "For you, yes."

He leads me by the hand, and I think we are going inside but he takes me to around the other side of the pool and I frown.

"Down here, I have a surprise for you." We wind down a path and over to the edge of the cliff.

A surprise...what is it? I smile as anticipation runs through me. Joshua leads me to an opening in the handrail that protects the cliff at the back of the property. I didn't even know this was here. You can't see it from the pool area. He opens the gate and I see a large set of stone stairs hugging the wall and disappearing down the side of the cliff. My eyes meet his and I bite my lip in excitement.

"What's down here?" I smile.

"Just something I wanted to show you." He smiles as he keeps leading me down the steps. We get halfway down and stop to look over the handrail and I gape in awe. There is a ledge that is probably the size of a tennis court naturally carved into the side of the cliff. I can see a table for two set under a big tree and the area is adorned with fairy lights. My eyes meet his.

"I thought we might eat down here tonight," he whispers. I smile and hunch my shoulders like a little kid.

We reach the bottom and are literally suspended on the side of a cliff on a natural rock ledge overlooking the water. There is an antique handrail around the perimeter and three large trees towards the back. Fairy lights light up their branches and there are lanterns that are lit hanging sporadically. Underneath the middle tree is a lone table set for two. Citronella lanterns line the perimeter and there is a large daybed at the back of the ledge that is obviously there all the time, but which has been covered in cushions. My eyes meet Joshua's and I smile. I kiss him on the lips and walk towards the handrail. Music is piped throughout the space through speakers.

"Why have we been hanging around the pool when this heavenly place has been just below us?" I whisper as I look over the handrail out to sea. Joshua walks up behind me and embraces me from behind as I hold the rail. He puts his hands over mine as the sea holds our gaze and he kisses me gently on the side of the face.

"I adore you," he whispers.

"I adore you, my beautiful Lamborghini." I sigh as my gaze holds his. God, I love this man. Our moment is broken by four of the kitchen staff emerging from the stairs, one carrying margaritas, another carrying a huge platter of grilled seafood, and the two behind bringing a large silver ice bucket with a bottle of champagne and champagne glasses. They hand us our cocktails, put the platter onto the table and set up the champagne stand and ice.

"What time do you want dinner, Joshua?" the head chef asks.

Joshua's eyes flick to me. "Give us an hour please."

The four men all line up and then bow in unison and disappear up the stairs.

I laugh out loud. "Oh my God, isn't this the dinner?" I ask as I walk over to the table and pick up a piece of the most beautiful lobster known to man.

"This is without a doubt the best date you have taken me on. I'm giving you a ten for this one." I widen my eyes to accentuate my point as I smile mischievously.

"I haven't taken you on many dates, Tash." He smiles nervously. "Yet," he adds.

"You don't think that my apartment is a date?" I hold my hand to my chest as I act offended.

He shakes his head as his eyes hold mine. "No, your apartment is home to me. Not a date."

I smile. He's beautiful. He is wearing brightly colored board shorts and a white tank...so very un-Joshua Stanton, so very relaxed. His large, ripped body is more tanned than usual due to our time in the sun and his dark eyes are intense as they look down at me. I have sandals on, so he is towering over me. How did I ever get this lucky? The song changes to *To Make You Feel*

My Love' and I gush. "Oh my God, this is one of my favorite songs.".

He smiles and takes my hand and pulls me up onto my feet and into his arms. We start to dance slowly to the beautiful words. "Do you know why I love this song so much, Joshua?" I ask as I pull back to look at his face.

He looks down at me and gently kisses my lips. "Tell me."

"When we were young, and I left you…" I hate this memory. "I couldn't stand the fact that you thought that I didn't love you, that I had hurt you. It broke me. I listened to this song on repeat for two years," I whisper. Hurt lingers in my psyche as if it was yesterday.

"I know," he whispers as his eyes hold mine.

I pull back to look at his face. Huh? How does he know that? Oh shit, the diaries. I smile broadly. "Of course, you know that." I shake my head as I smile and kiss his shoulder and lay my head on his chest.

"Tash, when we were young, did you know why I came to your tent that night?" he asks.

We stop dancing and stay still. I shake my head. This is very quickly becoming a night of confessions.

"I came to your tent not because I wanted sex. I didn't want sex."

"You didn't." I smirk, yeah right.

"I came to your tent because for the first time in my life I wanted to lie next to someone that I cared about, to hold you as you slept, to keep you safe."

I gently kiss his lips. "That's a lovely thing to say." I smile.

"I didn't mean for things to progress as they did. I never set out to pursue you," he whispers.

"I know, baby," I reply.

He kisses me gently again.

"I'm glad you did because we wouldn't have what we have today if you hadn't, Joshua." I smile softly.

Our lips meet again, and he gently dusts my forehead with soft kisses. "Natasha, I am a very rich man, but I didn't know the true value of wealth until you came back into my life. Everything was meaningless."

My eyes tear up at his words.

We stop dancing again. "Do you know how much I love you?" he whispers as he tenderly takes my lips in his, his tongue gently swiping into my mouth.

I smile again through tear-filled eyes and nod through the lump in my throat.

The song changes to *'The Power of Love'* by Gabrielle Aplin and I smile broadly. This is without a doubt my most favorite song of all time. Her hypnotic voice hums.

Dreams are like angels They keep bad at bay

"You are pulling out the big guns tonight, my Lamborghini." I smile as I kiss his shoulder. I am loving that he knows my favorite songs now.

"You think." He smiles as he kisses my forehead.

I nod as my eyes close on his shoulder. This is turning out to be the best night ever. He suddenly pulls from my grip and drops to his knee and my eyes widen.

"Natasha, you have been the biggest blessing in my life and it's one that I can't carry on without." He fusses around in his pocket and my eyes widen when he pulls out the biggest ring I have ever seen. I hold my hands over my mouth in shock.

Is this happening?

"I didn't even know what true love was until I met you. You

are the only woman I have made love to, the only woman I have loved...will ever love. I need you to marry me."

I stand still with my hands over my mouth in shock, my eyes filled with tears as my beautiful Lamborghini is down on one knee. He pulls my hand out and slides the ring onto my finger. Through tear filled eyes I hold my hand out and look at the ring on my hand.

"Are you going to answer me?" he asks nervously.

I'm in shock. "Is this real?" I whisper through my tears.

He nods lovingly. "Yes, Presh, it's as real as it comes."

I giggle and start to nod. "Yes, yes." I grab him in an embrace. "A million times yes."

He stands and grabs me and squeezes me hard, my tears rolling freely down my face. "I love you," I whisper.

"I love you too, so much," he whispers into the top of my head as he showers my face in kisses.

Holy shit.

I pull out of my fog and look at my hand. Bloody hell, it's huge. A thin rose gold band and an oval diamond...let me rephrase that, a frigging huge oval diamond. It is without a doubt the most beautiful ring I have ever seen. I shake my head with my hand held out. Joshua smiles and grabs me, his lips taking gentle possession of my mouth. I'm too excited. I pull out of the kiss and look at my hand again.

"I don't believe this." I smile as I bite my lip in excitement.

He shakes his head in amusement and walks over to the table and drinks his margarita in one gulp and I laugh.

"That was fucking nerve-wracking," he stammers.

"Oh, as if you were nervous," I tease as I pick up my margarita and sip it. "You knew what I would say." I smile.

"I didn't know what you would say. This life of mine is a lot to take on. Even for me." He widens his eyes to accentuate his point. I smile broadly and my eyes hold his as he gazes at me lovingly.

"We are getting married," I whisper.

He smiles broadly and nods. "Yes," he answers.

I hold my hand out to look at my ring again. "This is a big fuck-off ring."

He smiles broadly. "Only the best for my wife." He starts to undo the bottle of Dom Perignon.

I laugh and hold my hand over my mouth. "Wife...that sounds weird," I stammer.

Joshua screws up his face. "It does, doesn't it?" The cork pops. "Sounds old." He frowns as he pours the champagne into our glasses

He hands me my glass and I clink it with his. "To growing old." He smiles.

My heart melts and once again I tear up. 'To growing old," I whisper.

Joshua

Natasha has never been more beautiful, and I have never wanted her more. Her happiness is beaming from her like sunshine. She has been teary all night but really lost her shit when she called her mother. Even I may have had a moment at the happiness in her voice when she told her. We have just arrived at the beach to find the others. We see them at a beach bar and, holding hands, we approach the group who are sitting around a high table on stools.

"Where have you guys been?" Abbie questions with raised eyebrows.

Natasha's smile almost blinds me. "Oh, you know...just getting engaged." She holds out her hand proudly and the three girls all break into screams and start jumping around. I am then inundated with kisses from the girls as they continue to jump around in a circle like freaks.

Cameron shakes my hand and pulls me into an embrace as does Adrian. Ben throws ice at me and then shakes my hand.

"Congratulations. Did it go okay?" Adrian smiles.

"Yeah, it went well," I reply as I take a sip of my beer. I can't hide my smile. "This is a good day."

We look over at the girls to see Natasha in tears again. "What's with the waterworks?" Cameron asks.

I shrug. "I don't know. She's been in tears all night." I shake my head at her over-the-top happiness.

Cameron nods. "I would cry too if I had to marry you," he says matter of factly. Adrian laughs and hits his bottle with Cameron's.

"Did she notice the fairy lights?" Cameron asks.

I roll my eyes. "Yes, she noticed the fucking fairy lights." I smile. Yesterday, I made Cameron get up the tree and hang the fairy lights in preparation. I've never heard so much complaining in all of my life. Adrian's job was to get the girls out of the house for the day and he did that well, with not a complaint.

"She liked the ring," I mutter to Adrian as I swig my beer. "Thanks for helping me pick it."

"I knew she would. It's a beautiful ring." Adrian smiles as he slaps me on the back. "I won't ever get to pick one out, so I enjoyed it."

Cameron shakes his head. "You never know. When you marry your drag queen, she could want a big ring...to match hers."

Adrian fakes a smile at Cameron. "You're so funny," he

mouths. Natasha's eyes meet mine through the crowd and I melt. She smiles broadly and her dimples nearly split her face. Then she walks over to me and wraps her arms around me.

"Dance with me, my beautiful fiancée," she whispers.

I'm with my love and we are getting married. Anything from here on out is just icing on the cake.

CHAPTER 3

Joshua

NATASHA'S tight body grinds up against mine on the dance floor. She has a look in her eyes, the one that only she can give. She's so unbelievably hot, and she wants it from me... hard.

Wearing a bikini and a sarong, her hair loose and curly from the pool, her natural beauty is the ultimate aphrodisiac. "Josh, I need you," she whispers in my ear as she gently takes it between her teeth. I feel my already hard cock throb between my legs, and I close my eyes to hold off the arousal. How does she get me like this in public? So out of my head with need that I can't see straight. Her mouth comes to mine and she gently swipes her tongue through my open lips as her open hands run up and down my back, over my shoulders and down over my biceps.

"I want you in my mouth," she whispers as her gaze drops to my lips, and the throb once again clenches in my stomach.

"I want to taste you," she murmurs, and I can't help it, I crack my neck hard to the left.

"There it is," she whispers, her eyes holding mine as she licks her bottom lip seductively.

"There what is?" I question as I smile, she's so perfect.

"The fucking hot neck crack." She grinds her pelvis up against mine hard as she pulls me by my behind into her and I clench to stop myself. I need to get her home. She's going to orgasm here without me. I slowly grind her onto my pelvis and rock her onto me, up and down, up and down. She throws her both hands behind my head and practically climbs my body. That's it. We're out of here.

"We are leaving," I whisper as I bite her neck hard.

"After this song," she whispers. I frown as I try to make out what song is playing. *'As Long as You Love Me'* She kisses me gently and tenderly brings her two hands to my cheeks.

"As long as you love me?" I smile and she nods slowly. "I will sing it to you when we get home, Presh," I whisper into her ear. I have no idea what this song is.

She smiles warmly with those killer dimples. "Because that's all that matters, Josh."

I frown once again in question. "As long as you love me. That's all I'll ever need," she whispers. "As long as you love me, Joshua," she repeats again as she presses to get her point across.

My eyes close in reverence. That's all I will ever need too. "Fucking hell, you are going to cop it tonight," I growl.

I grab her hand and lead her to the door. "Are we not telling the others we are leaving?" she asks, looking around for them.

"They'll work it out," I reply. We leave the bar and start to make our way up the hill towards my house. It's hot and steamy and the streets are filled with people.

"Josh... sshh wait." Natasha stops dead still, and I turn to look at her in question.

"Can you see that?" she says breathlessly in excitement. I frown in question.

She gestures in front and behind us and looks at me excitedly. I look around.

"I don't see anything," I reply.

She smiles broadly and points at me. "Exactly my point. There is no one following us, there is no one in front of us. Nobody is driving us or guarding or eavesdropping on us and I don't have to watch what I say, and I could just have sex with you right here if I wanted." She throws her arms up in the air in excitement.

My heart drops. "Do you really hate it that much?" I ask.

She senses my hurt. "No, Josh, it is a small trade off to have you in my life, but I am very much enjoying it tonight." She kisses me gently. "Private time with you is a rare gift." We stand still for a moment, locked in an embrace and enjoying the peace and the time alone.

We continue up the hill and walk past a shop. "I need some water. It has to be 40 degrees," I mutter and I duck into the shop and buy some water as Natasha waits out the front. She's right, it is amazing not having anyone else around.

Natasha

I stand waiting for Joshua outside the shop. What a freaking awesome night. I hold my hand out in front of me to look at my ring again and I smile broadly. I love it, I can't believe he asked me to marry him. Is this really happening?

"What's a nice girl like you doing in a place like this?" Joshua asks sexily as he emerges from the shop. His eyes drop down my body and he gently cracks his neck.

Arousal fills me at the sound of his sexy voice. "Waiting for my fiancé," I reply smoothly.

He raises his eyebrows. "Engaged, that sounds old."

I smirk and look around. "You had better get out of here before he gets back, or he will pummel your ass. I don't want any trouble."

He walks up to me and slowly cups my breast with his hand. "Maybe it's your ass that needs to be pummeled." he purrs.

My eyes widen and I look around nervously. Shit, is anyone watching us?

"Why don't you let me show you why you shouldn't marry this guy?" he whispers.

I smile broadly as I take his bottle of water from him and take a drink. "You think I shouldn't marry this guy?" I ask.

He shakes his head. "No, I don't."

"He's a Lamborghini," I smirk.

"Pfft, he's a motorbike. The girl who gave him that name was deluded." He smirks.

I smile again, I like this game.

"What's your name?" he asks as he runs his hand down along my jaw and then down my clavicle to finally cup my breast with his hand. His thumb brushes back and forth over my nipple through my bikini top.

"Precious," I whisper as his touch steals my ability to speak.

His eyes drop to my lips and he gently swipes through my open mouth with his tongue.

"I bet you are," he whispers as his hand goes to the back of my head to hold me still.

"Precious," he whispers as he lifts my chin so that my face

meets his. "We are going to go over to the beach. I have something I want to show you, something I want to talk you out of."

I look around to the beach behind us as I play along. "But my fiancé will be back soon and I'm not that type of girl," I whisper.

He bends and gently kisses me again. I feel his hard arousal against my body. "Trust me, you are that kind of girl. I just want to talk to you, nothing more." Our kiss deepens and I feel giddy as his body starts to take me over.

"Just talk," I whisper into his kiss.

He nods. "Maybe steal a kiss or two," he whispers between kisses. "You can do that, can't you? Give me that before he comes back."

I nod and smile. "I suppose," I whisper into his lips.

He grabs my hand, and we walk across the road to the beach and down onto the sand. It is darkened but there are scatterings of people. Most are walking along the water's edge and others are at the back near the road. He leads me to the middle of the beach and lies down on his back on the sand.

"Lie on top of me," he whispers.

I look around nervously. There are people everywhere. "But my fiancé," I whisper.

"Your fiancé's not here," he snarls as he grabs my legs and pulls them over to straddle him. I fall on top of him. He grabs my head between his hands and kisses me deeply and slowly as he gently rocks me onto his hardness, backwards and forwards, backwards and forwards. As my eyes start to roll back in my head, he quickly moves me so that I am on the sand and he is on his side leaning on his elbow over me. His dark eyes drop down my body and he pulls my sarong apart, his eyes lingering on my white bikini that is glowing in the moonlight.

"What's in here?" he whispers as his fingers start to rub me through my bikini bottoms. His dark eyes watch my lips.

"Something you can't have," I whisper as I hold off a shudder of arousal.

He slips his fingers under the side of my bikini bottom and through my wet flesh, and his eyes close in pleasure. "Judging by how wet you are, it's something you want me to have. Something I'm taking if I want it." His strong fingers circle through my swollen flesh and over my clitoris. My head throws back into the sand. I can hear people talking all around us and here he is doing this to me so publicly. We need to stop.

"But my fiancé," I whisper again.

"You won't be thinking of your fiancé when I pump you full of my come, I promise you that." He pushes three of his fingers into me aggressively and I cry out and grab his forearm as if I am going to stop him, but we both know I won't. His fingers start to work me, and my legs start to open by themselves as I breathe heavily. His hand drops down and he undoes his board shorts and pulls his engorged penis out, then he aggressively grabs my hand and wraps it around him and my eyes close in pleasure. He's dripping with pre-ejaculate, so ready...so fucking hot.

His tongue once again dives into my mouth and he starts to work me even rougher, harder and I can hear voices all around. This is too intense... too public.

"Baby," I whisper as arousal starts to steal my brain.

"I'm not your baby," he growls as he lifts me and positions me above him and impales me in one move.

We stay still, his body deep within mine, our breathing so labored that we are panting. His hands drop to my hipbones and he starts to move me backwards and forwards slowly.

Subtly to the outside world but magnified between us and his dark eyes watch my lips as his mouth hangs slack.

He shakes his head and I know he is trying to hold off his orgasm. Oh, you're going to come alright, baby. I move from my knees and bring my feet to the sand in a squatting position, my feet up near his shoulders. I know this is his favorite position.

"Fuck me," I whisper.

He loses control and lurches deep into my body and sits up suddenly. I cry out at the change of position. His hands go to the back of my shoulders and he starts to ride me hard, lifting me up and down aggressively onto his hard length as his lips drop to my neck and he sucks me.

I cry out and lurch forward as an orgasm the size of a freight train hammers through my body.

"Fuck," Joshua growls as he holds himself buried deep inside me and shudders as a strong orgasm rips through him. We stay still, panting heavily, both breathless. My head drops to his shoulder and he showers my face in gentle kisses.

"I think I love you," he whispers, and he lifts my chin to bring my mouth to his where I am gifted with a beautiful kiss. "You can't marry this guy."

I wake to the sound of birds and the filtered sunlight that is seeping through the window, we must have forgotten to close the shutters last night. Joshua is next to me on his back and fast asleep. My eyes drop and linger on my beautiful man. His dark hair is in stark contrast to the crisp white bed linen. His large red lips slightly open as he breathes, and his skin is darker than usual due to all of our time in the sun. What an amazing week, unguarded time with my love, a wedding proposal and this beautiful place.

I look around at our opulent surroundings and the fine white netting hanging around the bed. My eyes go back to Joshua and drop down his body, with his large thick chest rising and falling, down to the tattoo of my name branding his side, over his ripped stomach and the fine trail of dark hair that runs from his navel down to his pubic hair, and his beautiful soft penis. It's not often I see it so lifeless. I have never met a man so blatantly sexual. I know my ex-boyfriends were nothing like Joshua and they weren't even actually getting sex. Joshua would never stand for that; he would have just taken what he wanted.

I smile, that's what I love about him, he knows my body better than I do... knows how much it can take, and what I need. Last night he pushed me until we couldn't go any further due to exhaustion. Our public display on the sand at the beach was followed gently and intimately in the ocean, and then by foreplay in the pool when we got home and then again in the shower before we went to sleep. Each time deeper and harder than the time before. I'm surprised he didn't crack the tiles in the bathroom. I lean up onto my elbow and gently kiss his chest.

"I love you," I whisper as I lie down and put my head on his chest.

His arms gently encase me, and he kisses my forehead. "Good morning, my beautiful girl," he whispers croakily.

"Good morning, motorbike," I reply, and he smiles broadly and closes his eyes.

"Mmm, that guy would have said anything to get you on your back on that sand last night."

"Would he have?" I giggle.

He nods slowly with his eyes closed. "Yes, he would have, serial sex deviant for sure."

I smile. "He seemed pretty hot to me; I would like another night with that man."

He kisses my forehead. "Yes, you would. That's why you're a beautiful slut."

We both smile. "I don't want to go home today, Josh, can't we just stay here?" I ask.

He shakes his head. "No, we will be back here soon enough. You will love LA, Tash. You just need to give it some time." He kisses me gently on the lips and heads to the bathroom. I go to the window and put my hands on the glass and stare out to sea. This place really is paradise. What does he mean I have to give it some time? Does he think I will hate it at first? My stomach drops. I have no idea what to expect or who to trust. I'm actually really glad the girls have come with us to help me adjust.

"What are the plans for the day?" I ask as I step into the shower.

Joshua gets in behind me.

"Murph is making us breakfast and then I am training while you lie by the pool like a mermaid."

"Mermaids are overrated," I reply flatly. "How come you never hear of mermen?"

Half an hour later we walk out onto the pool deck in Ben and Adrian's house where breakfast is being served and I laugh as I see everyone. They all cheer at our arrival. It's been a massive week here in Thailand. My whole life has changed.

"You all look like shit." I giggle.

"Shut up," Bridget retorts as she glares at me.

Adrian lifts his head from his hands. "Where did you two disappear to last night?" he asks.

"We went to celebrate alone." Joshua smiles as he picks up

my hand and kisses the back of it. My cheeks heat, it was more like a public celebration.

"Where's Cameron?" I ask.

"In the kitchen," Ben replies.

Joshua and I walk through the house and into the kitchen to see Cam. He is on the phone and his anxiety level is through the roof. Joshua frowns as he listens. Cameron hangs up the phone and drops his head into his hands.

I frown at Joshua in question and he shrugs in return. "What's up?" Joshua asks quietly.

Cameron's haunted eyes meet his. "The blood tests came back," he whispers.

"And?" Joshua replies.

"I'm not a Stanton," Cameron whispers.

What?!

Dear God, my world spins as my eyes fly to Joshua.

Joshua frowns. "What are you talking about? I thought you needed the blood tests for some university assignments."

Cameron shakes his head as he leans back onto the bench and runs both hands through his hair in frustration. "No," he whispers.

I start to hear my pulse in my ears as my cortisol escalates at a dangerously high pace.

"You've lost me," Joshua snaps. "What the hell are you talking about?"

"I did the testing for paternity because I knew that I didn't have the same blood type as you and I thought it was unusual," he replies.

Joshua frowns. "And?" he questions. I stand still, riveted to the spot. Oh my God, oh my God, *oh my fucking God*.

"You and Wilson have the same blood, but I don't."

What? Huh? I screw up my face in question. What does that

mean? My head is spinning. How can Joshua have the same blood type as Wilson? There must be some mistake. My heartbeat is thumping through my chest.

Joshua frowns again. "Speak fucking English," he snaps.

"It means there is no way genetically that you and I have the same father," Cameron replies.

I gently grab Joshua's hand in sympathy and he rips it from my grip angrily. I swallow the lump in my throat as fear fills me.

"Fuck off, that's bullshit," he snaps.

Cameron flies into a fury. "You think I am making this up? What are you fucking worried about? It's me that isn't a Stanton. Not you!"

I put my head into my hands. I'm confused. What the hell is going on? How is Wilson's blood type the same as Joshua's?

"Hang on. Wait a minute," I say gently, trying to defuse the situation. "Cameron, what blood type does your father have?" I ask.

"I don't know," he replies.

I frown again. "So how do you know you are not a Stanton?" I ask.

He shakes his head sadly. "I don't, but I know that Josh and I have different fathers. There is no way that we can be full brothers, and seeing that Josh and Wilson have the same blood type I am assuming it is me."

"What about Scott?" Joshua asks.

"He didn't get tested, remember," Cameron replies.

This is a nightmare. I hold my hand over my mouth. I think I'm going to be sick.

Joshua puts both of his hands over his face and I slump into the chair. What in the hell is going on? The lie I thought I knew is another lie... to cover God knows what lie. That fucking bitch Margaret. What has she done now?

"It's not true. That's bullshit," Joshua snaps.

Abbie comes around the corner. "You guys coming to eat or what?" She smiles excitedly as she pulls me into an embrace. "I can't believe you are getting married." She grabs Joshua into a headlock, and he forces out a smile. "You did good Stanton." She giggles.

"We will be out in a minute, babe." I fake a smile, and she picks up the napkins and disappears back out the door. Cameron's haunted eyes meet Joshua's and I die a little inside. Now is the time, I have to tell them now, but do I tell Joshua alone or with Cameron? And what do I know? I don't know the truth that's for sure.

"Let's just have breakfast and not tell anyone until we know the facts," I murmur. "It may be some crazy mix-up."

Joshua nods and puts his arm around Cameron to comfort him. Cameron is distraught and tears fill his eyes and Joshua drops his head to Cameron's shoulder. They stand still in an embrace and the hurt in the room is so thick that you could cut it with a knife. How could she do this to her two sons? You don't fuck around with people's paternity, bitch.

"Let's just go and have breakfast and we will sort out this mess when we get back to LA," I whisper. "Until we know the facts we can't jump to conclusions."

They both nod as they pull away from each other.

I head out to the table and everyone cheers loudly. Oh God, not now fuckers. I rub my forehead in frustration.

Adrian raises his glass of orange juice as Joshua takes his seat next to me. "To the happy couple." He toasts, and everyone repeats "To the happy couple". Joshua forces a smile and kisses me gently on the cheek. Perspiration starts to burn my armpits as my uncomfortable state becomes apparent. Cameron still hasn't returned to the table. Oh God, this is a nightmare.

My eyes flick around the table and I see Bridget looking sad up the other end of the table. I frown in question and she subtly shakes her head and forces a smile. Does she know? Has she overheard what we said? Something is definitely wrong with her; I can tell from her facial expression. Cameron eventually comes out and takes a seat on the other side of me and I grab his hand. Here I sit between two men who I love, both holding my hand for comfort, all three of us having no idea what the hell is going on.

"When are you getting married?" Abbie asks, oblivious to my inner turmoil.

I squirm uncomfortably. "Not sure," I reply.

Joshua keeps looking down at his breakfast. "Maybe in twelve months or something," I mutter.

Joshua looks up from his breakfast and frowns. "More like a month," he snaps. "I will not be waiting twelve months to get married. I've done it now, it's happening."

Everybody snickers over their breakfast.

I smile nervously and pick up his hand and kiss the back of it.

I am so uncomfortable.

"Okay, baby, whenever you want," I reply quietly, trying to diffuse his tension. The table breaks into chatter but my mind and stomach are in turmoil. What's going on here? What has Margaret done and how is Joshua going to react when I tell him what I know? Damn this bitch... ruining my heavenly engagement... and Joshua's freaking life.

I stare into space throughout breakfast, trying my hardest to get the words together in my head.

"I am so being the stylist to this wedding." Adrian smiles excitedly.

"Oh, get lost, I am," Bridget chimes in. "You can plan

Cameron's wedding."

"Well, you'll be waiting a while. I'm not getting married until I'm forty," Cameron sighs, defeated.

"Oh, get off it. When you meet her, she will wear your balls for earrings, like Natasha wears Joshua's." Adrian smiles.

I giggle and he clicks his juice glass with mine.

Joshua doesn't even respond and my heart drops as my eyes flick to him. I doubt he is even hearing this conversation, he's miles away. Oh God, what's he thinking about? This is horrific. I glance at Cameron and he too is sitting pensive and still. I start to eat for China while I notice Joshua hasn't eaten a thing.

After twenty minutes in this torture chamber, I need to get away, I can't handle seeing them like this. I stand and take my plate to the kitchen. "Thanks, Adrian. I'm going to head back and start packing." I smile as I gesture to the door with my thumb.

He stands and wraps his arms around me. "I'm so happy for you both." He smiles. "I have been on Team Natasha all along you know." He gently kisses my cheek and I melt. I really couldn't ask for Joshua to have nicer friends. Day by day I'm coming to love Adrian just as much as he does. Unable to help it I tear up. I want to run away. I don't want to have this damn conversation. It's only going to cause more hurt... hurt that isn't deserved. Adrian pulls back from our hug and frowns slightly at my tear-filled eyes.

"I'll walk you out." He gestures to the door and I reluctantly follow.

"I'll be there in a minute, Presh," Joshua calls after me.

"What's wrong chick?" Adrian asks as he pulls me into an

embrace and kisses my forehead.

I shake my head, unable to speak past the lump in my throat. "I'm just really happy," I push out.

He smiles broadly. "Me too."

I pull out of his grip and head back to the safety of our room where I start to pace as I wait for Joshua. For fifteen minutes I pace with my stomach in knots until finally he appears.

"You ok, Presh?" He sighs as he flops onto the bed and holds his arm out for me to join him.

I shake my head. "No, Josh. I know something." He frowns.

"What do you mean?" he asks.

My heart starts to hammer in my chest. "I have had a conversation with your mother about paternity."

He frowns. "What do you mean?"

I try really hard, but I can't help it and the tears of guilt break the dam.

"Answer me, Natasha!" he demands

I shake my head frantically. "I don't actually know what's true anymore and I haven't told you before because I didn't know whether it was true and..." I swallow the lump in my throat again. This is coming out all wrong.

"And what!" Joshua yells, making me jump.

"Margaret told me that she had a very hard time when Scott was a baby."

He walks over to the window and stares out to sea with his back to me. "Go on," he murmurs.

I twist my hands together in front of me nervously. "She and your father had grown apart and your mother thought he was having an affair." His eyes snap around to me, and I shrug. "But I don't know if that's true anymore," I whisper.

He slumps back onto the bed and runs both of his hands through his hair, unable to make eye contact with me.

"She told me that she had an affair and that you were another man's child."

Joshua's horrified eyes meet mine. *Dear God, help me.*

CHAPTER 4

Natasha

JOSHUA FROWNS. "WHAT DO YOU MEAN"

I swallow the huge lump in my throat. "I don't know if it's true."

"What are you talking about?" he sneers.

"Just like I said," I whisper, frightened.

"When?" he snaps.

The tears start to flow. "Your mother came to me when we were broken up." I drop my head in shame.

Joshua stands deathly still as he inhales deeply.

"You never thought, not once, to tell me this?" he yells.

I jump at his venom as I break into full blown tears.

"Joshua, I'm so sorry," I sob. "I didn't know if it was true or if it was a test to see if she could trust me."

He frowns as he listens to me. "You think this is a test?"

I shrug. "It can't be true, Joshua, you and Will have the same blood type. Her secret was a lie."

He frowns as he drops to the bed and puts his head into his hands.

"It wasn't my place to tell you. This is a family matter. I was so mad at your mother for telling me this."

He looks up at me as a thought crosses his mind. "She told you this before you came to me?"

Oh shit, my stomach drops. "Yes," I whisper.

"And that's the only reason you came to me!" he yells, making me jump again.

I nod. "I thought I murdered my father, Joshua. She told me this so that I could forgive myself and for that I will always be grateful to her," I whisper through tears.

He glares at me as he thinks.

"Joshua, I was dying... she was trying to help me in some fucked up way." My tears roll down my face as guilt eats me alive. "We don't even know if it's true!" I scream.

He stands and walks back over to the window as he thinks. "I was protecting you," I whisper.

He turns angrily. "You were protecting my mother!" he yells. He looks at me filled with disgust and storms past me out of the room.

He's not going to forgive me for this. What have I done? I drop to the bed in a fit of tears. All along I knew this was coming and yet I talked myself into thinking it would be all ok. This is anything but okay. I should have told him... but then it's not even true. Wait till I get my hands on that fucking bitch. I suddenly hear Max and Ben's voices echoing through the front door. "Natasha," Max calls.

I jump up and wave my hands around frantically. I don't want them to see me crying. I run to the walk-in closet and close the door behind me. For some reason I think if I squat down, they won't know I'm in here. I sit, squatting, with a deep sense of dread hanging over me and I eventually hear them.

"She must be with the girls," Ben replies as they leave through the front door.

I hold my hand over my mouth as I think. What have I done? I knew he would blame me and, you know what, he has a right to. I should have told him. I knew this was wrong and I should have never agreed with his mother to keep her secret. That bitch. What a liar. And now it seems that Joshua and I may in fact be cousins after all. Dad, I'm sorry, I've messed up again. I slump to my bottom and really let the tears flow as I wallow in self- pity.

The wardrobe door opens and Joshua towers over me. I put my head into my hands. I can't even look up at him. "Sweetheart, don't cry," he says gently as he puts his hand out to pull me up.

My haunted eyes meet his. "I'm so sorry. I should have told you." I slowly get to my feet as I shake my head in disbelief at the ugly turn of events.

"Yes, you should have," Cameron snaps from behind him.

Oh God, not Cameron too.

"What's going on?" Cameron demands.

My nervous eyes flick to Joshua and I swallow the lump in my throat. "I don't actually know," I whisper.

"What did my mother say to you?" Joshua asks gently, sensing my fear.

I swallow the nerves. "She came to me when I was blaming myself for Dad's death."

"And?" Cameron asks impatiently.

"She told me that when Scott was a baby your father was away a lot of the time and she was very lonely."

Joshua crosses his arms angrily in front of him.

"And that your father had lost interest in her sexually," I whisper.

"She said that. What, those words exactly?" Joshua frowns in disgust.

I nod nervously.

"Then what?" Cameron snaps again.

"I don't know if the next part is true." I shrug and pull my hands through my hair. "In fact, I don't know if any of this is true." My eyes flick nervously between them.

"What did she say?" Joshua asks calmly as he takes my hand in his in a reassuring gesture.

"That she had a very short affair which she had deeply regretted and that she'd finished it. Both your mother and father confessed to each other their infidelities and decided to try and work on their marriage."

Cameron and Joshua exchange looks and frown.

"Two months later she found out she was pregnant with Joshua, but she never thought the baby could be the other man's because they had always worn condoms. But then when Joshua was older, he had an accident and needed a blood trans-fusion, and it was discovered then that he was in fact the other man's child. She was devastated," I reply.

Joshua drops to the bed as he seemingly loses his balance and Cameron puts his hand on his shoulder in support. My heart sinks.

"When you fell off the horse," Cameron whispers.

I nod as the tears start to overfill my eyes again. "Yes, then," I reply.

"I remember something going on with my blood," Joshua whispers as he puts his hand over his mouth as if going to throw up.

"She said that is why she tried so hard to keep us apart from each other Joshua. She was scared that if we ended up together, we would have genetic testing for our children, and it would be picked up."

Cameron holds his temples.

"She said she was scared of this man," I whisper.

Both Cameron and Joshua's eyes flick to me. "She is still in contact with him?" Joshua growls.

I shrug, oh crap, do I tell them it's their dad's friend... no, that's going too far.

"I don't know," I whisper.

"What do you mean, scared?" Cameron demands.

I shake my head nervously. "I don't know," I cry.

"What did she say?" Cameron yells as his frustration hits another level.

"That she thought he was powerful and unstable and that he had a lot to lose if this comes out," I reply.

Joshua stands angrily and Cameron punches the closet door in anger, making me jump in fright.

"Why didn't you fucking tell me this in the hospital that day when I asked you?" Cameron demands.

I start to cry and shake my head. "I was scared, Cam, I didn't know if she had told me this to test my loyalty to her."

"Oh bullshit," Cameron yells.

I hold my hands on my head. "Your mother scares me, she's so mean... and I didn't know if it was true," I sob.

"You're a fucking liar!" Cameron yells. "You should have told us."

"Enough!" Joshua yells. "Get out, you do not speak to her like that... do you hear me?" He grabs Cameron by the t-shirt.

I hold my hands to my head. "Stop it," I yell.

"You will show her goddamn respect." He shoves Cameron up against the wall and I grab Joshua.

"Stop it. This isn't going to help," I yell. Oh my God, this is getting out of control.

"Our mother has put her through enough," Joshua sneers.

Cameron pulls out of his grip and glares at Joshua as he seemingly regains his composure. "Sorry, Tash," he whispers.

"No, I'm sorry," I whisper.

They both nod and sit defeated on the bed. "It gets worse," I whisper.

They both look at me. "I don't think your dad has AB blood." Joshua frowns.

"Why do you say that?" Joshua asks.

"Because Mum told me he has O Positive, but I'm not sure if she really knows."

Cameron frowns. "That's my blood type."

I nod. "I think everything your mother has told me is a lie. I don't know even what's true," I whisper.

"Fuck," Joshua whispers as he puts his head in his hands.

My heart sinks... what a terrible nightmarish situation.

I sit at the airport, waiting for our flight, with my eyes fixed firmly on Joshua. I have hardly seen him alone this morning since the damning information came out. He packed in silence and the only words he said to me were when I asked why he had a suit in his bag and he replied, "Because we will be photographed when we get to LA."

No anger, no animosity. No nothing. As if he didn't know me. I know he has a lot going on in his head at the moment, so I am just leaving him alone, but this is not exactly how I wanted to end our beautiful trip.

"Do you want coffee?" Abbie asks.

Abbie, Bridget and I are on the seats near the window.

Adrian is deep in conversation with Cameron at the back of the airport, no doubt being filled in on this morning's events and Joshua is sitting with the guards and Ben. He is still and silent. My eyes keep flicking to him.

"Yes, please." I smile. I am so very grateful my two best friends are in this with me. I would hate to be facing LA on my own.

Abbie rises and goes in search of coffee and my eyes flick to Bridget. Something is wrong with her.

"What's wrong, Didge?" I ask.

She smiles and takes my hand gently in hers as she looks around nervously. "Ben and I hooked up last night," she whispers.

My eyes widen. "What, really!" I look around and see Ben watching us with a serious look on his face so I quickly look away.

"Busted," I whisper.

"What happened?" I ask. Ben's hot, I can't imagine he would be anything but amazing.

She shakes her head. "Christ, this is a nightmare," she whispers.

"What do you mean?" I frown. "Oh shit, did you sleep with him?" I reply.

She screws up her face in disgust. "God no, what do you think I am?"

I wince. "Sorry, I didn't mean...what's the problem then?"

We are interrupted by Adrian. "We can board, ladies." He smiles down sympathetically at me and I know he knows, and that Cameron has probably been whining about me for the last hour.

I give him an awkward smile as Abbie returns without coffee. "What happened to our coffee?" I ask.

"Oh, they told me we were boarding so I just went to the bathroom."

"Oh, okay," I reply. I needed that damn caffeine fix.

Joshua comes over to us and holds out his hand. "Come on, Presh."

My heart skips a beat and I smile up at him. I don't think I have ever in my life been so grateful for him calling me Presh. I stand immediately and take his hand and he leads me onto the plane. We take our seats in silence and Joshua fusses about putting my handbag in the overhead bin. He then sits next to me and takes my hand in his. He is painfully quiet, and I know he doesn't want to talk. I just have to wait for him to open up to me. If I try to bring this up, he is just going to close off, that's Joshua's way. What is going on in that head of his anyway? I put my hand over his and sit still, staring out the window as I go over this morning's events in my head. What have you done, Margaret?

Six hours into the flight Joshua goes to the bathroom and on his return slumps into the seat next to Cameron who is diagonally across the aisle from us. Adrian and Abbie are in the middle of the plane and Bridget is a couple of seats behind us on her own. Ben and the guards are at the back of the plane playing cards.

"What's the next move?" I hear Cameron whisper to Joshua. Shit. I strain my ears to hear Joshua's reply.

Bridget flops into the seat next to me. Oh, damn it, I want to listen to what they are saying.

"So, Ben and I kissed," she whispers.

"Yes," I answer but I am trying to strain my ears to hear what Joshua is saying to Cameron.

"So, what's the problem?" I ask. Oh God, Didge, not now, I need to hear what's going on.

"He kissed me when we were dancing," she replies.

I smile and grab her hand. "This is good," I whisper.

She shakes her head in disgust. "So, then we got carried away and started making out on the dance floor," she whispers, mortified, and I bite my lip to stifle my smile... it must have been the night for public displays of affection. My cheeks heat at the thought that I had sex on a public beach last night. What was I thinking?

My eyes flick past her to the boys. What are they saying? "Okay, so what's the problem?" I frown again as I strain to hear above her.

"He went to the bathroom and then didn't come back for ten minutes and then when he did it was like a different person came back," she replies.

I frown. "Huh, what do you mean?" I ask.

"I think you should ring her now and demand answers," I hear Cameron assert.

Oh shit, are they going to call Margaret? What the hell is he going to say to her? Is he going to say he heard it from me? Will she deny it?

"He told me that he wasn't interested and that he must have had a brain snap," Bridget sighs.

I frown as I watch the boys. Joshua gets out his phone in slow motion and my eyes widen.

"Are you fucking listening to me at all?" Bridget whispers angrily.

"Huh?" My eyes flick to Bridget. "What did you say?" I ask.

"You're incredible. Thanks for the advice," she whispers furiously and gets up and goes back to her seat.

Oh crap, I rub my head in frustration. Now Bridget's shitty

with me too. Joshua dials the number and I sit still. Shit, shit, shit, this is a nightmare.

He hangs up. "Voicemail," he snaps angrily. Cameron replies something that I can't hear and then I hear Joshua. "No, I will wait till we get home." I sigh in relief. Thank God.

I sit still in a trance trying to imagine what story Margaret is going to spin. It seems more likely that Joshua and I *are* cousins but then Cam said that his blood is the same as his father's… if that's even his blood type. Mum's not exactly an expert on this subject. Joshua continues to sit with Cameron for the next hour and I am earning a medal for ear straining. Feeling guilty for my selfishness with Bridget earlier I get up with my iPad and walk back to her seat and sit next to her.

"Sorry, Didge." I grab her hand and she frowns and snatches my iPad from me and starts to type. Ben is not far behind us and she doesn't want him to hear.

She writes, "I know that your life is perfect now that you have Joshua but please remember that my life has been totally fucked in the process!"

I give her a sad face and take the iPad to write back. "Babe, I'm sorry for not listening. There is just some serious shit going on with the boys this morning and I was trying to listen to what they were saying. It wasn't fair to you and I'm sorry. Tell me about Ben."

She frowns as she reads the text and snatches the iPad from me and starts to type. "What's going on?"

Should I tell Bridget? I type. "Promise me on your life that you can keep a secret."

"I promise" she writes.

"There is a question over Joshua and Cameron's paternity."

She reads the text, and her horrified face meets mine. I nod as I narrow my eyes.

"I have no idea what is going on, but Cameron had blood tests done and he and Joshua can't genetically be full brothers" I write.

Her eyes widen as she reads the text. I write: "And I knew about it."

She holds her hand over her mouth as her eyes nearly bulge from her head.

"What the fucking hell?" she writes. "How?"

"Margaret told me a year ago that Joshua and I were not cousins and I have kept her filthy secret and this morning I fessed up to Cameron and Joshua" I write.

"Holy fuck!!!!!!!!!!" she replies.

I snatch the iPad from her and type furiously. "Now I know the bitch is going to turn on me because I told them."

Bridget's horrified eyes meet mine and she shakes her head. "I have no words" she types.

I nod sadly. "And now Joshua has hardly spoken to me since and I know he is furious. When we get back to his house it's going to be fucking Armageddon."

"Holy shit, does Mum know?" she writes.

I shake my head. "No and don't you dare tell anyone. Not even Abbie."

She nods. "You have my word."

I run my hands through my hair in frustration and type in another message. "What did Ben say?"

She shrugs sadly. "That he had a brain snap and that he didn't mean for it to happen."

I frown as I take the iPad from her. "Brain snap?! That's an awful thing to say. Screw him, Didge" I type.

She nods. "I know, right? What a prick!"

I nod and take her hand in mine and she takes the iPad from me and starts to type. "I don't want to go to LA anymore.

It's going to be weird now around Ben, and Joshua is going to be as cranky as all fuck. Sounds like pure hell."

I nod as I stare out the window. "It certainly does."

A couple of hours later I am woken by Joshua cupping my face tenderly as I sleep on Bridget's shoulder. "We are landing soon, Presh. I'm going to get changed," he says gently as he grabs my hand.

I sit up sleepily and squeeze his hand in return. "Okay, baby." I smile. I wait for him to finish and he emerges from the dressing room in the hottest charcoal suit known to man, a white shirt and navy tie. He looks edible, how on Earth did I ever get this man?

I rise from my seat and go to my hand luggage. Even though I know Joshua is not openly angry at me, I can feel his disappointment and I think that's worse. I would prefer he was raging mad, but then I think that's coming down the track anyway.

I go into the dressing room at the back of the plane to change. One good thing that did come from Adrian breaking up with Nicholas was that he needed intense retail therapy to keep his mind occupied and it seems I am his latest styling project. I have underwear to match my outfits, and shoes, bangles and lip gloss to match my handbags. We shopped daily for two or three hours when I finished work and Adrian spared no expense... or should I say Joshua's credit card spared no expense. The funny thing is I found out he styles Cameron and Joshua, too. They haven't been shopping for themselves for over three years. He does a good job, they always look frigging hot. Apparently, the look he is giving me is Olivia Palermo... whatever that is.

I put on my new underwear and a new ice blue dress. It's

gorgeous, made from silk and hangs just above the knee. It drapes and has a low V-neck front and capped sleeves. I think Adrian called it elegant sexy. I gently apply a full face of makeup and pull my dark hair back into a low messy bun. I frown as I pull out the high heeled strappy ice blue sandals. I have never been this matching in my life. I look like the damn queen. I then finish off the whole outfit with a cream-colored large satchel handbag.

I stand still and look at myself in the mirror in awe. I don't even look like me. I look... like I have money. This outfit was damn expensive, and I think the shoes alone were over 600 dollars. Adrian instructed me to wear this on the return flight to LA and I feel my nerves rising. I slowly open the door and exit into the plane to find everyone gathered together talking in the aisle. Cameron sees me first and does a low whistle and everyone's eyes turn to me. My eyes are only on Joshua who is sitting on an armrest.

He slowly looks up and gives me a sexy smile as he stands. "You look exceptionally hot, Miss Marx." He holds his head angled to the side as if assessing me.

I gently wipe my hands over my thighs nervously. "I thought if I was going to be a Stanton, I had better look the part," I reply awkwardly.

Joshua's eyes lock on mine and he gives me the best come fuck me look I have ever seen. "Did you now?" he replies.

Everyone else on the plane has disappeared and I inwardly smile to myself. He liked that answer, he liked it a lot.

"I like the sound of you being a Stanton," he whispers darkly with his eyes still locked on mine.

I give him a small smile. "Me too," I reply quietly. My eyes flick to Adrian who gives me a smirk and a wink. I love that man, this is all his doing. Joshua holds out his hand and I take it and he leans in and kisses me gently on the cheek. I feel like I want to jump in the air and punch the sky... this outfit is a direct hit... yes and exactly what I had hoped for.

We walk back to our seat and I hear Cameron and Abbie behind us make some joke about watching bad porn and I giggle.

We sit down and Joshua leans across and grabs my face and kisses me passionately.

"I love you, future, Mrs. Stanton," he whispers as he studies my face, his hand on my jaw.

I smile broadly as emotion fills my eyes with tears. "I love you too, Joshua, so much." Maybe everything is going to be okay after all.

Our moment is broken by the flight attendant's voice in the cabin: "Please fasten your seat belts and prepare for landing."

Fifty minutes later we are in customs waiting to exit into the airport. Ben is being his domineering self and throwing orders to all of the guards.

Max comes over to me. "Tash, when we get outside, I will be to your left, ok. Don't acknowledge the photographers or answer anything that they say to you. Keep a hold of Joshua's hand and walk as quickly as you can."

I frown at him and my eyes flick to Joshua. "Listen to him, Presh," Joshua says as he fiddles with his cufflinks.

I nod nervously. "What about the girls?" I ask.

"They will be in front with Adrian, Cam and a guard," Max replies. "Ben and I will be with you and Joshua."

My eyes flick to Ben as the other three guards start to get the luggage and exit with it on trolleys.

"Aren't we going with them?" Bridget asks.

"No, they will load the cars before we exit this room," Ben replies in a cool tone.

Bridget, Abbie and I exchange looks, frigging bizarre. "This is overkill. We are not Beyoncé you know." I frown.

Ben smiles and Joshua grabs my hand affectionately and starts to twist my engagement ring. "I don't know. You look pretty bootylicious to me." He smirks

My face drops. "That's what Gran used to call me," I murmur sadly.

Joshua hangs his head and kisses me gently. "I know, Presh," he whispers as he smiles gently. "I remember."

I frown. How would he remember? Oh, that's right, my diaries. I shake my head. Is there anything he doesn't bloody know?

The guards return from taking the bags out to the car and Ben once again starts shooting orders around. "Peter, I want you next to Bridget, please." Peter nods and moves around next to Bridget and she and I exchange looks. Adrian sighs, throws his head back and closes his eyes, obviously very sick of this routine. Cameron and Adrian then start to exit the doors with Abbie and Bridget behind them. The other guard walks next to Bridget on her left as requested, and then it is just the four of us. I remember the last time I was at this airport how oblivious I was to all of this. Adrian and I just walked through but now I know Joshua was trying to protect me and we had hardly any luggage that time.

"Let's go, sweetheart," Joshua says gently and my heart drops. I know he only calls me that when he feels sorry for me. He takes my hand, and we exit slowly and then I see it, a huge crowd of photographers behind the glass wall rushing towards us. Ben is in front slightly, holding his arms out so that we can keep walking and Max is directly next to me.

"Mrs. Stanton," they yell.

"Did you have a nice vacation, Joshua?" another yells.

Joshua quickens his pace and I struggle to keep up in these ridiculous matching shoes. Mental note, wear runners next time.

"Are you staying in LA permanently, Natasha?" another man yells.

What the hell? I hate that they know my name. We continue to walk quickly through the airport with these idiots clamoring around us. Joshua, with his head down, keeps walking with my hand in his but I can't help but notice all of the people around us looking at the commotion. At one point, Max puts his hand on my elbow to remind me to keep my head down. This really is ludicrous. Why in the hell are they interested in us?

We get to the doors where I see a large black SUV with tinted windows waiting for us. The driver opens the door and I climb in with Joshua behind me. Max gets into a car behind us and Ben gets into the front seat and slams the door in a rush. My heart is racing, and Joshua runs his hands through his hair in frustration.

Ben turns in his seat and smiles broadly at me. "Welcome to your new life in LA, Tash."

CHAPTER 5

Natasha

THE CAR TRIP from the airport to Joshua's house is uncomfortable to say the least. My hand is in his on his lap, but he is silent and pensive as he stares out the window. It is late afternoon and rain is sprinkling in a depressing way, like the mood in this car. Our moment of intimacy when Joshua saw my outfit has disappeared and with it so has my optimism.

What is he thinking about? My heart is aching for my beautiful man. Neither of us know what's going on but one thing is strikingly clear, his mother has lied to him. Deceived both him and Cameron. Which one of the boys is a Stanton? I want to comfort him and tell him it's a big mistake and that maybe he is adopted. Or maybe that his parents used donor sperm or something due to fertility problems, but we would both know deep down that it isn't true. The fact that she had this conversation in the past with me cements that information.

I am still unsure whether I have done the right thing or whether I should have just let them work it out for themselves. It would have come out eventually, the truth always comes out. Ben turns to look at Joshua and narrows his eyes as he thinks. He knows something is going on but obviously hasn't been told what. I'm going to try to change the subject.

"Ben, do you care for Bridget?" I ask. Stuff it, I need a distraction and at least I will have some answers for Didge.

"Why do you ask that?" he replies calmly in his beautiful South African accent as his eyes stay on the road.

I shrug. "Because she cares for you and I just wondered." The driver's eyes flick to me in the rearview mirror.

Joshua smiles broadly and punches Ben in the back of the shoulder over the seat. "I told you." He smirks.

I smile at Joshua. "Told him what?" I frown. "That Didge is into him." He smirks.

Ben drops his head. "I do care for Bridget," he replies.

"So?" I frown.

He pauses as he thinks of an appropriate answer. "So, I will be returning to Johannesburg eventually and..." He pauses again.

"And what?" I ask.

"Natasha, Bridget isn't the type of girl who would be easy to leave."

I smile. Oh wow, Ben really, really likes Bridget. I have big news for my beloved sister.

"Don't listen to Cameron, you fuckwit," Joshua sighs. The driver has a snicker to himself.

I frown at Joshua. "What does Cameron say?" I ask.

"He has warned Ben off Bridget for months, carries on like a big girl," Joshua tutts.

"I don't listen to Cameron," Ben snaps.

"But he has a point." I frown again.

"What's the point?" I ask.

Ben thinks about his answer again. "That your mother has already lost one daughter to overseas and she is not losing another one."

My heart drops. Oh, Cameron is thinking of my mum. I don't know whether to punch him or kiss him.

"Oh," I whisper, shocked. "I wouldn't worry. I don't think Bridget is thinking of marriage and babies anytime soon, Ben," I reply.

He nods and keeps looking straight ahead. "You should just go for it," Joshua asserts.

Ben shakes his head sadly. "No, I'm not starting something. I don't know what I was thinking."

Joshua sits up in his seat. "Did something happen?" he asks.

Ben keeps his eyes on the road. "No," he replies in monotone.

I smile broadly and nod my head at Joshua, and he smirks and narrows his eyes at the back of Ben's head. We continue up the road until we get to the large sandstone gates with the guard. It's so weird having a gated community. I smile at Joshua who is watching me intently.

"What?" I frown as I gently grab his hand in mine.

He smiles again and shakes his head as if amused about something. I smile. "What?' I ask again.

"I was just wondering if Carson is going to be waiting at my house when we get there."

My face falls. "Are you serious?" I gasp.

He laughs and shakes his head. "No," he replies.

Ben chuckles from the front seat. "Not funny, Joshua," I huff. "That man is not on my list of favorite people."

Ben turns. "I'm guessing you are not on his either." He

smiles. Joshua laughs out loud again as I fake a smile and narrow my eyes.

"You two are hilarious," I mutter under my breath. We turn the corner into the street with the beautiful trees and arrive at Joshua's space age palace gates. I can feel my nerves rise. It's been a long time since I have been here, and I wonder if anything has changed.

We make our way up the circular driveway toward the huge dark charcoal rendered palace. Fuck. I had forgotten how impeccable this place is, although I do have to admit that after being at beautiful Kamala for the last week, I am more prepared for this opulence than the first time I was here. The car pulls up and the girls' car is in front of us parked near the front doors and Adrian and two of the guards are taking luggage out of the trunk. The girls are waiting for me and have their best we-fucking-hate-you looks on their faces. I giggle when I see them and jump out of the car.

They rush me as Joshua gets out of the other side of the car. "This is bullshit," Abbie whispers as she links her arm with mine.

I nod and smile. "I know, right," I reply.

Bridget takes my other arm in hers and we start to walk over to the front steps. "It's like James Bond shit," Bridget whispers and we giggle. We turn and Ben walks past us with the bags into the house. He and Bridget exchange looks but he just glares at her.

"He's a cock," Abbie whispers as he goes inside.

Bridget drops her head in sadness and I whisper: "I've got gossip on that later."

Her eyes shoot up to me. "Tell me now," she demands.

I shake my head as Joshua approaches. "Ready?" He smiles

and I melt, for you, my love, I will always be ready. He takes my hand and we walk through the beautiful double doors into the house with the girls following us. The walls of the huge foyer are all white and the floors are dark polished concrete. A huge bright abstract painting hangs on the wall and a large pendant light hangs in the space.

"Joshua," Bridget whispers through her shock as her eyes look around the room.

"It's just a house, Didge," Joshua replies nonchalantly and as we turn the corner, we see Ben deep in conversation with Brigetta who looks over, catches my eye and smiles broadly.

"Excuse me," she says to Ben and then she comes over and gives me a huge cuddle. "Darling, you have come back." She holds me at arm's length to look at me and smiles again and then she grabs Joshua into an embrace.

"Brigetta, I have news. I am getting married," Joshua says gently to her.

"Ah," she cries. "Oh, my boy." She grabs me again and spins me around and then she hits Joshua in the chest as she tears up and shakes her head.

"You will be the death of me, son. Sick with worry I have been over you."

She then laughs out loud and shakes her head. My eyes wander over to the girls who are standing still watching the interaction.

Ben walks over. "Um, Stan, the police are on their way."

Joshua frowns. "What for?"

"Mike hasn't turned up for work for three days and Brigetta can't contact him."

Joshua rolls his eyes. "Has anything been taken?" He sighs.

"I'm not sure, but he worked his last shift here on his own,"

Brigetta replies. "So, I thought I had better call the police just in case."

Ben shakes his head. "It will be all good, he has probably just broken up with his girlfriend and done a runner."

I turn to look at the girls who are listening intently to the conversation. Joshua frowns and turns to Adrian.

"Murph, can you show the girls up to their rooms in the west wing? I just want to look around a bit."

"Sure thing," he replies and gestures to the girls to the sweeping split staircase and they exchange looks and giggle like schoolgirls. Can't they even pretend to be cool?

I grab Joshua's hand gently to show my support. "I won't be long, Presh. Make yourself at home." He gently kisses my lips and then disappears with Ben down one of the hallways toward his office. I turn and see Max standing awkwardly at the door.

"Hi Max."

"Hey, Tash." He smiles warmly.

"What's going on?" he asks as his eyes follow the boys up the hall.

I shrug. "Not sure. Someone didn't turn up for a guard shift or something and they are checking that nothing has been stolen."

He frowns. "Who?"

I screw up my face. "Mike?" I shake my head as I try to remember the name. "I think it was Mike."

He nods as he thinks.

"Can you and Joshua try to get along for my sake?" I ask. I know he wants to go and see what's going on.

"Natasha, I have apologized to Joshua numerous times and he has made it clear that if it wasn't for you I wouldn't be here." He sighs.

I narrow my eyes. "I'm going to talk to him, this is ridiculous."

He shrugs. "It's okay. Don't worry about it. I would rather guard you than him anyway."

"It's uncomfortable for me, Max, having a boyfriend and a guard that despise each other. It's damn uncomfortable." I shake my head. "You have no idea how it makes me feel."

He smiles as he gently puts his arm around my shoulders as we walk into the kitchen.

He smiles. "It will be fine, worrywart. It will eventually sort itself out."

"Get your fucking hands off her!" Joshua snaps from the other side of the kitchen where he stands with Ben.

Max's hand immediately drops from my shoulder. "Joshua," I stammer, embarrassed.

Joshua stands furious before us. "Let me make myself clear, Max. You do not fucking touch her. Got that!"

Ben winces from his position behind Joshua and pinches the bridge of his nose with his other hand on his hip.

Max stands defiantly before him. "Yes," he replies sarcastically.

"Joshua, Max and I are friends... that's all," I whisper horrified. How in the hell can he be jealous of Max?

"No, Natasha. Max is your guard." His angry eyes flick to Max. "And I don't trust him," he sneers.

Max shakes his head angrily. "I'm not putting up with this shit," he snaps. "I'm out. I quit!" He then storms from the room. My horrified eyes meet Ben's, and he shakes his head in frustration.

"Stan, calm down," Ben sighs.

"No. Fuck off. I will not have him pawing my fucking girlfriend. He's lucky I didn't sit him on his ass," Joshua snaps angrily.

I roll my eyes. I really want to throw a tantrum right now but I know Joshua has a lot on his mind and now is not the time to do it. Ben scratches his head in frustration and looks at me and I know that he knows something is going on that he doesn't know about.

"Has anything been stolen?" I ask flatly. Nothing would give me more pleasure than fighting you right now, asshole.

"Who knows?" Joshua snaps and then leaves the room in a rush.

Ben lingers in the kitchen and waits till he leaves. "Can you call Max and tell him not to be stupid and that I will call him later?" he asks.

I smile and rub his arm gratefully. "Thank you," I whisper.

"Don't touch *me*. I like my job," he teases as he pulls his arm from my grip and I smile stupidly.

"That was innocent, Ben. Joshua is overreacting," I whisper, mortified.

"I know. He's acting crazy." He sighs and heads off after Joshua. I walk out to the front garden and I see all of the guards checking things. Then I head over to the pool area to call Max. I need somewhere private. I dial the number and it rings.

"Yes," he answers, and I can tell he's walking briskly from his breathing.

"Max, Joshua has a lot on his plate at the moment and I can't tell you what, but I was hoping that you could just ignore him." I am talking in a rush to try and get the words out. I can't believe Joshua spoke to him like that.

"Natasha," he sighs.

"Ben asked me to call you and he said don't do anything stupid and that he will call you later."

He stays silent.

My mind is in overdrive and I know Joshua is going to be stressed as hell over the next few weeks. I need to keep them apart. "Have a couple of weeks off with full pay and you can both calm down. Go and see your folks."

He stays silent.

"And then when you get back, we will have a meeting and if you two can't come to an agreement then that's okay, but just don't do anything rash. Max, I know you can't get this money anywhere else. Please, for me will you think about it?"

"Natasha, I can't see this improving," he replies.

"Max, if I have to live this ridiculous life and have a guard, I want it to be you and you can guard me only when Joshua is at work and then I don't have to be with losers all the time. You won't even see him. Please, Max, don't leave. You are *my* body-guard, not Joshua's. I will talk to him, I promise. He's being ridiculous."

He stays silent as he thinks. I try to sweeten the deal.

"Take three weeks and we will talk about it when you get back, okay?"

"Fine." He sighs and I smile broadly and hold my chest in relief.

"Thanks, Max. I'm sorry about Joshua's behavior. I know this is hard for us to understand but when I left LA with you it affected Joshua more deeply than we thought. It will take time."

"Hmm," he grunts.

"See you in a couple of weeks." I smile hopefully.

"Bye, Tash." He hangs up.

Oh, thank God. Relief fills me and I go in search of my lunatic man. I find him in his huge office with Ben. I stand at the door.

Joshua has his back to me and is undoing the combination of the safe.

"No one could get into this safe. I can't get into it myself," Joshua mutters.

Ben sees me and smirks as I hold my finger up in a hush signal. "Seriously, what is Max playing at?" Joshua sneers.

Ben plays along with my game. "He is twice her age, dipstick."

"Nope, guns still here," he mutters as he finally gets the safe open and looks inside with his back to us.

"Guns." I frown. "Why do you have guns?" I ask, horrified.

Joshua's eyes snap back to me. "We just keep them in case we need them one day."

My eyes flick to Ben nervously. I'm just going to come out with it. "Ben, I called Max and asked him to take three weeks off with full pay to give Joshua time to cool down."

"You did what?" Joshua snaps.

My eyes hold Ben's and I can tell he wants to smile broadly but is holding it in. I need to stop this spoilt shit Joshua is pulling right now.

"Joshua, Max works for me, not you, and you are being ridiculous. Max is like a father to me and it is not how you portray it. We are friends," I announce as I try to act mature.

"You do not be friends with your bodyguard, Natasha, and he is too touchy," Joshua fumes.

I raise my eyebrows and fold my arms in front of me in defiance. "You're friends with Ben. What's the difference?" I ask.

Ben smiles and drops his head as he tries to stay out of the conversation. I really do like Ben and I bite my lip as I also stifle my smile.

"This is my first decision as the woman of this house, Joshua. I have given Max vacation pay and when he gets back the four of us will have a meeting." I signal at the space between Ben, Joshua and me. "And if you two can't figure this mess out then Ben will make a decision as to whether he stays or not. Ben is in charge of security, Joshua. Trust him to do his job."

Joshua narrows his eyes at Ben who gives me a quick nod. I can tell he was impressed with what I just said, and I smile broadly, feeling very proud of myself. We walk up towards the car museum at the end of the hall.

"Now I am going upstairs to find Bridget." I smile. Ben's eyes flick to mine as he opens the door.

"Want me to fix up a dinner date, Ben, just the two of you?" I throw him a wink and smile broadly. "I can book a romantic restaurant." I hunch my shoulders like a little kid. I am so match making these two.

Ben shakes his head sarcastically as he rolls his eyes. "Son of a fucking bitch!" Joshua yells from in front of us.

I spin around to see what he is talking about and there are empty spaces at the back of the garage closest to the door.

"Christ," Ben mutters. "Four cars are missing." My eyes widen... oh crap.

It's eight-thirty and Joshua is still with the police and Ben as they go over the crime scene, the girls are somewhere downstairs and Adrian has gone home. We are all exhausted and I am in my room waiting for my love. He's had a bad day and the weight is being felt throughout the silent house. I need to talk to Cameron alone about this Margaret nightmare and now might be the time. I walk down to the west wing of the house until I find his bedroom and knock quietly on the door.

"Come in," he yells.

I tentatively walk in and look around. His room is large. The walls are dark grey, and the bed is a huge four poster. My eyes are drawn to the red ropes and tassels on the four posts... *Cameron's into bondage*. Acting casual, I look around the rest of the room. It has its own lounge area off to the side, where he is watching television in boxer shorts on one of the armchairs. He cranes his neck to see who it is. I can see the disappointment when he realises it's me.

"Hi," I say nervously.

"What's up?" he replies as his eyes flick back to the television.

Oh God, can't he be more friendly. "I was just wondering if we could talk," I reply quietly. "I know you're mad at me and I understand why because I'm mad at myself."

His eyes meet mine. "Sit down," he replies, defeated.

I twist a small piece of material on the front of my t-shirt as I try to think what to say.

"Cam, I'm sorry. I should have told you that day in the hospital," I whisper.

His eyes meet mine and he nods.

I feel my heart drop. I love Cameron and we haven't been the same since he and I had those harsh words over Joshua in the hospital that day when Gran was sick. I feel my tears swell.

"Cameron, I know you resent the fact that I love your brother."

He screws up his face. "Tash, I don't resent the fact you love Joshua. I wouldn't want him to be with anyone else."

"Why have you been weird with me?" I ask through my tears. He just looks at me blankly.

"Cam, please can we talk, I am going to marry your brother and I can't have this underlying animosity coming from you. It hurts me."

He shakes his head. "Don't cry, Tash," he replies gently. I pull a really ugly face as the lump hurts my throat.

"I watched my brother nearly die and you wouldn't even talk to him and..." He shakes his head as he tries to articulate what he wants to say.

I nod sadly. "I know, Cameron, but I had to let him go so that he could see if he loved Amelie."

He shakes his head. "I don't buy that, Tash. I would never let someone go if I loved them."

I smile sadly. "Cameron, one day you will love someone more than yourself and you will do anything to give them a chance at real, deep happiness. I died a little every day I was away from him," I murmur.

He looks at me sadly as he thinks and goes to say something but then stops himself.

"What were you going to say?" I ask.

He thinks for a moment. "Were your parents like you and Josh?" I frown, not understanding.

"What do you mean?" I ask.

"Were they, like, crazy in love with each other like you and Joshua are?"

I smile and nod sadly. "Yes," I whisper.

He sits back in his seat as he thinks, and I see confusion on his face.

"Were yours?" I ask.

He shakes his head. "No, not at all."

I sit back as I understand the meaning of his question. He has never been around a couple like Joshua and me. He thinks this is abnormal.

"Cameron, there are too many mediocre things in life already... love shouldn't be one of them."

He nods sadly. "I guess," he replies.

"And just because your parents are not over-the-top affectionate doesn't mean they don't love each other."

He stares off into space somewhere, deep in thought. "What is it?" I ask.

"Have you ever been so deeply deceived that it makes you question if everything you thought you ever knew is a lie?"

"Not really Cam."

He looks back at me and I know he didn't expect that answer. "The thing is, when Joshua slept with Amelie... deep down I knew it was coming. He had feelings for her, and I had expected it all along on some unconscious level," I reply.

He frowns at me.

"Cam, it's not a bad thing. Amelie is beautiful and smart. I probably would have picked her if I was Joshua to be truthful." I widen my eyes at him.

Cameron smirks. "Well, you do hate horses."

I giggle and nod. "That's true. I definitely do."

"Joshua did the right thing sleeping with her and, to be honest, I am really glad he did because now I don't have any doubt that we are going to make it. I'm not insecure or jealous and he is better for it too because now he knows for certain that I am the one," I reply.

He smiles and holds out his hand to me in a peace offering and I take it in mine.

"Cam, I promise you as long as I draw breath, I will never hurt your brother again."

We sit still on the lounge, holding hands, and I can sense he still needs to talk.

"Can I ask you a question, off the record?" he asks. I nod sadly because I already know what it is.

"Do you think my mother is going to deny having an affair?" I shrug.

"Do you think our father knows?" he asks again.

I shake my head. "No, I don't think he knows."

I shrug. "I don't honestly know what the truth is anymore, Cam. I actually felt pity for her."

He frowns. "Pity, what do you mean?"

I shrug and frown. "Cam, I know it's stupid, but I've been thinking about it and I believe her. I still believe the story that she told me, and I think that perhaps your father has the odd blood."

He frowns as he thinks.

"But that would mean...?" He frowns again.

I nod as my eyes tear up. "Yes, I know what that means, and I doubt it, but it is possible," I whisper.

Cameron bites his lip as he thinks. "Gran would have never done that."

I shrug. "I don't know, Cam, but we have to support each other with this. We can't turn on each other." I shake my head as I imagine the shit fight that is going to go down with Margaret.

"Joshua said he is done with her," Cameron replies. I frown. "What do you mean?" I ask.

"He said he will never forgive her for putting you in that position."

"I'm not letting him use me as an excuse to not get along with his mother," I splutter.

Then I shake my head and stand. "What a nightmare. Come on. Let's go and find the girls."

He stands slowly. "Sorry I've been an ass."

I smile broadly and punch him playfully in the stomach. "Sorry I have been a drama queen bitch."

He smiles broadly. "You have, but I'm kind of getting used to it by now." He nods as he grabs my arm and twists it behind my back, and I laugh loudly.

I escape and walk towards the door and my eyes flick to the large navy-blue velvet quilt and the red tasseled ties. Mmm, Cameron Stanton, I'm thinking you are a naughty boy like your brother.

———

We find the girls sitting on the lounge near the kitchen downstairs, drinking coffee.

"Hey." Cameron smiles as he walks in and flops into a lying position on the lounge between them. Then he attempts to puts his feet onto Bridget's lap.

She holds her hands up without thinking to let him put his feet on her and I smile. "Who do you think stole the cars?" Abbie asks Cameron.

Cameron shrugs. "I don't know. Most probably the security cameras were disabled two weeks ago."

"At least they didn't get my Lamborghini," I comment.

"Oh, fuck off," Abbie snaps as she rolls her eyes. "You sound like fucking Kim Kardashian."

We all laugh. "Yeah, at least they didn't get my Lamborghini." Bridget copies me in a fake Kim accent.

Cameron's phone rings and he looks at the screen and smiles broadly. "Hello," he says sexily into the phone.

The girls and I exchange looks. He's talking to a girl.

"I got back today," he coos. His voice is different... soft and cajoling. He listens for a moment.

"What have you been up to?" he asks.

He listens and then smiles sexily. "Really?" he replies as he raises his eyebrows.

The girls and I exchange looks again.

He sits up slowly and bites his thumbnail as he listens, then smiles, stands and walks into the kitchen to escape our ears.

Abbie kicks Bridget and points at him and we all giggle silently. "What are you wearing?" he asks.

Bridget's eyes just about pop out of her head.

"Yeah, that's too much," he replies sexily in a hushed voice.

He listens again.

"Naked and on your knees." He listens for a moment. "I will be there in twenty," he whispers huskily and then he hangs up and disappears upstairs.

We all burst into giggles. "Naked and on your knees," Bridget whispers. "Who says that?"

I smile broadly. "His brother."

"Oh, my fuck, they probably have it written down... like in a journal of hot talk," Abbie laughs.

Bridget throws her head back onto the lounge chair. "Oh God, do you think Ben has that journal?" Bridget sighs.

I hold my hands up in a stop signal. "Oh my God, Didge, I forgot to tell you. Ben likes you," I whisper.

"What?" she snaps.

"He said that he stopped it because you wouldn't be an easy girl to leave."

She frowns. "He said that?" I smile broadly and nod. "Oh, fuck off, that's pathetic," Abbie snaps.

"What's pathetic?" Joshua asks as he enters the room.

"I was just saying that I can't wait to start our life here together," I reply nervously to throw him off the scent.

Joshua smirks. "I agree. That is pathetic Marx."

The girls and I burst into laughter and I wrap my arms around Joshua's waist. He is still in his suit, although his jacket has been ditched hours ago.

He kisses my forehead. "I'm going to bed." His eyes hold mine in a silent invitation and I smile.

"I'm coming," I whisper.

His dark eyes drop to my lips and he licks them in anticipation as I feel that familiar pulse in my core. My man needs his sleeping pill.

CHAPTER 6

Natasha

"THE POWER OF LOVE" by Gabrielle Aplin rings out and my sleepy eyes struggle to open. It takes me a minute to realize it's my new phone ringtone and I scramble out of bed and dive into my handbag on the dressing table.

"Hello." My voice is groggy.

"Hi, love. Did I wake you?" Mum's soothing voice coos down the phone.

I smile broadly. "Yes, but it's okay. I miss you," I mumble as I sit naked on the end of my bed.

"I just called to check everything is alright. I spoke to Bridget last night and she told me that Joshua's cars got stolen."

I blow out a breath and run my hand through my hair. "Yeah, they did."

"Is Joshua okay?" she asks.

I shrug. "Not sure, he had a bad day yesterday and when we

got to bed we didn't really talk about it. I've woken up and he is not here, so I am assuming that he is at the gym."

"Are the girls okay with you? I'm sure you and Joshua want to be alone."

I sigh. Mum thinks the girls are here for a holiday. She has no idea that the idiots committed the world's dumbest crime and that they were in fact forced to come with us.

"It's okay, Mum. Cameron is already here. Joshua and I have the rest of our lives together alone." I smile into the phone. God, that sounds good.

"You okay honey?"

I stay silent. Why does she always read me like a book? "Yes. Why?" I reply.

"You just sound off," she breathes.

I stand and walk over to the mirror and look at my reflection. "No, I'm good. Maybe a bit jet lagged," I reply as I stare at my lying face.

I can hear her smile. "I will let you go then, sweety. Go back to bed. I love you."

"Bye, Mum. I love you too." I hang up the phone.

I look at my reflection in the mirror. Mum was right. I am off. I have a sinking feeling that everything is not as it seems with Joshua and me. Last night when we came to bed and made love... actually that's not true, we didn't make love. Joshua fucked me, no emotion, no passion, no tenderness, it was like he needed a release as a sleeping pill, and I was the closest thing he could find. I could have been anybody and he would have taken me the same. It was like he didn't know me. It has never been like that before. Even through all of our shit when I didn't know what was going on between us there was always love and tenderness after we had both orgasmed, a gentleness in him that I love. Not last night...nothing like it...what does that mean?

I take a shower while deep in thought, then I put a sexy nightdress on and hop back into bed and surf the net on my iPad as I wait for his return. Forty minutes later the bedroom door opens.

He smiles as he walks in. "Hey Presh." "Hi," I breathe. "How was the gym?"

"Good." He keeps walking into the bathroom.

Hmm. I get up and follow him into the bathroom and find him getting into the shower. I lean up against the vanity as I watch him soap up.

Something is definitely wrong. He hasn't commented on my sexy apparel or asked me to join him or tried to take me on the sink... unusual behavior for my beautiful man. I stay still watching him for ten minutes with my mind in overdrive and eventually he gets out and starts to dry himself.

"Josh."

He bends to dry his legs. "Yes," he replies without making eye contact.

"Are we okay?"

He looks up. "Why wouldn't we be?" he asks and we both know there is a double meaning to that question.

"Can we talk about me not telling you about your mother?" I ask nervously.

He throws his towel into the washing basket briskly and exits the bathroom. "There is nothing to talk about," he replies flatly.

I follow him like a puppy. "Josh, I'm sorry, okay. I didn't know what to do and I didn't know if it was a test."

His eyes meet mine and he smiles sarcastically. "I'm glad

you passed it, Natasha." He turns his back on me and starts to dress. Fuck. I knew he was pissed off.

"Come on, Josh. Don't be smart. Try and see this from my point of view," I reply.

He pulls on a pair of shorts and throws a t-shirt over his head. "I have and that's why I'm not fighting with you." His eyes challenge me to say something and I can tell he wants to fight. He has that bat shit crazy look in his eye.

I swallow my nerves. "I would rather you scream at me than fuck me like you don't know me," I whisper.

His eyes lock onto mine. "You don't like to be fucked like I don't know you?" he sneers.

I cringe at the venom in his voice and I shake my head. "No, I don't."

"Well, I don't like to be fucked over like I don't know you." He glares at me and then leaves the room in a rush.

My heart races and I close my eyes as regret fills me. He has every right to hate me right now. Yesterday when he found out about this nightmare, he was in shock but now the hard and strong ramifications are coming my way. I should be grateful that he is just angry and not disowning me but the fact that I have disappointed him is like a knife through my chest. I blow out a breath as I search through my case to find something to wear. It's going to be a long day.

Half an hour later I lie on Bridget's bed. "What do you mean, he's got the shits? He was fine yesterday." She tuts as she puts her clothes onto hangers and in the walk-in robe.

I shrug. "Obviously he is over the shock and is now angry," I reply.

She shakes her head. "I still can't believe this crap. So tell me, what exactly did Margaret say to you?"

"She said that when Scott was a baby Joshua's dad had an affair and was away a lot of the time and that one of his friends would come to the house to check on them."

Her eyes widen. "One of his friends?" she repeats.

I nod. "I know and that they started hanging out and then one night he kissed her, and she told him to leave but he didn't, and he stayed in the car out the front of the house for hours and then when he knocked again at 2 am she didn't have the willpower to reject him."

"Fuck," Bridget whispers. "It's like Dynasty."

I nod again. "And get this, she said she fell in love with him and was going to leave Robert when he got back two months later but then this guy told her not to be stupid because he never loved her anyway."

Bridget stops what she is doing. "She said that?"

I nod. "And I don't know if I'm being stupid, but I believe her," I reply.

She frowns. "So how is Cameron involved? I don't get what he has to do with this."

I blow out a deep breath. "So, when Joshua was in hospital for the drug overdose Cameron saw his blood type. I still remember the moment when he spotted it."

She stops again. "You saw him see it and you didn't say anything?" I shake my head.

"No."

She winces and I nod.

"So, Cameron obviously started doing a bit of research and realized that Joshua and he had different blood."

"Right," she replies as she hangs things up in the wardrobe. "Go on."

"Remember when Gran was sick in the hospital and that kid was sick and needed Josh's blood?"

"Yes," she nods.

"Cameron asked me then what I know, and I denied knowing anything."

Bridget grabs her temples. "Fuck, this is messed up shit, Natasha."

"I know and I tried to smooth it with Cameron last night and explain," I reply.

"What did he say?" she asks.

I shrug. "I know he's mad at me and it is just going to take time, but I think we may have turned the corner."

Bridget nods. "Fair enough, I would be mad at you too if I was him." I nod.

"So, what did Josh say?" she asks.

"Well, yesterday when I told him he was quiet, and I thought it would be okay, but then last night he had sex with me as if he didn't know me."

She points the coat hanger at me. "At least he had sex with you. That's a good sign, right?"

"Mmm, I suppose. But then this morning I called him on it, and he is openly pissed off with me."

Bridget nods and walks back into the closet. "Hmm, I think I would rather him fight with me and get it over with than pretend not to be angry," she replies.

I pull the pillow over my head. "Oh God, I'm such a fucking idiot," I scream into it.

"I know," she replies. "Just take it. You deserve it so just take it. Let him fight with you and be prepared for a couple of days of shit. You are lucky he is even here."

I nod sadly. "I know. I just didn't imagine that we would be fighting on our first week in LA." I sigh.

She smiles. "Natasha Marx, I wouldn't expect anything less than drama with you. You're a walking fucking sitcom."

I laugh and nod. "It's true, I am. But it's not the 'Bold and the Beautiful', it's 'The Stupid and the Ugly'."

She laughs again and Joshua pokes his head through the door. "I'm going, Tash."

I frown and sit up. "Where are you going?" "To work," he replies.

My face drops as I see his edible navy suit and tie.

"Oh." I stand and walk to the door.

"Bye, Didge," Joshua calls to her as he walks down the hall. I grab his hand. I need to make this right before he goes.

"Do you want to go out for dinner tonight, just the two of us?" I ask as I nearly run to keep up with him.

He shakes his head as he walks forward powerfully. "No"

"Can I come to your office for lunch?" I give him a stupid hopeful smile.

He looks down at me as he keeps walking and shakes his head again. "No."

"Can I come to your office and strip?" I widen my eyes and try to be cute.

"No, definitely not." I see a trace of a smile on his lips. Ha, I'm getting to him.

"Do you want to go to a strip club tonight with the boys and I do a pole dance for you?"

He can't help himself and he smirks. "You will do a pole dance for me in a strip club?" He raises an eyebrow in question. I bite my bottom lip to stifle my smile and I nod. That is without a doubt the stupidest thing that has ever come out of my mouth.

He thinks for a moment and seemingly remembers he is mad at me.

"No," he replies.

I pull a dejected face. "So, I will just wait here for you then?"

"Yes," he replies.

"So, I won't leave the house and will just sit around and think about you all day then?"

"Yes," he replies, and I see the underlying smile again.

"So, I will just masturbate all day then and get my tight pussy so wet and soft that when you get home tonight you can just put my legs over your shoulders and put that beautiful big cock into the hilt."

He smirks and then breaks into a smile. "Goodbye, Natasha." He bends and quickly kisses me and heads down the stairs.

I lean over the balustrade rails and watch him walk down the stairs. God, he's simply delicious.

"Bye, honey," I call in an exaggerated voice as I do a wave in the air.

He looks back up and I can see that smirk again.

"I will be waiting here when you get home... because I'm like a wife now," I call as I throw both of my arms in the air and show him my ring. He shakes his head in embarrassment and smirks again.

"I love you, Mr. Stanton," I yell again as he exits the door. I smile broadly to myself and turn and see Cameron standing in the hall watching me.

"What the fuck are you doing, you fruitcake?" He frowns.

I laugh at my stupidity and widen my eyes at him. "Sucking up, what does it look like?" I reply.

He smirks. "Did it work?"

I shake my head. "Nah, he will be cranky again by the time he gets home."

He smiles and shakes his head. "Like I said, fruitcake."

I smile and shake my head around like a freak. "Being normal is so last season, Cam. Get with the times. Joshua's favorite food is fruitcake."

Joshua

I sit at my desk, swivel slightly on my chair and think. I'm procrastinating. I don't want to be here today, but then I don't want to be with Natasha at home either. Adrian is snowed under with staff issues and I am trapped in my office like a mouse. My intercom buzzes.

"Mr. Stanton, Mr. Stanton is here to see you." Eliza's voice echoes through the speaker.

"Send him in," I reply.

Cam walks in casually. "Hey"

I sit back in my chair and link my hands on my head. "What's Tash doing?" I ask.

He smiles as he takes a seat. "What's it to you? I thought you were mad at her."

I smirk. "I am, but I want to know what she's doing," I reply.

He frowns. "They were talking about shopping or something equally boring."

"They are leaving the house?" I ask.

"Um... yeah, so." He frowns at me like I'm from another planet. I immediately call Ben.

"What's up?" he answers.

"Who is with the girls?" I ask.

"Peter and Frank," he replies.

I frown. Those two are useless. "Can you go home and take them shopping?"

"Oh fuck, man, come on," he replies.

"Max isn't with them and those two are idiots. I need her safe."

"Stan, you're killing me. Stop this nonsense with Max. I am not going shopping and shit all the time."

I frown. "What's up your ass?" I ask. I never have to ask Ben to do anything twice.

"Nothing. I am not hanging out with Bridget and the girls that's all. I'm your guard, not hers."

I smile and look at Cameron and shake my head. "I'm asking you to guard my future wife, not bone Bridget, although somehow I don't think you would be complaining if that's what I was asking."

"Fuck off, man," he snaps in his heavy accent and I smile.

Cameron narrows his eyes and does his hand in a choking gesture.

"Send the other two here and you and Richard go with the girls," I reply.

"Fine," he snaps and then hangs up.

I smile broadly. I've never seen Ben like this. I think he actually does like Bridget.

"Are you calling our mother dearest or am I?" Cameron says in a defeated voice.

I tap my foot up and down as I think. "I will. When are you working this week?"

"I am on for the next five days, so in a week's time would be good," Cameron replies.

I nod and pick up my mobile and dial the number. "Hello darling," she answers.

My heart drops at her calling me that. "Hello," I reply. I close my eyes as dread fills me and Cameron stands and walks to the large windows. He stands with his back to me as he stares at the view and listens.

"I've organized my plane to pick you up in a week," I reply flatly.

"Darling, it doesn't suit me next week. I have things on," she replies.

I narrow my eyes in contempt. "Change your plans," I snap.

"Joshua, is something wrong?" she asks. "You tell me," I sneer.

She remains silent and Cameron turns to face me, looking ill.

"Cameron and I have a small matter we need to discuss with you."

"What is it?" she replies. "Our paternity," I reply flatly.

The phone goes silent and you could hear a pin drop.

"I don't know what you are talking about," she whispers nervously, and I sit back in my chair.

I narrow my eyes at Cameron. "Okay, if you don't know anything about it, I will call Dad and he can fill us in," I sneer sarcastically.

"No! Joshua, please don't call your father," she pleads.

I shake my head at Cameron as my blood runs cold... it's true.

Everything we feared is true.

"I don't know what she has told you, Joshua, but it's not true. You know you can't trust anything that comes out of that woman's mouth."

I stand in a rush as my anger hits crescendo. "That woman is about to become my wife!" I scream.

Cameron's hands fly to his head in a panic.

"Do not dare disrespect Natasha!" I yell. "This is your doing, not hers, and I will not have you slander her one more fucking time!"

"Joshua," she whispers.

"Be ready for my plane!" I scream and then anger steals my ability to speak and I hang up.

I put my elbows on my desk and my head into my hands. "That went well," Cameron mutters.

I nod, too angry to speak. I can't believe she tried to turn this on Natasha. Typical.

"Fuck, what did she say when you mentioned Dad?"

"She panicked and said please don't call your father," I reply.

Cameron shakes his head. "So, it's true." I nod. "Unfortunately, Cam, I think it is."

It's 4.45 pm and I am just going through my emails for the day when my intercom sounds.

Eliza speaks. "Mr. Stanton, Miss Marx is here to see you."

I smile. The crazy bitch won't take a hint. "Send her in," I sigh. The bodyguard opens the door, and she walks in wearing a black coat, her high heels clicking on the marble tiles. She smiles warmly and her dimples immediately defrost my anger. Just the sight of my precious girl makes my neck tight and I crack it to release the tightness.

"Hello baby," she smiles.

"Hello." I smile defeated, she's not going to let me fight with her, and it's strangely comforting.

"I wanted to come and see where you work." Her eyes flick around the office.

I smirk as I sit back in my chair. "Did you now?"

She nods again and her eyes look around the room and up to the ceiling. "Your office is very nice."

I frown, not understanding what she is doing.

"Are there cameras in here?" she asks.

I smile. "No."

She bites her lip nervously. "I thought I would come and show you what I bought today."

I raise a brow in question.

She drops the coat, and my eyes drop down her body. She is in a black suspender belt, lace bra and G-string... fucking perfection.

She holds her hand out and I take it in mine as I stand. She does a twirl on the spot and I feel my cock harden.

"You like, Mr. Stanton?" she asks.

My eyes hold hers and I reply. "I do."

"I know that you're disappointed in me but I'm not letting your mother come between us again."

I smirk.

"Do you want to be friends?" She raises an eyebrow in question as she places her hands on her hips.

I can't resist and my lips drop to the part where her neck meets her shoulder and I kiss her gently. "Are you trying to bargain your way out of my anger, Miss Marx?" I run my lips back and forth up her neck.

She drops her head to the side to give me greater access. "Maybe?" she whispers as she smiles into my kiss and runs her tongue through my open smiling lips.

"Maybe?" I repeat. "What does that mean?" I ask as she kisses me more urgently and I feel my cock start to thump as I see our reflection in the window. The sight of her in that lingerie in my office nearly makes me come on the spot. She is standing on her toes to reach me and in the process flexing every muscle in her legs and ass. So fucking hot...

"It means I have a closing argument for you," she whispers as she tiptoes to kiss my neck. She bites me and goose-bumps scatter up my arms.

"What's the closing argument?" I whisper huskily.

She slowly unzips my pants and without breaking eye contact drops to her knees in front of me. My hands instinctively go to the back of her head.

"I would like you to blow in my mouth," she breathes and then licks her lips as she frees me from my pants and gently licks up the length of my penis. I run my hand gently over her hair as my cock oozes pre-ejaculate. Fuck, I love this woman.

"And then I want you to bend me over your desk and fuck me like you hate me!" she whispers.

I grab a hand full of hair and impale her mouth with my cock. "Stop talking and start sucking because you are about to fucking cop it." I growl as I fill her mouth to the hilt and hiss as I pull out, again deeper, and she runs her tongue over the end of me as she pulls out and my eyes close. Fuck, she gives good head. Deeper and deeper, she takes me as she fondles my balls and I watch our reflection in the window until I am so crazy with lust that I can't stand it anymore. I don't want her mouth, I want inside her.

I drag her up by the arm and throw her across my desk and rip her underpants from her body. There she lies... my beautiful kryptonite. I spread her with my fingers so that I can see her beautiful weeping pink flesh and pull her breast out of her bra to get the visual of the whole package. I look up at the door as I realize that it isn't locked and it only fuels my desire even more. Anyone could walk in here at any moment, and the thought of someone seeing us like this turns me inside out. I pull her apart again and start to stroke myself slowly and vigorously, one... two... three... four... my cock weeps.

Her dark eyes watch me and her back arches off the table. "Joshua," she begs, and I start to run my head backwards and forwards through her until I can hold it no longer and I feed my cock into her hot flesh.

"That's it," she whispers as her eyes roll back in her head.

My eyes close as I try to control the orgasm that is hammering up on me. I grab her shoulders with straightened arms for leverage and I let loose: long hard punishing stokes where she can't speak. Pure desire fills her face, her mouth hangs open and she tries to deal with the brutality of my flesh ripping through hers. I rip her shoes off and bring her feet up to my shoulders as once again my eyes flick to the door. Fuck, we are going to get caught. Adrian will be here any moment. I bring one of her feet up to my face and while my cock works at a piston pace, I slowly lick her instep underneath her foot.

"Ahhh," she cries as she tries to rip her foot from my grip.

My body is now out of control and I couldn't stop if I wanted to. The desk is banging, and she puts her hand up and clutches at the air as she comes silently around my cock. The muscle contraction is so intense that it doubles me over and I pump her, one... two... three times with my hands wrapped around her shoulders, and I come in a rush into her beautiful hot body. I lean and drop my head to her shoulder as I try to catch my breath, my heart hammering in my chest along with hers.

And she kisses me, the gentle tender kiss that is Natasha. The most powerful gesture in my world is the tender kiss in the afterglow of lovemaking from this beautiful creature. Nothing is more important than this, what we have. I thank

God every day that she has come into my life... that she makes me feel like this. I feel myself being overwhelmed with emotion and I close my eyes and my lips instinctively drop to her neck as I try to gather my thoughts.

"You're totally right. I do give a great closing argument," she whispers.

I smile broadly into her neck. "Yes, you do."

"I'm like the queen of closing arguments." She giggles.

"Shut up." I smile as I kiss her again on the neck and do up my fly. Then I stand and pull her up into a standing position and quickly retrieve her jacket and put it on her. "Stop seducing me in my office. Anybody could have walked in," I mutter, disgusted that I lost my head. I bend and pick up her G-string and put it into my pocket.

She pushes me back into my chair and sits across my lap like a child with her arms wrapped around my neck.

"I love you," she whispers as she kisses me again gently.

I smile and peck her on the lips. "I love you too."

She starts to do crazy little kisses all over my face and I screw up my face to escape her.

"Does that mean you can take me on a date tonight... just us?" she whispers as she raises her eyebrows in question.

I smirk. "I suppose," I reply.

She smiles broadly and kisses me again and my office door opens. "I'm out," Adrian asserts as he puts his head through the door.

"Oh, hi, Tash." He smiles.

She smiles nervously and immediately stands as Adrian flicks me a knowing look.

"Hi, Adrian." She smiles. "Are you ok?" she asks him.

"Yes, mother, I am ok." He rolls his eyes and shakes his head.

I smile at their interaction. Natasha cares for Adrian and has taken to being a mother hen to him.

"Do you want to come over for dinner tomorrow night?" she asks.

He smiles broadly. "Who's cooking?"

She smiles and shrugs her shoulders. "I don't know. I was hoping you would."

I stand and shake my head. "You should learn to cook, Presh," I reply.

She smirks. "That's why I'm marrying you. I need a slave, Stanton."

I narrow my eyes and slap her hard on the behind. "Behave," I murmur as I turn and start to shut down my computer. She walks over to the door and starts to talk to

Adrian and I finish up for the day.

The thing is, after the day I have had I should be in a much worse mood than I am. Lucky for me my girl knows what I need better than I do, and a deep sense of contentment sweeps over me. Having her here with me and on my side is all that I need.

CHAPTER 7

Natasha

"WE WILL HAVE THE SALMON, thank you."

"Yes, will that be all?" the waiter replies.

Joshua nods and hands over the menu. "Thank you."

It's 8 pm and we have escaped the crowd at our house and are at the back of a swanky restaurant in a curved booth. The ambience is dark and romantic with candlelight flickering gently on our faces. I am wearing another of Adrian's sexy black dresses and sky-high stilettos and Joshua is in his standard charcoal orgasmic suit. The rest of the gang are hitting the clubs tonight and Joshua has taken me on the date that I desperately wanted. Our security guards are seated at the front of the restaurant and are eating here too.

Joshua's eyes flick to me as he tops up my wine glass.

"So, is this a full-service date?" he asks.

I smile. "Maybe. Depends what the definition of full-service date is." I take a sip of my wine. *Bloody hell, that wine is good shit.*

He smirks. "I think you know the definition of full service, my beautiful slut."

I smile and pick up his hand and kiss the back of it. "Well then, yes, this is a full-service date, Mr. Stanton," I whisper darkly.

"Have you put any thought into where you want to move to?" he asks.

I shrug my shoulders and blow out a breath. "Not really."

"I was thinking we might move into an apartment for a while," he says matter of factly.

I frown. "Why?"

He shrugs. "I don't know... privacy."

My heart drops. I knew he didn't want to live with the girls. "Does it bother you having the girls staying with us?" I ask.

He shakes his head. "No more than it bothers me Cameron is living with us."

I frown. "I thought you liked living with Cameron?"

"I do," he replies.

"So, what's the problem then?" I ask.

"I like your apartment."

I giggle as I nearly choke on my wine. "You like my shitty apartment?" I splutter as I wipe my chin.

He smiles and shakes his head. "I know it's stupid."

I nod and laugh loudly. "That's downright ridiculous. What do you like about my apartment?"

He shrugs and smiles. "I like that it was small and cozy, that once we were inside the rest of the world didn't exist, no guards, no housemates. Just us."

My heart melts a little and I pick up his hand and kiss it again. "You can say the most romantic things when you want to, my beautiful Lamborghini."

He smiles as our eyes connect and he runs his thumb over my lip and leans in and kisses me gently on the lips.

"I like your house and I don't want to move," I reply as I pull out of his kiss.

He frowns. "I thought we agreed that we would move."

I nod. "And we will when we have children and settle down. What's the rush? We have forever, you have a beautiful house, and your cars need that garage. I can't imagine houses like that with those facilities are common."

He nods as he thinks and sips his wine.

"Why can't we just stay there and kick everyone else out?" I frown.

"What do you mean?" he asks

"Buy Cameron a house and find an apartment to rent for the girls."

He frowns. "You would do that?"

"I don't want them living with us either you know. I'm used to being alone with you and I would prefer it to stay that way," I reply.

He smiles warmly and grabs my hand onto his lap as he thinks out loud. "Would Bridget be okay? I mean living with Abbie?" he asks.

I frown. "Hmm, actually, on second thoughts we may need to get two small apartments next to each other. Bridget won't want to live with Abbs alone."

He narrows his eyes. "Maybe Didge can live with Cam. I don't want her alone," he mutters.

I screw up my face. "Um hello, the reason she wouldn't want to live with Abbie is because she would have to hear sex and I'm pretty sure that the sound effects would be much worse in Cameron's place."

"True, good point," he mutters.

"What's happening with Ben?" I ask.

"Nothing. I asked him today. He's not going there with Didge. Said it was too complicated and he couldn't be assed."

My heart drops. "Oh, he said that?"

He shrugs. "Yeah, tell her to forget about it. It's not happening."

I nod. "That's shitty. She likes him."

Joshua shrugs. "How it is."

He spins his glass by the stem as he contemplates telling me something and after a moment's silence, I hear the words. "I called my mother today."

I stop with my glass midair and my eyes widen. "Oh," I mutter. This can't be good.

He watches his glass as he continues to spin it. "Do you want to hear what she had to say?"

Oh shit, not really. "Only if you want to tell me. I understand if you don't want to talk about it," I reply.

He nods and takes a sip of his wine and I hold my breath waiting for him to speak.

"She asked me to not call my father." My heart drops. "Oh," I whisper.

His eyes stay glued to his spinning glass as I watch him. "Joshua, things sometimes happen." I frown as I try to articulate my words. "Don't just look at the end result."

He looks up at me and frowns. "What do you mean?"

I shrug. "When she told me the story, I felt real pity for her and for the first time I saw her as a woman who had made mistakes."

His eyes watch me, and I can hear his brain ticking.

"Nobody is perfect, Josh. Look at us. I broke your heart and then you slept with Amelie and you didn't mean for it to happen." I shrug my shoulders. "Unexpected things happen sometimes, Josh."

He shakes his head in disgust and I grab his forearm over the table. "A baby could have resulted from that, Joshua. You and Amelie could have had a baby together very easily and it would have ruined our whole future."

He fakes a shiver. "Don't even say that," he murmurs.

"What I am trying to say is, whatever has happened with your mother I don't think that it was ever intentional and that she didn't find out until it was way too late to tell anyone."

He closes his eyes. "Tash," he whispers in frustration.

"Just listen to her. Don't judge her until you know all of the circumstances."

He shakes his head in frustration and our meals arrive. "Here you are." The waitress puts our meals down. "Will that be all, sir?"

"Yes, thank you," Joshua replies.

I give him a sad smile as I rub his forearm again. "Josh, I'm not taking sides on this one. I need to stay out of this because you two will work this out eventually but if she and I fight again I doubt we will get past it."

He shakes his head as he cuts his fish. "I can't believe you're defending her. Don't bother, she's a witch."

I drop my head to hide my smile and what I really want to do is point at him and scream *oh yeah baby, you nailed it in one*, but I bite my tongue. I'm so taking the high road with this one.

He takes a bite of his food. "Leave my mother to me anyway. You just concentrate on organizing the wedding."

I smile broadly. "What do you want me to organize?" I whisper.

He shrugs. "I don't know. Whatever needs to be organized."

I bite my bottom lip in excitement. "I've never done this before."

He frowns. "And I have?" He shakes his head like I'm an idiot.

"Well shit, I don't know what to do," I mutter as my head starts to spin.

He smiles as he eats.

"Where do you want to get married?" I ask.

"Wherever you pick," he replies nonchalantly.

"When?" I ask.

"A couple of weeks."

I screw up my face. "A couple of weeks? I need to lose like five kilos before I get married."

"Stop eating McDonald's then," he mutters under his breath.

I fake a smile. "Ha, ha, you're so funny." Fuck, Operation slimdown is back on with a frigging vengeance. I sit still as I try to comprehend what to do first, this is overwhelming.

He stops eating. "What is it?' he asks.

"I can't do it in a couple of weeks," I murmur in a panic.

He smiles sympathetically. "When would you like to get married, Presh?" he asks gently.

I think for a moment. "I would like to get married in fourteen weeks."

He smiles. "In May?"

I nod. "Yes."

He gets out his phone and scrolls through his calendar. "How's May the 21st?" he asks.

I bite my bottom lip to stifle my smile. "Perfect."

He smiles again. "And where would you like to get married, Presh?"

I think for a moment and narrow my eyes. "Kamala, on our ledge," I reply hopefully.

He picks up my hand and kisses the inside of my palm. "Sounds like a date."

Our eyes meet and I am overcome with emotion. My eyes start to fill with tears. After all we have been through this is finally happening.

He smiles and points to my plate with his knife. "Eat your fish," he mutters.

I drop my head and smile as I pick up my knife and fork. May the 21st... May the 21st... May the 21st... May the 21st... this shit just got real.

"Where's Bridget?" I ask Joshua as I come down for breakfast the next morning.

"Out by the pool," he replies as he shakes his protein shaker.

I walk out and find her sitting on the edge of the pool drinking her coffee, her feet dangling in the water.

"Hey babe." I smile. "Hi," she replies.

I sit next to her and put my arm around her.

"You okay?" I ask as I drop my feet into the water.

She nods. "Yeah."

I know that's not true. "Don't lie to me. What's up?" I ask.

She takes a sip of her coffee and looks straight ahead. "I just had the talk with Ben."

My heart drops. "Oh, how did that go?" I ask.

"I asked him what was wrong and why he was angry with me." I nod and frown.

"What did he say?" I ask.

She looks down and contemplates telling me the next part of the story.

"Well?" I urge.

"He told me that in another circumstance he would be pursuing me but, in this life, he is not going there."

I listen and take her coffee cup from her to take a sip.

"Oh," I whisper.

"I feel like an idiot," she snaps.

I put my arm around her as I listen. "I really liked him," she sighs.

I frown. "When did all this start? Have I been living under a rock?"

She shrugs and blows out a breath. "At the hospital with Gran for weeks we sat together and laughed when he was trying to cheer me up." She shakes her head. "I can't explain it, but we just clicked, or so I thought."

I nod and sip her coffee again.

"And then on the night when you got really drunk."

I cringe at the memory of my daggy dancing on Joshua's phone. "Oh God, that night." I sigh as I run my hands over my eyes in embarrassment.

"He drove me home and walked me up to my door." I smile as I imagine the scenario, she is setting for me.

"I was quite drunk too and he came into my apartment to check it and I wanted him. Never have I wanted someone so badly."

My heart drops again.

"He was saying goodbye and I was looking up at him hoping he would kiss me. He slowly ran his pointer finger across my lips down over my jaw and down between my breasts and right down to my pubic bone, I nearly orgasmed from one finger."

I cringe. Oh God, this is awful.

"The way he looked at me." She stops and thinks as she stares straight ahead.

"How did he look at you?" I ask.

"He wanted me too. I know he did," she whispers.

I drop my head. I've seen that look. Joshua wore it a lot in the early days.

"He kissed me on the forehead and left without saying anything," she whispers.

"And then what happened?" I ask, confused.

"From then on we both knew that there was some serious chemistry between us, but we just kept it at bay."

"Until Kamala," I reply.

She nods. "Yes, until Kamala."

"Hmm." I put my arm around her again.

"He raised more arousal in me in that five minutes on the dance floor than I have ever felt in my life."

"He *is* gorgeous," I whisper, defeated.

"And now he doesn't want me and I have to be here and under his protection and I can't even fucking get away from him."

"Oh Didge, I'm sorry." We clink the tops of our heads together. "Why don't we get you an apartment on your own and your own guard so you can distance yourself a bit from all of this?"

"Really?" she asks. "Would Joshua be okay with that?"

I smile. If only she knew that Joshua wants them all out. "Yeah, maybe you just need some privacy."

"I can't live alone with Abbie, Tash," she sighs.

I giggle. "What's wrong with Abbs?" I tease.

She looks at me deadpan. "Could you live with Abbie?"

"Definitely not." I smirk.

She laughs. "Abbs is the best friend anyone could ask for...

but she would be the world's worst roomy."

"Oh God, I know, right," I reply. I wince.

The door opens and Abbie walks out into the pool area with two cups of coffee.

"What's so funny, bitches?" she asks.

"We were just saying what a terrible roomy you would be." I smile.

She nods. "This is true."

"I am going to get you two your own apartments next to each other," I reply.

She sits down and hands Bridget the fresh coffee. "Where's mine?" I ask.

"You have one," she replies.

"This is Bridget's cold coffee," I scoff.

"So why are you drinking it?" she asks.

"Actually, yes, why are you drinking my cold coffee?" Bridget frowns.

I look down at it and smile and shrug. Actually... I have no frigging idea.

Adrian

"What are you looking for?" Joshua asks me as I search the pantry.

"Oregano," I reply as I move things around on the shelf as I search.

"What's that for?" he replies as he helps me look.

"To degrease the engine of my car, what do you think?" I reply as I continue searching.

He fakes a smile and hands me a jar and I take it and smirk. "Thanks."

"Bitch," he mouths before he takes a seat at the counter to

continue reading the paper. It's Tuesday night and true to Tash's promise I am cooking everyone dinner, Italian. This was supposed to be Cameron's task, but he has been held up at work, so I've been roped in. Natasha is lying on the lounge watching television in her flannel pajamas and the girls are at the table stalking someone on Facebook.

"Oh my God, get off it, you slapper." Abbie scowls as she looks at a picture.

Bridget laughs out loud. "Who is this skank?" she gasps. "Who cares?" Joshua snaps as he flicks the page while rolling his eyes.

"Oh my God, Adrian, look at this picture." Bridget holds up her phone and I walk over and take it. Apparently one of their friends' boyfriends has been caught sleeping with this woman and they are scoping out the competition. The woman in the photo, let me rephrase that, the scrubber in this photo has taken a topless selfie in the bathroom mirror.

"Revolting." I frown as I hand the phone back and fake a shiver. Joshua's eyes flick to Natasha and he watches her for a moment.

He then gets up and walks upstairs while I continue to stir my pasta sauce. Two minutes later he walks into the kitchen and holds Natasha's glasses under the tap, washes them and then dries them on his t-shirt. I watch him walk over to her and put them on her face. She smiles lovingly up at him as she sits up and he sits down and then she lies back down with her head on his lap and he puts his feet on the coffee table. No words are exchanged, and he starts to play gently with her hair as they watch TV. I smile and turn back to my sauce.

I want that, I want someone to get my glasses without me asking. I want the comfortable silence. I want the love that is so obvious between them. Theirs is an extraordinary bond and I'm so happy that it has happened for two of my favorite people.

"Oh no!" Bridget laughs as she sees another bad picture and the girls both erupt into laughter.

Cameron walks in and sits on the table. "Hey," he smiles.

Everyone answers without looking at him and carries on with their business.

"Don't anyone get excited I'm home," Cameron grunts. "I've been slaving my guts out all day saving lives to keep us in the lap of luxury you are all used to." He sighs as he lies back on the table.

I shake my head at him. "Yeah, right, because you pay for everything," I reply flatly.

He smiles cheekily. "Wouldn't matter if I did, nobody would appreciate it anyway," he replies in a raised voice.

"Shut up," Abbie scoffs and bursts into laughter again at another picture without raising her eyes to him.

I smile broadly and turn back to my sauce. How did I get here with this group of friends where four has turned into seven so easily and everyone is comfortable being completely themselves in pajamas? I am grateful that Joshua has brought these women into my life, I adore the three of them. They are genuinely good girls... and funny. They make me laugh constantly with their stupid antics. Cameron gets a message on his phone.

"Brennan is having a party on the weekend and wants us all to go," he announces as he reads it.

"Oh," the girls coo as they pull an excited face to each other.

"No," Joshua replies flatly. "Why not?" Cameron asks.

"I'm not taking my girl to a pussy party." Joshua shakes his head in disgust at the suggestion.

The girls giggle. "Pussy party?" Abbie gasps. "What the hell is a pussy party?"

Cameron smirks. "Pussy on a platter," he replies as he widens his eyes in jest.

"Oh Joshua," Natasha scoffs. "We can go. I'm not being a closet girlfriend."

Cameron frowns. "What's a closet girlfriend?" he asks. "It's a girlfriend that a guy keeps at home in the closet

and nobody knows she exists. He just pulls her out at bedtime for sex," Bridget replies as she goes back to her phone.

Cameron nods seemingly interested. "I need me one of those closet girlfriends. Where do you get them?"

I shake my head. "You already have about ten," I reply.

I see Ben walk outside with a security guard and I go to the door.

"Dinner is about fifteen away."

"No, I've eaten," he replies. "Thanks anyway."

"You okay, man?" I ask. Ben has been noticeably absent lately. "Yeah, just rebooting all the systems. I still can't work out how he got past the security gates."

I nod. "I will save you some for later." He winks and keeps walking.

I walk back inside to see Cameron answering my phone. "Hello Nicholas." He smiles. "It's Cameron." He listens for

a moment. "How are you?" He laughs at something. "Yeah, I'm good."

My eyes widen as the whole room stops still. I scratch my head uncomfortably. Fuck.

"Yes, he is right here." Cameron smiles as he hands me

the phone and then punches me so hard in the stomach that I am nearly winded.

I take the phone as I hold my stomach and walk outside to escape the listening ears. My heart thumps heavily in my chest.

"Hello," I answer as I walk over to the pool. My mind goes back to the very first time he rang me when I was out here on the deckchair.

Silence... "Hello Adrian," he whispers huskily.

My eyes close at the sound of his voice and I find myself unable to answer him. I don't have it in me to be angry with him tonight.

"How are you?" he asks quietly.

"I'm okay, and you?" I ask.

"I could be better," he replies. Again silence.

"I want to come and see you," he whispers.

My eyes close again. Why do I care so much about this bastard? "Why?" I ask.

"Because I miss you and me," he pauses.

"Nick, don't, there is no point." I sigh as I shake my head. "Please?"

"We have nothing to say, Nick. You have stated your case. I get it."

"Adrian please, I'm as confused as you. I can't work this out alone."

My anger starts to simmer, and I shake my head. "You will always be confused." I reply flatly.

"No, that's not what I meant," he stammers.

"That's what you said, Nicholas."

"You're twisting my words," he replies.

"And you're twisting my fucking heart. Leave me alone," I snap.

"No, I won't."

"Nicholas, stop this. Go back to writing your books and your life in France. We have been there, and it didn't work. Let's leave it at that."

"I will be in LA in a week," he snaps angrily.

"Don't bother. I won't see you. It's a waste of your time."

"You will see me and if I have to kidnap you," he snaps angrily.

I shake my head in frustration. "Who do you think you are? I don't want to see you!" I snap.

"You're lying!" he sneers.

"And you need to get over yourself!" I reply angrily.

"I will be there in a week and we are going to sit down at dinner and talk about that twisted heart of yours."

I narrow my eyes. Why the hell did I say that? *Fucking psychologist.*

"Goodbye, Nicholas," I reply.

"See you soon, my love." He hangs up.

I rub my hands over my face. Oh, this is just perfect. I storm inside to see everybody in the same position and my sauce burning. "What the hell are you idiots doing? Stir the fucking sauce!" I snap angrily.

Joshua and Cameron laugh, and the girls all jump up and run to the kitchen to help. Bridget starts to stir the sauce frantically.

Natasha puts her arm around me and gives me a gentle smile, sensing my fragility.

"Are we good?" she asks as she kisses my shoulder.

I nod. "Yes, I'm good," I reply, although in all honesty I'm just not sure. Men. It would be so much easier if I just liked women.

Natasha

I stand at the mirror with my stomach in my throat as I put on my hot-pink lipstick. I'm nervous... no, that's an understatement, I'm in a near panic. I am going to a pussy party tonight... with Mr. Pussy himself. What the hell goes on at these things?

"Knock, knock," Adrian calls from the door. "Come in," I answer.

He sticks his head around the door and his eyes drop down to my toes and he gives a low whistle. "You're hot, Natasha Marx."

I smile and look back at the mirror. "Is this okay?" I ask nervously.

"I hope so. It cost a bomb." He walks around behind me and puts his hands on my hips, and we look at our reflection in the mirror.

I am wearing a white dress that is short and tight. Hot pink stiletto strappy sandals and a hot pink clutch match my lipstick. My dark hair is out and full. I even went to the hairdressers today to get a blow dry, something I never do.

Adrian is in navy pants and a white shirt and looks gorgeous as usual. I put my hand on my stomach.

"Where are the boys?" I ask.

"Downstairs having some drinks before we go. Are you okay?" He smiles.

"I'm as nervous as hell," I whisper as I hear male laughter echo from downstairs. "I don't fit into this world, Adrian. Why did I think this was a good idea?"

He smiles broadly. "Stop. It will be fine, and we will all be there. You're the hottest girl in LA. I do hope you are wearing glass boots though?"

I frown. "A stage up from glass slippers?"

He smiles again. "About three stages up from glass slippers, my beautiful Cinderella."

"Oh God." I put my head into my hands. "Can you make me a margarita, please? I need something to calm my nerves."

He kisses me gently on the cheek. "Sure, chick. Where are the girls?"

"In their room," I reply and with that he disappears.

Ten minutes later, I tentatively walk down the hall and over towards the handrail. I hear different male voices. Oh God... who else is frigging here? I wish the girls' rooms weren't so far away. I don't know if they are downstairs or not, but I have to walk past the stairs to see. I slowly walk down the stairs and a group of about ten men are in the lounge room drinking... oh crap.

I stop in my tracks and close my eyes. *You can do this.* I slowly start to walk again, and Joshua glances up and sees me. Standing in the group of men with his legs wide and his hand in his pocket, a slow sexy smile comes over his face. He is in dark jeans and a black V-neck shirt, and his hard muscular body oozes sexual power in that casual outfit. From his ridiculously expensive watch on that ripped forearm to the dark clipped no fuss hair. And those broad shoulders and that tight ass seal the deal. *How in the hell did I get this god?*

Joshua Stanton is one hell of a delicious package.

He puts his head on an angle and slowly cracks his neck and I smile on the inside. I will never tire of that.

"Here she is," he announces and the men all turn to face me.

"Hello," I smile meekly.

My eyes flick around the group. Ben smiles warmly and

Adrian winks in our special we know a secret wink. He bought this whole outfit for me on one of our shopping trips.

"And this is my beautiful Natasha." Joshua smiles as he holds his hand out for me and I feel myself melt. I take his hand and hold my breath as I walk down the bottom three steps. He gently kisses my cheek and puts his arm around me protectively. Oh crap, I feel like the freak from the show on display, everyone's eyes are on us.

The men all smile and start to shake my hand and introduce themselves, Markus, Andrew, Ricardo.

Then I get to a familiar face. "Carson." He smiles as he takes my hand and shakes it.

Oh shit, I smile nervously. "I remember." What I don't remember is him being so good-looking last time.

He looks uncomfortable. "Sorry about last time we met," he murmurs.

Oh God, he had to bring that up. "Me too, forgive my rudeness," I mutter as my eyes flick to Joshua.

Joshua eyes are locked onto me and he smiles warmly in appreciation.

"Let me get you a drink, Presh." Joshua leads me over to the bar where a jug of frozen margarita sits. What I really want to do is pick up the whole jug and scull it while it pours all over my face and down over my clothes. Abbie comes laughing out of the kitchen with Cameron and Brigetta and they walk over to us at the bar. Trust her not to be intimidated by this situation and I instantly feel some of my nerves dissipate. Cameron runs his hand up my arm to my shoulder and smiles warmly.

"You look beautiful tonight, Tash," he says gently, and I smile. Since Cam and I had that talk we have definitely turned a corner.

Abbie screws her face up and hits him on the arm. "Why

didn't you tell me I look beautiful, dipshit?" she whispers so the others can't hear.

He looks at her and replies flatly: "You look beautiful, Abbie."

"It doesn't count now. You have to say it when you see me, asshole."

He rolls his eyes at Joshua who seems amused by the banter between the idiots and he passes us our margaritas.

A low whistle sounds and I look instinctively up at the staircase. "Hello yellow," Carson whispers loudly and the boys snicker.

Bridget is slowly coming down the stairs wearing a short bright yellow dress and white short boots and carries a white clutch. Her long honey hair is out and blow dried from our salon appointment this morning, and she is literally glowing. I don't think I have ever seen her look so good. My eyes immediately flick to Ben whose eyes are glued to her. He smiles softly as she walks down the stairs. Carson rushes to the bottom of the stairs and holds out his hand to her. She nervously smiles and takes it. He does an exaggerated bow and kisses the back of her hand.

"You are the most divine creature I have ever seen. Who are you?" he purrs.

Bridget smiles nervously. "My name is Bridget," she whispers as the whole room looks on.

"Well, Bridget," Carson purrs. "You are my date for the night. I am not letting you out of my sight."

She giggles nervously, unsure what to say.

My eyes widen and flick to Ben. He stands stock still, glaring at Carson, his jaw ticking in anger.

Hmm, this night just got very interesting.

CHAPTER 8

Natasha

JOSHUA and I approach the double front doors of the white three-story mansion, the venue for the pussy party. What in the hell goes on at this place to earn it that name? Bridget and Abbie were in the car in front of us with Cameron and Carson and have already gone in. Adrian and a few of the other boys are in cars behind us. Security guards are lined up along the huge circular driveway in front of the house and are greeting everyone by their first name. Are they bodyguards for the people inside? Crap, I am so out of my depth here.

"See you in there," Ben says as he sees someone he knows across the lawn.

"Okay," Joshua replies.

Ben walks over and shakes the burly security guard's hand and they both laugh out loud at something that is said.

Large white paper lanterns line the pathway and the sound of dance music echoes from around the back of the house.

Joshua looks down at me. "What?" He smirks.

"Nothing," I reply as I try to act casual and swallow my fear. "We can leave anytime you want," he says as his eyes stay forward on the crowd.

I nod. "Okay."

"Don't tell anyone anything," he whispers. I frown.

"This place is the gossip capital of the world. Anything you say can and will be used against you."

My horrified eyes meet his.

He smirks and bends to kiss me gently on the cheek. "Just so you know, this is the life I don't want anymore."

I bite my bottom lip and nod.

"It is you who wanted to come here, remember?" he murmurs. I nod again.

His eyes hold mine as he senses my trepidation. "I would rather be at home with you in your pajamas," he whispers.

I smirk. "What is it with you and my granny PJs, Stanton?" I reply.

Raising his eyebrows, he shakes his head. "I have no idea actually." His hand runs gently down to my behind and he smirks as he winks.

We walk through the doors and are passed glasses of champagne by a woman walking around with a circular silver tray. We follow the crowd through the house. Loud dance music thumps through the space and Joshua grabs my hand and leads me through the crowd to the backyard. As people move to the side to let us through, I notice them all do a double take at Joshua and then me, then instantly say something to whoever they are standing with. I glance down at myself to check all my bits are tucked into this skimpy outfit. This is uncomfortable... *God*. We walk out another set of double doors to the huge backyard and the resort pool and my eyes fly around nervously. I see the girls across the pool and a wave of relief hits me and I go to walk off, but Joshua keeps hold of my hand.

"Don't go anywhere. I want to introduce you to some people."

"Ah, okay." I swallow my nerves again. You have got to be kidding. I don't want to meet anyone. I want to binge-drink until I forget why I am here.

Joshua leads me around the pool by the hand and, unlike inside the house where people were pretending to be polite, people are now just blatantly staring. Beautiful women in next to nothing and men who look like they stepped off a modelling shoot are interested in me, what's wrong with this picture?

"Hi Stan," the girls all remark as he keeps walking with my hand in a death grip.

He nods. "Hello Stan."

He nods and smiles in return, fuck. These women are all gorgeous. Why did I want to come here? Oh my God... and this is the pussy on demand that Cameron was talking about. I'm so screwed! We walk towards a group of men and they all turn. "Stan, you made it out, old boy," one man says in a throaty voice, and handshakes happen all around.

Like Joshua's prized pig I am then introduced to about 100 people. The men are all very interested, maybe too interested, and the women are just downright catty and look me up and down and then exchange looks. I finally can't take anymore and pull out of Joshua's grip. He frowns in question.

"I am just going over here with the girls." I smile.

He nods. "Don't go anywhere I can't see you, Presh." I frown.

"Am I under investigation or something?"

"No, I know what these people are like and I don't want you to have to put up with it."

"Joshua, just do what you normally do here, and I will

hang with the girls. I don't want to listen to boy talk all night," I reply.

He bends as he gently holds my jaw and kisses me tenderly and I smile.

"Okay, my Lamborghini?" I ask as I smile into his kiss, a little relieved that we are still the same.

He smiles and rubs his hand down my hip and around to my behind but then his eyes catch something over my shoulder and he slowly drops his hand from my behind and takes my hand in his.

I turn immediately to see who is there.

Shit, the model. What's her name again? I have seen her in photographs with Joshua on numerous occasions. She is wearing a skin-colored tight dress and perfectly matching stilettos and has a figure to die for. Her long thick layered caramel hair hangs effortlessly around her shoulders. She's beautiful.

"Hello Stan," she murmurs with a trace of a hopeful smile on her face.

Joshua seems uncomfortable. "Hello Mills," he replies.

Crap, Heidi Mills. Oh, how cute, fucking nicknames. I want to vomit in my mouth.

Her eyes flick to me. "Hello." She smiles.

Joshua interjects. "Mills, this is Natasha, my fiancée."

Her face drops as her eyes flick between us and I see an emotion I know too well. Pain, this woman is in love with my Lamborghini.

She forces out a smile. "Congratulations," she whispers. Joshua grimaces, knowing how uncomfortable this situation is.

"How have you been?" he asks her.

She smiles again. "You know me, always happy." She fakes a smile as she lies through her teeth.

Why do I feel pity for these women? He nods. "That's good."

Her eyes flick to me again. "How long have you two been together?"

I go to speak but Joshua cuts me off. "Natasha and I went out seven years ago and have just recently reconnected."

She swallows the lump in her throat and nods, and I can see her thinking... that was Joshua's way of telling her that I am the girl in his tattoo and, yes, I was his first love from Australia. I slowly go to pull my hand out of Joshua's and he grips me hard. He wants me to stay.

"May I?" She grabs my hand to look at my ring and her face falls again when she sees the huge rock.

"It's a beautiful ring," she murmurs. "Thank you." I smile.

"Did you pick it, Joshua?" she asks as her eyes flick to him.

He smiles sarcastically. "Fuck off, Mills, that's none of your business."

My heart drops in pity for her. Joshua obviously doesn't want to play nice and is tired of this conversation.

Joshua then leans down and kisses me again gently on the lips. "We are heading over here, Mills. Catch you later." He then pulls my arm out of the socket as he walks me over to the girls.

"How long did you date her?" I ask as I am pulled along. "We never dated," he snaps.

"I've seen photographs of you together at functions." "We are friends," he replies as we get to the group. "Friends with benefits?" I ask.

He scratches his head in frustration but doesn't answer my question. We arrive at the girls and Abbie and Bridget smile and kiss me on arrival. Joshua stands still across the group from me with his dominant stance in full play, legs wide, one hand in his pocket and Corona beer in his other hand. My eyes flick to Heidi on the other side of the pool. She now stands with six other beautiful women and they are deep in conversation. What was his relationship with her? How well do they know each other? That stupid insecure feeling sinks in. *Stop it.*

The dance music starts to blare from the DJ inside and the lights get dimmed and the space is lit up only from the lanterns and party lights. This is some frigging party with recognizable super models and actors everywhere. The prerequisite to gain entry must be to pass a cool and beautiful persons' test. There are two bars in the backyard making cocktails and waiters walking around with trays of tequila shots. Joshua has two when the tray goes past us. I have never been anywhere quite like this, it's just like in the movies. I know the girls want Joshua to buzz off so we can do some serious fan girl gossiping. I keep seeing them widen their eyes at each other when they see something they want to talk about.

"Joshua, go and hang with your friends, baby. I will stay just here with the girls."

His eyes hold mine as he does an internal risk assessment. "I'm fine. I have to get used to all this if we are going to stay

here. Let me figure this out by myself; you have nothing to worry about. I will come and find you in an hour or so" I say.

He nods and his eyes flick to Abbie. "Don't leave Natasha or Bridget alone."

She smiles and clicks his bottle with her glass. "Okay, boss." He smirks at her idiocy. I think Abbie is growing on him.

"Natasha and I can look after ourselves,"Bridget announces, annoyed at his suggestion.

He puts his arm around her shoulder. "I know, Didge. These people just aren't wired like you two, that's all."

"And I am?" Abbie asks, affronted.

Joshua smirks. "Yes, Abbie, everyone here is wired just like you. I know you will be okay here."

Bridget narrows her eyes at me in annoyance. "Go away, Joshua, you're just cramping our style now," I whisper, horrified.

He kisses me gently on the lips as he smirks. "Over to the wall there, do you see the two men?" He points to the high rendered wall around the back of the huge backyard and to two men in suits lingering on the outskirts.

I frown. "Yes."

"They are your guards for the night."

I frown. "Where's Ben and the boys?" I ask as my eyes flick around.

"Ben attends these parties by my side as a friend. He is not working when he is out with me."

Bridget's and my eyes meet across the group. "Why is that?" I ask flatly.

"Because in the past I have needed a guard I can trust to party with, so Ben just accompanies me as a friend and if I need him, he steps in, but if you want anything, go to the boys at the back."

Hmm, that was code for I take Ben to my strip joints and he has seen me have sex with a copious number of women, so he gets special treatment. I skull the rest of my champagne. I did not like that answer one little bit.

"Don't get drunk," Joshua reprimands me.

"Listen, fun cop, go away!" I snap. He's really beginning to piss me off now.

"I will be over there with the boys." He points across the party to a group of men all laughing loudly and I nod.

"Okay, God, I get the point!" I reply, exasperated, and he finally disappears through the crowd.

"Oh my fuck," Bridget gasps as soon as he is out of hearing distance.

"I know, right," I answer.

"It's like the parties you read about in magazines," says Abbie as she grabs my arm.

"Did you see that Andrew Menzies is here? He's really short in real life."

My eyes flick around. "No, where?" He is an actor who has just recently become a hot property of Tinseltown, and he is in about five of leading movies at the moment.

"What do you make of the Ben comment?" Bridget asks me as we wait for our cocktails ten minutes later.

"That he goes to strip joints with Joshua and is part of this social clique," I reply flatly.

"Hmm, that's how I took it too," she replies.

"Who is the girl talking to Joshua?" Abbie whispers as the waiter hands over our margaritas.

We all turn to see Joshua over near the boys talking to a blonde and my eyes narrow. I swig my drink without tasting it. Fuck. We are now standing over near the bar under a large tree lit up with fairy lights and have moved from our position that Joshua left us in.

Ben walks over to us. "Are you girls okay? Can I get you a drink?"

Bridget narrows her eyes. "I don't want anything from you Ben," she snaps.

Abbie smiles into her drink and I wince at Didge. Oh shit, she's getting all bitchy now.

He glares at her. "Well, that's good because I was only offering drinks," he snaps. "Anything wasn't on the table."

She fakes a smile and Abbie giggles.

"Witty," she murmurs, and I drop my head to hide my smile. I stand still, watching Joshua as he talks to the girl, and then

Cameron and two other girls join them, and he says something and the girls all burst into laughter. *What's so fucking funny?* Joshua's eyes keep flicking back to the space where we were as he tries to locate me. Oh, I'm watching alright, Mr. Funny Guy, don't bother looking for me.

"How often do you guys come to these parties?" Abbie asks Ben.

He shrugs. "We used to come most weekends before we went to Australia."

"Beeeeennnnny." A girl with huge boobs and beautiful black long hair calls from across the pool.

He nervously looks her way. "Hey Hen," he replies, and she does an exaggerated wiggle on the spot with her hands above her head. Obviously, she is one of his girls and is excited to see him out.

This time it is Bridget who sculls her drink without tasting it.

If looks could kill Ben would be dead on the floor. "I will be over here if you need me," Ben replies.

"I won't be needing you Ben," Bridget snaps angrily.

He glares at her again and we all wither a little under his glare. "Fine," he snaps.

"Fine," Bridget replies, and he storms off.

"I hate fucking pussy parties," Bridget whispers angrily as she sculls the last of her margarita.

"Me, too," I whisper into my drink as I keep watching Joshua and his harem. A group of men approach us and start to talk to Abbs, and they all introduce each other, but still my eyes don't leave Joshua. Bridget's eyes follow mine.

"Stuff this," Bridget whispers with her eyes on Joshua as Abbie talks to the men. "What's he doing?"

I narrow my eyes. "Being witty and gorgeous it seems." "Oh shit. I hate it when they do that," she replies flatly.

"What do you reckon they are saying?" I ask.

"Who cares? Look at Joshua looking around for you."

"Screw him, I'm hiding. Let's go inside," I whisper, exasperated.

"Okay." She grabs my hand and leads me around the other side and into the house where the dance floor is, and we see a low leather lounge in the corner and slump into it to people watch.

An hour later Didge and I are feeling quite happy with our cocktails in our pole position from the corner and have seen enough action for the xxx channel. We have even seen a tray of cocaine go past. Heidi Mills drops into the chair beside us.

"So, I'm Heidi," she introduces herself to Bridget.

Bridget fakes a smile. "Hi," she replies as they shake hands. "Natasha, I would love to show you around LA and introduce you to some people." She smiles.

Oh God, you are the last person on Earth I want to hang around with, but it is nice of you to offer. I raise my eyebrows in surprise. "Thanks," I reply. "I'm really busy at the moment but down the track that would be great." I smile as I lie through my teeth.

Bridget knowingly squashes my foot with hers and I elbow her discreetly.

Heidi stands. "I'm going to get another drink. Do you guys want one?" she asks. We both shake our heads and she shimmies past us.

"Oh my God, check it out." Bridget hits me on the leg, and I look up to see Cameron sit at the counter on the stool in the next room. A beautiful brunette comes around and walks in between his legs, with her back facing us. We giggle and take a drink off a passing tray. Bridget's phone beeps a message.

Where are you bitches?

Oh shit, we forgot about Abbie. We instantly text her our coordinates and continue to watch the Cameron show.

His hand slides up and down her legs as he talks to her and she seemingly giggles on demand. I sit riveted as I watch him. He's more like Joshua than I care to admit. The girl puts her arms around him and leans in and he kisses her.

Abbie bounces into the seat next to us. "Oh, you're dead meat. Stanton is looking for you."

I smile into my drink. "Good." "What's Ben doing?" Bridget asks.

"Who fucking cares," Abbie snaps. "He's an asshole. Worry about what that other hot guy is doing."

Bridget frowns. "Who? Carmichael?"

I laugh into my drink. "Carmichael. His name is Carson." "Whatever!" Bridget snaps.

Our eyes go back to Cameron as another blonde girl walks up to him and puts her arms around him and the girl who is already between his legs. Cameron's hand immediately falls to her behind.

"No!" Bridget whispers wide eyed.

We then watch in shock as Cameron slowly tongue kisses one girl and then turns and kisses the other.

Abbie giggles. "Go Cam," she chants.

My eyes meet Bridget's in horror. We are on another planet in this place. For ten minutes we watch two girls practically dry hump Cameron on his stool until he finally stands and leads them both out the front door by their hands.

"I guess we know what Cam is doing tonight," Bridget murmurs.

My stomach drops. How many times has Joshua done just

that? Picked up more than one girl and taken them home from one of these pussy parties. Past tense, past tense, past tense, I try to remind myself. I see Ben through the hallway looking around, obviously for us.

"I'm going out to see Joshua." I frown. "Okay," they reply.

"You guys coming?" I ask.

"No, we are good here."

I walk out to the backyard and see Joshua talking to a group of men. One hand is holding his drink and the other is in his pocket. His eyes narrow when he sees me, and he runs his tongue over his front teeth. He's angry.

I walk over to him and gently link my arm through his. "Hello." I smile.

His eyes flick to me and the men all continue their conversation. "I will be coming alone to the next party," he murmurs into his drink.

I roll my lips as I think of an answer. "Because I was dancing?" A waitress walks past, and I grab another champagne off the tray.

"No, because I told you to stay where I can see you," he replies.

I smile. "I won't let you leave the house to come without me anyway."

His eyes drop to mine. "Like you could stop me," he whispers, annoyed.

I smirk. "I could easily stop you if I wanted to." He sips his drink as he raises his eyebrow.

"I would just tie you to the bed," I murmur into my drink. A trace of a smile kisses his lips.

I smile broadly.

"Natasha, what do you think of LA?" a man from across the circle asks me. Huh? My eyes flick across the group.

"I love it so far." I smile nervously. "It will be better when I go to work though."

"Oh, what do you do?" another man asks. "I'm a psychologist," I reply.

"Oh, healthcare like Cam," someone replies.

I smile and nod as my mind flicks to Cam. "Cameron left with two girls," I whisper to Joshua and his eyes hold mine as he thinks of a reply.

"Cameron's single," he mutters.

What in the hell is he doing at this moment? Two girls are probably taking turns at sucking his dick. Oh my God, eww. Gross.

The men keep talking about Cameron's new role. "What then?" Joshua whispers as he moves us back from the crowd a bit.

My eyes flick up to him and I frown in question as he pulls me from my disgusting Cameron thoughts.

"You have me tied to the bed. What then?" he asks.

Oh shit, he wants to play dirty talk and I've got nothing... hmmm. Quick, think of something. I troll my brain for something sexy.

"I would sit on your face," I blurt out. Oh God, that sounded shit. I inwardly wince.

He smirks sexily. "Really? Could be hard for me to breathe." Umm. "I wouldn't care if you couldn't breathe because I would be sliding up and down on your face getting myself off while I hold onto the bed headboard." I nearly giggle at the ridiculousness of my last comment. Where do I come up with this shit?

His eyes hold mine.

I lick my bottom lip for effect. "You see when a woman needs an orgasm, she has no regard for anything that goes on around her. Her mind is focused on one thing only," I whisper.

His eyes darken and drop down to my legs and then back up to my breasts. "And how would you get your orgasm?" he whispers.

"I would turn around and suck that big dick of yours while I kneel over you. That big cock would touch the back of my throat while my eyes close in need."

He slowly cracks his neck, and his eyes drop to my cleavage and then back up to my lips.

Ok, he liked that. I inwardly high five my dirty talking skills, it's been a while. "And then I would crawl down your body and mount you reverse cowboy position."

His eyes darken further.

"So you could see my body struggling and my legs would have to be spread so wide to take in that massive cock of yours. And you would feel how deep inside my body you are, feel the quiver of my muscles contract around you as you slide home," I whisper.

He lifts his chin as he cracks his neck again.

"In... out... stretched to the hilt," I whisper as my eyes linger on his beautiful big lips.

His mouth hangs slack and I know he is picturing just what I am telling him. His arousal is obvious.

"And you can film it," I whisper.

His eyes widen. "I can film it?" he asks.

"On your phone you can film it, and we can watch it on the television in our room."

His darkened eyes drop to my body and then my lips as his chest starts to rise and fall deeply.

"Again and again," I whisper as I lean in close and kiss him gently. I can feel his erection though his pants and pride hits me that I can get him like this without touching him.

He smiles and gently kisses me again as he brings his hand

gently to my jaw. "You do give a great closing argument, Marx. We are going home." His hand wraps possessively around my waist and he pulls me into his body. "Now. I need to fuck!" he growls into my ear.

Bridget walks up and stands beside me, and Joshua blows out a frustrated breath. Our moment is temporarily broken.

"Do you both want margaritas?"

Joshua sighs. "Yes, please," we both murmur and he walks off.

"Carson just asked me to dance with him and then he tried to kiss me," Bridget blurts out in a rush.

"What?" I reply.

"Yep." She nods. "And then when I was walking off the dance floor I see Ben glaring at me all possessive-like and I just wanted to punch him in the nose."

I nod. "Maybe you should have," I reply.

"Do you think I should just forget Ben and kiss Carson?" she asks.

I frown. "It's a hard one. What would Abbie do?" I bite my lip as I think.

"She would go for Carson." I nod again. "He is exceptionally hot," she murmurs.

"Meh." I shrug. "Doesn't do it for me. I prefer Ben."

"Ben's a prick!" she snaps.

"Mmm, there is that unfortunate fact." I nod.

I see Heidi Mills around the other side of the pool. "Oh look, it's the American stick insect," I mutter flatly.

Bridget clinks our glasses. "Bridget Jones." She smirks. I nod and smile at the stupid movie lines game we play.

"Oh shit, she's coming over to us. God, buzz off. Don't tell her anything," I whisper, annoyed.

"Are you both having fun?" she asks.

I nod and fake a smile. What do you want bitch? "Do you live around here?" Bridget asks.

Heidi chuckles. "Oh, I love your accent. You're Australian too. I couldn't hear it over the music inside."

"I'm Natasha's sister," Bridget replies.

Her face drops. "Oh," she replies. Abbie comes out and walks around to us and I don't think I have ever been so happy to see her in my life.

"Hi," Abbie announces. "Who are you?" She smiles, being her best passive aggressive self.

Heidi seemingly sums up Abbie. "I'm Heidi." She fakes a smile as Abbie throws me and Bridge a look.

Joshua returns with three drinks. "Fuck off, Mills," he growls.

My mouth drops open in shock. "Joshua," I gasp. "Don't be so rude!"

Abbie's hand immediately goes to her hip as she narrows her eyes at the girl.

"She's not somebody you should be associating with, Natasha," Joshua sneers

"You don't know that, we could become friends," I gasp. This rude behavior is unacceptable. I don't want to be friends but if I did, he has no say in it.

"Well, seeing she just hit me up for a lunchtime meeting tomorrow in a hotel for sex with no strings, I'm thinking not." He narrows his eyes at her in contempt.

My heart drops and my horrified eyes meet hers, *what?*

"Stan," she gasps. "Stop talking!"

"You did what?" I snap. Of all the nerve, what a bitch.

"You've got a hide," Abbie growls. "Fuck off now, you bitch, before I punch your ugly face in."

Bridget gets the uncontrollable giggles into her drink.

Joshua glares at her and I put my hand on my hip angrily.

"Seriously go away, Heidi, you make me sick," I sneer as I shake my head in disgust.

Heidi huffs and storms off through the crowd, furious that Joshua has called her out.

I stand still... in shock. What the hell just happened? Abbie and Bridget can't control it anymore and burst out laughing and even Joshua is trying to hold it in.

I bite my lip to hide my smile.

"Punch your ugly face in," Joshua repeats. "Who says that?"

"I do," Abbie snaps as she takes Bridget's drink from her and sips it.

That's it, I can't hold it anymore and I burst into laughter.

"What's so funny?" Adrian asks as he walks up.

"Abbie just told Mills she was going to punch her ugly face in," Bridget laughs.

Adrian chokes on his drink. "What?" he gasps. "Her face is anything but ugly."

"We had an incident," Joshua murmurs as he shakes his head in annoyance.

Adrian shakes his head in disgust. "I bet you did," he sighs.

Carson walks over and grabs Bridget's hand. "Bridget, would you like to go and get something to eat?"

"Huh?" she whispers as her eyes flick to Joshua and me. She spots something across the pool and my eyes follow to where she is looking. Ben is talking to that girl with the long black hair.

Bridget gets a new bout of bravery. "I'm going to go to a bar with Carson," she announces.

Joshua's and Adrian's eyes meet.

"Ah... Didge," I reply. Oh hell, what do I say to this?

"You had better take a guard," Joshua replies. "I will ask Ben who he wants to send with you."

Bridget's horrified eyes meet mine and she puts her hands on her hips angrily. "I will not be taking a guard with me!"

Carson stands back and winces. This is uncomfortable. "Why don't you go with her Abbie?" Adrian asks.

Ben walks over. "What's the problem?" he asks.

Joshua looks uncomfortable and pauses before he answers. "Bridget wants to go to a bar."

Ben's eyes flick angrily to Carson who withers under the glare.

Oh shit.

Ben then seems to regain his composure and lifts his chin defiantly. "No, Bridget, you won't be going anywhere. We don't have enough security here tonight to cover two locations."

My heart drops for Bridget. This situation is totally messed up. "Oh, fuck off, Ben, you have like ten men here," Abbie snaps.

Bridget shakes her head in disgust at Ben. "I know what you're doing!"

Oh shit, this is about to get ugly.

Ben grabs her by the upper arm. "I would like a word," he sneers

She rips her arm from his grip. "Stop it," she whispers angrily.

He pulls her away from the group over to near the back of the wall and they continue their heated conversation.

"Why is Ben being such a cock?" Carson asks.

I look at him deadpan. Now that's the pot calling the kettle black. You are the biggest cock I have ever laid eyes on. Adrian seemingly reads my mind and snickers under his breath.

Bridget comes back to the group and kisses all of us on the

cheek. "I'm leaving with Carson," she announces, and Abbie smiles broadly and winks at her.

My eyes flick to Ben who is openly furious, and my eyes meet Joshua's across the circle, and he smirks into his drink. Ben deserved this but the loser in me feels sorry for him.

"What guard am I taking, Ben?" Bridget asks sarcastically as she lifts her chin in defiance.

Ben's furious eyes hold hers. "I will send Peter. I'm busy tonight." His eyes flick to the girl with the dark hair across the pool.

Bridget narrows her eyes in anger, and I can see the red fumes shooting from her ears. "Fine," she snaps.

Bens smiles sarcastically. "More than fine, it will be great." Bridget huffs and grabs Carson's hand to further infuriate

Ben and he takes the bait as he openly clenches his fists beside his body. Oh jeez, this is uncomfortable. We all stand still and hold our breath, unsure of what is going to happen as Bridget disappears through the crowd hand in hand with Carson. I can't help but wonder what Ben would do if he didn't work for Joshua and I'm thinking Carson might be out cold on the floor. Joshua hands Ben another drink and he gulps it down as they move away to talk.

Abbie smiles broadly. "Go, Didge," she whispers. I shake my head.

"She's an idiot," I reply.

"Nice girls come last, Natasha," she snaps.

"Nice girls win in the end, Abbie, mark my words. You can't have your cake and eat it too," I murmur.

"That's bullshit and you know it, Natasha Marx."

CHAPTER 9

Natasha

I WAKE FEELING VERY second hand. When we got back from the party this morning at 4 am Joshua had his wicked way with me and bent me over every hard surface in this bedroom and the bathroom. It seems alcohol gives him superhuman stamina... I'm bloody sore. No man can have sex for that long, surely. I rub my hand through my hair as I remember the activities and I shake my head and smile. God, he's an animal.

He's not here. I look around the room and by the position of the sun peeking through the blinds I know it's late. I need to get up. I wish we lived alone so I could go searching naked for my man. I'm sick of being so damn respectable. I am missing our little apartment love bubble too, where nakedness was the norm and sex on the dining table was a prerequisite.

I shower, dress, make the bed and go in search for him. As I am walking toward the kitchen, I see Bridget sitting at the counter. She subtly shakes her head and widens her eyes as if warning me about something. I frown in question, am I inter-rupting a fight with Ben? And then I turn the corner and see it and stop dead in my tracks, Margaret is sitting at the counter and spins her chair around to see me. Her chin lifts defiantly and her cold eyes meet mine.

Oh crap, what the hell is she doing here? This is going to be bad. Really bad. I feel my stomach clench with nerves and I tentatively walk into the kitchen. Is it too late to run? Why didn't bloody Bridget text and warn me?

"Good morning," I say meekly.

"Good afternoon, don't you mean?" she replies coldly. My nervous eyes flick to Bridget who wisely is staring at her coffee in its cup. I'm pretty sure the coffee is not going anywhere, Bridget. I glance at the clock and it's 11.30 am. Oh God, this is a disaster. *Where's Joshua?*

I walk over to the coffee machine and slowly make myself a cup of coffee in silence. What should I do? I don't want to talk to her alone before she talks to Joshua... or do I?

"So, you are all living here?" Margaret asks Bridget. "Um, yes," Bridget replies.

Oh God, this looks bad. It must seem like all of my friends are here in LA freeloading off of Joshua... well we all are sort of, but it is not by choice.

"Hmm, how nice," she sneers.

I stand with my back to her at the coffee machine trying to think of a getaway plan and I slowly stir my sugar... actually, I need another one. I pile another heaped teaspoon into my coffee and stir it. I will try anything to sweeten this conversa-tion. I walk back and lean my behind on the counter facing the two women. Bridget flicks her eyes to the door and I throw her a filthy look. Don't even think of leaving me here, bitch.

"Your mother told me that you are engaged," she replies in monotone.

Oh shit, didn't Joshua tell her that? Why wouldn't he tell them? I have been so wrapped up in myself and my family I didn't even notice. This just gets worse by the minute.

"Yes," I whisper.

She fakes a smile. "How lovely for you. You must be very happy," she sneers.

I start to hear my pulse in my ears as my anger starts to grow.

I fake a smile back. "I am." My eyes hold hers. Bring it on bitch, I'm ready.

Bridget drains her coffee cup and appears uncomfortable. "What are you doing here?" I ask too sweetly, as once again our eyes lock.

"My son sent his plane to pick me up. We have some things that we need to discuss." She sits back in her chair. "But you already know that, don't you?" she sneers.

Bridget stands. "Um, I'm just going to..." She points to the door with her thumb.

"Sit back down!" I snap. Bridget drops into her seat immediately and you could hear a pin drop. "And why would I know that?" I ask.

She smiles and widens her eyes animatedly. "Oh, there it is, the innocence that Joshua loves. You really should become an actress, Natasha. You're very good."

Fury starts to pump through me and my eyes meet Bridget's.

The moment is broken as the front door opens and closes and

I hear Cameron's voice. "Hey," he calls. I don't think I have ever been so relieved to see him in my life.

He throws his keys onto the counter and his eyes flick between the three of us.

"Mother," he says uncomfortably, and he walks over to her and kisses each of her cheeks. By his body language I can tell he's furious too. This is going to be a bad day all round.

I walk to the kitchen and start to make Joshua a protein shake. I have noticed he is not eating as much. He's obviously under a lot of stress.

"How was your flight?" Cameron asks.

"Long," Margaret replies. "You look tired, Cameron. Have you been working too hard?"

Bridget's and my eyes meet, and she smirks. Fucking two women all night long probably is hard work, I wonder if he got paid an overtime allowance.

Joshua walks in and my eyes find him across the room. He's wearing a three-piece navy suit... his armor, a white shirt and tie, dressed for a business meeting. My heart drops. I don't want him to have to go through this shit. I smile gently, hoping that he will feel my love across the room.

"Mother," he says, his voice void of emotion. "Hello Joshua," she stammers.

He walks past her to me on the other side of the kitchen and kisses me gently. "Good morning, my lovely Natasha." He smiles as he brushes the hair from my face.

I melt and feel a wave of emotion pulse through me that only he can arouse.

"I made you a shake," I whisper as I hand it to him.

"Thank you, very thoughtful." He takes it from me and takes a sip as his eyes hold mine. He bends and kisses me again, then turns and walks from the room.

"Cameron, can I see you in my office for a moment?" he calls.

Cameron and Margaret both stand. "Not you, Mother. I will call you when I want you."

He keeps walking and I drop my head. He can be such a cold prick when he wants to be.

I slowly stand. "I'm going upstairs," I whisper quietly as I look at the ground.

She doesn't reply and I can't even lift my head to look at Bridget. What a nightmarish situation. I feel sick to my stomach. I know Margaret has brought this all on herself...but I can't help but feel sorry for her.

Joshua

I sit at my desk as fury pumps through me. Cameron walks in behind me, shuts the door and flops onto the leather chesterfield lounge.

He holds his hands over his face. "Over this day already. I haven't even slept yet," he moans.

"You knew we were meeting with her this morning.

Couldn't you get some sleep, for fuck's sake?" I snap.

He rubs his face. "Something came up that I couldn't refuse."

I glare at him. "About that, Natasha saw you with the two girls last night."

"Oh God," he sighs.

"Can you just try to tone it down around her? She's not used to this, Cameron."

"I know," he sighs.

"She's going to be my wife!"

"I fucking get it, shut up. Fuck!" he snaps.

"I don't want her seeing that shit from her brother-in-law!"

He sighs, lies back and throws the back of his forearm over his face and my phone rings.

"Stanton," I answer.

"Umm, hello Mr. Stanton."

"Yes."

"This is Matthew from Elders Real Estate." I frown. "Yes."

"I sold you the property Willowvale and you asked me to keep in touch."

I breathe in. I don't need this nonsense today. "Yes, what is it?" I ask as I roll my eyes.

He pauses on the other end. "I may be speaking out of turn here but rumor has it you had a bit of trouble with the ex-property manager, the veterinarian."

I run my tongue over my front teeth in contempt. Who is this prick?

"What about it?" I snap.

"I just thought I should let you know that she is trying to buy the property next door to your farm."

I sit forward in my seat. "What do you mean?" I ask. "Apparently, she has contacted all of the surrounding properties and offered huge money to buy their properties," he replies.

"Has she now?" I reply in a monotone as I think.

Cameron frowns at me and I narrow my eyes as I roll my pen on the desk under my fingers while I think.

"Are you there?" he asks.

"Yes, sorry, just thinking. Block the sales," I reply.

"Um, I don't have the power," he replies.

I cut him off. "I will be down for a meeting with you tomorrow but contact all of the properties and let them know if they want to sell, I will always top the price."

"Um."

"Do it!" I snap. "You will be paid well for the trouble."

"I just thought you should know sir," he answers.

"Thank you. I will see you tomorrow afternoon." I hang up and stand in a rush. "Bitch, what's she playing at now?"

"Huh?" Cameron frowns.

"Amelie is apparently trying to buy a property next to Willowvale."

Cameron screws up his face. "Why?"

"To fucking piss me off, that's why!" I snap.

"Does it really matter?"

"Yes, it matters. I want to live there with Natasha and my kids one day. Natasha will not be running into that bitch on the school run!" I snap as my anger erupts.

He shakes his head. "She's tapped man... fatal fucking attraction." I put my head into my hands on my desk, this is another nightmare that I don't damn well need. "Don't say anything to Mother. Let her do the talking," I sigh.

Cameron nods. "Got it."

"I want to hear what she has to say before we tell her anything," I add.

"Yep. Do you want me to get her?" he asks. I look at him deadpan. "If you must."

Cameron stands and his eyes search mine. "Promise me that whatever she says won't change anything between us."

A lump in my throat forms and I drop my head.

"Promise me, Josh," he repeats.

I nod, unable to speak.

"And nothing will change with Dad," he replies.

"He's not the father of one of us, Cameron."

"Bullshit! That's semantics."

"Is it?" I ask. "Seems like a lot more than that to me."

"He obviously knows nothing about this," Cameron sighs.

I nod and my stomach drops. My father is a good man. My anger erupts again.

"Go and get her." Cameron nods and leaves the room.

Two minutes later my mother walks into the room with Cameron behind her. I am seated at my desk and she sits nervously on the leather chesterfield lounge with Cameron. She adjusts her skirt and folds her legs.

"Joshua, I didn't appreciate your tone when you told me to wait outside. I am your mother, and you will show me respect."

My eyes hold hers and I run my tongue over my front teeth, is she kidding?

"Respect is earned," I reply.

She scratches her head nervously. "What's this about?" she asks.

My eyes flick to Cameron. "You tell us," Cameron replies. "Stop playing games you two. I did not fly all the way from Australia to play charades. Spit it out!" she demands.

I stand up from my chair and walk around to lean back on my desk and I fold my arms in front of me. "It has come to our attention that we do not have the same blood."

She swallows nervously. "How?" I smirk. "Does it matter?"

"To me, yes."

"I had blood tests carried out because I saw Joshua's chart in the hospital. I am unsure if you are aware, I'm a qualified doctor," Cameron sneers sarcastically.

"Cut the tone!" she snaps.

"Cut the shit!" I yell. "You tell me how in hell we have different blood!"

Her face falls. "Joshua," she whispers. "I love you."

I quickly look away from her. I don't want to hear this.

She stands and walks over to the window. "What did Natasha say about this?"

My eyes meet Cameron's, here we go. "She has said nothing. Only that I should talk to you," I reply in a monotone.

She fakes a smile. "She must be loving this, driving a wedge between me and my boys. It's what she has always wanted."

I inhale deeply. I knew she would try and turn this against Natasha.

"This has nothing to do with Natasha, Mother! How dare you bring her into this?" Cameron yells.

My eyes meet his and I silently thank him. He's with me on this.

"Start talking," I sneer.

On cue she starts to cry, and Cameron covers his face. He can't stand it when women get upset, he's just not wired that way.

I stand still watching her, void of emotion.

Cameron stands and goes to her. "Please don't cry," he whispers as he pulls her into an embrace. "Tell us what's going on," he whispers.

"It's terrible. This whole situation is just terrible," she sobs into Cameron's shoulder.

I sit for five minutes while she gets herself together and finally, she takes a seat on the lounge and Cameron sits next to her and takes her hand in his. He's such a soft touch.

"When I was twenty-one and after I had Scott..." she pauses.

"Yes," he whispers.

"I... it... was a very difficult time for me."

I should have more empathy for her, but I just don't. I lean on the desk with my arms folded in front of me.

"Your father was away for months at a time and had lost interest in me. I was quite sure he was involved with another woman and his heart was somewhere else."

My stomach drops.

"Go on," Cameron whispers.

"I had a friend that would come to the house and check on Scott and me." Her eyes rise and meet mine. "Don't hate me, Joshua," she sobs.

I drop my head.

"His marriage had ended, and we relied on each other for support. Your father was away for four months."

I feel sick to my stomach and my eyes close in pain as I imagine the scenario she is setting.

"After much resistance I fell in love with this man and we began an intimate affair."

Cameron pulls his hand from hers and she drops her head.

"I thought he loved me. I was going to leave your father for him," she sobs.

The room is silent except for the sound of her crying. "How long?" I say in monotone.

"Six weeks," she whispers.

More silence...She sobs. "I told him of my plans to leave your father, but he was outraged and told me that he didn't love me and not to be a fool, it was just sex to him."

I rub my hands through my hair as nausea fills me.

She starts to cry uncontrollably. "I was crushed. I had thrown my marriage vows away on a man who didn't love me. I ended it immediately."

She becomes inconsolable and starts to really cry and I can see Cameron's heart breaking with every tear that she sheds.

"Go on," I reply.

"When Robert came back, he admitted that he had been having an affair and that he wanted to start again. I was so grateful to be given another chance."

My eyes watch her as my fury starts to reignite.

"We knew we had problems but were determined to work them out for the sake of Scott. We were so young, Joshua. We made mistakes. Both of us, your father and me."

I stand and go to the window behind my desk and look out onto the pool area. I just want this conversation over.

"Eight weeks later I found out I was pregnant. I had always worn condoms with this man so I knew it couldn't be his. I was overjoyed. I was being given a second chance with my husband."

Cameron's eyes meet mine as my eyes cloud over. We both know what this means. I drop back into my seat as pain starts to fill me. I'm not a Stanton.

"Joshua, remember when you were seventeen and you fell off the horse?" she asks.

I nod through my glassy eyes.

"You cut your leg deeply on the fence and you lost a lot of blood and needed a blood transfusion."

I nod with my head dropped.

"The doctors came to me and told me that you had a very rare blood type and that there was no physical possibility that you could be your father's child."

Cameron stands immediately and comes around behind me and places both of his hands on my shoulders in support.

I'm not a Stanton.

"Joshua, I didn't know what to do. Your father and I were finally so happy, and we had worked so damn hard to get to that place. How could I break a young boy's heart, Joshua?"

My broken eyes meet hers.

She sobs as the tears run freely down her face.

I stare at her, unable to speak through the tightening in my chest.

"I didn't know what to do," she whispers in a barely recognizable voice.

I keep staring at her.

"What would you have done in that situation?" she yells. "If I had told you the truth back then I would have messed up your whole life and you were already going off the rails at that point. Remember the partying, the fighting, the women?"

Cameron squeezes my shoulders and I put my hand over his.

"I decided to not say anything. No good could come from that kind of information. Your father loves you, Joshua."

I drop my face into my hands as the tears start to flow... who am I?

I hear Cameron sob behind me as the deafening silence fills the room.

"Get out," I whisper through the lump in my throat. "Joshua, no," she cries.

"Don't tell me no!" I yell as I stand furiously.

"Explain to me how Wilson has the same blood as me!" Her face drops.

"What?" she whispers.

"Wilson and I are 100% brothers, we have the same blood. You were sleeping with this man for six fucking years. Do not dare insult my intelligence with your lies one moment longer. Are you still sleeping with him now?"

"What?" she whispers again, and I can see by the look on

her face she didn't know this previously. "No," she shakes her head frantically.

"We have the tests. Who is he?" I scream. "Joshua, calm down," Cameron whispers.

I pick up a paperweight from my desk and throw it across the room in anger. "I will not fucking calm down. Tell me his name!" I scream.

She starts to shake her head nervously. "Joshua, stop it, you're scaring me."

I regain my composure as the angry tears roll down my face.

And she sobs again. "It can't be," she whispers.

"Does he know?" My broken eyes meet hers. "Does your husband know that two of his children are not biologically his?"

She shakes her head as her tear-filled eyes silently beg for forgiveness and time stands still.

"Please don't tell him," she whispers.

I stand. I can't be here any longer. "You have seven days to tell him or I will."

"Joshua, no," she cries.

"I want the name of my biological father in an email with contact details."

"Joshua, no," she cries. "Please... Joshua." She goes to grab me, but I push her away.

I stand still. I have never been so angry, so hurt. "Get out of my house and get out of my life. I'm done." I leave the room in a rush.

Natasha

I sit quietly alone in the party room with the door just slightly ajar. Joshua's office is diagonally across and three doors down the hall. I have cleared the house from everyone. The girls have gone to Adrian's for the day, I have given Brigetta the day off, and the guards are out the back in their office. The only voice I can hear raised is Joshua's. Ten minutes ago, something hit the wall with a thud... God knows what that was. What the hell is going on in there?

I sit silently waiting, wondering what I am going to say to him... them, when they emerge. A deep lead ball sits in my stomach. I have seen people at work for this very matter but when it's your own family it's completely different. The door slams and I hold my breath and close my eyes. Here we go. I sit for ten minutes as I watch the gap through the door. Joshua hasn't come down the hall so he must be still in his office and then finally I hear the door open and hear Cameron's and Margaret's voices.

"I can't believe this," Cameron sighs.

"Where is he? I need to see him," Margaret whispers.

"You heard him. He doesn't want to see you."

"He will never forgive me, Cameron. What will become of our family?" she sobs.

My heart drops and I know that my Lamborghini is somewhere in this house hurt. I put my hand over my mouth. Shit, what do I do?

"The driver will take you to a hotel," Cameron sighs.

"Why can't I stay here?" she whispers.

"You know why," he snaps. "Stop your shit."

She cries and then I hear her voice muffled. Cameron is obviously cuddling her.

"I don't want to leave," she sobs.

"Just go, Mum. Please." He sighs, their voices go out the front door and I sneak out into the hall. Where is he? He didn't walk past the door, my eyes flick around the hallway and then to the end door, the garage. I walk down the hall and slowly open the garage door and close it behind me. It's darkened so I flick the light on.

I walk down between the cars, but I don't see him. I walk to the other side of the Lamborghini. My heart drops, my beautiful man is sitting on the floor leaning up against the car, his head in his hands... crying.

Tears instantly fall to my cheeks and I walk over and drop to sit silently next to him on the floor.

I have no words. "Josh," I whisper.

He keeps his head down but pulls me onto his lap and I wrap my arms around his neck.

"I'm here, baby. It's okay," I whisper into the top of his head.

He sits deathly still as his head stays buried in my chest and the pain I feel coming from him is so strong.

I don't know what to say. What could I possibly say to make this situation better?

For forty minutes we sit on the cold cement floor. Finally he speaks. "Can we run away?" He smiles sadly.

I smile through my tears. "We can. Where do you want to go, my Lamborghini?"

He shakes his head as he stands and pulls me up by the hand. "Anywhere but here." He sighs.

CHAPTER 10

Adrian

I SIT STILL as I watch Joshua. He's standing at the end of my desk going through the pile of mail in my in-tray.

"I'm finishing early and going away for a couple of days," he remarks casually as he flicks through the letters.

"Where are you going?" I ask.

"Willowvale." He throws the letters onto my desk and they land with a thud.

"Why are you going on a Tuesday afternoon?" I frown.

"I have to see an estate agent. Apparently, bitch face is trying to buy a property adjacent to Willowvale." He pinches the bridge of his nose and inhales deeply.

I screw up my face. "Who? Amelie?"

He nods and walks over to the window with his hands in his suit pant pockets and stares out at the view.

I blow out a deep breath. "Fuck, man, what next? Does Natasha know?"

He shakes his head.

I lean back in my chair as I think. "Why don't you let me handle the real estate? You have enough shit on your plate at the moment."

His eyes stare straight ahead deep in thought.

I run my hands through my hair. "I don't think now is a good time for you to leave town."

"Why?" he asks.

"I think you should sort this stuff out with your mother."

"What's the point?" he replies in a monotone. "It's not going to change anything... my whole life has been a lie."

"Joshua, stop it, you're being melodramatic," I snap. "Do you have any idea what I would give to have my mother back here on Earth?"

He turns and his eyes meet mine.

"Don't take her for granted, Joshua. You will regret it one day." I sigh.

"Cut her funds," he says flatly.

"Payments?" I widen my eyes in shock. "Joshua, it's a couple of million dollars a year. This will seriously hamper her lifestyle."

"I don't give a fuck. Actually, I want her bank accounts traced. Let's see how she spends my money."

I shake my head. "Joshua, stop it. Why would you want to know that?"

"Just do it," he snaps.

My phone beeps a text. Natasha.

Wardrobe emergency!!
The king has told me to pack for polo.
What the hell does one wear to polo?
I don't have a spotted brown dress

I smile broadly. She's referring to Pretty Woman. Joshua's love is slowly turning into the sister that I never had. I love this girl. I quickly shoot back a text.

The buzzer sounds as I throw my phone back onto the desk. "Mr. Murphy."

"Yes," I reply.

"Your eleven o'clock appointment is here," Brittany replies.

I frown and open my diary screen on my monitor. I didn't know I had an appointment this morning. "What's the name?" I ask.

"Nicholas Anastas, sir."

My stomach drops, shit. I sit back in my chair and shake my head as my eyes flick to Joshua. He smirks.

I blow out a deep breath. "Send him in," I reply flatly. "I'm going," Joshua smiles as he raises his eyebrows.

"Sit down. You're not going anywhere," I snap. "I'm marching him immediately."

"Why don't you take some of your own advice?" Joshua snaps.

"Like what?" I ask.

"About taking people for granted," he replies. A knock sounds at the door.

"Shut up, Stanton," I murmur.

He smirks and walks over and opens the door.

"Here you are, sir," Brittany smiles as she opens the door for Nicholas.

"Thank you, Brittany," Joshua smiles, suddenly all perky. "Nicholas," he says in a rowdy voice. "Great to see you." He shakes his hand and holds his arm out in a welcoming gesture. "Come in, come in."

Nicholas turns and his eyes meet mine, and there he

stands, six foot two of Greek god perfection. The instant physical attraction I have to this man overwhelms me, it's so damn inconvenient. He is wearing a navy three-piece suit, his dark wavy hair tucks behind his ear, and he is immaculate from head to toe.

I drop my head to hide my distress as my heart races out of control. Why does he affect me like this?

"Hello Adrian." His eyes search mine. This is the first time I have seen him since that dreaded morning when he said goodbye.

I regain my manners and stand to greet him and shake his hand. "Hello Nicholas."

"How long are you here?" Joshua asks as I return to safety behind my desk.

"Umm." His chest rises and his eyes flick to me. He's nervous. "That depends," he replies quietly.

I pick up my pen and hold it between two hands. "On what?" I ask flatly.

"On you, Adrian."

I roll my eyes. "Don't start your shit, Nicholas, you know the score." I throw my pen onto the desk angrily.

Joshua narrows his eyes at me. "That will be my cue to leave then." He shakes Nicholas's hand. "Lovely seeing you, mate. Come by the house. Natasha would love to catch up."

What's Joshua playing at? I'm going to kill him. Nicholas nods, obviously flustered at my sudden outburst. We both stare after Joshua as he leaves the room.

His eyes meet mine. "What's with the attitude?" he says calmly.

"I told you not to come here," I reply.

"Well, I have, and you are giving me half an hour."

"I'm at work and very busy for the next couple of days."

"Make time!" he snaps.

I scratch the back of my head in frustration. "Take a seat," I sigh.

He sits down and looks around. "Nice office." I nod.

"Yes."

"How long have you been here?"

I raise my eyebrows. "Do you really want to know the answer to that question? Are you here to talk about my office?"

He rolls his lips as his eyes hold mine again. "I'm sorry about before," he murmurs.

Hurt fills me, and I drop my eyes to my desk as I run my pointer finger along the edge.

"I thought I was ready," he replies quietly. I stay silent.

"I had no idea I was going to fall in love with you, Adrian." I lift my eyes to meet his and hold my chin as I think.

"I handled it badly," he whispers.

"Is that it?" I ask.

He frowns. "What do you mean?"

"Is that all you've got to say? As I mentioned I'm very busy today," I reply.

His face drops. "Why are you being such a cold bastard?"

I fake a smile. "Really? You're calling me a cold bastard? How ironic."

He holds his head at an angle. "Adrian, please, can we just talk about this?"

"No," I snap.

"Why not?"

"Because it will get us nowhere," I reply.

"Do you still have feelings for me?" he asks quietly.

My stomach drops. "No," I reply flatly. "I've met someone else."

His face drops. "You're lying," he whispers.

"Am I?" I ask.

"I know you are. I know you wouldn't have moved on from what we had so quickly."

Once again hurt rips through me. He knows me a lot better than I care to admit. I need to get away from this shit.

"Nicholas, I don't have time for this. Please leave."

"Can we have dinner tonight?" he pleads.

"No."

"Why not? Just as friends."

"I have a business dinner on tonight," I reply.

"Can I be your date?" he asks hopefully.

"Fuck. No. Stop it!" I snap.

"Can't we be friends?" he murmurs.

"I have enough friends, I don't want another friend."

"I'm not going anywhere until you agree to have dinner with me," he pleads.

"Stop it. You're acting crazy. We are finished, and it was your decision! End of story," I snap.

His sad eyes look right through me. "I made a mistake," he whispers.

I close my eyes as pain once again lances through me. "You did."

"Just dinner," he stammers.

I stand in a rush. "Leave me alone, Nicholas. I can't fucking compete with a dead man!"

His face drops and his eyes tear up as his chest rises. I drop my head in shame that I just said that out loud.

"Please, Nicholas, leave me be. I can't do this," I whisper.

He closes his eyes and swallows deeply. He stands and waits for me to look up at him... I don't and two minutes later I hear my door quietly open and close.

And once again the enigmatic Nicholas Anastas has left my life... and once again I am left feeling empty and gutted.

Natasha

Bridget and I lie by the fire that Abbie has just lit for us in the lounge room. It's cool outside and has a distinct winter feel.

"Why haven't we been having the fire going all week? It's frigging freezing in this museum." Abbie frowns as she flops down next to us.

"I don't know if the boys even light it," I reply. "They are not exactly domesticated."

Bridget looks around at our surroundings. "I can't believe this is your life now." She gestures at the ridiculously high ceiling and we all stare up at it in silence as we lie on the floor in the huge room.

"What if you never come back to Australia, Tash?" Bridget whispers sadly.

My heart sinks. That thought had crossed my mind more than once too. I don't know if I will ever get Joshua to leave LA and the bad thing is, the longer I am here... the further my dream of living in Australia seems, I'm starting to like LA. Bridget grabs my hand and Abbie flops her legs over ours.

"You guys going to be ok for the next couple of days here without me?" I ask.

"Are you going to be ok is the question?" Abbie asks. "Joshua seems to be on edge."

I nod. "He is on edge, I'm worried about him."

"How's frigging Margaret?" Bridget sighs.

"That's my worst nightmare. I feel sorry for her," Abbie replies.

"She's a trollop," Bridget sneers.

"Stop it," I snap. "She's Joshua's mother; don't speak about her that way."

"Don't defend the mole," Bridget snaps. "She has put you and Joshua through hell for years."

Cameron walks to the door and stands still as he watches us. "What are we doing?"

"Cooking pancakes, what does it look like?" I reply flatly.

He smirks and comes and lies down across me and puts his head on my stomach and joins us in our ceiling staring.

"Is your mum okay, Cam?" I ask.

"No, she's messed up."

"Can you go and stay with her after we leave?" I ask.

He shakes his head. "Nope. She can go to hell."

I frown. "But you were cuddling her the other day."

He sighs. "I can't stand women crying, that's all."

Bridget puts her hand over onto Cameron's forehead and pats it. "You can be quite cute when you want to be, Cameron Stanton."

Abbie laughs and he flicks Bridget's hand off his face. "Fuck off, don't touch me," he groans.

The front door opens and closes, and we hear Joshua's voice. "Can you get Murray to get Natasha's Lamborghini out of the garage, please?"

"Yeah, sure. Where are you going?" Ben replies.

"Natasha and I are going to Willowvale for a couple of days," Joshua replies.

"And when were you going to tell me this?" Ben snaps.

"I'm telling you now," Joshua answers angrily.

"I can't plan rosters if I don't know what's going on, Stan. We have more than one location to guard then."

"I didn't tell you because I am not taking security. I need a couple of days alone with my girl," Joshua replies.

I smile to myself. I need a couple of days alone with you too, baby.

They turn the corner and stop dead in their tracks when they see us.

"Hey," everyone calls.

Joshua glares at us. "Interrupting something, am I?"

I giggle. What must we look like in a pile on the floor? "Get your head off her stomach," Joshua snaps.

Cameron rolls his eyes and sits up. "Glad you're home, Happy Jack."

I smirk. Joshua really is on edge at the moment. "You are not going anywhere without security," Ben asserts as his eyes find Bridget across the room and he glares at her.

"Watch me!" Joshua sneers as he angrily undoes his tie. "Are you packed?" he snaps at me as he reefs his tie so hard I am surprised he doesn't break his neck.

My eyes flick to the girls who are smirking. "Yes," I reply meekly.

"Good, we leave in ten." He then storms through the room and disappears up the staircase.

Cameron smirks. "It sucks to be you, Tash."

Hmm, it sure does. I nod and slowly pick myself up off the floor and Ben stands exasperated with his hands on his hips.

"Just have someone follow us discreetly down there, Ben. He needs some privacy at the moment," I whisper quietly.

Ben frowns. "Why? What's going on?" he asks.

Oh shit, he doesn't know. "Joshua has some family stuff that is worrying him, and he needs to get away. You stay here with the girls and send someone else."

"I can't do my job properly if I don't know what's going on, Natasha," he replies.

"I know, I'm sorry," I sigh. "I will talk to him, I promise. Can you just make security minimal for a couple of days please?"

A knock sounds at the door.

"It's not safe, Tash," Ben replies as he frowns at the door and looks at his watch. He opens the door and two large muscle up men stand before us. Ben raises his eyebrows in question. "Can I help you?" he asks.

"Yes, I'm Detective Ford and this is my partner Detective Taylor. We are here to see a Joshua Stanton and a Ben Stathem."

Ben's face drops. "That's me. Please come in and I will get Mr. Stanton." He holds his arm out and the two detectives walk into the lounge room.

I fake a nervous smile and my panicked eyes meet the girls. The three stooges get up from the floor, walk over and the detectives introduce themselves to everyone. Abbie shakes the first guy's hand and then when she gets to the second guy, Detective Taylor, they seemingly forget we are all here.

"Hello. I'm Abbie," she breathes, appearing nervous. Bridget's and my eyes meet, this is new. I've never seen Abbie get nervous before.

He smiles warmly, taking her hand in his, and he seems all flustered too. "The pleasure is all mine." His eyes hold hers. "My name is Rick."

I frown at their exchange. Rick is tall with blond curly hair and appears super fit... super freaking hot actually. Pity about the small fact he is here to interview us about a murder that he thinks we are involved in.

Bridget and I frown at each other. Joshua comes back down the stairs with a renewed purpose.

"Hello," he says calmly.

Rick speaks first. "Mr. Stanton, we are here to check in with you as required by the Australian Police Force."

"Yes, of course," Joshua murmurs as his eyes flick to Cameron. "Come into my office."

Abbie bites her bottom lip in anticipation and Joshua, Ben and Detective Ford all head down the hallway. Cameron takes off upstairs, not wanting to be involved in any of this. *Thanks a lot, Cam.* Rick, however, stays glued to the spot staring at Abbie.

Bridget widens her eyes at me. Fuck, I know, what is she doing?

She holds out her hand again and he takes it in his. "Lovely to meet you, Rick," she whispers.

Oh God, give me a break.

He hands her a business card. "If you think of any reason why you need to call me, please feel free," he smiles sexily.

She smiles nervously and Bridget frowns, huh? What the hell?

Why would she need to call you, dipshit?

"Thank you, I will," she replies.

Rick then turns and walks down the hall to meet the others and I grab her by the arm and lead her into the kitchen.

"What do you think you are doing?" Bridget whispers angrily.

"What?" Abbie snaps as she rips her arm from the vice grip I have on her.

"You don't screw the cops, Abbie," I whisper.

"I'm not screwing anybody," she snaps. I raise my eyebrows in question.

"Yet." She smiles. "Although I am having a drought and he is gorgeous. Maybe I will."

"No," Bridget snaps. "I frigging mean it. He could bring us undone," she whispers angrily.

"God." Abbie shakes her head in disgust at us. "You two are the biggest drama queens I know. Calm down."

The car horn beeps from out the front. "I'm coming, I'm coming," I sigh as I look for my sunglasses around the bedroom. Where in the hell have I put them? The horn sounds again. Bloody hell, shut up. I finally find them and make my way downstairs. The Lamborghini is parked in the driveway and everyone is gathered around it.

"Joshua, are you sure you don't want to marry me instead?" Abbie asks as she hangs in the window looking at the beautiful interior of the car.

Everyone laughs and Joshua looks at her deadpan. "Positive, Abbs."

I smile and put my hands on my hips as I circle the beast.

This doesn't even look like a frigging car.

Joshua throws me the keys. "You're driving, Presh," he says.

I look at the keys in my hand and I see the beautiful silver key ring with the initials:

NMS

I smile broadly and hold it out for Bridget to see. She pretends to swoon as she picks it up and smiles. She turns to Joshua. "You really are a little bit beautiful, Joshua Stanton."

I smile broadly as my eyes flick to him. "Don't I know it?" I reply.

Joshua shakes his head and gets into the passenger side of the car, unimpressed.

"What about me, am I beautiful?" Cameron asks.

Bridget looks at him flatly. "No, you're an idiot."

He grabs her in a headlock, and she squeals in laughter as they start to wrestle, and he pushes her over, so she falls into the hedge.

"See, an idiot. That's what an idiot would do." She squeals as she giggles. Ben grabs her hand and pulls her out of the bush.

I nervously hop into the driver's seat. "It's very low." My eyes flick to Joshua.

He smiles broadly and I melt. That's the first genuine smile I have seen from him in a week.

"Are you sure that other cars can even see you in this thing?" I ask.

He nods. "Start the engine." He points to the ignition.

I bite my bottom lip as I start the car and I laugh loudly.

Joshua's eyes light up in excitement.

"I'm like a bad ass gangster," I yell out the window and Ben laughs.

"This doesn't feel safe," I murmur as I adjust the rear-view mirror.

"It's not meant to be; it's designed to frighten the hell out of you." Joshua smiles.

I nod as I practice the blinkers. "Hmm, it's working," I mutter under my breath. I slowly go round the driveway and everyone waves. I squeal loudly in excitement and Joshua laughs.

"Look out, drivers, here we come." I laugh.

"Stop talking, concentrate and watch the road," Joshua murmurs and the fear in his eyes makes me laugh again.

"Oh, are you scared, Stanton?" I squeal.

His eyes flick to me and he smirks. "Maybe."

. . .

I sit in the car across the road from where Joshua is talking to a real estate agent who we have called in on our way to Willowvale. They have emerged from the office and are standing on the sidewalk finishing their conversation. Joshua is wearing my favorite army green cargo pants with a black V-neck jumper. The way he is standing, back facing me with one foot up on the curb, I can see every muscle in his broad back and that tight behind... excellent viewing just quietly. Oh, and that clipped dark hair, a walking goddamn orgasm.

He's been quiet, too quiet, and I need to take his mind off things. Ben's words about us not being safe are playing on my mind. Joshua was attacked once on his way back from Willowvale. A little earlier when I bought coffee for us in a cafe I kept looking around nervously to see if people were following us now. I quickly glance around the street to see if anyone suspicious is lurking. I thought the security would have been following us by now, but apparently not.

My recurring nightmare comes into my mind. What if someone had Joshua and I had to try and defend him? I wouldn't have a frigging clue how to do that. Maybe I should take some self-defense classes and learn how. The image of me being gang raped brings a ball of fear to my throat and I internally hear the sound of the metal bar hitting Joshua's head. I close my eyes. *Stop it, Natasha, it's not real.*

How can a nightmare frighten someone so much? I now know for sure that my dreams are stress related. I have had my nightmare twice this week, the first time since my place got broken into the night before we went to Kamala.

Joshua finally walks back across to the car. He smiles warmly at me through the windscreen and I feel my heart skip a grateful beat. I have never loved him more than I do now. The way he has handled this whole nightmare has only cemented our relationship and how strong it really is. I honestly thought that when he found out that I knew about his mother it was going to be hell to pay and we would start all of our ridiculous games again. But no. We are finally past the nonsense infiltrating our precious relationship.

"Sorry, that took longer than I thought." He bounces into his seat.

I bend down to the cup holder and produce a protein smoothie and the coffee I bought him at the shop.

"Here you are, babe."

He smiles and his eyes twinkle. "You're looking after me very well these days, Presh."

I smirk. "Isn't that what wives do, look after their husbands?"

His face falls. "Not always," he answers quietly as he takes them from me, and I know he is thinking of his own mother and father.

Shit! Why did I frigging say that? What an idiot!

Trying to recover the situation I quickly answer. "Well, that's what this wife does, future wife," I stammer as I correct myself.

He smirks and bends over and pecks me on the lips. "Lucky me."

"Yes, you are lucky actually. I'm hot property you know." I widen my eyes to accentuate my point.

He smirks as he pulls the car back onto the road. I made him swap and drive. I'm just too nervous... wrong side of the road in a space machine... not a good combination.

Ten minutes later, we are driving up the beautiful driveway toward Willowvale and I feel my nerves flutter. All of the staff here know Amelie, and they all know what went down. If this place wasn't so sacred to Joshua it would be the first damn thing

I would change. It would be so gone, and that sold sign would be swinging in the breeze.

Joshua's eyes light up and he starts to look at me. Oh jeez, he wants me to be excited now.

"What?" I smile.

"We are home." He smiles broadly.

"You think this is home?" I question, slightly horrified.

He nods. "This is my favorite place on Earth. I love it here. I want you to love it here as much as I do."

My stomach drops. Oh shit, I need to get over myself and start liking this country life crap. I look around at all the space. What the hell do you do out here? I'm telling you one thing. If he thinks for one minute, I'm wearing jodhpurs he's got another think coming, my behind would look like a stocking full of marbles in those things.

We pull into the parking area and Joshua laughs out loud when he sees an old dog trotting up the road towards us. He quickly gets out of the car and bends to pat it. I sit with my eyes glued on the mansion in front of me. This is ridiculous wealth. The house isn't a house, it's a frigging castle minus Mr. Darcy. Actually, no, that's not true. My Mr. Darcy is right here. I smile inwardly as I watch him pat the dog.

Joshua comes around to my door and opens it for me. "Out, Presh." He holds his hand out for me and I climb out of the comfort of my luxury car. Joshua gets our bags, and we walk slowly up the stairs.

"Where is everybody?" I ask as I follow him, remembering how many people were here last time.

"I have given everyone a few days off. I told you I need some time alone," he replies.

I fake a smile and nod nervously. "Oh, right." Shit, are we safe? This place is like a perfect setting for a horror murder massacre. No neighbors, out in the country, no one would hear me scream... *stop it, Natasha.*

I follow him into the house and my eyes go straight to the ceiling. It is really beautiful.

Joshua walks to the huge staircase. "Come on," he calls, and I follow him tentatively up the stairs and down the huge hallway towards his room. He keeps walking past it and I stop at the door and peer in... *the scene of the crime.* Joshua had sex with Amelie in that room, on that bed. My head drops at the visual that rolls around in my pea brain.

"Tash, don't," he whispers, well aware of what is going through my mind. He drops the bags and comes back and cuddles me. "Sweetheart, don't think of it," he whispers into the top of my head.

There's that word again... *the pity sweetheart.* I put on a brave face and nod. *Stop being a baby.* "I know," I whisper as I pull out of his grip.

"I have had the master room redone, new bed, paint and bathroom. But change it to whatever you like. Actually, change the whole house to whatever you like." He pulls me into the bedroom.

My eyes flick around the huge space, a large modern bed with light grey velvet padding on the headboard that matches the huge triple ottoman at the bottom of the bed. All white bed linen and walls, and all along the length of one wall is a huge window bench seat in the same grey luxurious material and four double bay windows that go off it. A large double comfy looking sofa lounge in the same beautiful material is in the corner with a lamp and a small, mirrored table next to it.

On the far wall is a picture in black and white with a silver pendant light hanging over it and I walk over to try and make it out. I squint and then my eyes widen when I work it out. It's me in bed naked from the back, taken on the first night we were together, the photo that Joshua had on his phone. My eyes flick to Joshua. "Why would you want this photo in our bedroom?"

"Because it is my favorite picture in the world. When I took it, I thought that I only had that night with you." He runs his finger down the picture following the shape of my hips and down my legs. "I was gutted that night thinking I had to let you go."

I smile softly. "And yet you didn't," I whisper.

He shakes his head. "You didn't let me go."

"I will never let you go, Josh," I reply.

He kisses me gently as he holds my face, his tongue slowly sliding through my open lips. "Do you know how much I love you?" he whispers.

I smile and emotion steals my ability to speak.

"I fucking adore you," he whispers. "You are everything to me. This money and this life mean nothing to me if I don't have you."

I smile as tears fill my eyes.

"Even though you are a crybaby," he whispers into our kiss.

I smile as he kisses me again. "Josh," I whisper.

"Hmm," he replies as his lips drop to my neck.

"We're going to be okay, you know. This is our family now, right here in this room, in this house. Our love and our children will block everything else out."

I feel him smile into my neck. "Our six children," he whispers into my skin.

"Maybe." I smirk.

"Let's make some tonight." He lifts my top over my shoulders.

"No," I mutter.

"No?" he repeats.

I shake my head. "No knocking up, Stanton."

He smirks. "Run us a bath and I am going to find us some wine. Three hours of hot water therapy is just what I need." He kisses me and stretches my bottom lip with a stretch as he pulls away from me. A flutter of nervous excitement runs through me, Mr. Stanton is in the house and I can tell he's feeling bad.

CHAPTER 11

Natasha

TRUE TO OUR word we are on our third hour in the bath, our second bottle of Crystal Champagne and about our tenth top-up of hot water. The room is steamy and warm, and Joshua is in front encircled by my legs, his head on my chest between my breasts. With each glass of champagne, he relaxes and talks just that bit more... too bad I am also feeling inebriated and so damn relaxed that I may slip into a coma at any minute.

My psychology skills are down the gurgler. I pick up the sponge and squeeze it over Joshua's chest as I brush my lips over his temple. He frowns slightly as he thinks of something.

I kiss his cheek and wait for him to speak. One thing I have learned tonight is that if I don't ask, he will tell me. If I do ask... he shuts up.

"I'm a bad person," he whispers.

I frown as I kiss him again on his temple. "Why do you say that?" I squeeze the water over his chest from the sponge.

"I'm glad she's dead." He sighs.

I frown. "Who?"

"The prostitute," he replies.

"Oh," I whisper. TC, the bitch.

"When the police told me she was dead I was relieved."

"I understand why," I whisper into his temple.

He turns and looks at me in shock. "You do?"

"That whole situation is a nightmare," I whisper.

"It is," he sighs as he looks forward again.

"We are innocent. Nothing can be proven, Joshua." I kiss him again on the side of his cheek reassuringly.

He nods. "Fucking Starsky and Hutch didn't help the situation." He takes a drink from his crystal champagne glass.

I laugh out loud. "Starsky and Hutch." I giggle. "I thought you said they were dumb and dumber."

He widens his eyes. "Yeah, that too," he says flatly. We sit for another ten minutes as we slip into another comfortable silence.

"I think it's true," he murmurs as he stares into space.

"What is?"

"I think my father didn't love my mother."

I frown as I continue to wash him. His thoughts are jumping all over the place.

"He was never home when I was a child, now I think about it and compare it to how I feel about you." He pauses.

I wait for him to keep speaking.

"I wouldn't leave you for one night. I couldn't stand being away from you. As soon as we kids went to bed I would hear his car leave."

His eyes drop down as his hands slide up and down my shins as he thinks. "He couldn't have loved her," he murmurs almost to himself.

I don't know what to say so I stay silent and he brings my feet around onto his stomach and rubs them onto his semi-hard cock. God, he feels good, even with my feet.

"Tell me about your tattoo." I smile into his temple.

He drops his head back to my shoulder and looks at me. "Which story do you want? The one I tell everybody or the truth?"

I smile. "Let's start with the one you tell everyone."

He smiles and turns and kisses my arm. "So, I met this smoking hot girl this night, had the most un-fucking-believable sex and we had such a bender that we ended up in a tattoo parlor at 6 am and I woke up with this. Her name was obviously Natasha. I don't remember ever getting it."

I smile faintly. How many women has he told that story to?

He kisses my breast.

"Tell me the other one," I murmur.

He rolls over so he is lying with his chest rubbing on my pubic bone. "So, I met this smoking hot girl who I had known forever... but not really at all." Our eyes are locked. "And I couldn't stay away from her no matter how hard I tried."

A trace of a smile brushes my lips. "Go on," I whisper.

"And then one night I kissed her and for the first time in my life I didn't want to fuck."

I frown. "You didn't?"

He shakes his head and then takes my nipple into his mouth and sucks it seductively. "I wanted to lie next to her, for her to hold me, to want me. I wanted to protect her and then the feelings got out of control and grew so strong that the need to be inside her turned me inside out. So much so that I was totally consumed with need for this woman." He stops and smiles to himself. "And when she let me make love to her for the first time..." He pauses and looks into space. "It was the first time I had ever made love too. Up until then I had only had sex. I didn't even know what making love was. It was the best and worst day of my life. I realized I was desperately in love and then I knew I couldn't have her."

I lean up and gently swipe my tongue through his wet lips. "And the tattoo?" I whisper into his kiss.

"I wanted a mark on the outside of my body to match the mark I had for her on the inside of my body."

I smile softly at him. Dear God, I love this man.

"I had been to the tattoo parlor three times to discuss what he was going to do and then on her 21st birthday at 9 am I was waiting at the door when it opened. If I couldn't have her, I was not going to let myself ever forget her and what she had taught me. It took six hours to do."

My eyes gaze into his. How did I ever get so lucky as to have this man love me?

He kisses me with such intensity and emotion that he rolls us slowly so that I am on top of his large body. His hand grabs the back of my head hard as he holds me to him and kisses me aggressively, passionately. Instinctively my body starts to rub itself back and forth over his large erection that is lying thick up against his stomach. His tongue takes possession of my mouth as he holds me almost brutally to his kiss. He grabs my thighs, spreads me over him and his hands start to slide up and down my wet body.

His eyes meet mine. "Fuck me," he whispers as he cracks his neck. It seems our little game of truth or dare is over.

I can hardly breathe from want of this man and he aggressively grabs my hipbones and drags my flesh over his. "I need to be inside you, my precious girl."

My eyes close and my head throws back.

"Now!" he snaps. Bloody hell, he was half asleep three minutes ago.

Goosebumps scatter over my body. That was Mr. Stanton's voice and I know I'm going to be blessed with his aggression. He lifts me and holds the bottom of his shaft up and grabs my hip and impales me to the hilt. My head throws forward with the sharp sting of his possession. "Joshua," I whisper as the air is forced from my lungs.

"Squat!" he snaps as he pants, trying to control himself. I slowly bring my legs up and his head drops back to the side of the bath as his mouth hangs slack and his dark eyes watch me struggle to take him.

He lifts me slowly and slides back in and my eyes close. "You like that?" he whispers.

My body shudders and I nod. "Answer me!" he snaps.

"Yes," I whimper.

"I'm in the mood for some pain, baby." His eyes drop to where our bodies meet. "You with me, can I have it?" he asks.

He lifts me again and my insides start to liquefy as he brings me back down firmly and circles my hips with him deep inside of me, my head thrown back.

"Can I have it, Natasha?" he growls.

"Yes," I pant. "Take it," I breathe.

He smiles darkly and lifts me and slams me back down and I cry out. Up and down, he slams me so aggressively that I don't think I can take it and my legs are as far open as they can go. He sits up and his open mouth is on my neck and his rock-hard cock is pistoling at such a fast pace in and out of my body I can do nothing but hang on.

He stops and rearranges my legs so that they are up on the side of the bath and then he grabs my shoulders from behind as leverage and starts to really fuck me... oh dear God... he's so damn good at this. The water is sloshing all over the bathroom and I start to scream. He's going to rip me in half. He brings his palm down to my stomach and his thumb down to my clitoris and starts to circle it in precise timing with his deep pounding. My eyes roll back in my head and I start to shudder. My body contracts hard around him and I cry out.

"You. Are. Such. A. Hot. Fuck," he growls as his own orgasm rips through him so ferociously that he is thrown forward. We stay still, panting, and I smile into his perspiration clad chest.

"Seriously," he whispers into my neck. "Having sex with you is..." He shakes his head as he tries to catch his breath and articulate what he is saying. "You blow my fucking mind, Natasha. I can feel every single muscle inside you." He pants.

I try to talk through my breathlessness. "Baby, with a muscle as big as yours, you could feel it in the next room." I smile.

He bites my neck hard and I wince to escape him. "Now I need a shower to wash off my bath," he murmurs.

I smile into his kiss. "I like being dirty with you, Mr. Stanton."

I wake to a bang and I frown. The bathroom light is still on and Joshua and I are on top of the blankets on the bed. *What time is it?* I unwrap myself from Joshua's grasp and walk to my handbag and get out my phone: 1.50 am. God, we fell asleep. I hear it again, a distant bang. What is that? I wrestle through my bag and retrieve my pajamas and gown and quickly dress. It's frigging freezing. The fire is just dying down to embers. I turn on the lamp so I can see and quickly put some wood onto it. It crackles loudly in a thank you.

My eyes flick to Joshua who is on his back and out cold. One hand is behind his head and the other is on the family jewels, his deep sleeping position. He needs a good night's sleep, I know he hasn't had one in over a week.

I'm starving. Our three-hour bath and lovemaking put us into such a relaxed state that we fell asleep before eating dinner. I sit nervously on the ottoman in front of the fire and watch the red glow. I should just go downstairs and get something to eat. Yeah, why not? I can do that. I walk to the door and peer down the huge, darkened hall. Fuck this house, castle, whatever it is, it's like the frigging Amityville Horror on acid. People would pay good money to come on a haunted tour of this place.

I go back into the room and retrieve my phone and turn the flashlight thingy on. Just find the light switches and turn the lights on... not hard, Natasha. I start to shake my hands nervously. I look at Joshua sleeping like a baby... should I wake him up? No, he needs to sleep. I walk back over and peer down the hall. If Joshua thinks I am getting up to breastfeed six kids in the middle of the night in this museum, he can think again.

I start to slowly walk down the wide darkened space. Yep, this is totally messed up and for some stupid reason I get a feeling someone is behind me. I can see a light on down the end of the hall, and I start to run towards it. I get to the end of the hallway and flick on the light switch and hold my chest as I pant. I smile to myself. Stop it, you idiot, you're just scaring yourself. I turn on all of the light switches and the house lights up like Christmas. That's better.

I walk downstairs proudly with my heart beating loudly in my chest and find some more light switches, flick them on, then head into the kitchen. I look around the huge silent kitchen. To the left is a huge double oven and, on the counter, next to that are two knife blocks with long carving knives in them.

A loud bang sounds in the distance and my eyes widen.

What the fuck was that? Goosebumps scatter over my body, my eyes flick to the knife blocks and I grab a knife. Shit, shit, shit. I walk over to the kitchen window, stand on my tiptoes and peer out. I can't see anything... darkness. Where are the guards? I don't even know if they arrived. *It's not safe, Natasha.* Ben's words run repeatedly through my mind. What's that noise... what's that noise? I look down at myself... what the hell? I am in the Amityville Horror house holding a carving knife in the middle of the night alone. Halloween movie times ten.

I want confirmation that the guards are here. I need to know my man is safe. I'll call Bridget. She will know what time they left. I dial her number and it rings. Ring... ring... ring... ring.

"What's wrong?" Ben's voice snaps as he answers the phone.

I frown and look at the time on my phone. 2 am. "Um... Ben?" I murmur.

"What's wrong, Tash?"

What's he doing answering Bridget's phone in the middle of the night? Oh my God... I smile broadly.

"Umm." I'm so shocked I raise my eyebrows and am speechless

"Is something wrong?" he snaps again.

"No," I smile. "I was just a bit scared and I thought I would call to see if the guards are outside, that's all."

"Where is Joshua?" he snaps.

"He's upstairs asleep, Ben. It's okay. I'm scared of ghosts, not people. I just heard a noise."

"Oh God." He sighs under his breath.

I bite my bottom lip to stifle my smile. "Are the guards here?" I ask.

"Hang on and I will call them and check."

"Okay," I answer.

I hear him put the phone down and I listen as he dials from

another phone... obviously his.

"Where are you?" he snaps. "Circle the outside of the house and do a check, please."

He listens. "Yes, Natasha is up." He listens again. "Call me back when you've done it." He hangs up.

He picks up the phone to me. "Tash." His voice becomes gentle. "Are you okay?"

I smile. "Yes, thank you."

"They are out the front in the guard's office at the garage. They have been walking around the house all night."

I put my hand on my chest in relief. "Thanks Ben," I whisper.

"Is Joshua okay?" he asks.

"Yes, he's just exhausted."

He stays silent and I know he wants to know what's going on with him and Cameron, but it's not my place to tell him.

"Is Bridget there?" I ask. He stays silent. "Ben?" I ask.

"She's asleep," he says quietly.

A broad smile beams from my face... oh my God... they hooked up.

"She left her phone in the kitchen, that's all," he mutters.

I smile again and I know he's lying. Bridget would not go to bed without her phone, that phone and she are attached at the hip.

For some reason I get a visual of him sitting in her bed, naked, on her phone to me now.

"Do you want me to come down there?" Ben asks.

I smile. "No, you stay there and look after my sister," I whisper. He stays silent as he thinks.

"Not a word, Natasha," he murmurs. "Please."

I smile. "You have my word, Ben, and please don't tell Joshua I called you frightened."

"Yes, of course," he replies.

I smile broadly. "Good night, Ben," I whisper.

"Good night, Tash." He hangs up. I hold my chest and smile broadly. Oh my God, oh my God. Bridget and Ben. Bridget and Ben.

I go to the fridge and get out the platter that was obviously prepared by the cook for us earlier and head back to our room while smiling like an idiot. I leave all of the lights on. Stuff it, it's not like Joshua can't afford the power bill. This place is frigging scary. I turn back and look at the knife on the counter and go back and pick it up. I'm just going to keep this hidden in our room... just in case. *I should probably learn how to use the damn thing.* I get halfway up the hall and once again start to run. This place frigging freaks me out.

At this moment I am missing my little apartment that would fit into Joshua's bedroom alone. I make it, close the door behind me and lean on it in relief with my heart beating furiously. Instant silence and calm again in my love bubble with my man asleep like a baby.

I put the food on the ottoman in front of the fire and go and sit next to Joshua on the bed. He's in his deep sleeping position. I smile. Do all men sleep with their hand on their dick? Carbon copies, actually that's not true. In fact, it couldn't be further from the truth. My last two boyfriends openly loved me from the very beginning, did everything in their power to try and get me to love them back, and yet this man is the ultimate onion. I have had to peel him back, layer upon layer, even to get acknowledgement that he wanted to spend time with me.

From the beginning the sexual attraction has been undeniable and so damn hot that my body never had a chance of refusing it... not that my heart would have let me. Unlike my feelings for the other men in my past, I need intimacy from

Joshua, crave it. Just like I crave the animal inside him whose only goal is to fuck hard and mate, damn the consequences. He will take what he wants from my body, when he wants it and I love it.

I hold my hand up and look at my ring and I smile as a deep wave of gratitude flows over me. He loves me, he loves me with the same intensity that he resisted me. All consuming passion that every woman should feel at least once in a lifetime. For a lifetime. I bend and gently kiss his cheek and run my hand gently over his short dark hair, over his chest and down through his dark pubic hair and then over his thigh. He told me tonight in the bath that he couldn't stand being away from me for a night. I smile again. I can't stand being away from him at all. I know that will wear off and we will slip into comfortableness like everyone does. But I think because the fight has been so hard, the prize is that much sweeter and that much more valuable, to both of us.

I walk over to the ottoman, pick up the cheese platter and

go and sit on the window seat and look out into the darkness. I sit for ten minutes eating cheese like a mouse in silence and am interrupted from my calm when the dog starts to bark downstairs.

I don't think anyone could see me where I am sitting in the semi darkness but I'm not sure. So, I get up and grab my phone and turn the lamp off next to the bed and go back to the seat and sit in the darkness. What's out there? The dog goes off again and I know it's an intruder warning bark. I see the dog trot around the side of the building downstairs, and I watch in silence... and then I see it. A red glow of a cigarette as it gets inhaled at the side of the outhouse down the back. I see it go up and glow red as it is inhaled and then go back down in between puffs.

I frown. Ben said they were in the office in the garage at the front of the house. Why would they walk around to the backyard and behind the outhouse to smoke? That's weird. Should I go and check that it's them? *Stop being stupid Natasha!* I shake my head in disgust at myself and go and crawl into bed next to Joshua. If there was someone down there, the bloody guards would know about it. What an idiot I am, talk about drama queen. I'm even imagining things now.

My sleepy eyes open to silence. Where's Joshua? It's daylight but very early, maybe 5 or 6. I roll over and my eyes go to the side table where there is a note:

Presh, gone for a ride. Won't be long.

I smile. My boy is doing what he loves. I slowly hop up and go to the window and sit on the thick padded window seat, my new favorite place, and stare out over the green paddocks. A sense of calm comes over me. This is what he loves about it here, the stillness. He has never had the LA party life here in Willowvale. His fake friends don't come here. There are no cameras, no excuses... no lies.

I make an internal decision. If Joshua wants to relax here, then the very least I can do is learn to love it as much as him. I shower and dress in my favorite faded tight jeans with a chunky cream knitted sweater and my runners and I head downstairs. I walk out the back door and look around. Where is this guard office thingy? I walk around the side and up onto the asphalt driveway and see a door at the back of the garage and tentatively walk up to it.

The door is open, and two men are inside. "Hello." I wave

meekly as my eyes flick around the space. A large office with a kitchen, dining table and chairs, lounge and television and a very large selection of guns hanging on the wall. I frown. Hell, why do they need all these guns?

"Hello, Natasha," the two men reply.

I smile nervously as my eyes stay glued on the guns on the wall. "Thanks for watching us last night." My eyes flick back to the men.

"No, we have just taken over. The night-shift pair finished at 7 am."

"Oh." I nod. "Will they be back tonight?"

"Yep," one of the men replies. "They will be back at ten."

"Ah, okay," I answer. "Have..." I frown as I feel stupid asking the next question. "Do they smoke?" I ask.

They frown and exchange looks. "No," one of them replies. "Why?"

I narrow my eyes as I think. "Last night someone was smoking outside my window and the dog was barking. I just wanted to check it was them."

The older man smiles. "One of them must have taken it up. They would have checked why the dog was barking. It's fine. Don't worry."

I smile in relief. "Which stable is Joshua at?"

"He's in the east stables. Would you like me to drive you there?"

I bite my lip. "Is it far away?"

"No, about five hundred meters down the hill to the east." He points down a dirt lane and I look in that direction.

"I might just take a walk down there." I smile as I shield my face from the sun.

"Okay, we will watch you but call us if you need anything," he replies.

I nod and head off in search of the stables. Ten minutes later, I am regretting declining the lift as it is a long way down the hill and to the left. In a paddock I catch sight of Joshua riding his huge black horse. I smile and then I frown as I watch him. Is he trying to kill it? I have never seen someone ride a horse so fast, like sprinting, and then he keeps pulling it back and changing direction. They then run full pelt in the new direction until changing direction again. What the hell is he doing? I would definitely buck him off if I was that poor horse. This is why I don't ride horses, you never know who has tortured it before you get on and what score they want to settle with the human race.

I continue walking to the stables as I watch him give it to this horse. He hasn't seen me. He slows and I can hear his voice cajoling the huge beast.

"Whoa Jasper, whoa Jasper," he coos. I smile, this is his beloved Jasper.

He slowly gets down and fiddles with the bridle and Jasper puts his head affectionately into Joshua's chest and butts him. He smiles and slaps it hard on the front forequarter. They are both breathing heavily, and both absolutely wet with perspiration. Yep, he's totally trying to kill the horse. Not everyone likes to train like a madman, Joshua. He looks up and sees me and breaks into a breathtaking smile which I return. They walk over to me and he kisses me gently.

"So, explain why you are trying to kill the horse." I frown.

He frowns in disgust. "His name is Jasper."

"Oh, yes, that's what I meant to say," I murmur.

He wipes the sweat from his forehead. "What do you mean?" he pants as he wipes his wet hands onto the behind of his jodhpurs.

"Why are you making him run so fast that he will have a heart attack?" I ask.

He smiles sarcastically. "He is one of the most athletic horses on the polo circuit. He's much fitter than me. Not everyone's a wimp."

I don't even know what to say to that. Hmm.

I follow him into the stables and watch as he takes off his wet t-shirt and starts to take the saddle off Jasper. The way he is moving in those frigging skintight orgasmic cream riding pants with his skin dripping sweat is calling to my libido on a level that I totally understand.

I sit still, watching my very own private stripper dream show. This scene should totally be in the next Magic Mike movie. As he moves his arms above his head as he tends to his horse, every muscle is rippling on his back and I can see the muscles in his buttocks and thighs flex as he twists and turns. My eyes drop to my name written down the length of his body and I start to feel a familiar pulse between my legs as desire fills me. I want this man. I walk over to him.

"Joshua," I whisper.

"Hmm," he replies as he continues to brush his horse.

"I want you to take me back to the house and ride me as hard as you have just ridden this horse," I whisper.

His eyes meet mine and he gives me one of those come fuck me looks he does so well. I feel my insides liquefy. I love that look. "Get back to the house, Marx." He then turns and picks up his riding whip and hits me hard across the buttocks and I yelp. "Now!" he snaps.

"Joshua," I gasp.

He hits me hard again. "Shut the fuck up and do it," he snarls darkly.

CHAPTER 12

Natasha

I STUMBLE out of the stable and Joshua whips me again. "Oww, stop it," I whisper as I put my hands on my behind to protect it. He rips my upper arm nearly out of the socket.

"I said get to the house," he sneers in my ear as he pushes me forward up the track towards the house.

A rush of adrenaline hits me hard and I put my head down and walk... I like this game.

"Faster," he sneers, and I keep walking at a quickened pace. I can't go any bloody faster. He whips me again.

"Oww, that hurts." I frown as I rub my behind.

He pushes my back and I stumble forward as I giggle. Fuck, he's taking this whole ride me hard thing to another level. I'm half frightened. We continue up the track until we get to the house.

"Up the stairs," his cool voice says calmly, and he gestures up the stairs with the whip.

Lose the whip. I'm not into the whip. That bastard stings. My eyes drop to the large erection I can see through his tight pants and I feel a rush of moisture hit me. Joshua likes this game too and I inwardly high-five myself. He cracks his neck hard and I walk upstairs with him right behind as anticipation starts to overtake me.

"I want you naked and on the bed with those fingers in that tight pussy of mine," he says darkly.

My eyes flick to him again.

He cracks his neck hard once again. God, I love that. "Now, or I'm going to whip that naked ass so hard you won't sit down for a week!" he purrs.

My eyes widen. Shit, he means it. I nervously kick off my shoes and start to undress and he walks into the bathroom and gets into the shower.

"You had better be wet when I get out or there will be hell to pay," he calls.

Crap, I take off all my clothes and pull back the blankets on the bed I have just made and lay myself in the center.

The shower turns off, and I smile to myself. That was the quickest shower in history. I can hear him drying himself double time and he walks to the door of the bathroom with a towel around his waist. His eyes drop down my naked body and he licks his lips.

"Legs spread," he murmurs. I spread my legs. "Wider."

I put my legs flat to the bed.

"Show me," he whispers darkly as his eyes stay fixed on the flesh between my legs.

Goosebumps start to scatter over my flesh, and I spread myself wide for him to see.

"Very nice," he whispers as he puts his hand out and runs his fingers through my open lips.

"Fingers in," he murmurs as he slowly unwraps his towel and takes his large erection in his hand.

Oh God. My eyes close at the sight of him. He is without a doubt the most virile magnificent beast I have ever seen.

I slowly ease one finger into myself and he strokes his cock to the end.

"That's it," he whispers as he strokes himself again.

My eyes stay riveted to his body, the power emanating and bouncing off the walls from him.

"More. Two fingers," he whispers as his strokes get stronger. My eyes drop to his cock and the pre-ejaculate dripping from the end. Goosebumps scatter. I want him. I slowly ease two fingers into myself and then back out, and my back arches off the bed.

His strokes get almost violent and my breathing picks up to a pant. I can see every muscle in his torso flex as his powerful strokes move his whole perspiration sheened body. His body starts to lurch forward to meet the punishing rhythm as his eyes stay riveted to my fingers disappearing into my body.

"Give it to yourself. I want three fingers," he growls.

I frown in hesitation. "Now!" he snaps. "Don't make me whip you."

I slowly add another finger and groan as I feel the burn of the stretch. His eyes flicker with excitement. "Faster," he whispers.

I'm so wet that I'm throbbing, and my fingers are sliding easily in and out of myself. My back arches off the bed again as I feel an orgasm approaching. He grabs one of my feet and holds it wide in the air.

He starts to work himself with such power that I can hardly breathe as I watch him. *Dear God, he's beautiful.* The perspiration, the muscle, the throbbing large cock, the look in his eyes and the feeling of my fingers are too much and I lurch forward as I orgasm. He just goes harder, long hard strokes, and the bed is moving from the force of his power.

"On your knees on the floor," he growls.

Huh? He grabs me by the arm and rips me onto the floor and down to my knees and grabs my hair in a vice-like grip and strokes himself centimeters away from my mouth. The grip on my hair is painful as he rips my head back and slides his cock into my mouth and my gag reflex kicks in as he pushes it to the back of my throat.

"Suck!" he demands. His dark eyes show me a level of arousal that I love.

My eyes close and I swirl my tongue around the end of him and he growls in appreciation as he comes in a rush into my mouth. His body jerks as his body empties itself into my mouth. His harsh grip on my hair releases and he strokes my hair gently as he pants, and I lick him clean.

I rest my head up against his hip as I pant. Fuck... what was that?

"Good girl, now on your knees on the bed," he purrs. My eyes meet his in question.

"I'm far from finished with you, my precious girl." He bends and kisses me and as he tastes his arousal his kiss turns animalistic and he picks me up and throws me onto the bed.

"On your elbows and knees."

My eyes widen. Oh shit, what's he going to do?

He picks up the whip and whips his hand in a threat and I jump into position. My breathing is labored as I watch him walk around behind me. His cock is hard again. He bends and picks me up and positions me towards the side of the bed.

"That's it," he murmurs almost to himself. As he walks

around behind me, I watch his legs and cock through my legs. His fingers slide through my wet swollen lips and he hisses.

"So fucking perfect," he growls as he slaps me hard on the ass with the whip and I cringe and close my eyes. He bends and slowly bites one of my butt cheeks and then the other as I hold my breath and then his tongue is on my back entrance and he forces my body forward onto the bed.

"Joshua," I whisper muffled into the blankets. He pushes me forward again to silence me.

He slowly licks every inch of me, and I can't breathe. This is too much, too intense, too intimate. He spreads me with his hands and pulls me back onto his face and my eyes roll back in my head. *Good God... what this man can do.*

His fingers drop to my wet flesh and he inserts three fingers into me, and I cry out, his magical fingers in the front, his perfect tongue in the back.

I open my eyes to see his cock once again hanging heavily between his legs. I can actually see the pulse in the veins and start to quiver, and he immediately removes his fingers.

"I want you coming around my cock next time. Don't fucking come!" he growls.

I close my eyes, like I could stop it. He spreads saliva around my entrance and continually runs his fingers back and forth over the opening as I hold my breath. I can hear him thinking.

"I don't have any lube," he whispers to himself.

My eyes widen into the blankets. Oh shit, this is going to hurt.

There is only one reason he would need lube.

His fingers go over me again with pressure and I close my eyes to the pleasure. Why does this feel so good? "Mmm." My body whispers involuntarily.

"I need this ass," he growls as he pushes his thumb into me, and I cry out. My eyes roll back in my head. Oh fuck, I think I need him to take it.

He slowly pumps his thumb in and out of me and I know he's trying to calm himself down. He's too amped up.

He starts to breathe heavily, and my eyes once again drop to the huge muscle between his legs, dripping with pre-ejaculate. I can still taste his semen in my mouth.

"You're lucky I don't have any lube, Presh," he growls as he slams into my vagina so hard that I face-plant into the bed. He rips me back by the hair and onto his cock as his thumb pumps in and out of me, his cock working at a piston-pace. I can't move, I am so paralyzed with pleasure. He's going to rip the orgasm from my body without me moving a muscle.

I close my eyes and ride the wave of pleasure that my beautiful animal is dishing up. My legs keep opening by themselves and he rips me back up to him by the hipbones. His thumb picks up speed and I start to lose my head and thrash into the sheets and scream in ecstasy as the orgasm is ripped from my body.

"Fuck!" he yells and with one... two... three hard pumps I feel him harden even further and jerk inside me. He slowly moves my body back and forth over his to totally empty himself. I am wet with perspiration and panting just like the horse.

He softens and gently kisses my back as he rolls me over. "I fucking adore you," he whispers.

I pant, exhaustion kicking in. "Who knows, I could get into this horse-riding thing after all," I breathe.

With a trace of a smile, he kisses me softly on the lips. "Shut up and kiss me."T L SWAN

. . .

The wind whips through my hair as we go over the rugged terrain in the four-wheel-drive wagon. It's Friday and Joshua is giving me a tour of the huge grounds of his beloved Willowvale. I hate to admit it, but this place is seriously growing on me. Privacy, until you never have it you can't ever appreciate what it truly means. To me it means Joshua being himself, laughing freely, joking around in unguarded conversations and a gentle side to him that not many people get to see.

We have had the most wonderful four days here and have slipped into a little routine very quickly. Joshua rides and takes care of his adored horses, while I read and relax. I have even made friends with a stray ginger cat that comes to the house and then in the afternoons and nights we have quality time together in the bath and around the grand fireplace... I could very easily get used to this relaxed loving lifestyle.

Joshua points over to a paddock on the left. "I was thinking I could build your mother a house over on the hill, anything she wants."

I look at him. He really is pulling out all stops to make me try and move here. "Hmm," I mutter.

"And Bridget could have a house down here too if she wants," he carries on.

Oh God, he really is on a mission.

"Hmm," I reply again, acting uninterested. I smile to myself. "What about Abbie? Can she have a house?" I ask as I raise my eyebrows in question. Let's see how desperate he really is.

He narrows his eyes at me. "Abbie wouldn't want to live here," he snaps.

She so wouldn't but this is fun. I smirk and he gets a hold of my game.

"No, Abbie is not living here." He smirks. "And neither is Cameron so don't ask me."

"Oh," I reply in a defeated voice as I smile. We continue driving along the dirt road through the huge paddocks.

"So, this is all your land?" I ask as my eyes wander over the hills.

He nods as he drives nonchalantly. "Yes, but I don't come all the way out here very often."

For ten minutes we keep driving and I am in awe. This is a huge property. We drive over a hill and into a valley and Joshua stops the car as he sees something. His wrist is resting over the steering wheel as he narrows his eyes and runs his tongue over his top front teeth. My eyes flick to the paddock where his eyes are fixed. What's he looking at? All I see are more horses.

"What is it?" I ask.

"Nothing," he snaps and then does a three sixty turn and starts to speed back toward the stables. I hold on for dear life. What the hell is wrong with him?

"What are you doing? Why are you driving like a frigging maniac?" I ask as I am propelled up and down on my seat as we go over bumps at high speed. Christ almighty, I could die here. He pulls up at the stables' offices and jumps out of the car furiously.

Huh? I jump out and run in after him.

He bangs the office door open. "Why are those fucking horses on the bottom paddock?" he yells as he points his hand toward the paddock we have just come from.

I screw up my face as I look between him and the two men in the office. What's he talking about?

"Um...Joshua, calm down," the older man replies.

"I will not calm down! Tell me why those fucking horses are on my land!"

Huh? What's wrong with those horses? Have they got rabies or something? What's going on here? This is confusing.

"Who approved this?" he screams.

My eyes flick to Joshua and the veins are practically popping from his forehead in anger. *Jeez, settle petal.*

"She has nowhere to put them," the man replies.

"My fucking ass!" Joshua screams. "She has more than enough places to put her horses, she's a fucking veterinarian."

My face drops. Oh shit, those are Amelie's horses. "Get her on the phone," Joshua sneers.

The two men look at each other uncomfortably and the older guy takes out his mobile phone and starts to scroll through his contacts. The younger man looks at me as Joshua storms out of the office. I fake a smile. *Awkward.* I stand still on the spot not sure where I am supposed to go.

The man dials a number and waits. "Hello, I have a furious Mr. Stanton here."

He listens. "Yes, he has seen them, and he wants to speak to you."

He listens and nods again and walks out onto the landing and hands the phone to Joshua.

"Where are you?" he screams. He listens. "You have one hour to get your horses off my land or I am putting them out on the road!" he yells and then he listens.

God, talk about an overreaction. I frown at him in question. "I don't want to hear your shit," he yells.

My eyes flick nervously to the two men who are standing at the door listening. Yep... he's losing it, and this is getting embarrassing. "I don't give a fuck about your ten horses. I will go and shoot the bastards myself!" he screams.

My eyes widen.

"You have one hour!" he yells and hangs up.

He points angrily at the two men. "You do not help her and

her fucking horses, do you hear me! You both work for me. Not her."

"Joshua," I whisper as I grab his hand to try and calm him down and he snatches it away angrily.

"Natasha. Not. Now!" he screams.

I start to feel my cheeks heat in embarrassment and my eyes drop to the ground.

He storms out and starts to walk at a brisk pace down to Jasper's stable. I don't really want to go with him after the way he has just screamed at me, so I sit on the step of the office landing.

"Jason, organize a trailer for Amelie, please," the older man asks.

"She has nowhere to put them Alf, you know that."

"Surely she can find somewhere."

"Nobody is offering agistment locally, I have already been looking for her," the younger man replies.

"Seriously, not my problem. I'm not losing my job over this," the older man replies.

My new ginger friend, the stray cat, comes up and rubs itself on my leg and I stroke it as I sit deep in thought. This is just bad timing for Joshua. He can't handle not being in control at the moment. I'm just going to stay out of it. This is none of my business. It is ridiculous though, they are not hurting anyone on the bottom paddock.

"Would you like a coffee, love?" The older man smiles gently, realizing that I have stayed with them rather than follow the psycho chicken on a raging rampage.

"Yes, please." I smile thankfully. "White and one please."

He makes it and brings it out. "We haven't formally met, dear. My name is Alf. I am the stable manager, and this is Jason, my leading hand."

I smile. "Hello." I shake both of their hands. "My name is Natasha."

"We know who you are." Alf smiles.

Oh God, these men are probably Amelie's best friends and hate my guts.

"Is it okay if I sit here?" I ask nervously. "I don't want to intrude."

Alf smiles warmly. "It's fine dear, we are staying out of this, too."

I smile gratefully. "Oh good," I whisper.

"You are from Australia?" Jason asks.

I nod. "Yes."

"I am going there one day." He smiles.

Oh, I like these men. "It's a beautiful country," I reply.

"I was offered a job as a jackaroo on a huge cattle station a few years back but I knocked it back."

"How come?" I frown.

"It was a fly in and fly out farm and there were no women on the property. I'd go mad." He laughs.

"Sex maniac," Alf grunts and I smile. We see a saddle get thrown across the grass out of the stable that Joshua is in. Bloody hell, he's raging like a lunatic. Obviously, Amelie's saddle. My eyes flick nervously to the two men as they look at each other.

"How two people can go from being best friends to absolutely despising each other beats me," sighs Alf as he shakes his head.

I frown and keep patting the cat, best friends? Joshua told me they were friends... not best friends. Why does he hate her so much? I put my head on the side as I think, the same reason he hates Max. I frown and then widen my eyes.

Lightbulb moment.

Joshua really did see her as a friend and he feels that she betrayed him, like he feels Max betrayed him when he sided with me. Did I start this hate of betrayal in him when I betrayed him at nineteen... well, not really but he thought I did. Fuck... and now his own mother has hit him with the ultimate betrayal. Betrayal, betrayal, betrayal... how many times can you say that word in one sentence? I continue patting the cat as I think. I'm onto something here. Joshua has a definite personality pattern. I need to talk to him about this, but I will let him cool down first. A bridle gets thrown out of the stable at full pelt. He's really losing his shit in there.

Alf shakes his head. "That man of yours is losing his mind," he sighs.

I fake a smile. "Mmm." Shit, he really is, not even joking.

"Are you ok with him? Are you frightened at all?" he asks.

I smile and frown. "Yes, I mean no, I'm not frightened." What an odd thing to say.

A white wagon comes down the track with dust bellowing behind it.

"Oh shit," Jason murmurs.

"I will take you back to the house, lass," Alf says to me.

"Why?" I ask.

"Amelie is here, and it won't be pretty," he replies.

My eyes flick to the stable that Joshua is in. He's too mad to remember that I am even here. I think I need to calm him down. "No, I would like to stay," I murmur as I stand and walk toward the stable.

The car pulls up and she jumps out angrily. She's covered in mud and has obviously come straight from work. God, she's frigging beautiful, *bitch.*

Another one of her bridles comes flying out of the stable

and lands near her car. "What do you think you're doing?" she yells.

Joshua emerges from the stall like the devil himself. "What does it look like?" he screams.

"Having a temper tantrum is what it looks like. You child!" she yells back.

"Oh shit," sighs Alf behind me and I bite my lip to stifle my smile. Yep, she's got him. He is totally acting like a child.

Joshua rushes her and my eyes widen, and I quicken the pace as I walk toward them. "You get your fucking horses off my farm."

"Joshua, be reasonable. I need some time," she replies.

"You are out of time!" he yells.

I finally reach them. "Hello Amelie," I murmur as I try to diffuse the situation.

Her eyes flick to me. "Hello Natasha," she replies through her anger.

"Natasha, get to the house!" Joshua yells as he points to the house.

I frown, fuck off asshole. Don't speak to me like that.

"Why can't her horses stay in the bottom paddock? You're being unreasonable, Joshua," I reply.

"Because I fucking said so!" he screams at me.

I start to hear my angry pulse in my ears... *go time*. I narrow my eyes at him and he glares back.

"Jason, get the float," he yells.

"Where will I take them?" Jason replies.

"Out onto the fucking road. I don't care!" he screams as he starts to storm towards the house.

I stand still and my eyes flick to Amelie. Hot furious tears are forming in her eyes and she swipes them angrily with shaking hands.

I look back at the crazy man storming towards the house. "Natasha, get here!" he yells as he keeps walking.

I frown, as if I'm going to come with you, asshole... and you call me a drama queen.

"What can I do to help, Amelie?" I ask. God, I feel sorry for this woman.

"I don't want your pity, Natasha!" she snaps.

I nod. "I know. Can I help you load the horses or something?" I ask.

She shakes her head and starts to pick up her things that Joshua has thrown out of the stall.

I bend and pick up a bridle.

She picks up the heavy saddle and struggles to her car and I run and open the back door for her.

"You're too good for him," she snaps as she throws the saddle into the back of the car.

Right at this moment, I kind of have to agree.

"He's just stressed out. Don't worry about him," I murmur as I throw in the bridle.

I blow out a breath. "Where are you going to put the horses?" I ask as I wipe my hands on my jeans.

She rubs her head in frustration. "I have a client who is away at the moment. I will have to keep them there for the minute." Her accent really is lovely.

Alf walks over and shakes his head sympathetically at her. "Don't, Alf," she snaps.

"I told you this would happen," he says quietly.

"I know, I know," she mutters. "I had no choice."

"Natasha, don't make me come and get you!" Joshua screams from up the hill like a madman. Is he kidding?

"He's trying to ruin my life," Amelie snaps furiously to Alf.

I frown. "How?"

She shakes her head. "It's not your concern," she snaps.

"That's it!" Joshua screams as he starts to head back down the hill to retrieve me. Oh shit.

"I'd better go," I whisper. "Sorry." My eyes meet hers.

She tears up again and gets into her car angrily and I start to storm toward the imbecile who is raging like a lunatic coming down the hill.

"What do you think you're doing?" he sneers as I approach him.

I glare at him and continue to walk past him toward the house. If he thinks for one minute, I'm taking that shit he has another think coming.

"Answer me," he snaps as he walks up next to me. I keep walking angrily. He has got to be joking.

"When I tell you to get to the house, you fucking do what I say!" he sneers.

I stop on the spot and glare at him.

The thing is that I know he is stressed out beyond belief and I should just ignore him, but just how much shit can I take before I crack?

"Don't talk to me," I snap as I storm past him. "Fine! Don't talk to me!" he screams.

"Suits me!" I yell in reply.

I've said it before, and I will say it again. It's a total mindfuck dealing with a cantankerous stubborn mule. It's 6 pm and Joshua and I haven't spoken a word since our blow up over Amelie this morning. I am in the study reading on my iPad and he came in from outside about an hour ago. If he thinks I am putting up with his shit for one minute he is sadly mistaken.

The door to the study opens. "Who's cooking dinner?" he asks.

My eyes rise to him above my iPad. "Not me," I reply and drop my eyes back to the screen.

He stays at the door and waits for me to look back up at him. I don't.

"Well, I'm not either," he replies.

I keep reading and acting like I am uninterested in what he has to say.

"Do you want to go out for dinner?" he asks.

Hmm, typical. I have to practically beg to go out to dinner every other night because he doesn't want to be photographed but when I am fuming mad, he brings it out to dangle like a carrot.

"No, thank you," I reply. I so do but I am not falling for his bribe.

"Fine, I will go alone then," he replies and leaves.

For fifteen minutes I sit in the study while he is upstairs. He wouldn't go without me, would he? No, surely not. I continue reading.

He pops his head in the study door. "See you later then," he replies. My horrified eyes drop down to his clothing. He is going without me. Of all the nerve. I narrow my eyes and return to the book I have been pretending to read for five hours.

"See you," I murmur under my breath.

He walks out of the study. God, I'm off him. I start to fume.

He comes back in. "What are you mad about?"

I screw up my face. "You can't be that stupid?" I reply in a monotone.

His eyes hold mine. "I'm not putting up with Amelie's shit, Natasha."

"I don't expect you to, Joshua, but you acted like a child throwing a tantrum," I reply.

He narrows his eyes at me.

"I will not be spoken to the way you did this morning, and I don't give a damn who you are. I was embarrassed that my fiancé was ordering me around like I was one of his staff."

He blows out a breath. "I apologize for that. I was angry and I didn't mean to take it out on you."

I put the iPad down.

He shakes his head in frustration. "It's just her," he mutters.

"You know what? This little victim routine you have going on here is getting old." I shake my head in disgust.

"What do you mean?" he snaps.

"Stop blaming her for everything. You were on that bed upstairs with a hard dick. It takes two people to have sex, Joshua, and if you were not aroused this couldn't have physically happened."

He cuts in and shakes his head and I can see he doesn't like where this conversation is going. "Natasha."

"Stop it," I yell. "I don't give a damn that you slept with her, but you need to man the fuck up and stop playing the blame game."

"What?" He screws up his face.

"Stop blaming everything on everybody else." I stand and point my finger at him angrily. "You fucked Amelie, just admit it, and now you are making her pay."

"Bullshit," he sneers.

"Is it Joshua?" I yell. "Seems pretty factual to me, wake up and smell the coffee. You can't stand it when people... namely Amelie, don't do what you want and expect them to do and then you get downright nasty in return."

He shakes his head. "You have no idea the shit she has caused for me in the last twelve months." He sighs, defeated.

Empathy wins. "No, Joshua, I don't. Because you tell me nothing, but I do know that she doesn't deserve to be treated the way you treated her this morning... and neither did I," I reply quietly.

He walks in and drops onto the black leather wingback chair. "I'm sorry," he murmurs. "You are the last person I want to treat badly."

I stand and walk over to him and crawl onto his lap and put my arms around his neck and he drops his head sadly. I feel guilty for upsetting him when he already has so much on his plate but that behavior was plainly unacceptable.

"Joshua, you need to learn to accept that people don't have to always do what you tell them to and when they go against what you want, you can't be angry. It's pointless. Nobody can determine things out of their control. Amelie is her own person and Max is his own person. Please stop being a control freak and having a personal vendetta against them."

His eyes flick to me. "Are you finished my therapy session, Dr. Marx?"

I smirk. "For tonight, Mr. Stanton. Would you like to make another appointment?" I bend and gently kiss his lips.

"No. I'm good." He smirks.

CHAPTER 13

Natasha

I SIT as I watch him walk around the side of the court... field? "What do you play polo on?" I ask Adrian, who is leaning on the car's hood next to me.

"Field," he murmurs into his coffee.

I nod as I take a sip of mine and continue watching my man on the other side of the field as he prepares for his game. Orgasmic doesn't even describe that polo outfit. Our little game of horse and jockey last week has me all steamed up for those jodhpurs and that broad back. Of course, the small fact that I know exactly what that body is capable of, mind-blowing pleasure, only adds to the deal.

He's been withdrawn since our fight over Amelie the other day. I know he's disappointed that I sided with her and I have explained that I didn't but his behavior is not on. He grudgingly agreed that he lost his shit with her but still is silently disappointed with me. Does he really think I will defend him even if I think he's in the wrong?

Security has never been so tight. Ben is walking next to him as they talk and there is a guard discreetly on each side of the field.

"What's with all of the security?" I ask.

Adrian's eyes flick around to the guards. "This is one of the only scheduled things that Joshua does. He can always be found here so they take extra precautions."

I frown as my eyes flick to him. "Has there ever been an issue?" I ask.

He shakes his head. "No, just those idiots over there." He points with his chin and I look over to the field next to us and see three photographers with long lenses on their cameras.

"Do they want photos of Joshua?" I frown.

"Yeah, among other things. There are about four or five players here who are followed by the paps, so it's open slather," he murmurs into his coffee again.

"Bloody hell," I whisper. "Stupid people."

"Thanks for coming with me today." I bump Adrian with my shoulder.

He smiles warmly. "That's okay, Cinderella. I haven't been to a game for a while." Joshua is playing near LA so Adrian has met us here. We go home tonight.

Up past the side of the car walks a handsome man. "Adrian." He smiles as he puts out his hand and then kisses

Adrian on the cheek as they shake hands.

My eyes scan up and down the fine specimen, mmm, who is this?

Adrian's eyes flick to me. "This is Natasha, Joshua's fiancée." He gestures to me. "And this is Ross."

We shake hands. I have heard that name before. Who is this guy? "Hello." I smile.

"Ah, I have heard a lot about you." He smirks.

Oh crap, what's he heard? "I wouldn't believe any of it." I smile nervously.

He winks and smiles. His body language reveals that this guy loves himself. "So, has he got you on lockdown?" he asks.

I raise my eyebrows in question. "What do you mean?" I ask.

"You know, under heavy guard, gorgeous and new in town. I imagine after the attempted hit he would be nervous to say the least." He smiles as his eyes go to the field in front of us.

I fake a smile. *How does he know that?* "No, not really," I mutter.

"Adrian, why didn't you go to Macey's art show last week? She was disappointed you weren't there," he asks.

"Damn," Adrian murmurs. "I totally forgot about it. I've been busy."

"See you do need me to keep your calendar for you." He gives Adrian a sexy look as he puts his hands into his pockets.

Adrian smirks as his eyes hold Ross's. "You being in charge of my calendar is the last thing I need," he replies.

Who is this guy?

Ben walks over. "Murph, I need you and Tash for a moment."

Adrian smiles. "Sure, excuse us Ross." He grabs Ross's elbow affectionately as he brushes past him and Adrian grabs my hand to take me with him and follow Ben.

Ross glares at Ben and I feel uncomfortable... okay. "What took you so long?" Adrian asks Ben.

"I didn't see you. This may come as a surprise, but I don't watch you all the time you know," Ben replies flatly as he maneuvers through the cars.

Adrian smirks.

I frown. I'm lost. "Huh, what's going on?" I ask.

Adrian scratches his head uncomfortably. "That was Ross." He shakes his head. "We used to date."

"Fuckwit," Ben murmurs under his breath.

I smile broadly. "Did you just save Adrian from having to talk to an ex, Ben?"

Ben shakes his head in exasperation. "No, I saved myself from having to hear about it later."

Adrian rolls his eyes and I smile.

We stop at another of Joshua's cars at the other end of the field and sit on the hood.

"I'm going to get some water. Do you guys want some?" Adrian asks.

"Yes, please," we both reply and he walks off.

Ben and I sit in silence and I can't help but want to ask what's going on with him and Didge since we went away. Last time I saw them together they were hating each other's guts and now... who knows?

I watch in awe across the field as Joshua's stable hands bring Jasper around and fuss over the expensive horse and Joshua mounts him gracefully. Even without Joshua's money and celebrity status he has an inner power that is undeniable. If I met him in the street, I would think to myself... this guy is somebody.

"How does Ross know about the attempted hit on Joshua?" I ask as my eyes flick to Ben.

Ben frowns at me. "He doesn't."

I raise my eyebrows. "Yeah, he does. He just asked me if Joshua was jumpy after the attempted hit."

Ben leans back on his hands and frowns as he thinks, and Adrian walks back over to us with our bottles of water that he hands over. "Did you tell Ross about the hit on Joshua?" Ben asks Adrian as he takes his water.

Adrian frowns. "No, he probably heard it through the grapevine."

"Have you told anyone?" Ben asks.

Adrian shakes his head, and the game begins at the sound of the whistle. I frown as I watch the field. Oh shit, the horses bang into each other as they sprint, and I wince. This is aggressive and very fast.

"Joshua has told nobody," Ben whispers almost to himself as he stares straight ahead.

I nod. "He wouldn't have told anybody. He doesn't tell people things that they are supposed to know, let alone something like that," I reply.

Ben crosses his arms in front of him as he thinks. "How does that fucking idiot know that?"

I get the giggles at Ben's accent. "What's funny?" He smirks.

I smile broadly. "I like the way you say fuck. It's funny."

"The way he fucks is funny as well I imagine," Adrian murmurs dryly as he takes a sip. My eyes flick to Ben and his rugged handsomeness. Somehow, I just don't think that's true and my beloved sister comes back to mind. What's going on with them?

Ben shakes his head as he drinks his water, unimpressed, and then takes out his phone and calls someone.

"Hey, can you go around to Ross Markham's house and have a look at which security system he has?" He listens. "The address is in the filing cabinet under cock." I smirk. Ben really hates this guy. He listens and then laughs. "Thanks," he replies and hangs up. We keep watching the game. Joshua is very good at this. In fact, all of these men are very good at this, and ridiculously good looking.

"There are a lot of good-looking men here," I murmur.

"Sure are." Adrian nods.

"Apart from me you mean?" Ben replies flatly with folded arms as he watches the game.

I smirk, every day Ben reveals just a little more of himself and I am beginning to really, really like him. Ben glances at his watch and stands. "I will be around the other side," he murmurs.

"Okay," I answer.

I watch Ben walk around the other side of the field and my eyes flick to Joshua on the horse as the quarter ends. He rides to the sidelines and dismounts his horse. His stable hand walks over to him and gives Jasper a drink and hands Joshua a bottle of water. As people fuss around, Joshua takes a drink and turns and looks for me. I give him a small wave and he nods and turns back to his horse and crew.

I smile at the ground. Joshua Stanton looking for me will never grow old.

The game is over, and I am waiting by the car for Joshua with two security guards and Adrian. He is still finishing up. I watch as Maria walks with the three girls around the field so that they can talk with their father. Maria kisses her husband and the girls all rush Joshua. He picks up the smallest child and lifts her onto his shoulders as the other two wrestle with his legs. He breaks into a full-blown loud laugh and I find myself smiling broadly as I melt. Okay... that's it. I'm out. I can't take anymore. This man is trying to pop my damn ovaries. Just when I don't think this guy can be any more perfect...he goes and turns all paternal. The internal sound of those eggs being released from my pounding ovaries is deafening.

I smile as I watch him with the girls. I never even knew this side of him existed. He is so gentle and loving with them and if this is what he will be like with our children, damn it, I'll have ten of the little buggers.

I lie with my head on Joshua's chest in the afterglow of our lovemaking as he intermittently runs his fingertips back and forth over my arm, with his lips resting on my temple. He has just made beautiful gentle love to me and I feel totally cocooned in our bed by his love.

I smile into his chest. "I love you," I whisper.

I feel him smile above me. "I love you too," he replies.

"We can have six children," I breathe.

I feel him smile again. "You say that like it was ever a question," he replies.

I smile.

"That was always happening, Marx." He picks up my hand and kisses my fingertips.

"Joshua," I ask.

"Yes, Presh," he replies.

"Do I have any say at all in the way our lives turn out?" I ask.

I feel him smile broadly again.

"Funnily enough, no," he murmurs. "I've got it all planned out."

I bend and bite him on the chest. "What do I have a say in?" I tease.

He smiles into the darkness again. "Right now?" he asks.

"Yes, right now." I act serious as he rolls me onto my back.

"You get to choose whether I stand or kneel as I fuck you doggy style."

I giggle loudly as he brings my leg up around his hip. "What's it going to be?" he asks.

"Standing please," I smile. "I would like my life to be given to me hard."

"Got it." He bites me on the neck as I squeal in laughter. "Hard life, coming straight up!"

The sound of the echoing alarm rips me from my sleep.

"Fuck," Joshua snaps as he jumps from the bed. Huh? I sit up in a start. It's the middle of the night. What's going on? We arrived back in LA from Willowvale late tonight after dinner and have woken to an alarm that is sounding through the house. It's deafening. Joshua tries to switch on the lamp, and it doesn't turn on.

"Fuck, the power's cut," he whispers.

My eyes widen, huh? What the hell. I am suddenly wide awake and sit up immediately. Shit, shit, shit.

"Get in the bathroom!" he snaps.

I jump out of bed and start to try and find my clothes in a panic in the darkness.

"Get in the fucking bathroom and lock the door," Joshua whispers angrily.

"I have no clothes on, Joshua." I start to jump around in fear and Joshua grabs me and pushes me through the dark room into the bathroom, naked.

"Lock the door!" he snaps.

"No." I grab his arm and try to pull him in with me. "Stay in here with me," I plead.

"Stop there." I hear Ben's voice yell out over the alarm.

Oh crap, what's going on? Joshua and I stand perfectly still as we try to listen. A glass vase smashes and Joshua roughly pushes me into the bathroom as I try to hang onto him. No, what's going on?

"Joshua, stay here with me, please," I beg as I hold onto his arms to try and force him to stay with me. A loud banging sound comes from downstairs and a few different men's voices ring out.

He pushes me in and slams the door shut. I start to jump up and down as I freak out.

I hear a second guard's voice ring out and then someone running up the hall and then a gunshot. Oh fuck! I hold my hands over my mouth and then another three gun shots... then silence.

My heartbeat is thumping in my chest hard and the house is silent except for the deafening alarm. Oh dear God, who had the gun? Why is there silence? Who's down there? I start to shake my hands frantically in front of me as adrenaline pumps heavily through my body. Fuck! I put my ear up to the door and try to listen. Please be okay, Joshua. Where are you? Oh God, Bridget and Abbie, where's Cameron?

My hands go to my chest as I try to control my erratic heartbeat and tears of fear start to roll down my face. Why is it so quiet? Is Ben okay? My recurring nightmare of Ben and Joshua dying comes straight to my mind. *Don't let it be true.*

I hear a downstairs door slam and then more yelling, but it seems to be coming from outside in the backyard. I need to know what's going on, so I slowly open the bathroom door to try and hear but it's muffled. Something is definitely happening in the backyard. I suddenly hear glass smashing downstairs and I quickly close the door again and lock it. Fuck, this is hectic. Where is my phone? I need to call the police. It's on my side table so I slowly open the door again and my eyes search the darkened room. Is anyone in here? Oh my God, this is terrifying. Where is Joshua?

I run to the bedside, grab my phone and run back into the bathroom and lock the door. I am breathless with fear. What's the number for the police here? It's 000 in Australia... what is it in America? Is it the same as the television shows? I shake my hands as I try to remember... is it 555... 999... 911. I hold my hands to my temples. Think Natasha, think. I can't think over that fucking alarm. Shut the hell up! 555, 999, 555... I dial the number 911 and it rings.

"Fire, ambulance or police services?" a calm voice answers.

"Police." I yell.

"Hold the line."

"Hello, Police." The person answers.

"We have been broken into, and there are gunshots. Please come," I stammer.

"Ok, ma'am, please stay calm. What is your address?"

My eyes widen, what is the fucking address? "Umm, I don't know," I whisper in a panic. "I am in Brentwood. My fiancé is Joshua Stanton. We are at his house and someone has broken in. There were shots fired."

"Stay on the line, ma'am." She seemingly rings someone while I nearly hyperventilate. Another gunshot... omg... what's happening?

"They are shooting! Hurry up!" I stammer. "I need a police car here now," I scream.

"Calm down, ma'am, and stay on the line. Is anyone injured?"

My eyes are nearly bulging from their sockets. How in the hell is this woman staying so calm? "I don't know," I yell. How many times does she get these phone calls?

The bathroom door bangs, and I scream and jump into the shower. "Are you there, ma'am?" the woman replies.

"Omg," I stammer.

"Natasha, it's us." I hear Bridget's voice whisper through the door. I nearly collapse in relief and open the door and Bridget and Abbie run in and slam the door behind them and flick the lock.

Bridget grabs me in relief. "Eww, you're naked," she remarks as she cuddles me. "Get dressed."

"Are you there, ma'am?" the operator repeats.

"Yes, I'm here," I whisper.

"Who's that?" Abbie snaps.

"Police," I whisper.

Abbie snatches the phone off me. "Listen. Get someone here right now. Someone has been shot and we are in a fucking bathroom," she yells.

My hands go to my chest. "Who has been shot?" I stammer with wide eyes.

Bridget shakes her head. "I don't know. We heard someone groaning after a gunshot."

My eyes widen. "What the hell... was it Joshua?" I whisper.

"No, I don't think so," she answers.

"Yes or no?" I snap.

"I don't fucking know," she yells.

Oh my God, oh my God, oh my God. I sit on the toilet and put my head in my hands. The alarm stops and it becomes eerily silent. Bridget takes my hand as I am gripped with fear.

"Natasha," I hear Joshua's voice yell out and I hold my hands to my chest in relief.

"He's okay," I whisper. "He's okay." Tears of relief start to roll down my face, a knock sounds on the door and we all jump.

"It's me, baby," Joshua's voice calls through the door. I open it and fall into his arms in a fit of tears.

"What happened?" I cry.

The hall light switches on and the girls come out of the bathroom and then the bedroom light flicks on.

"Can you two put some fucking clothes on?" Cameron snaps and I look down and Joshua and I are totally naked. Oh jeez, how embarrassing.

"Shut up!" Joshua snaps. He pulls out of my arms and retrieves my nightgown and wraps me in it, then wraps a towel around his waist.

"What the hell was that?" Cameron stammers. Joshua starts to pace with his hands on his head.

"Where's Ben?" Bridget whispers wide-eyed.

"He's okay," Joshua answers. "Everyone is okay."

"Oh, dear God, who was here?" I whisper.

"I don't know." Joshua shakes his head in frustration.

The blue and red lights flicker through the window... thank heavens, the police are here.

Adrian

I stand at my office window as I watch the media circus below clamber around Joshua's car as it arrives at the entry to the underground parking garage and waits for the guard to open the gate. The break-in at his house last night is all over the news this morning. This is the last thing he needs. I buzz my receptionist.

"Can you get coffee for Joshua and me please, Ella?" I ask.

"Yes, sir," she replies politely.

Two minutes later Joshua is entering my office at the

same time as our coffee. "Thank you, Ella." Joshua smiles as he takes it from the tray.

I wait for her to leave and my eyes flick to my dear friend. "Are you okay?" I ask.

He nods and walks over to the window to watch the photographers who are the size of ants below.

"What happened?" I ask.

He turns. "I don't know. We were all asleep and three men cut the power and then broke into my house."

I frown as I listen.

"They obviously weren't aware that the alarm system has battery backup," he murmurs into his coffee as he takes a sip.

"Oh my God," I whisper.

He shrugs. "Natasha's a basket case. She didn't sleep all night and kept having those fucking nightmares that she gets."

"Christ," I murmur. "The news said that there were shots fired."

He nods. "We think someone was shot."

My eyes widen. "What do you mean?" I ask, horrified.

He blows out a deep breath. "One of my guards had a gun and was using it to control the situation but one of the men ran at him and tackled him into the table near the landing and they fell onto the glass vase."

I hold my hand over my mouth in horror. "He was either shot or cut on the broken glass because there was blood everywhere in the foyer."

I shake my head in shock. I can't believe this.

Joshua flops onto the lounge in my office. "Ben has booked us all into the Montage in Beverly Hills for a few days until the house is cleaned up. He's at home getting everyone there now."

"What was Ben doing there? I thought he worked yesterday," I ask.

Joshua frowns. "I don't know actually, but I'm glad he was." He shrugs. "He must have filled in another shift for someone overnight."

"Any idea who is responsible for this?" I ask.

He shrugs. "The police said it could be just a random robbery."

His eyes meet mine. "But how would you know?"

I shake my head. "Have you watched the news?"

He shakes his head.

I blow out a breath. "The call Natasha made to the police has been recorded and they are playing it again and again."

Joshua shakes his head in disgust. "Fuck this place... I'm over it. Why would people want to listen to that? And so much for the authorities not giving out information."

"Yeah, I know. It would have been hacked. Natasha sounded terrified." I sigh.

"She was... is," he murmurs into his coffee. I lean on my desk as I watch him.

"What?" he questions.

"I did that bank account trace thing for your mother that you wanted me to do." I don't know whether now is the time for this conversation.

His eyes meet mine. "And?"

I bite my lip as I try to articulate what I want to say. "So, I would transfer your mother one million dollars every four months."

Joshua raises his eyebrows. "And?" he asks.

"Well, on every occasion for the last two years that one million dollars has been transferred to someone else's account the very next day without being touched."

He frowns.

I walk to my filing cabinet, remove the file and hand it to him. He snatches it from me and stands immediately. He walks to my desk and starts to flick through the statements as he slumps into my seat.

I need another coffee so I buzz Ella. "Can we have two more coffees, please?"

"Sure thing," she replies.

Joshua sits entranced as he goes through the statements. "My father gives her a damn lot of money too," he murmurs to himself and then shakes his head at the realization of what he has just said.

"I know what you mean but he's still your father, Joshua," I reply.

"She goes through some cash. What does she spend it all on?" He frowns.

I shrug. "From what I can see, designer clothing and spa treatments. She has a very expensive massage once a week."

Joshua's eyes meet mine and I know we are thinking the same thing. He brushes his tongue over his top front teeth in contempt.

God, I would hate to be Margaret at this moment. Ben arrives at the same time as our second coffees.

"Hey," he remarks as he walks in and sits on the lounge.

"What are you doing here? I want you with Natasha," Joshua murmurs without his eyes leaving the statements. "Yeah, well she's having a fit over you being here without me," Ben snaps. "It's not worth the drama."

Joshua frowns as he looks up. "What do you mean?"

Ben shakes his head. "She's going all fucking crazy." He runs a hand over his forehead in frustration and I smile.

Somehow, I think Ben was glad to escape Natasha this morning.

I smile broadly. "What's my girl doing?" I ask.

"She's my girl," Joshua murmurs as he keeps reading.

"She started demanding to see the guard roster for Joshua and then she started stomping around the house like a mad woman and screaming at the girls to get their stuff because they were keeping me from guarding you."

I smile as I imagine the scenario.

"She called Max and asked him to come back immediately."

Joshua's eyes flick up immediately.

"She did what?" he snaps.

"You heard me. She called Max and asked him to come back so I could guard you fulltime."

Joshua shakes his head.

"Smart girl." I nod.

"And then she started having a hissy fit at Cameron and demanding that he has his own guard too, which he refused, and then the two of them got into a screaming match. Abbie told Natasha to calm down and shut the fuck up." Ben shakes his head at the dramatics, and I laugh.

"Oh, and I forgot the best part. She marched down to the guards' office and demanded answers as to how someone got to the power box without being noticed and she put them all on warning of being fired."

I bite my lip to stifle my smile. "Did I tell you that I love that girl?" I reply.

Joshua rolls his eyes. "Every day, so shut up." He then throws the bank statements onto the table and stands and puts his hands into his pockets. "We need to trace where that money is going."

I nod. "Done."

He frowns at me in question. "Well?"

"It's going into the account of someone named James Brennan," I answer.

Joshua closes his eyes and drops his head.

Ben and I exchange looks. I told Ben yesterday what was going on. "Do you know that person?" I ask.

Joshua's furious eyes meet mine and he runs his tongue over his top front teeth for the second time today.

"James Brennan," he repeats as he raises his eyebrows.

I frown. "Yes"

"James fucking Brennan!" he yells.

Ben and I exchange looks again. "Who is that?" I ask.

With a scarily cold voice Joshua replies. "James Brennan is my father's best friend."

CHAPTER 14

Joshua

MY FURIOUS EYES meet Adrian's, and he frowns.

"I don't get it," he murmurs.

I put my hands on my head as I think. Why would my mother be transferring money to my father's friend's account unless... Fuck. I close my eyes in regret.

"What?" Adrian snaps.

"He's blackmailing her," I whisper.

"Who?" Adrian frowns. "Go back. I'm confused. What you are talking about?" I snatch the statements from the desk and storm into my office with Adrian and Ben hot on my heels.

"Leave me alone, please," I snap as I drop into my seat and spin in my chair to turn my computer on.

Ben nods and leaves the room immediately but, unfortunately, Adrian has never been in the army and has absolutely no regard for my requests. He stands next to my desk with his hands on his hips.

"You think he's blackmailing her?" he asks. I nod as I bite my bottom lip in thought.

"What about?" he frowns.

I shake my head. "Think about it."

Adrian leans on my desk as he thinks and shrugs.

"He has something on her, and she is paying him to be quiet," I sneer.

His eyes widen as he works it out. I'm furious. I dial Natasha's number.

"Hi baby," she answers. "You okay?"

I shake my head as I try to calm my anger before I speak to her. "Hi Presh. I have to ask you something."

"Ahuh," she says.

"When my mother told you, she had an affair did she tell you anything about who it was with?"

She goes silent.

"Did you hear me?" I reply.

"Umm, Josh, does it really matter?" she murmurs.

"It does," I snap.

She blows out a deep breath. "She said it was with a family friend, Josh."

I close my eyes as bile rises from my stomach. Adrian walks around in front of me to see what I am doing, and I angrily point to the door. "Get out, Murph!" I mouth.

His face drops in disappointment and he quietly leaves the room.

"Babe, I have to go," I reply.

"Josh, what's going on?" Natasha asks.

"Nothing, I will talk to you tonight," I reply.

"Don't leave your office without your guards, okay?" she asserts.

"Natasha, not fucking now!" I snap. God, I'm not in the mood for this shit.

"Jesus, you're a grouch. See you tonight." She hangs up.

I put my elbows on the table and my head in my hands.

Could this situation get any worse?

My door opens and Cameron saunters in, seemingly without a care in the world. "Listen, tell your future wife to stop nagging me. I'm not having a guard so she can just back the fuck off already," he snaps.

"Shut up!" I yell.

He frowns as he flops onto the couch. "What crawled up your ass and died?"

I pinch the bridge of my nose as I try to hold it together. "Seriously, just go Cameron," I whisper. "I can't do this right now."

"What's wrong?" he frowns.

I shake my head as anger renders me speechless.

"Stan, what is it?" he asks again with worry in his voice.

"James Brennan is blackmailing Mother. She has transferred six million dollars of my money to his account over the last two years."

He frowns. "What?", he whispers.

I nod as I hold my forehead in my hand with my elbow on the desk.

"So, does that mean?" His voice trails off as he thinks out loud.

"I'm guessing he is the one with the AB blood type," I reply.

"You think James is your biological father?" Cameron gasps.

I nod solemnly.

"Oh my God, what about Dad?" he sighs.

"I know," I murmur into my hands on the desk.

Cameron thinks of something and puts his hand over his mouth to hide his smile.

I shake my head. "You think this is fucking funny?" I snap. "You are such an imbecile."

He bubbles up a chuckle. "No, but you do realize that this means that you lost your virginity to your sister?"

My eyes widen as I connect the dots.

He laughs again. "You are one incestuous bastard."

"Shit, don't ever tell anybody that," I mutter.

He shakes his head. "Seriously, this is messed up complicated shit. What are you going to do?"

I pick up my phone and dial my mother's phone number.

It rings three times.

"Hello Joshua," she answers quietly.

The hurt in her voice cuts through me. I want to go back to a time when I loved my honest mother... but I know that's not possible. She is gone, along with the fantasy life I had.

"Who?" I snap.

"Joshua," she whispers as I hear the tears in her voice.

"Who?" I yell, unable to control my anger.

"It doesn't matter," she sobs.

"I know who!" I yell.

"What?" she whispers.

"James fucking Brennan!" I scream and Cameron puts his head into his hands, unable to handle this situation.

She starts to cry. "Please, Joshua, I'm begging you. You can't tell your father."

Contempt and hate fill my every cell. "Which one are you talking about, you dirty whore?" I sneer.

She sobs loudly and Cameron walks out of the room, obviously unable to handle this conversation.

She stays silent on the phone as she tries to compose herself.

"Both," she whispers.

I close my eyes as the hatred starts to drip-feed into my blood stream. I feel the cold of the poison start to pump through me.

"Let me get this straight!" I sit back on my chair and swivel as I think. "You continually slept with your husband's best friend and one of your best friends' husband for over seven years."

She stays silent.

"And you had two of his children," I sneer. She still stays silent.

"And now you give him my fucking money!" I scream.

She starts to cry. "Joshua, how do you know that? Please calm down."

I swivel on my chair. "You have twenty-four hours to tell Dad, Wilson and Scott."

"Joshua, please!" she begs.

"This time tomorrow I am calling them all!" I scream and hang up furiously.

I sit at my desk with my heart pumping hard in my chest. Never have I been so enraged. So hurt. I feel sick to my stomach.

Cameron walks back in, quietly closes the door behind him and sits down on the chair at my desk. His haunted eyes meet mine. "Did you have to call her a whore?" he growls. "I don't want you speaking to her like that."

"If the name fits," I mutter under my breath. I grab my

phone and scroll though my contact list until I get to a name that I now despise, James Brennan.

I dial the number and it rings.

"James Brennan," he answers. My eyes narrow. I have only ever had respect for this man... yet another lie in my pitiful life.

"This is Joshua Stanton," I reply.

"Hello Joshua," he says jovially. "To what do I owe this pleasure, young man?"

"You have seven days to repay my six million dollars or I am going to the police to have you charged with blackmail," I sneer.

He stays silent on the other end of the line as he thinks.

"I will email you the bank account to put it into," I reply coldly.

What kind of man sleeps with his best friend's wife?

"I could destroy her," he growls.

I close my eyes in regret. "You already have."

It's 7 pm and I have been stalling at work as I try to calm myself down before I go home to my girl. I don't want to be angry around her. This isn't her fault, and my mother has caused enough discomfort for Natasha for this lifetime.

I stand in the lift to our floor at the Montage in Beverly Hills and to be honest I am looking forward to having my own space with Natasha. This roomy thing is getting on my nerves. I have two guards with me, and I know Ben has stepped up security again. Who was it that broke into my house last night? I just wish we had confirmation that it was a random robbery gone wrong and then I will be able to relax again.

We get to our floor and walk down the corridor where I see a guard outside each of the rooms, obviously where the girls and Cameron are. This is ridiculous and I feel my anger rising again that we all have to live like animals in a petting zoo.

Ben hands me a card which I swipe and enter. "Thanks," I mutter as I close the door and I turn and see her. Instantly a smile comes to my face.

Natasha is wearing a white robe and her hair is in a messy bun.

She is makeup free and breathtaking.

She leans up onto her toes and puts her arms around my neck. "Hello, my beautiful Lamborghini," she purrs as her lips meet mine, then she undoes her robe and lets it fall to the floor.

I smile. "Now that's a greeting I like." I bend and inhale her scent deeply. Being with her makes me feel instantly at ease.

"We are alone in an apartment, so we won't be needing clothes." She smiles.

I grab my tie and start undoing it. "Good." I smirk.

A knock sounds at the door. "Room service," someone calls from the other side and I roll my eyes as Natasha dives for her robe.

She quickly redresses and opens the door. "Please, this way." She smiles as she gestures with her hand to the table. My eyes flick around the apartment. This is nice. Very old Hollywood. I walk to the bedroom and check it out. Mmm, I could live here.

The room attendant puts down five trays on the table while another brings in a bottle of champagne and an ice bucket and opens the bottle. My eyes flick to Natasha in gratitude. She knows me better than anyone. I give her a wink and the waiters all leave the room.

Natasha pours me a glass of champagne and passes it to me as she gently kisses my lips.

"I got you dinner, baby."

I smile softly. "I'm not hungry, Presh. You eat it." I sit down at the table.

Her face falls. "I know you haven't eaten today."

I smirk. "How do you know that?"

"Because I know you. You can't eat when you are stressed," she replies softly.

My eyes drop to the salmon on the plate. I could think of nothing worse than eating that right now.

I blow out a deep breath. "Tash," I whisper sadly.

Her face falls and she comes over and sits across my lap like a child and wraps her arms around my neck. "Please, just eat it." She pulls a cute face. "For me?"

I drop my head.

"Josh, I know it's hard to see the forest for the trees at the moment. This is overwhelming, but you need to know that even though everything outside this room is a nightmare..." She kisses me gently and I feel myself melt a little. "What's in here..." She puts her hand on my heart. "Between us... is so pure and so perfect that it counteracts anything negative in our lives. I love you so much, Josh, and we are so blessed to have each other." She kisses me again. "It doesn't matter what goes on out there...because we have perfection in here," she whispers.

I pull her close to me and smile into her neck as I inhale deeply.

I love this woman.

"And I have a surprise for you if you eat." She stands and goes back to her seat opposite me.

I raise my eyebrows. "A surprise?" I ask.

She takes a bite of the bread roll she has just buttered and hands it to me.

I take it. "What's the surprise?" I ask.

"I thought I would give you a two-hour massage when we are finished." She raises an eyebrow in question.

I smirk and grudgingly pick up my knife and fork and start to eat my dinner like the pussy whipped man that I am. She is right...as usual. I need to get some perspective on this situation and not eating does not help.

I smile at the beautiful woman sitting across from me and she smiles back. "Thank you," I murmur as I place my cutlery back onto my plate. I lead her into the bathroom and am blessed with the site of a double massage table in the center of the bathroom surrounded in darkness and lit only by candles. God, she knows me well. I need this tonight.

I slowly undo her robe and it falls to the floor; my eyes drop to her lips as my hand drops instantly to between her legs. I don't have it in me for foreplay tonight. I want to fuck...and I want to fuck hard.

Her head throws back as I impale her with two of my fingers. I need all of her. Tonight's the night I'm taking it. Blood rushes to my cock at the thought and I bite my bottom lip to stop my hips from pumping by themselves.

"Shower," she whispers.

Hmm, I inhale deeply as my lips drop to her shoulder and I kiss her gently. I lick from her collarbone to her neck and up to her jaw. Natasha's eyes close and she throws her head back.

"Joshua, shower," she whispers again.

I step back from her and start to rip my shirt out of my pants aggressively as I undo the buttons double time. I crack my neck hard. Natasha rips at the fly of my pants to undo them quickly, sensing my desperation. I need to bury myself so deep inside that beautiful ass that I can't see straight. I rip my pants down in one quick motion. The thought of what I'm about to do to this beautiful body of hers is almost too much to comprehend. I've waited eight years to take her there.

We step into the shower and under the hot water and instantly I push her soft body up against the wall and bend my knees to rub my shaft through her dripping wet flesh. Fuck, she's perfect. Her mouth is open and soft, like her body. My eyes close in pleasure at the visual of her. I will never get enough of this beautiful creature. I am the only man who has ever seen her like this, and I am the only man who will ever see her like this. It's too much to handle and I crack my neck hard again. Natasha Marx and her beautiful tight cunt is enough to send any man insane with lust...and love. How did I ever get this blessed?

"Josh," she whispers frantically.

I bring her thigh around my hips to give me better access and I slowly sink in one finger as I twist my hand. My eyes close at the feeling of her soft wetness, she whimpers softly, and the sound goes straight to my cock. Unable to hold myself back, I push another two fingers into her, and she winces as her body instinctively pulls away from me.

"Oww, baby, gently," she whispers into my mouth.

Shit, I shake my head. I need to slow down. I instantly

remove my fingers and kiss her neck gently as I try to calm myself down. I can't hurt her. It's my biggest fear that in my heightened arousal I will hurt her. I can't ever lose control with her. She's so soft and gentle, so tight... so everything I ever wanted. Take it slow, take it slow. I inhale deeply, take it slow. I slowly pick up the soap and turn her body away from me.

"Let me wash your back, sweetheart," I whisper gently.

She turns and kisses me over her shoulder and her eyes search mine.

I frown. "What?" I ask.

"Why do you feel sorry for me?" she whispers.

I frown. "What do you mean?"

She turns in my arms and slowly runs her tongue through my mouth. "You only call me sweetheart when you feel sorry for me," she whispers.

I smile. "Do I?" I whisper.

She smiles and nods. "Why do you feel sorry for me tonight?"

My eyes hold hers and my chest rises and falls. How does she know me so well?

"Tell me," she whispers into my lips.

"I want to hurt you," I whisper as my lips find hers. My tongue dives deeply into her mouth as my hands grab her ass and bring her up to rub her onto my erection.

"You would never hurt me, Joshua. I trust you... with my life. It's ok, you can have what you want," she whimpers.

My heartbeat starts to pump in my ears. "Let me massage you tonight, Presh. I need to really touch you, baby."

She smiles and kisses me slowly as her hand drops to my penis and she slowly strokes it in an upstroke. My eyes close and I hiss in ecstasy.

"Do you know how much I love you, Joshua?" She kisses me again as her hand milks a burst of pre-ejaculate.

I smile into her lips. "Do you know how much I fucking adore you, my beautiful girl?"

She nods and turns off the tap. "I'm ready for my massage, Mr. Stanton."

My eyes hold hers. Is she? Is she really ready? I can't hold it back any longer. I need this.

Natasha

I lie on the massage table and Joshua smirks as he slowly pours oil onto his hands, then rubs them together to warm it up. I drop my head and smile into the hole in the table. Unlike the last time I had a massage I can actually relax this time. The room is steamy and darkened, lit only by the ten candles surrounding us. His hands start at my left foot and he kneads it between his fingers.

"This is just what I needed tonight, Presh. You know me so well," he purrs.

I smile again into the hole in the table. I was hoping I could relax him this way. Cameron told me today about James Brennan and the way Joshua was losing it. I knew I had to bring out the big guns.

Joshua's smooth oil covered hands rub up and down one calf muscle and I feel myself sink into the table more deeply. Mmm, this is good. For twenty minutes he stays focused on my legs and rubs back and forth, and my body moves with his rhythm up and down the table. With a white towel around his waist, Joshua pours more oil directly onto my behind and I sigh at the contact. Strong hands rub my buttocks in circular movements and I feel myself smile once more. Oh yeah, I needed this too.

He massages me deeper, up my back and then over my shoulders for another half an hour by which time my skin is dripping in oil. I put my head to the side and watch him as he rubs me. He's concentrating, his eyes are hooded and dark and I know that massaging me is not the only thing on my strong man's mind. He brings his body up parallel to my face and starts to really rub deeply into my back and my body slides forward with every deep rub of my arms, shoulders and back. This is heavenly. I start to feel a deep relaxation sweep over me that I haven't felt in a very long time.

"Roll over, Presh," he murmurs, concentrating deeply. I smile softly as I roll over onto my back and our eyes lock in the darkness. Dear God, I love this man. He starts to rub my chest, kneading my breasts in a circular movement. My eyes close involuntarily and my lips fall open. He bends and very gently takes them in his. "So perfect," he whispers.

I smile into his mouth and I feel his warm fingers slide over my oiled sex, and he inhales heavily as I feel his arousal start to intoxicate the space. When Joshua Stanton becomes aroused it can be felt in the next room. I am one lucky bitch. Backwards and forwards his hand rubs over my lips and my legs have parted by themselves. One hand kneads my breast and the other kneads my sex. His hands are strong and start to really rub me deeply as his eyes stay locked on mine. My eyes flick to the towel and I can see his large erection lying up against his stomach through the towel. A burst of creamy arousal bursts the dam and he hisses gently as he feels it rush to meet his fingers. I turn and undo his towel and am blessed with the sight of his hard as rock penis, the beautiful cock that pleasures my body so often. I know every thick vein that runs its length, and it hangs heavily between his legs.

I take him in my mouth and lick up the length of it. His eyes close at the contact and my legs fall open in a silent invitation. With his fingertips he starts to circle over my swollen lips, backward and forward over my clitoris, and my back arches off the massage table as my body chases a deeper touch. In slow motion I watch him stop and pour more oil onto his hand and then directly over my vagina, and it runs down between my legs. He then rubs me hard and deeply from my sex down to my behind, long deep circular movements, and my body bows off the table to meet him. I close my eyes and start to suck him hard. I am blessed with the taste of pre-ejaculate... fuck he tastes good. I groan at the sensation on my tongue and feel his teeth gently bite one of my nipples. Holy shit, this man is hot. He keeps rubbing me deeply and my body is writhing on the table. I need him inside me... now.

"Joshua," I whisper around his cock as my legs hit the massage table as I open them as far as they go.

"I got you, baby. Let me take my time." He bends and gently kisses me again.

I swallow and nod softly as his mouth goes back to my breasts. Oh shit, I moan softly. His thumb starts to slowly push in and out of my sex and I lift my body so that he can get deeper. Oh God, I need this hard tonight. He watches me with dark eyes as his other fingers drop lower on my body. They start to rim my behind and I instinctively open my legs again. His thumb pulsing, his fingers exploring, it's too much to bear and I start to feel the building of an orgasm. I start to quiver and try to hold it off.

"Let it go, baby," he whispers. "I need you soft and open tonight." He slides a finger in, and I groan. He's been touching me a lot here lately and I have grown to like it, something I never thought I would. I moan and close my eyes as his thumb and two fingers start to pump my openings in perfect timing. Fuck, this feels good. My eyes drop to his cock as I watch the pre-ejaculate drip from the end of his penis... oh shit. I start to quiver, and he stops immediately. I pant and lift my head from the table to see what he is doing. "Baby, what are you doing?"

His eyes meet mine. "You will be coming a different way tonight."

I pant and a pang of fear fills me. Fuck. I nod nervously and he smiles a dark smile and takes my lips aggressively in his.

"Roll over," he whispers.

Oh shit, I gently roll over and watch as he pours more oil over his torso and down over his penis. He gently strokes himself four times and I nearly orgasm on the spot. Watching him there in the candlelight covered in oil and pulling himself is the most erotic thing I have ever seen.

"Head down," he murmurs, and I drop my head to the table. Mr. Stanton is here, and he is taking no prisoners.

He gets onto the table above me and, starting at my feet, he rubs his body over me and slides it up toward my head. I feel his hard shoulders and then his chest... his perfect cock slides up and down my body. Again and again, he slides back and forth. Oh God, this is too much, I have never been this aroused in my life. His penis catches between my cheeks and he stops and slides it up and down as his mouth goes to my neck from behind and he bites me gently. His arousal is off the charts. I can feel his breath quiver as he tries desperately to hold it together.

"I need you here," he whispers into my ear from behind as his finger impales me.

I nod and drop my head into the table as he starts to really ride me with his finger and then another. "Open," he whispers darkly and holds his body off mine. I slowly open my legs even further.

"You're so fucking perfect here," he growls into my back.

How in the hell does he make this feel so good? This is something I never thought I would like.

"Once we start there is no pulling back," he whispers. I turn and my nervous eyes meet his.

"I love you," he whispers as he kisses me gently again, sensing my fear.

I am instantly mollified and nod as I give him a soft smile. "It's okay, baby, I won't want to pull back," I whisper.

He applies more oil to my behind and his penis.

I turn back to the table and he rolls me to my side facing away from him, his front to my back. He lifts my top leg and puts the flat of my foot onto his outer thigh and his bottom arm underneath my head, then he pulls my body close to his. He starts to run his open mouth up and down my neck as his top hand reaches around and massages my clit in a circular movement. My head throws back onto his shoulder once again as my arousal starts to thump heavily between my legs. Very slowly he brings his hand down to grab the base of his cock and guides it to my entrance as I hold my breath.

"It's okay, baby," he whispers into my ear and I turn and kiss him with everything I have. I want this to be good for him, he deserves this to be good. He has been so patient and is trying so damn hard not to hurt me. I have never loved him more than I do at this moment.

"Kiss me through it," he whispers into my cheek and I nod and turn and take his lips in mine again.

He pushes forward as his top hand pushes me back onto

him. Oh shit, this fucking hurts. I close my eyes as I try to block out the pain.

"Baby, kiss me" he whispers desperately, knowing that he's hurting me. I slowly take his lips in mine and he keeps circling his fingers on my clitoris. I feel my body relax and he slowly adds just one finger to my sex and starts to pump me with it. I feel my arousal start to climb again and I drop my head back to his chest as I pant, and he pushes forward again as his front hand pushes me back.

"Ah," I whisper as I close my eyes and hold my breath.

"Nearly there, baby," he moans in an unrecognizable voice.

God, I have never seen him like this.

"Kiss me," he growls as his arousal hits a new level and I turn, and he takes my lips in his in hard erotic, passionate kissing. I feel the last of my body's resistance fall away and he slides home in one deep movement. Oh dear God. I pant to try to deal with the overwhelming sense of his claiming.

He drops his head to my shoulder and moans. "Oh fucking hell, Natasha."

I smile. I did it, we are doing it. I can do this. I turn and kiss him over my shoulder again and my arousal hits a new level. This is new uncharted territory and I feel like I might just lose my mind.

"Fuck me," I whisper.

His eyes meet mine and he cracks his neck hard. I giggle and throw my head back to his chest. God, I love this man.

He lifts my upper leg and holds it in the air as his body starts to pump me slowly and I moan in pleasure. He hooks my leg over his forearm and starts to pulse his fingers into my sex gently in time with his cock. Oh dear God, I'm in heaven.

As I get more aroused, he gets rougher, until we are hard at it and the sound of our bodies slapping together echoes through the room. I have never felt anything so good... so intimate... so perfect. We are both screaming as we start to hit the climax and I shudder deeply as I am hit with the strongest orgasm I have ever had, and he growls as his body lurches forward in the most perfect orgasm I have ever seen.

We lie still, covered in perspiration, panting, and I smile broadly.

Joshua is breathing heavily and can't talk. He smiles into the side of my forehead.

I smile broadly. "I think I'm actually good at that."

He smirks and takes my lips in his. "You blow my mind, Natasha Marx. You are one seriously hot fuck and yes, you are very, very good at that."

I smile, I like that answer. I like it a lot.

CHAPTER 15

Natasha

BOUNDARIES... what are they and do I have any left?

I'm pretty sure they and any physical restrictions I had put on myself flew completely out the window last night. There are no secrets anymore, no lies, no betrayal... at least not between the two of us anyway. As for the rest of the world, I'm not so sure anymore. We both lie on our sides facing each other and Joshua gently runs his fingertips in a circular pattern on my upper arm. I smile softly and he leans in to kiss me gently on the lips.

"What are you thinking about?" he asks.

I shrug as I smile into my pillow. "Just you."

He smirks. "What about me?"

I bite my bottom lips to stifle my smile. "Just thinking how you are the master magician."

"How so?" he smiles softly.

"Last night. How did you do that?" I bend and gently kiss him on his beautiful broad chest.

"Do what?" he asks as his hand tenderly cups the back of my head.

"Turn something that I was so sure that I was going to hate into something so beautiful and intimate?" I shake my head in disbelief. "I think last night was the biggest shock of my life."

He leans in and kisses me gently, then rolls onto his back and splays my body half over his. "Have we ever had anything but intimate and beautiful between us, Presh?" His eyes hold mine. "Together we are intimate perfection," he whispers into my hair.

I melt and kiss his chest. "No, I can't say that we have." I smile broadly. "We are, aren't we?"

I need a day at home with my boy. "Can you stay home with me today?" I ask hopefully.

"No, Presh," he whispers into the top of my head.

"I want to spoil you and I think you need some R and R, Josh."

He smiles. "Do you now?"

"What have you got going on today?" I ask, already knowing the answer. Cam told me yesterday.

He stays silent for a moment while he forms his answer in his head. "I am having James Brennan charged with blackmail."

My stomach drops, oh crap. I was hoping he had changed his mind on that. I stay silent.

He pulls back to look at my face. "What?" he frowns. I shrug.

"You don't think I should?" he asks, affronted.

I blow out a heavy breath. "No Josh, I don't. Not yet anyway."

"Why ever not? The bastard is living the high life on my

money," he snaps as his anger simmers dangerously close to the surface.

"Think about it, Joshua. If the paparazzi can get hold of the recording of the 911 call I made to the police when we were getting burgled what do you think they will do when they get hold of this information? And you know that they will."

He sits up in a rush, obviously annoyed at my opinion. "This is something that needs to be kept behind closed doors, Joshua, for your father's sake," I sigh.

He stands and walks over to the window and looks out as he processes my words. My eyes drop to his large naked body and I ache for his broken heart.

I sit up slowly and pool the blankets around my waist. "Joshua, this was your father's best friend and I know that you are angry and hurt but you need to let your dad deal with this the way he wants to. This isn't just about you."

His dark eyes meet mine. "I despise James Brennan, every fucking thing about him."

Pity fills me. "I know, honey, and I'm sorry you have to go through this shit." I drop my head as I search for the perfect thing to say... not a damn thing in my empty frigging head.

"What if she doesn't tell him? Dad I mean," he murmurs. "What then?"

I shrug. This thought has crossed my mind too. "I'm not sure."

He walks over and sits on the bed. "Do you think I should tell him?"

I shrug again. "You need to just take your time and not rush into anything that you may regret." He nods again as he chews his thumbnail deep in thought.

I stand and walk over to him sitting on the end of the bed

and pull his head into my body. "You know what we should do today?" I smile.

"Do tell?" he mutters flatly into my stomach.

I widen my eyes in excitement and his lips curl into a trace of a smile. "We should go and buy our wedding rings and a suit for you to wear to get married in."

He smirks as I bend to kiss him. "What do you think?" I smile into his lips.

"Can we get married today?" he asks hopefully.

I shake my head. "No, we cannot get married today. I don't even have my dress yet. Adrian, the girls and I are getting it next week."

"I've got heaps of suits," he replies flatly.

I roll my eyes. "Josh, you have to buy a suit that you only wear twice in your life."

He frowns in question.

"You wear it on the day you get married and then on the day you get buried." I smile at the wonder on his face.

He smiles softly as his eyes hold mine. "I want to be married. I want this to be legal."

I melt. "Oh God, me too. I have never wanted anything so much," I whisper.

He stands with new purpose. "Ok, Miss Marx, good distraction tactics. Let's go get some wedding rings and that suit I am only going to wear twice in my life."

When I told my man that I wanted to go shopping I had no idea he knew how to execute my idea to damn perfection. We are in a luxury shoe store and I am tottering around on the most ridiculously high stilettos known to man. Joshua is sitting on a velvet chair in full control and directing me as to which ones he wants me to try on.

His dark eyes watch me in my short black dress. I wore it purposely to keep the blood from the brain in his head detoured to the brain in his dick... Distraction 101... I got this shit.

"Turn around," he whispers as his eyes drop to my legs. I turn to see the much anticipated neck crack in the mirror as he watches me from behind and I bite my lip to stifle my smile as I look down at the shoes.

"Yes, we will take those." He nods to the salesclerk and she adds it to the other ten boxes on the counter. The four shop assistants' tongues are literally hanging onto the floor as they watch Mr. Orgasmic with his bottomless credit card in full throttle action. They are running around trying to please him and are deep green with envy. I hate to admit it, but I am loving every minute of this. These shoes are ridiculously expensive and not something I would ever buy but you know what? I don't care because this is keeping his mind off things and he has the money, so why the hell not?

His eyes scan the shop again and I feel my cheeks heat as I start hearing the word Kardashian run though my head. "That's enough, baby." I frown, suddenly embarrassed.

He stands and smirks at me, knowing exactly what's going through that pea brain of mine, and he casually throws his arm around my waist. "We haven't started yet, my beautiful girl."

I smile and my eyes flick to the salesgirls on the other side of their desk who are all melting right alongside me. Unable to help myself, I smile broadly.

"Let's go get those wedding rings," he murmurs as he slides his credit card across the glass countertop.

"Okay," I whisper. I lean up and kiss him gently on the

cheek as he pulls me into him, then he heads out the door to talk to Ben briefly. My eyes, and those of the sales assistants, follow him across the shop and I feel a wave of affection sweep over me. Their eyes flick back to me and they seem embarrassed at me catching them checking out my man.

"I know, right," I smile.

The blonde girl smiles in relief and shakes her head at me. "You are one lucky lady. When do you get married?"

I smile at her honesty. "Three months," I reply.

She smiles warmly at me. "You make a lovely couple."

"Thank you." I beam. You betcha, baby, and he's all mine, so eyes off the merchandise.

"Yes," Joshua answers his phone. We are in the back seat of the car on our way home after buying wedding rings, and Ben is driving. That did not go down as I had expected. I had thought we would go into a jewellery shop on the street, peruse glass cabinets and pick out rings from the display but, no, I keep forgetting. We are in Stanton Land now, a land where luxury is mandatory, expected and delivered on a silver tray with champagne, much to my delight. We went to a plush high rise office and mirrored cabinets on wheels were rolled out to our leather seats while we drank champagne out of crystal glasses. We were shown 'exclusive pieces' as they called them. This was the master jeweller's office that had made my engagement ring for Joshua.

I smile as I watch him. When we came back here for that week to pick out a new house, Joshua had consulted the master jeweller and he had made a ring for me in a rush so Josh could give it to me before our expected return two weeks later.

I feel regret knowing the pain I put Joshua through in that

week when I lost my father. I frown at my thoughts and my eyes fill with tears. I turn away to stare out the window. I know a thing or two about deep pain. *Dad, I miss you. Where are you now?* A lump in my throat forms as I contemplate how sad my wedding day will be when he is not the one who will be walking me down those steps to the altar and telling me I look beautiful. He won't be the one to be giving speeches and he won't see how happy I am. He won't be welcoming Joshua to our family. My eyes close in pain—I hate this. *Why did you have to die? It's not fair that you left me when I needed you the most.*

Joshua grabs my hand across the backseat and my eyes flick to him. He frowns as he speaks on the phone as he senses my inner turmoil. My cloudy eyes flick back out the window. If only I could turn back time and if we only knew Dad had a heart problem, we could have saved him. My thoughts go to Brock, a beloved brother who I have lost contact with. We have hardly spoken since Dad's death. You hear of families breaking up and you never once think that it will happen to yours. I need to make this right with him. I need to make him see how happy I am. Out of all of this nightmare with Joshua and his family, one thing has become glaringly obvious to me. Family is the most important thing in life, and I want what's left of mine to be happy and united. I need to fix this so I'm calling Brock as soon as we get home.

Joshua hangs up, undoes his seatbelt and slides over next to me. He puts his arm around me and pulls me into him and my tears drop onto his suit. No words are needed between us; he knows the only reason I get sad. He knows it's the only thing he can't fix in my world. If he could, I know he would. He gently kisses my forehead and stays silent. The sad truth is my wedding day is going to be the happiest day of my life, but it will also be one of the saddest days in my life and there is not a thing that we can do about it. I imagine all brides must feel like this when they have lost a parent.

After ten minutes I pull back and wipe my eyes. "Sorry," I whisper as I shake my head. What's happening to me? "We just bought wedding rings. I should be happy."

He smiles gently as his eyes hold mine. "Don't ever apologize to me for being emotional. It's the emotion in you that I love."

I smile softly and kiss him as I grab his jaw and run my thumb backwards and forwards through his stubble as my eyes search his. "I love you," I whisper, grateful for this beautiful man who knows me so well.

He smiles. "I know you do."

"I don't mean to be sad," I whisper into his neck.

"I know you don't." He smiles and picks up my hand and kisses the back of it. "We can go home, the house has been cleared and the detectives have given us the go ahead," he replies.

I nod. "Oh." For some reason I feel slightly dejected. I wanted another night in our hotel room with just the two of us. Maybe he's right and we should move to an apartment somewhere for a while.

"I told them we wouldn't be back for a few days. I want you to myself some more," he whispers as his lips kiss my cheek.

My overly emotional eyes tear up again because he can read my mind so well. "Thank you," I whisper gratefully.

He pushes the hair from my forehead as he looks at me. "I think that it's you who needs to be spoiled for a while, my beautiful girl."

I smile shyly as my fragility hits home. "Maybe I do," I whisper.

. . .

True to Joshua's promise I have been just that, spoiled rotten. We have stayed at the hotel for an extra five days in our own little love cocoon. Joshua has been dealing with the paternity news and me... well... I don't know, but for some reason buying those wedding rings on Monday has opened a can of worms and had me thinking all about my father and his absence from my life. I'm sad to my bones that both Joshua and I have lost what we have always known. Things will be forever different from here on. Joshua and I are healing each other; we have talked for hours and hours. From deep, deep soul-searching conversations to the mechanics of female contraception. I actually think he's a better therapist than me and this is exactly what we have needed: time alone to regroup. Unfortunately, our love bubble finishes today. Joshua is at the gym and then returning to take me to our home.

Today he has to make a decision on what he is going to do about James Brennan. The asshole hasn't returned the money, exactly as I thought. Thankfully though, our long daily discussions have made Joshua much better prepared to deal with the situation than he was last week. My phone rings, the name Brock lights my screen and I smile. I have been trying to get him all week, but I have had to wait for him to call me back from Afghanistan. My nerves flutter in my stomach, this is an important conversation.

"Hello, Brock." I smile.

"Hi, Tash," he replies softly, and then a silence falls on the line.

I'm just going to come out and say it: "Brock, I don't want to fight with you anymore." A lump in my throat forms. "I miss having you in my life."

He sighs. "Tash"

"Joshua makes me so happy, Brock, and I know you two

have had your issues but that's because you are so alike." I blurt the words out in a rush to get them off my chest.

"We are nothing alike," he snaps coldly.

"Brock, I love both of you and I know both of you. You *are* alike whether you want to admit it or not." He stays silent as he listens.

"He's going through a lot right now," I whisper.

"Like what?" he asks.

I puff out my cheeks in nerves. "He has just found out that Robert is not his biological father."

"What?" he replies.

My heart drops and I nod. "It's true," I whisper. "Margaret had an affair and I killed our father for nothing," I add through tears.

"Tash, you didn't kill Dad. Stop it. I don't want you thinking that," he replies quietly.

I am silent as the tears run down my face and I swipe them angrily from my face. "You said that I killed him," I then blurt out, silently angry that he said that to me at such a dark time in my life.

"Tash, I didn't mean that shit. I was being a fucking idiot. I don't even know what I was saying back then." I stay silent as I listen. "You're not cousins," he replies, and I can hear him deep in thought.

I shake my head. "No, we are not." And I feel excitement rise a little in my stomach now that he knows the truth.

"Doesn't change anything. I still can't stand him," he mutters.

My heart drops. "Brock, I swear to you on Mum's life that when we were young, I wanted this relationship just as much as he did. He never pushed himself onto me. Not once. Brock, we fell in love and we couldn't help it."

He stays silent.

I need to get him on my side. "I'm so happy, Brock. He adores me and he treats me so well," I continue.

"He's a womanizer, Natasha," he mutters.

I shake my head. "Brock, no, he's not. I mean he was, but he isn't anymore." I screw up my face as I hear how that would have sounded. *God, I'm blowing it.* "He loves me and spends all of his time trying to make me happy. You know we are getting married, right?" I ask.

"Yeah, Mum told me," he replies flatly.

I bite my bottom lip in nerves. "Will you give me away, Brock?"

"Tash." He sighs, defeated.

"Please," I beg. "I need your approval." My tears start to form. "I love him so much and we are so happy. I wouldn't be with him if he didn't treat me well. Deep down you know that."

He stays silent.

"I know you're finished with your deployment in four weeks. Can you come straight here to LA and spend some time with Joshua and me? Mum is coming over for the wedding and Bridget is here. We need to regroup as a family, Brock. This is a special time. Please don't let Dad's death destroy our family, it is not what he would have wanted. He would want us to be happy and getting along." Tears overflow from my eyes.

He cuts me off. "I thought you were getting married in Thailand?"

I smile. He stays silent. "Let me think about it." He sighs.

I smile broadly. At least he's thinking about it. "I love you," I reply.

"I love you, too." He sighs again.

"I swear to God if he hurts you, Natasha," he threatens.

I smile again. "I don't know much in this fucked up world,

Brock, but I know one thing with every cell in my body. Joshua Stanton will never ever hurt me. He is my soulmate, and we are deeply in love. We are so happy, I promise."

"Oh God, that's pathetic," he responds, and I can hear him smiling. I know I've got him.

"So, I will see you in four weeks?" I ask hopefully.

"I'll see," he mutters but I know that's a yes.

"Bye, Brock. Please be safe over there." I put my hand over my heart as relief fills me.

"Goodbye, Tash, you too."

I've worked it out. Yep, Albert Einstein has finally figured it out. The reason Joshua and I like small spaces and apartments is because we are in the same vicinity as each other. This house is so big that even the distance from the kitchen to his office is miles apart. I feel like he's not even home half the time. I have just got off the phone with Adrian, Cameron and the girls. I'm cooking dinner tonight for everyone and today I had an epiphany. If I'm going to be a Stepford wife... ahem... Stanton wife to be exact, I'm going to be damn good at it. I'm going to bake cookies and shit... like Martha Stewart on crack.

I am lying on the bench reading through Brigetta's recipe books.

"What about Lobster Vol au Vent?" I call out to Joshua who is reading the paper while lying on the lounge.

He flicks the paper down and looks over the top of it. "Really, Vol au Vent?" He frowns. "Keep reading," he replies dryly.

Hmm, I keep turning through the pages looking for something that is relatively easy to make but tastes really difficult to make, the ultimate sensory illusion. I narrow my eyes. "This cooking is tricky business, you know?" I mutter.

Joshua puts the paper down and smirks. I smile and raise my eyebrows in question. Crap, I'm shit at this already. He wisely holds his tongue and goes back to his paper.

"What about Beef Ragout?" I ask.

He raises his eyebrows again in question.

I shrug. "I just feel like something meaty," I add.

He smirks. "Whatever takes your fancy, Presh. Meaty is... different I suppose."

Hmm, I hate it when they say whatever. I need a decision, so I have someone to blame if it turns out shit.

Joshua's phone beeps a text on the bench and I pick it up and read it. It's from Ben.

Are you and Natasha free to have a meeting with Max and me now?

Hmm. "It's Ben. He wants to know if we can meet with Max and him," I call out as I read the message.

Joshua looks at me deadpan and I smile a little too sweetly and fake bat my eyelashes.

"Fine," he mutters. I text back.

Sure. Come in now.

So here we sit around the dining table: Joshua, Ben, Max and me. Ben is the first to speak. "So, I think we just need to air out this situation and work out if you two can work together because Natasha and I are tired of being the meat in the sandwich."

His eyes flick to me and I stifle a smile and look at the

ground. Ben's being tough and has obviously gone over this conversation in his head.

Joshua inhales deeply as his eyes bore into Max. Shit. I interject. "Joshua, I would like Max to keep being my guard. He was very good to me and my family after my father died and we became friends," I announce.

Joshua runs his tongue over his top teeth as his eyes flick to Max again as he thinks.

Ben's eyes flick between the two men who are staying silent. "I think that Max has crossed a line and, Joshua, because you are unwilling to forgive it is damn uncomfortable around here," Ben contributes.

Max crosses his arms angrily in front of him. "Don't tell me if you were guarding Natasha that you would have left her alone in another country, Ben. That's complete bullshit and you know it."

Ben scratches his head uncomfortably.

"I wanted you to bring her to me," Joshua snaps.

I screw up my face. *Hello, I'm sitting right here.* "Joshua, Max tried repeatedly to get me to go back to you and when I refused, he had no choice. He had to make a decision to guard me or know that I was going to run off the first chance I got and be alone," I reply.

Joshua's angry eyes turn to me and I wither under his glare.

"What exactly has brought this to a head?" Ben asks. Oh God, he had to bring that up, didn't he?

"I will not have him pawing Natasha," Joshua sneers.

Ben frowns and Max rolls his eyes and sits back in his chair in disgust.

"I don't paw her," he snaps.

"What's with walking around my house with your arm around her then?"

I frown. Oh God, this conversation is turning to shit.

Max shakes his head in frustration. "We were talking, and I didn't realize I was doing it. We are friends."

Joshua sits forward in his chair. "Well, I realize you are doing it and I don't fucking like it." His angry eyes hold Max's.

I hold up my hands in a stop signal. "Let's just calm down, shall we. Joshua, Max puts his arm around me because I have set the precedent. I often link arms with him as we walk or talk, or I will grab his hand if we are crossing a busy road. It's how I am with people I trust, and it means nothing. I would do the same to Ben or Adrian or Cameron," I reply.

My eyes flick to Ben and he frowns slightly as if to say leave me out of this and I nearly break into a smile.

"Let me make this clear to you, Natasha," Joshua sneers as he leans into the table in anger. "I will not have my wife's security guard touching her in any way. So, you and Max make the decision right now because I can tell you if I catch him with his arm around you again it will be fucking Armageddon."

"Joshua," I snap, talk about an over-reaction. Max shakes his head in frustration.

"Fine, but I only want Max as my guard," I assert.

Joshua's eyes flick to me again. "Why? He is part of the team that looks after us and you should be happy to have whichever guard is assigned to you."

I roll my eyes as my anger starts to pump. "Assigned to me?" I repeat. Who in the hell does he think he is?

"Yes, assigned to you," Joshua snaps as his eyes hold mine. "This is my household, and these are my staff."

"Well, this is just fucking great, isn't it?" I snap. "I choose Ben then, asshole."

Joshua narrows his eyes. "Ben is my guard. He is unavailable," he replies.

I shake my head. "Nope, if I don't get to pick my guard you sure as shit don't get to pick yours. You can hang out with the losers that you expect me to."

"Um, excuse me," Ben interjects, sensing that this conversation is turning into a power trip for both Joshua and me.

"No offence, but I am not guarding you, Natasha. I am staying with Stan and Max is staying with you. We are both happy with our designated roles."

My eyes flick back to Joshua who folds his arms in front of him as his eyes flick to Max. "I understand the terms and I am happy with them. I will be guarding Natasha when you are at work and will not be over-friendly or inappropriate at any time," Max replies flatly as his eyes flick to me. I smile gratefully at him.

Joshua stays still and silent as he thinks. I know he wants to get rid of Max and we are railroading him, but I don't care. Max doesn't deserve to be fired for protecting me and in the long-term future this will all be forgotten.

"Max is the best guard we have. If you want Natasha to be safe and protected, you need someone experienced that she likes, and you know that."

Joshua nods as he drops his head and looks at the ground, sensing that he is losing this battle.

Joshua's eyes meet Max's. "Don't get me wrong. I am grateful that your loyalty lies with Natasha, but you need to understand that this is a family unit now and not me against her or her against me. I need to know that all of my staff are on the same page and there is no underhandedness between us."

For the first time Max smiles. "I understand that, and I am very happy that this is turning into a family unit. You have my word that you can trust me, and I will do what's right for everyone in the future and not just Natasha," he replies.

Joshua nods and his lips show a hint of a smile. "Thank you," he replies softly.

Max stands and holds his hand out and Joshua stands, and they shake. An over-the-top smile beams from my face and I jump out of my chair. What I really want to do is cuddle all three of them but I am going to stick to this over-friendly thing, so I punch Ben in the arm instead and he smiles warmly. That went really well if I do say so myself.

It's 7 pm. Dinner is on and our friends will be here soon. Between us, Joshua and I have deciphered the recipe for Fettuccine Carbonara. I took the easy way out and picked the simplest recipe I could find. Joshua is sending a few emails before they get here, and I am lying on the lounge in his office. All this Martha Stewart stuff has made me tired before the guests even get here.

A soft knock sounds on the office door. We both look up and my heart sinks. Robert Stanton, Joshua's father, stands in the doorway, wearing a suit and an obvious broken heart. Joshua, who is sitting behind his desk, immediately drops his head as tears flow from his eyes. I bring my hand up to my neck as I am overcome with emotion.

"Hello, son," Robert whispers.

CHAPTER 16

Natasha

ROBERT STANDS tall as he waits for Joshua's reaction, but Joshua's head stays down. A lump in my throat forms, blocking my vocal cords. I've never seen my beautiful Joshua so gutted.

"Come and hug your old man," Robert says quietly.

Joshua brings both of his hands over his face and the tears drop onto my cheeks.

Silence and time seem to stand still.

Robert walks into the room. "Joshua, look at me," he whispers. Joshua's haunted tear-filled eyes meet his.

"It's okay, son," he whispers.

Joshua screws up his face as he fights the tears, then he shakes his head and wipes his face angrily.

"It's okay, it changes nothing," Robert continues softly, sensing his son's distress.

Joshua stands furiously. "It changes everything. I'm not your son," he yells as he breaks into full blown tears. "I'm not your fucking son," he sobs. "My whole life is a lie."

I hold my hand up to my mouth as pity and hurt fill me. Oh dear God, he's so hurt.

"Don't you dare say that," Robert replies. "I love you and you will always be my son."

I sob loudly and screw up my face as I try to hold in my tears. "I don't give a damn what blood type you have. You are my son! Do you hear me? I will not let a blood test determine that!" he whispers.

Joshua puts his head in his hands and Robert wraps his arms around his broken son. They stand in an embrace, both in tears about a circumstance that they have no control over, both gutted by a woman they loved and trusted. For the first time I see Joshua as a broken child and not the powerful man that he is. This is devastating for him.

Cameron walks to the door and I see his face drop. I stand and quietly leave the room and as I turn the corner I see Scott and Wilson. Oh my, all of the Stanton men are here in LA.

My man needs some time alone with his family.

It's Sunday and Adrian, the girls and I have arrived back at Adrian's apartment after wedding dress shopping all day. Joshua has spent most of the weekend at our house with his father and brothers and I have been making myself scarce by hanging out with my gang... um, our gang. It's weird. I adore Adrian and I know Joshua thinks the world of the girls. The boundaries of our friends are being blurred.

I think Joshua's little speech to Max the other day has cemented in my head what I have always felt. This is my treasured and very much deserved family unit.

I haven't really had any time with Joshua alone to talk but he has come to bed in a good mood every night if you know what I mean. I don't know what that means but I think we are definitely taking his mind off his problems when in bed together.

"Just weeks till you're married, Tash." Adrian smiles

I flop onto his lounge. "Makes me nervous just thinking about it."

"I love that dress," he replies.

I put my hand over my heart and pretend to swoon. "Oh my God, so do I. I can't believe we found that on our first day shopping." The girls sit on the floor opening the boxes that the newly purchased bridesmaid's shoes are in and my eyes flick around the surroundings of Adrian's beautiful luxury apartment and I smile.

"Remember how you told me I needed a bathroom renovation on the first time we met?" I ask.

Adrian puts his hand over his face in embarrassment. "Oh, don't remind me. I know, how rude," he murmurs as he shakes his head in disgust at himself.

"I thought I might have hated you then." I smirk.

He shakes his head. "I knew I offended you."

"Totally. I thought to myself who does this guy think he is, Donatella fucking Versace?" I reply.

He smiles broadly.

I hold my hand up in the air and gesture around the space. "But now I see your apartment I know that you put Donatella to shame. You have amazing taste, Adrian."

He looks around his beautiful apartment proudly. "I do, don't I?" He winks cheekily and Abbie sticks her finger down her throat in disgust. "Pity I don't pick men as well as I pick furnishings and wedding dresses."

I smile warmly to hide a tinge of sadness. Adrian has been a little down this weekend and I know that Joshua and Cameron having their large family around is only reminding him of what we all know. He doesn't have a family anymore and even though the Stantons are totally messed up at the moment, everyone is alive and dealing with this nightmare together. I want Adrian to go back to Nicholas. I know he still loves him, and I also know how totally unproductive and heartbreaking it is taking the high road to loneliness. They both deserve better.

The girls stand and start to parade around the lounge room in their shoes.

"We should have gone higher." Bridget frowns as she looks down at her feet. "My legs look short and dumpy."

Adrian rolls his eyes. "I told you there are 167 stairs to climb down and I am not scraping your ass off the steps when you fall over."

Abbie holds her hand up in the shape of a bird's beak and opens and closes it a few times to simulate him nagging.

"Did Joshua get his suit?" I ask as I walk into the kitchen and flick on the jug. "Who wants tea?" I call. Joshua wanted to pick his suit through the week with Cam and Adrian. I wasn't invited.

"You will be happy with the result. He's the easiest man on the planet to style," he calls.

I smile. "That's because he looks orgasmic in everything," I mutter as I exit the kitchen.

"That does help," he replies under his breath.

Abbie's phone beeps a text and she smiles. "My ride is downstairs. Are we leaving the shoes here?" she asks as she points to the boxes.

"Yeah. Who is your ride?" Adrian frowns.

Abbie's eyes flick between us. "Oh, just this guy I met. He's really nice and really hot. I am just going to hang at his house tonight," she replies nonchalantly.

Bridget and I exchange looks and narrow our eyes at each other.

The only guy I know who has interested her is the damn cop. "You're not seeing the frigging cop, are you?" Bridget frowns.

Abbie frowns. "No. Maybe." She winces. "Sort of." She shrugs in a who cares gesture.

"You called him?" I exclaim. "Abbie, you can't date this frigging guy. He's investigating a murder that your fingerprints are involved in. This is a recipe for disaster."

Adrian frowns. "Huh? What did I miss? Who is this guy?"

Bridget shakes her head. "You are not going out with this fucking guy. Abbie, stop it. Adrian, this guy came to the house to see Joshua and Ben about TC."

Adrian rolls his eyes as if in pain. "Of course he did," he mutters deadpan.

"Listen here, my beautiful but boring friends. The cop whose name is Rick is smoking hot and I'm turning into a fucking nun in that mansion." Her eyes flick to me. "It's alright for you. You get to have sex everyday with Mr. Multiple."

I smirk. Okay, she's got me on that one. She points to Bridget. "And I know for a fact the Ben banged the hell out of you for about four hours last night."

My mouth drops open and my eyes flick to Bridget. "What?" I shriek.

Bridget's horrified eyes meet Abbie's. "He did not!" she exclaims nervously and starts to wobble uncontrollably in her heels as she gets distracted.

"See you can't walk in those heels. How are you going to walk in anything taller?" Adrian butts in with his observation.

"Oh yes, he did and you fucking loved it if your moans are anything to go by," Abbie replies.

Adrian bursts out laughing as my eyes narrow at Bridget. "You and Ben," I say.

She frowns. "It was Carson."

I narrow my eyes again. "Liar, Carson went to the Philippines for a week on Friday for business."

Adrian laughs again. "That's why Ben has been in such a good mood."

Bridget's eyes light up and she momentarily forgets her denial. "Why, what did he say?"

"Bridget!" I yell. "This is true." I knew it. I knew she didn't leave her phone in the kitchen.

"Oh God, yes it's true. We are just fooling around a bit—it means nothing. But we are not telling anyone," she sighs, defeated.

"Why not?" Adrian asks as he gets up to get the tea.

"Ben thinks that it will jeopardize his job if things don't work out," she replies.

I nod. Something like that had crossed my mind, not that his job would be in danger but that he might resign.

Bridget lies back on the lounge. "Oh my lord, he's so hot in bed," she whispers so that Adrian can't hear from the kitchen.

I smile broadly and Abbie puts on her jacket. "Well, a hot cop is just what I need. I hope he brought his handcuffs home."

I frown. "Don't tell me you would let a stranger cuff you?" I ask, horrified.

"Totally," she replies. "It's all the better being a little scared and I haven't had sex for six weeks."

Adrian returns from the kitchen carrying a tray of tea and coffee. "Maybe it should be him that is scared then," he mutters.

Abbie smiles her sneaky slut smile. "He should totally be petrified." Her phone beeps again and she smiles as she reads it. "Oh, and he's being all dominant with the messaging," she purrs.

"What did he say?" I frown.

"Hurry up and get that hot little ass down here. I have plans for it." She smirks.

Unable to help it we all break into broad smiles.

"Yeah, I'll pay that. He'll do." Adrian smirks as he blows on his hot coffee, then stands and kisses her on the cheek. "Be safe, babe," he murmurs.

Abbie inhales like a kid in a candy store and breezes out of the apartment and I smile broadly.

"What are you smiling at?" Bridget frowns.

"Do you know how worried I have been about her? She hasn't slept with anyone for weeks and has been all agreeable. I can't handle it. I wanted my annoying sex-crazed disobedient friend back, and today she finally arrived," I reply.

Bridget smiles. "This is true." Her eyes flick between Adrian and me. "Can you guys keep quiet about Ben and me, please? It's only early days and I don't want to bring it out until we know what's going on."

I frown. "How did this happen? Last time I saw you two together you had a massive fight and then you left with Carson."

She picks up her coffee from the tray. "Yeah, well then I felt like shit and I couldn't stand the thought of him going home with that big-boobed bitch and, let's face it, Carmichael is a huge nob," she replies.

"Huge," I mutter.

"Gigantic," Adrian agrees.

"So, I call Ben and asked him to pick me up from the club we were at." She shrugs.

Adrian is now lying on the lounge. "And then what happened?" he asks.

Bridget drinks her coffee and shrugs again. "We had a huge fight in the car and were screaming at each other and he told me I'm not allowed to sleep with anyone else because it's all he could think about doing and couldn't and he couldn't handle watching me do it with someone else."

Adrian and I smirk at each other.

"So, I just jumped him in the car." She smiles. "I thought to myself, fuck it. I want him and he wants me, so who cares. I thought to myself what would Abbie do in this situation so I just straddled him at a traffic light and started kissing him until he couldn't refuse."

Adrian holds his coffee cup in the air to symbolize well done.

I smile and frown. "So, you had sex in the car?" My horrified eyes meet Adrian's. "At a traffic light?" My eyes widen. "Bloody hell, Bridget, that's dangerous."

"No, he took me back to his apartment to show me what he is really capable of."

I smile again as I listen. I like this story. "And?" I question.

Bridget points at Adrian. "Not a fucking word. You're swapping to our side of the friendship fence."

Adrian laughs and holds up his hands in self-defense. "Of course."

Bridget simulates sliding down the lounge. "Seriously, he is off the charts."

I smile broadly. "I knew he would be."

"So how many times have you been with him?" Adrian asks.

Bridget seems embarrassed. "Every night since."

My mouth drops open. "He has been sneaking into your room like a frat boy?" I frown.

She screws up her face. "Sort of."

Adrian laughs. "How do you sort of sneak into a room?"

She rubs her face with both hands. "Not a word, you two!" she repeats.

"Yes!" we both yell in frustration.

"Every night I go to bed and then I ask him to come and say goodbye to me before he leaves and then when he gets to my room, I just sort of talk him into staying. He has been getting up and leaving at four in the morning so he can arrive back at eight."

I smile in satisfaction. I knew those two would be so good together. "That's how he saw the burglars the other night. He was leaving as they were coming in."

I frown. "Shit," I whisper, horrified. "So, if Ben hadn't been leaving they would have gotten in."

Adrian reads my mind. "Security has been doubled, babe. Don't worry." Adrian puts his foot onto my lap in a comforting gesture and I rub it through his sock as I think.

"What are you doing tonight?" Adrian asks Bridget.

She smiles shyly. "I'm going out for dinner with Ben. He has the weekend off and then I am staying at his house."

Both Adrian and I smile at her obvious excitement.

Adrian and Bridget then start talking but I am lost in my own little world. They would have got in. The power was cut and Ben wasn't on duty. They would have killed Joshua. I sit up in a rush, thinking I need to go to him. I need to make sure he's safe.

"What are you doing?" Adrian frowns.

I shake my head. "I'm worried they are going to get Joshua."

I sigh as once again I rub Adrian's foot, deep in thought. "I can't even bear to think of that."

"Tash, I promise you, I have got this. Security has been

doubled and, to be honest, the police think it was a random burglary anyway. Please remember there are ten million dollars' worth of cars in Joshua's garage," Adrian replies.

I nod. "True," I whisper.

Bridget smiles. "Tash, you know Ben wouldn't have had the weekend off if he was worried about Joshua's safety."

God, I'm overreacting as usual. "Yeah, you're right. That's true." I nod, feeling a little better.

Adrian gets a text and, after reading it, texts a reply and Bridget stands and looks out the window. "I'm off too. I can hear Ben calling me."

I roll my eyes. "Oh God, is this going to get soppy?"

Bridget smiles broadly. "Perhaps." She walks over and kisses Adrian's forehead and then mine on her way to the door.

"See you tomorrow guys."

"Bye," we both call.

My phone rings and the name Lambo lights up the screen. "Hi babe." I smile.

"Hello, my beautiful girl," Joshua smiles down the phone. "Did you get your dress?" he purrs.

"I did." I smile like a schoolgirl.

"And?" he asks.

"And you are going to have to wait till our wedding to see it."

"Mmm." He sighs sexily. "I'm waiting for you. What time are you coming home?"

"Um." My eyes flick to Adrian as he watches television. "What are our plans for the night?" I ask.

"I got us a box at the Lakers," he replies.

I screw up my face. That sounds exactly the opposite of what I want to do tonight. "Is Adrian coming?" I ask and then I hold my hand over the phone. "Are you going to the basketball game?" I mouth.

Adrian frowns and shakes his head.

"No, I just texted him and he doesn't want to come," Joshua replies.

"Why don't you go with your brothers and dad and I will hang with Adrian? You can pick me up on the way home."

"Why? What are you guys doing?" he asks.

I shrug. "Nothing probably. We'll eat something I suppose. I'm just not really in the mood to get dressed and go out. You go and have fun with the boys."

He thinks for a moment. "Are you sure?" he asks.

I roll my eyes. "Yes, I'm not a baby."

"Um, ok. I just don't want you to think you are not invited."

I frown. "Don't be stupid. Call me when you finish."

"Okay, is Max with you?"

"Yes, he's outside with Jason," I reply.

"Ok, Presh. See you in a couple of hours. I love you," he speaks quietly down the phone and I know he has just walked away from the others so they can't hear him.

"Okay." I smile.

"Tomorrow we find apartments for our guests," he replies.

"Yes." I smile gratefully. "That is a good plan."

"So I can fuck you wherever I want to," he whispers.

I smile deviously. "You already fuck me wherever you want to, Mr. Stanton."

Adrian puts his hands over his ears and pretends to vomit. Oops, I forgot he was listening.

"So I do. I meant location," he whispers darkly.

Four hours later Adrian and I are in a Mexican restaurant and on our fourth frozen margarita. Our guards are seated up the front. We are dagging it up in our jeans and clothes from today.

I must look like a wreck and it feels bloody good not to be getting chased by idiots with cameras. We are eating the biggest serves of nachos I have ever seen.

"I know we have gone over this but why don't you call Nicholas?" I ask.

He sips his drink. "I nearly did last night actually."

I smile as I wipe my mouth with a serviette. "What stopped you?"

"I don't want him to think that I am after anything," he replies.

"Can't you be friends?" I frown.

He shrugs. "Maybe, I haven't scoped that out."

My phone rings and the name Jesten lights up the screen. I roll my eyes and answer the call. This is about the fourth time he has called me and I can never answer it because I am always with Joshua.

"Sorry, I have to take this," I whisper to Adrian.

He waves me off in an *I don't care I'm drinking* kind of wave. "Hello, Jes," I answer.

"Tash, I wish you'd answer your damn phone. I have been trying to get in contact with you." He sighs in relief.

I frown. "What's wrong?"

"We haven't spoken since you chose the dickhead over me and I thought..." He goes silent as he rethinks his wording.

I narrow my eyes. "He's not a dickhead!" I snap.

Adrian smiles as he licks some salt from his glass and clinks his with mine.

"Who is it?" Adrian asks with a frown.

I write the name Jesten on my napkin and he smirks at my annoyed face.

"Jes, if you care to remember, last time we saw each other, you had the audacity to tell Joshua that I loved every minute of the sex we had, and you knew that was a downright lie. We have never even kissed, Jesten," I blurt out angrily. "Why did you do that?" I ask, hurt. "I thought we were friends?"

"You would love every minute of it," he replies, ignoring my last question.

"Oh God, are you even listening to me?" I respond.

"I had drinks with Simon last night," he volunteers.

I frown. "Simon, my Simon. Since when have you and Simon been close?" I didn't even know that they knew each other.

"He's been coming to the prison and we got to know each other," he replies.

"Oh," I answer. I did not expect that combo of friends. Mr. Nerd meets Mr. Bad Boy—what a combination.

"Simon told me you are marrying the psycho," he snaps.

I bite my lip as I start to fume. I can just imagine those two gossipy bitches on a Joshua-sledging fest.

"Yep!" I snap. "I can't wait." Don't give me your attitude, dickhead. I'm not in the mood.

"Natasha. You can't be serious?" he growls.

I screw up my face. "What?" I snap.

"Natasha, he isn't good for you!" he replies angrily.

"What?" I shake my head in frustration. "Oh, and you are?" I sneer. This guy is pissing me off.

"Yeah, I was a lot better than him. Money isn't everything you know," he scoffs.

I roll my eyes at Adrian and he smiles broadly. He's loving this. "Listen, Jesten, I was hoping we could be friends but I am marrying Joshua because I love him, and it has nothing to do with money and you and he are never going to get along so let's just leave it at that. Okay?"

"When's the wedding?" he asks.

"Ten weeks," I reply.

"We'll see," he murmurs almost to himself.

"What's that supposed to mean?" I snap.

"You won't fucking marry him!" he screams.

"Yes, Jesten, I will," I reply coldly.

"Are you in LA?" he asks.

"Yes, where do you think I am?" I scoff. What's with the twenty questions?

He stays silent on the phone as he thinks.

"I have to go. I'm out to dinner with a friend," I reply.

"What friend?" he asks.

"Adrian, you know my friend Adrian," I reply.

"No," he snaps. "Who is he?"

I roll my eyes. Now he's getting jealous of Adrian.

"Goodbye, Jesten."

"Tash, don't go," he whispers in a panicked voice. "I think I love you. I can't stop thinking about you... and about what we could be together. Come back to me."

My heart drops. Jesten and I did have a connection and the truth is I am sad that we can't even be friends. "Jes," I whisper. "Don't."

"Please," he begs.

"Jes, I'm not the girl for you. I'm in love with another man. You and I were just friends. I would like it if we could stay friends."

He stays silent and I know I have to get off the phone. "Bye, Jes, take care."

I wait on the phone for a reply but again silence and I slowly hang up.

I put my head in my hands. God, I hate hurting people's feelings.

"Tough, huh?" Adrian asks.

I pick up my drink and drain the glass. "Who was he again?" Adrian asks.

"You know that prison warden guy who cage fights with Joshua, the one who told me to think of him while I had sex with Joshua."

Adrian bubbles up a chuckle. "Oh yeah, the dude with the big balls."

I smile. "That is pretty tough, hey."

Adrian widens his eyes. "I thought Joshua was seriously going to kill him that night."

I nod as I shovel another corn chip into my mouth. "Yeah well, they had another couple of fights after that as well."

"When?" Adrian frowns.

"At the fight ring and then again one night at my house."

Adrian frowns. "Your house, what the hell? I didn't hear about this."

I shake my head, why did I mention that? "Jes and I became really good friends in that time Joshua and I were apart and he came around one night professing his love and Joshua turned up in the middle of it and Joshua lost his shit".

Adrian nods as he sips his drink. "So Jesten is your Amelie?"

I smile sadly. "Yeah, I suppose he is, I haven't thought of it before but that's exactly what he is."

I frown as I think. "Please explain to me why Joshua hates Amelie so much?" I shake my head. "I thought they were friends, and he is just so mean to her."

Adrian holds my eyes. "She is fatal fucking attraction that's why."

I frown and hold up my arm for more drinks. "What do you mean?" I ask.

"She won't let go. She is trying to make Joshua go back to her."

I frown, huh? This is news. "What do you mean?"

"Well, when Joshua gave her the money he just wanted her to go away but she just won't. She has turned up at his polo games and she started going out with the LA clique so she could see him when she was out."

I frown, money... what money? I need to play along and trick Adrian into thinking I already know this. When would he have given her money? My eyes widen in realization, when he gave me the money. Joshua paid two divorce settlements, not one. I start to hear my pulse in my ears and fury fills me.

I act uninterested and continue shoveling food into my mouth. "This is when he paid me and her the money?" I murmur with my mouth full.

"Yes," Adrian replies, thinking I already know this. "The twenty million guilt money."

What?!

"Fuck off. He gave her twenty million dollars?" I snap furiously. Adrian's eyes widen in horror. "You didn't know this?" he whispers, mortified that he has just opened his mouth.

"No, I didn't know this." I look around angrily. "Where are our fucking drinks?" I snap.

"Oh my God, don't you say anything," Adrian whispers as his face falls. "He will kill me."

I narrow my eyes. "No, of course not," I snap. "As if. You swapped sides of the friendship fence, remember."

He drains his glass and rolls his eyes at his predicament. "Do you mean to tell me that that bitch took twenty million dollars and she can't afford a fucking horse paddock?" I scoff.

What a hide.

Adrian shakes his head. "You don't know the half of it. She's trying to buy a farm next to Willowvale."

I frown. "Why?"

"She's so deluded that she thinks that if she is around Joshua, he will see what he's missing and go to her with open arms," he replies. "Joshua gave her that money because he felt guilty taking the life from her that she was used to. The mansion, the horses." He shakes his head in disgust.

The waitress arrives with the tray of drinks and I take mine gratefully. "Thank you," I murmur, deep in thought.

"Cameron thinks she's unstable."

I frown again. "Why?"

He shakes his head. "She just does weird things."

"Like what?" I ask.

He looks around as he thinks. "I don't know. At first she would just turn up at his office all the time crying and shit and then when Ben stepped in and wouldn't let her get access to Joshua, she started sending him naked pictures of herself."

I sit back in my chair uneasily. "Go on," I reply in a monotone. He sits forward and looks around to see if anyone can hear us.

"You can't tell anyone this shit."

"Go on," I snap.

"She started sending him movies of her masturbating and getting herself off."

I screw up my face in horror.

"In some movies she was in his horse stables, naked on his horse saddles, with massive dildos and crazy sex toys."

"She's trying to tap into his kink," I whisper to myself.

"Yep, totally," Adrian whispers.

"What the hell! That *is* unstable behavior," I whisper, mortified. My mind goes to him acting like a lunatic in the horse stables that day. I don't blame him. He thinks if he gives her an inch, she will take a mile. Why didn't he just tell me this?

"He ended up getting a restraining order put on her," he replies.

"Is she on any meds?" I ask.

Adrian shrugs. "Since we have got back from Australia there has been nothing. I think now that you're here she realizes it's all over and he won't tolerate her shit anymore."

"God, we know some bizarre people. don't we?" I sigh.

"Yeah, I do feel a bit sorry for her." He shrugs.

I frown. "How come?"

"Even though she was such a bitch to all of us, she really did love Joshua, and he has only ever loved you."

My heart hurts for her. I know how it feels to go crazy over this man. There were times when I felt like I couldn't breathe if I couldn't have him. "God, Adrian, what a nightmare." I sigh.

He shrugs. "She's harmless."

I nod. "Well, that's a good explanation of why he hates her." I smile broadly. "Not what I expected but a very good reason."

I pick up Adrian's phone as I feel the alcohol start to pump through my blood.

"Let's call Nicholas." I smirk.

"Let's not." Adrian smiles into his drink.

I scroll though his numbers until I get to the name and dial the number. Adrian doesn't stop me so I'm thinking he secretly wants me to do this. It answers first ring.

"Hello, Adrian," Nicholas answers hopefully and I put my hand on my heart and close my eyes in a happy gesture.

"Nicholas, it's me Natasha," I reply. Adrian covers his face with his hands.

"Oh, hello, Natasha. Is everything alright?" he asks gently.

"Everything is great." I smile as the waitress brings us more drinks. Holy shit, I need to stop, I'm feeling very tipsy. "I'm having dinner with my dear friend Adrian." I reach over and grab his hand over the table, and he takes it in his and picks it up and kisses the back of it. I smile broadly. "We thought we would call and just say hello. So, hello." I giggle.

I can hear him smiling over the phone. "Hello," he replies.

"What are you doing?" I ask.

"I'm just coming back from my run," he replies. "It's early morning here."

"Are you in Australia?" I ask. "Not France?"

"No, Australia. I don't go to my French house that much anymore," he replies.

I hold my hand over the phone. "He's in Australia," I whisper to Adrian loudly and he nods and smiles. "Adrian and I are drinking margaritas." I laugh.

"I can tell." He replies cheekily.

"Would you like to speak to Adrian?" I ask.

"That would be nice," he replies and once again I put my hand over my heart as if to swoon.

"I will put him on." I hand the phone to Adrian and he blows out a breath nervously.

"Hello Nicholas." He listens for a moment and then smiles broadly. "Yes," he replies. "Have you?" Nicholas just told him that he has been thinking of him, I just know it, and I start feeling very proud of myself. I'm the matchmaker master. I should charge for my services. I don't want Adrian to feel self-conscious by me listening, so who can I call? Mum. I pull out my phone and scroll through to the Ms and I dial the number.

It nearly rings out and then a familiar voice that isn't Mum's answers.

"Hello, Natasha," the soft sad voice says.

I frown and then look at my screen. Margaret. Oh shit, I've called Margaret by mistake.

I screw up my face. "Hello, Margaret." She stays silent. "I thought I would just call you and check on you," I lie.

"Thank you, dear, I'm okay," she replies quietly.

I frown and by the tone of her voice I can tell that she's not, and I instantly feel uneasy.

"Where are you?" I ask.

She stays silent. "Does it matter?" she answers.

"Yes," I answer and for the first time since this whole thing has come to life, I find myself actually thinking of what this woman must be going through alone.

"I'm in a hotel in LA," she whispers.

I frown. "LA," I repeat. Why would she be in LA? And then her words come into my head: *This man is dangerous, and my life will be in danger if this comes out.*

More silence.

My alcoholic fog instantly dissipates. "Margaret, are you scared of James Brennan? Is that why you are in LA?" I ask.

More silence... and unfortunately, the silence is speaking to me more than words at the moment. Adrian frowns at me as he over-hears my conversation

"Give me your hotel address. I am coming to see you," I reply.

"No, please, Natasha, don't tell anyone I am here. I'm alright," she whispers.

"I am not with Joshua. He is out with the boys. I will come alone. Actually, I'm with Adrian. We are coming over, so give me the address."

She thinks for a moment. "I will text you the address. Please, don't say anything," she begs.

"You have my word," I reply.

CHAPTER 17

Joshua

I SIT in the restaurant surrounded by my family, the men in my family. We are eating before we make our way to the Lakers game. There's an elephant in the room and its name is paternity. Wilson and I have not spoken at all about the news that we are not Stantons. If we acknowledge it... then we have to believe it. What does that mean for the only family we know? Wilson and I are on either side of our father and Scott and Cameron are seated opposite us at the round table.

"Boys, I want to talk to you about this news that has just come to light," my father replies.

My eyes drop, I don't.

"I do too," Cameron adds.

Both my eyes and Wilson's meet across the table and he instantly tears up. My father grabs our hands. "This doesn't change anything between us. The four of you are all my sons and you will stay my sons. We have been dealt a situation that is...not ideal...but it will only hurt us if you let it." My eyes rise to meet Cameron's across the table.

"Fatherhood is not semen...or sex. I think it is raising a son who is a good person, a son I love."

I drop my head again as I listen.

"Can we just try to forget this news and carry on as if we don't know it?" he asks. "It doesn't change anything so why acknowledge it?"

Cameron and Scott nod their heads.

"I'm choosing to ignore this news. I have four sons and nothing at all has changed and I want to know if anything has changed for any of you?" he asks. "And if it has, how can I help you?"

Cameron shakes his head. "Definitely nothing's changed," he replies. "It could have been any of us. In fact, I wish it was me instead of you two because I think I could have handled it more easily."

My eyes meet Cameron's over the table, and I smile softly.

He would definitely have handled this better than me.

Scott shakes his head. "Of course, it doesn't change anything. You two are still fucking annoying." He smirks.

We all smile.

I nod. "I would like that," I reply softly.

"Me too," Wilson replies.

My father raises his glass in the air. "To the unbreakable Stantons," he toasts.

I feel my eyes well up as I raise my glass. "To the unbreakable Stantons," we all reply.

Natasha

We drive up the street, way off the main strip, and I frown at Adrian. "Are you sure it's down here?" Adrian asks the two guards in the front seat.

Max shrugs as he turns to look at us. "That's the address Tash gave me."

"Huh," I mutter as he pulls over to the side of the road.

"It's there." He points to a dodgy looking hotel on the right.

The four of us all frown as we peer out the window at the uninviting premises.

"This is where she's staying?" I frown.

"Looks like it." Max sighs as he gets out of the car. We tentatively follow and Adrian grabs my hand in a reassuring gesture. A car of two more guards pulls up behind us and I turn and give them a soft smile. Max's phone rings.

"Yes," he answers.

My eyes flick to the car behind us and I see the driver on the phone. He's ringing to check what the hell we are doing. What *are* we frigging doing?

"Yes, into the hotel on the right, level 4, room 62," he replies into the phone as his eyes flick to the car with the person in it who is on the phone.

As we approach the door Adrian takes out a tissue to open it, so he doesn't have to touch the handle and I shake my head at him.

"You're such a princess," I scoff, and the guards snicker.

"I can see the germs from here, it's like a lab experiment," he whispers.

We walk into the unattended foyer and the elevator isn't working so we walk over to the stairs at the side of the foyer.

"I don't like this," Max whispers to the other guard. "This could be a trap."

I screw up my face. "Oh, for Pete's sake, this is Margaret, you wimps! Stop watching too many horror films." I shake my head in disgust at my three yellow companions. "You boys are snobs," I whisper.

Adrian smiles broadly. "Oh, and you're so gangster."

I giggle. "Well, somebody around here has to be," I whisper. Max shakes his head at me and puts his hand on his gun under his jacket and I roll my eyes. Now I've seen it all. We continue up the darkened stairs until we get to the fourth floor and find the room we are after, and I frown at Adrian.

"This is weird," he whispers.

I nod. "I know, right." And I knock gently on the door.

"Come in," Margaret's sad voice calls. Adrian and I exchange looks and frown. Shit, she's really here. I was hoping I had the address wrong. Max steps in front of me and opens the door and nods at Margaret.

"I just need to check the room, Ma'am," he says sternly. She drops her head and nods.

Oh my God, my heart drops. I have never seen her like this. She is in a tracksuit with no makeup. Her hair is undone, and she is deathly pale. She sits alone and broken on the small single bed.

"Is there a bathroom?" Max asks.

"No," she answers quietly, and Adrian drops his head in pity. Fuck. This is the first time I have seen Margaret, the real Margaret, without the façade of money and her expensive outfits. I feel nothing but pity. What a sad lonely woman she is.

We wait in silence as Max checks under the bed and in the small wardrobe and then he nods, seemingly satisfied.

"Can you give us a minute, please, Adrian?" I ask.

"Sure." He nods. "I will be just outside." He walks over to Margaret and kisses her gently on the cheek, sensing her fragility.

I drop to the bed next her and pull her into an embrace. "Margaret," I whisper.

She shakes her head as she tries to hold back the tears and drops her head again.

"What are you doing in LA?" I ask into the top of her head.

She shrugs without answering.

"Why are you staying in this terrible place?" I ask as my eyes look around our surroundings, and then it dawns on me. "Do you have any money, Margaret?" I ask.

She shakes her head in shame. "James has taken all of Joshua's money and Robert put a stop on all of my accounts."

"Why are you in LA?" I whisper.

"It's safer here," she replies.

I frown. What in the hell is that supposed to mean? I keep watching her. She thinks she's in danger, but from who?

"Do you think that James Brennan is going to hurt you if you stay in Australia?" I ask.

She fakes a smile. "He's going to kill me wherever I am." Her eyes fill with tears. "It's only a matter of time," she whispers.

I frown as my blood runs cold. "No, he won't." I shake my head. "He's all talk."

She smiles at my innocence. "Dear Natasha, always finding the good in people." She grabs my hand and holds it in hers. "He's nearly killed me before and next time he will succeed, I have no doubt about that."

I frown. "When has he nearly killed you?" I'm lost, what the hell is she talking about? Is she having a psychotic episode?

"It doesn't matter anymore," she whispers as she stands and pulls back the dirty floral curtains to look down at the road.

Fear fills me. This is uncharted territory seeing her like this. "You need to tell me the truth about what is going on right now!" I demand.

Her tortured eyes meet mine as she contemplates my request. "Enough lies. You told me before that you fell in love with him and that the affair lasted only weeks," I reply.

"I was telling the truth," she whispers sadly.

I frown. "Then how is Wilson James's son also? It doesn't add up!"

She twists a piece of her jacket between her fingers as she thinks out loud. "Men don't always need consent to take what they want," she murmurs.

My stomach drops as my eyes meet her tear-filled ones. "Tell me," I whisper.

"I'm a bad person," she whispers.

I shake my head as I pull her into an embrace. "No, you're not, Margaret. Nobody is a bad person. You can make bad decisions but that doesn't mean you are bad."

She stays in my arms and I know she so desperately needs someone on her side. I can feel it.

"Tell me, please. I will not judge you. Psychologists are a different kind of person, Margaret. We are trained not to judge, we couldn't do this job if we held judgement. And trust me whatever you think is your worst secret, I have heard worse and then some." She bursts into full-blown sobs and I know I nearly have her.

"Please trust me," I whisper into the top of her head. She pulls back and coldly resolves to tell me.

"The affair happened as I told you. I fell madly in love with him and wanted to leave Robert." She stares off into space as if she is right there in the moment.

"Yes," I whisper.

"Robert came back from his trip and confessed to his affair and apologized to me for leaving me alone so much. They were words that I had wanted to hear for such a long time." I smile sympathetically. "He asked me if we could start again for the sake of Scott. He didn't want his son to grow up in a broken home and I knew that I owed it to Scott to try."

Her scared eyes meet mine and I give her a reassuring smile. "Yes, go on," I whisper.

"I told Robert that I had been unfaithful and that I had been desperately lonely and that I still loved him. We decided to put the past behind us and move forward together, we were so young."

I nod. "Did he know it was James?" I ask.

She shakes her head. "He never asked; he didn't want to know who," she replies.

I nod my head. This is common for men, if they know who they can't move past it.

"I went to James and told him my plans and he went crazy, totally lost control, and then he hit me." She stops as if remembering the pain and closes her eyes. "And then he broke down crying and sobbing. I felt so guilty." She sobs.

I go to the cabinet and find her some tissues and pass them to her and she wipes her nose as she thinks.

"And then I did the stupidest thing I have ever done in my life," she whispers.

I already know what she is going to say.

"He begged me for one last time. He wanted to make love to me one last time and I was in love with him also. He was so broken." She looks down at the ground as she thinks. "We made love that day and I had in effect betrayed Robert all over again and he knew it. I gave him the ammunition he needed."

I frown.

"Two months later Robert and I had gotten back on track and the feelings we had for each other had returned and I was just newly pregnant with Joshua. I thought I had put it all behind me. James had left me alone and had gone back to his wife."

I smile and nod.

"James called me this day out of the blue when Robert was away and asked me to meet him. His wife had found out and he needed to talk to me to get our stories straight. I agreed to meet him in a hotel room as we didn't have anywhere else, we could go that was private and I would never allow him to come to my house."

I nod. "Yes."

She stands and walks back over to the window and wraps her arms around her as if cold.

"What happened then?" I ask. This story is true. I can tell by how uncomfortable she is telling it.

"He told me that if I didn't have sex with him, he was going to tell Robert everything. That I was previously going to leave Robert, that I loved James, the whole sordid story. When I refused..." She stops.

"He took it anyway," I whisper and her eyes meet mine.

"I didn't want it." She shakes her head as her eyes tear up again. "He told me that if I fought him, he would take me so roughly that I would lose Robert's baby. He would make sure that Robert's baby didn't survive."

Oh God, this is fucked up. That was Joshua in her stomach.

She drops her head in shame.

"How long did this go on for Margaret?" I whisper through my dread.

"Up until the day I paid him Joshua's money. I hated him, I

thought of killing him so many times. I should have." Anger lights her eyes as she lifts her chin defiantly. "I wouldn't hear from him for months and I would be so grateful but then as soon as Robert went away, he would demand his sexual favors and if I didn't agree he would beat me. I was hospitalized three times when the children were young. The doctors thought it was my husband. They had no idea he wasn't even in the country at the time."

Oh my God, I drop my head in pity. "How did you?"

"The children always had a nanny. I had to have one so I knew they would be safe when Robert was away. At least I could guarantee their safety."

"Margaret," I whisper.

"He always wore a condom. I had no idea that Wilson was his until Joshua threw it in my face."

My eyes widen in horror.

She fakes a smile at me. "So, you see, Natasha, Joshua was right. His mother is a dirty whore and now I have lost the husband that I do love and my four sons. My life is not worth living."

I stand still as shock courses through me. Margaret's the victim in all of this. It's always the ones who are so vulnerable that pretend to be so together. *The best form of defense is attack.* What do I do? *Fuck... what do I do?*

I watch her for a moment. I can't leave her here like this. "Right." I stand and go to the door and open it in a rush.

"Adrian, can you come in here, please?" I ask.

He stands up from his seat in the hall and walks into the room.

"Can you help me pack Margaret's things, please?" I ask him as I close the door behind him.

His eyes hold mine for a moment and he nods. "Yes, of

course." He bends and starts to pick up her things and she shakes her head.

"Natasha, no. I'm staying here," she answers defiantly.

"You are coming with me." I point at her. "If you think for one minute, I am going to let you be a victim to fucking James Brennan one more time you can think again."

Adrian stops what he is doing and stares at me as he pieces the puzzle together. His eyes widen.

I bend and start to throw her things together and I point a hairbrush at her. "You are coming with me as a guest in my house and tomorrow we go to the police and that asshole is getting charged."

She shakes her head. "He will kill me, Natasha."

I shrug my shoulders. "You know what, I would rather take my chances on that than you take your own life through shame. If I leave you here tonight that's exactly what you will do!" I shake my head angrily. "And I'm not having that on my conscience!" I yell.

"I'm okay," she snaps.

"You are as far from okay as one could possibly get!" I scream as my anger erupts. This man has ruined her life. How dare he?

"If Adrian has to drag you kicking and screaming out of here, he will," I yell.

Her eyes flick to Adrian and he smirks, and she smiles softly. "Pack," I yell.

Joshua

I stand in the kitchen as I make the coffee for everyone. Dad is in the kitchen and Cameron, Wilson and Scott are sitting on the lounge as we discuss the game.

I take out my phone and dial Natasha again. "Hey." She answers on the first ring.

"Where are you?" I frown. This is the third time I have called her. She should be here by now.

"I'm out the front, coming in now," she replies.

"Okay." I hang up.

I pass the coffees around and we sit and I yawn. I'm really tired.

Natasha walks in and smiles nervously.

"Here's my girl." I smile as I hold my hand out for her and she takes it and bends to kiss me softly on the cheek. My father smiles at our interaction. He adores Natasha.

Adrian walks through the door. "Hi." He smiles.

"Where have you been, soft cock?" Cameron calls. "It was a good game you missed."

Natasha walks back out of the room and returns, pulling someone by the hand into the room, and I frown. She pulls my mother into view and we all fall silent. What's she doing here? I didn't even know she was in the country. My anger immediately starts to pump.

"Get out!" I snap as I jump to my feet.

"Joshua!" Natasha snaps as she puts her arm around my mother protectively.

"How dare you turn up at my house?" I reply.

She drops her head as her eyes fill with tears and my heart hurts. She looks bad. I've never seen her like this. My eyes flick to my father and his eyes are glued to her as well.

"Margaret is staying with us for a while," Natasha announces.

"Like hell," I reply.

Natasha's eyes flick to Cameron. "Cameron, she's not fit to be staying alone at the moment." Cameron frowns and immediately stands, goes to her and puts his arm around our mother, understanding whatever that code stands for.

"It's okay, Mum. You can stay," he says softly. His eyes flick to me and he subtly shakes his head.

"Margaret, let's get you to bed, honey," Natasha says softly as she smiles at her. I frown. What the hell is going on here?

My mother's haunted eyes meet mine and then flick back to Natasha for approval. Natasha smiles warmly. "You're safe, Margaret. It's okay. This is a safe place," she says softly.

I frown at Dad and my brothers. "No," I snap.

"Joshua!" Natasha asserts. "Enough! This is my house too and Margaret is staying here as my guest. I just found her in a two-star hotel across town on her own, frightened half to death." Her voice raises with her anger. "You two are two of the wealthiest men on the planet and yet she has no fucking money! Tell me why!" She looks at Dad and me.

Robert drops his head in shame and guilt fills me.

"Now, I am taking Margaret to her room and tomorrow we are going to the police and having that fucking asshole charged and we are uniting as a family."

Wilson shakes his head. "I want nothing to do with her."

"Well, tough luck!" Natasha yells, losing her temper. "She is my mother-in-law and my children's grandmother and I will not have her disrespected one fucking minute longer."

The room shrinks at Natasha's venom. She's furious and my eyes flick to Adrian in question.

"You know, I have had an epiphany. I would give anything on earth to have my father back. It doesn't matter, all this bullshit you are all going on about. We can get through this... together...the Stantons are not being brought to our knees by James Brennan. Margaret has suffered enough at the hands of that monster and I for one am standing by her in her time of need."

My heart skips a beat, and my eyes fill with tears. I don't think I have ever loved Natasha more than I do at this very moment.

Natasha angrily wipes the tears from her eyes. "That's what families do...we stand together...and defend each other. Don't let this monster do this to us!"

I look at the floor and Natasha quietly grabs my mother in an embrace and leads her out of the room. We all sit, still and in shock. Why is Natasha on her side now?

"I don't get it," I snap. "Natasha wouldn't let me go to the police before. What's changed?"

Adrian stands. "I think the charges against him have changed," he murmurs.

"To what?" Robert snaps.

Adrian's eyes meet his. "To rape."

Dear God.

CHAPTER 18

Joshua

NATASHA IS WRAPPED AROUND ME, dozing in her orgasmic state of consciousness. I kiss her gently on the forehead. "I have to get up," I murmur.

"Hmm," she replies sleepily.

I peel her off me and she grips her legs around mine tighter.

"You can't get out of bed yet," she murmurs into my chest.

"I've got to go to work, Marx." I smile.

"Mmm, we need to talk," she mutters sleepily. I smile.

God she's beautiful when she's half asleep. "About what?" I reply.

"What do you want for a wedding present, Joshua?" she says into my chest as she kisses it.

I think for a moment. "A baby," I reply.

Her eyebrows instantly rise, and she pulls back to look at my face.

"What?"

"You asked me what I want, and I told you," I reply.

She frowns as she looks at my face. "You're serious?" she whispers.

"Deadly," I mutter deadpan. That wasn't the response I had hoped for. I get up and walk into the bathroom and she calls to me.

"I'm too young."

I shake my head as I get into the shower. "Whatever," I reply.

Aren't women supposed to be the maternal ones? I will be getting kids when I'm fifty.

Fifteen minutes later, I stare at my reflection in the mirror of our bathroom as I fasten my tie, having just showered for the second time this morning. I smirk. It was worth it as always. My girl does come up with the goods every time. I am in a suit and will be leaving for work soon. I hear Cameron's voice in my bedroom. Frowning I go out to see what's going on.

Natasha is naked and the blankets are pulled up around her chest as she speaks to Cameron who stands at the end of the bed.

"So, will you be able to prescribe those for her?" Natasha asks. "I can't, I'm not registered to work here," she adds.

Cameron nods as he thinks. "Yeah, I'm going in now. Just keep her here until I get back in about an hour."

My eyes flick between the two. "What medication are you putting her on?" I ask flatly. Natasha explained the whole sordid story last night and to be honest I am having trouble believing any of it ever occurred.

"I'm concerned about her, Joshua. She needs to be on a mild anti-depressant," Natasha replies.

She rustles around in the bed and my eyes flick to her. Naked, soft and open under those blankets, her dark long hair falls softly around her shoulders and her beautiful brown eyes and dimples are on show. I feel my cock twitch in arousal. Here we go again. Will this need I have to be inside her ever subside just a little so I can think?

"I don't even think it's true," I murmur as I bend and pickup Natasha's pajamas from the floor.

"Why?" Natasha snaps.

I shrug. "James is a wealthy man. I can't see him using domestic violence as power over a woman," I reply.

Natasha and Cameron's faces both fall. "You can't be serious," Natasha snaps.

I stand still. "Deadly," I reply as I put my hand on my hip.

"That is without a doubt the stupidest thing that has ever come out of your mouth. Are you telling me that men with money don't hit their wives or use stand-over tactics?" Natasha snaps, outraged.

I shrug. "Well, you don't hear about it," I reply.

Natasha sits up, the blankets nearly fall, and she catches them just in time. I raise my eyebrows at her in annoyance.

"Oh, and I suppose you think that people who have a mental health issue can only be depressed if they have a terrible life," she snaps again.

I shrug.

Cameron shakes his head at me in disgust.

"People who live with domestic violence and mental health conditions who have money are just better at hiding it from the world. It happens in all walks of life, Joshua. You don't have to have a depressing life to be depressed and it makes me sick that you would stand here and defend him when you know he was definitely taking her money...your money." She sits up again angrily and grabs the blankets again as they nearly slip and the protective instincts kick in.

My eyes flick to Cameron. "Do you mind?" I snap. He frowns in question.

"I don't like you in my bedroom talking to my girl while she's naked."

He rolls his eyes. "Well, let me fucking finish what I was saying," he snaps.

"I'm right here, Joshua," Natasha snaps.

"Yeah, and the only man you talk to naked is me. Get out Cameron, Natasha will be with you when she's dressed."

"God," Natasha gasps, exasperated.

Cameron shakes his head and walks out. "Call me when you're dressed," he mutters.

Natasha jumps out of bed angrily and snatches her pajamas from my hands. "Are you serious? I can't talk to Cameron with you in the room?" she snaps. "I had a fucking blanket on," she adds.

"Same shit," I snap.

She quickly dresses and walks into the bathroom to pull her long hair back. I stand still and watch her until she returns. "Are you going to speak to your mother before you leave?" she asks.

I roll my lips as I think. "I don't know what to say to her."

"Joshua," she whispers sympathetically as she puts her arms around my neck gently and kisses me. "Just listen to her, baby. She needs you to listen."

My eyes drop to the floor. "I don't know if I can hear it," I murmur. My hand goes under her pajamas pants and I cup her behind.

She smirks. "Really? You're jealous of Cameron now?" she asks with raised eyebrows.

I smirk. "No, but he won't be looking at you naked, soft and flushed from the sex we have just had. I know what's under those blankets." I kiss her gently on the lips.

She smiles softly. "I love you."

"You smell like sex," I whisper.

"I smell like my future husband," she whispers darkly.

I feel my heart skip a beat. "I love you, too. Please wear clothes around my brothers. I can't stand them looking at you," I murmur.

She kisses me again and smiles broadly. "Maybe I should get you some anxiety medication today while I'm at it?"

"Mmm, maybe you should," I reply in a monotone.

I make my way down to the kitchen as Natasha and Cameron discuss my mother's diagnosis. I see my father and mother sitting at the table and chairs out by the pool, deep in discussion. My eyes flick to Wilson who is sitting at the kitchen bench.

"What's going on out there?" I point to them with my chin.

He shrugs. "I don't know man, but Mum's crying and Dad's furious."

I watch them out of the window for a minute and she is shaking her head as he speaks. I wonder what he is asking her.

"Where did Dad sleep last night?" I ask as I make a protein shake.

"In his room I think, but I know he was in Mum's room for a couple of hours last night. He's worried about her," he replies as he looks out the window.

My anger simmers dangerously close to the surface. "Do you believe this story?" I ask Wilson.

He nods. "Unfortunately, I do. Cameron and Adrian hacked the hospital records in Melbourne last night and she was telling the truth."

I clench my jaw in anger. "Does Dad know this?" I ask. He nods and sips his coffee.

"One time when he was in England the bastard broke four of her ribs," he murmurs as he watches them.

My eyes close. How could this happen under all of our noses? "Dad said he remembers it. When he got back, she still had a foot-shaped bruise on her from being kicked, but she told him that she had been mugged."

The lead of hate starts to drip through my bloodstream.

He's going to fucking pay for this.

I rub my hand over my face. "I called her a whore," I whisper.

"You only said what we all were thinking," he replies.

I blow out a breath and walk into the pool area and they both turn to look at me. I bite my lip as I try to articulate what I want to say. "I'm sorry for the way I spoke to you, Mum," I whisper nervously as I approach them. She gives me a sad smile and I shake my head. "I just...I was hurt and lashed out. I didn't mean any of it," I say quietly. They both nod. "Please stay as long as you like. You are always welcome here."

"Thank you," she whispers, and Dad nods his head, unable to speak. This is too much, guilt fills me, and I shake my head, I can't deal with this. I need to get out of here.

"I've got to go to work. Call me if I'm needed." I walk inside and grab my keys and head for the door where Ben is waiting for me. He gives me a stifled smile.

"Where were you last night?" I ask.

He doesn't look at me. "I had a date," he replies as he walks in front of me.

My eyes follow him out the door. Fuck! I knew it.

"With whom?" I ask as I walk around to the car. He's never missed a Lakers game since he started with me.

He shakes his head and opens the car. "Does it matter?" he replies.

A car pulls up and Abbie leans over and kisses the driver. Ben and I exchange looks and I roll my eyes. Ben narrows his eyes at the driver as it pulls away and shakes his head angrily.

"Hi." Abbie beams as she walks toward us. "Was that the fucking cop?" Ben snaps.

She stiffens under his glare.

"Yeah, so?"

"Are you stupid?" he sneers.

"I won't say anything!" she replies. "I don't know anyone here. I'm going crazy, Ben."

He nods as his anger erupts. "Listen here, you are in LA only because you put you and Bridget into a stupid position and now, you're fucking the cop who is investigating it." He shakes his head in anger. "Now I've seen it all."

I roll my eyes. I don't need this shit this morning. "Joshua!" Abbie exclaims. "I can see who I want. Tell him I can do what I want."

I shake my head and hold up my hands. "Ben's in charge of this one. I've got enough on my plate."

She crosses her arms angrily in front of her and huffily walks inside. We get into the car and drive off in silence.

My eyes flick to Ben as he drives. He looks at me and then back at the road. I keep watching him and his eyes turn to me again.

"What?" he asks.

"I'm going to ask you once and once only, Ben."

He bites his bottom lip as he waits for the question with his eyes on the road.

"Are you making love to Bridget or are you fucking her?"

He lifts his chin defiantly as his eyes stay on the road. He stays silent.

"Does it matter?" he replies flatly.

"Yeah, it does actually," I reply.

He rolls his eyes and shakes his head to himself.

We continue up the road in silence and his eyes flick to the rearview mirror as he checks the security behind us.

"You know I know a thing or two about this," I murmur.

He looks at me deadpan.

"About what?" he replies flatly.

"Being in love with a Marx girl." I smirk.

He shakes his head and keeps his eyes on the road, and we continue to drive in silence.

My phone rings. It's Adrian. "Hello."

"Are you coming in today?" he asks.

"Yeah, on my way," I reply.

"See you soon," he replies before hanging up.

"They're not wired to fuck around, Ben," I mutter.

He swallows as he thinks and then his eyes flick to me again. "Well, why are they wired to fuck so damn well?" he snaps.

I smile and shake my head as I stare out the window.

"I don't know, but I know it will do you over if you let it."

His eyes stay on the road. "I'm not letting it," he replies.

"So, is that why she's at home in your bed with her guard outside your house instead of mine?" I reply.

"She's going crazy in that fishbowl," he snaps.

"You think I'm not?" I reply. "All I want is my house to myself with Natasha and I currently have seven extra people staying with me and a very bad case of Jerry Springer playing out before my eyes."

"Bridget and Abbie are looking at some apartments this afternoon," Ben replies.

"Good," I reply.

"Are you going with them?" I ask.

He shakes his head. "No, I'm staying with you. Their guards can take them. I think Tash wants to go along."

I frown. "I don't like Natasha being out and about on her own without me or you with her. It makes me jumpy."

He nods. "Me too," he replies.

"Has there been any news on Coby Allender?" I ask. "That sick bastard makes my blood run cold."

"I'm due to call them on any updates of the case today," he mutters as we turn into the carpark of my office.

"Call them first thing. I want to know what's happening." I sigh. God, I'm just so sick of this bullshit.

He nods and we make our way to the office.

The day has been uneventful. Adrian is killing me with emails and details. He saunters into my office. "Have you put any thought into that conference in London?"

I shake my head as I open his fortieth email this morning. "No." I don't look up from my screen.

"You okay?" he asks, and I lift my eyes to meet his.

I shrug and shake my head. "I don't think I have ever been

so shocked in my life as I am at this newest revelation. I can't get my head around it," I reply in a monotone.

"Me too." He sighs. "You should have seen Natasha with your mum last night."

I frown. "What happened?" I ask.

"We were out for dinner and Tash called Nicholas and I was talking to him." I smirk and he rolls his eyes at me. "Tash called your mother to check on her and she didn't sound too well so Natasha hauled us all to the other side of town to find her. You should have seen the hotel she was staying at. It was atrocious."

"God," I sigh as guilt fills me. "Transfer her some money today. It makes me sick what that bastard has done."

"Natasha took one look at your mother and her psychologist instincts kicked in." He shrugs. "She's very good at her job, Joshua. You should see her in action." He smiles softly.

"I would hate to think what could have happened," I whisper as I hit the delete button repeatedly. "If you guys didn't go to her when you did. Thanks for going with Tash."

"Can you find me a male version of Natasha, please?" he mutters as he sits on my desk.

I smile. "If there were any other versions of Natasha around, male or female, I would want them too," I reply.

"Greedy bastard." Adrian smirks. "Don't forget we have Laura's wedding down the coast this weekend."

I frown. "Shit." I blow out a breath. "Really? That's this weekend?" I shake my head. "I don't have the energy to go to a wedding. I hate fucking weddings."

"Yeah, well you are. I've done the gifts and you and Tash are staying the night on Sean's yacht in the bay," he replies.

I smirk. "Murph, what would I do without you?" I ask. He looks at me deadpan. "I hate to think."

I swing on my chair as I look out the window, deep in thought, and Adrian puts some files away in my filing cabinet.

"Oh, and you bought that house next to Willowvale. You will need to go down and sign the contracts on Thursday or Friday," he replies.

My eyes meet his. "What's her go? Why would she want to live next door to me?"

Adrian shakes his head as he continues filing. "I don't know, something to do with that big cock of yours probably," he mutters dryly as he slams a drawer shut.

I throw my pencil at him as I lean back and put my feet on my desk. "You're an imbecile." I sigh.

Ben walks in. "We've got a problem," he snaps.

I put my head back onto my chair. "Enlighten me, Ben, on which problem this is about. The shit around here just gets better and better by the day." I sigh as I blow out a deep breath.

"I just rang the prison and Coby Allender had a visitor on the weekend."

Adrian frowns and stops what he is doing. "And?" I reply.

He throws some photos onto the desk. "It's the dude that broke into Natasha's apartment."

My face drops and I sit up immediately.

"I sent the security vision through to them this morning and it's him. It's fucking him."

My eyes widen as I look at the black and white images taken via the jail security system spread over the table.

"Holy shit," Adrian whispers.

"The police are ecstatic. They haven't had a definite link to him before, but this proves without doubt that they are working together. They have issued a warrant for his arrest and are going around there as we speak to get the bastard."

I shake my head. "God." I frown at the photos as I put my hand over my mouth. "How many women did these sick fucks murder?" I ask.

"Twelve, and like weird-shit killing too. Tortured, raped and cut up," Ben replies as goosebumps cover my flesh.

"And they wanted Natasha," I whisper.

"Thankfully she has been guarded all the time. They may have gotten her if you two hadn't gotten back together," Adrian gasps.

"See, this is why I hate her doing psychology in a jail. You're messing with fucked up psychopaths' minds. She's not doing that shit again. Over my dead body is she doing that shit again. What does she expect going to the fucking prison?" I stand in an outrage and rub my hands through my hair.

My intercom buzzes. "Mr. Stanton, Robert Stanton is here to see you."

Adrian pats me on the shoulder in a symbol of sympathy. "I've got stuff to do. We will go out for lunch to discuss this."

"Yeah, okay." I sigh as I watch Adrian leave the room.

Dad walks in and smiles at Ben and me. "Hello," he greets us softly. I've never seen my father so broken. This was one of his closest friends that did this to his wife.

"I will be outside." Ben gestures to the door. "No, I want to see you too, Ben," Dad replies.

Ben's and my eyes meet. I knew this was coming. Ben nods and sits at the table.

I sit back down at my desk and my father sits opposite me.

"I want to have James Brennan taken care of," he announces.

"Yes, I agree," I reply. "He's not getting away with this."

Dad looks at Ben. "Do you... have the contacts?" he asks nervously.

"Yes," Ben replies flatly.

"Can you call? How does this work?" Dad asks him.

"No," I snap. "Ben is not getting involved in this one."

Ben's eyes meet mine. "Joshua, it's what you pay me for," he snaps.

"Your role in this family has changed and you know that," I reply.

Ben shakes his head angrily in disgust. "It's what I'm trained to do," he snaps.

"And you should have thought about that before you fell in love with my sister-in-law."

"I didn't say I was in love with her," he replies.

"You didn't have to!" I reply. "If you are becoming a part of this family that's it, no more fucking hits, no more dealing with the underworld. You leave your military training in the past. You are already being investigated for the prostitute's murder. I will not have Bridget alone with two kids while her husband is rotting in jail."

Ben drops his head angrily.

"Well, I hope nobody is going to jail." Dad frowns. "You pay good money to not get caught I would expect."

I nod. "Do you have the money?" I ask.

He nods. "Yes."

My eyes hold his. "Do you have untraceable money?"

He thinks for a moment and then shakes his head. "No," he answers.

My eyes meet Ben's. "How much is in the safe at home,

Ben?"

Ben narrows his eyes as he thinks. "I don't know, about two million I think."

My eyes flick back to my father. "It's yours. You will need to pay before you leave the country, organize it while you are here. We can't get that much money into Australia without being noticed," I reply. "Ben, give my father the contact numbers. That is as far as you can get involved in this one," I reply. Ben nods angrily like a naughty child.

"You will need to stay in the US until it is done," I mutter.

My father nods. "Yes," he replies. "I will get a hotel for your mother and me. We won't burden you any longer."

My eyes hold his. "Are you two going to be okay?"

He shakes his head. "I don't know. How do you get past something like this?"

My stomach drops. What a nightmare.

My father stands. "Thank you, Joshua." He nods at Ben and leaves the room.

Ben stands still and defiant with his eyes fixed on me. "What?" I snap.

"I'm not changing my whole life to be with Bridget."

My eyes hold his. "Yes, you are, go with my father and give him the money and stay with Natasha until I know they have this sick fuck in custody."

He nods and walks toward the door. "Ben," I call. And he turns to look at me. "I don't want you involved in this because I want you and Bridget together. You have my full support, but you need to leave that life behind. Bridget needs you to leave that life behind," I say.

His eyes hold mine for a moment and he nods, turns and walks out of the room.

I scrub my hand over my face in frustration. What next?

Natasha

It's late afternoon on Thursday and Joshua and I are on our way to Willowvale with three security cars trailing behind us. They have linked Coby Allender with the breaking and entering at my house in Australia and apparently when they went to arrest the guy they couldn't find him but what they did find was much worse. Photographs of me were strewn all over his apartment, along with photos of the other victims that have since been murdered. I can't believe this shit. I've hardly slept since I found out. I keep having those stupid nightmares and Joshua is beside himself with worry.

The guy hasn't left Australia through a commercial flight and he doesn't have money for a private one so we shouldn't be worried, but until they have him in custody, we are all a little jumpy. I haven't told Joshua yet, but my head is starting to thump, and I am trying desperately to hold off a migraine. I was hoping I had turned the corner with that shit... obviously not.

"We just have to pull into the estate agent's for a moment," Joshua remarks casually as he looks for a parking space.

"Did you buy that house?" I ask.

His eyes flick to me as he tries to remember if he has mentioned it before. "Yes, I thought it would be good for your mother or Bridget," he replies.

I fake a smile and hold his eyes with mine as I raise a brow in question.

He stares at me for a moment. "I am buying the damn house to stop Amelie buying it," he snaps in frustration.

"Oh," I mutter, acting surprised.

He shakes his head. "Let's just do it and we will talk about it later." He sighs, defeated.

I nod and act uncaring. The truth is I'm glad he's buying the house. I'm not living next door to the silly bitch. No way in hell. He picks up my hand and kisses the back of it. "I won't be long. Don't get out of the car," he murmurs.

I roll my eyes and nod.

"Do you want a coffee?" he asks.

"Yes, please," I reply as he gets out of the car.

Joshua walks to the group of guards who are now congregated on the sidewalk and hands over some money. One of them nods and disappears into the café.

I blow out a breath and throw my head back onto the seat. Just how long are we going to have to live like this? I can't stand all of this security. I know exactly why Joshua hates it so much. He's had to deal with this a lot longer than me. I shouldn't whine, at least I have security. My blood runs cold as my mind goes to the young women who have been murdered and I get a visual in my head of them being tied up, tortured and raped... alone. *That could have been me.* What they would have given to have security with them, protecting them. God, I hope they catch the bastards.

I wrap my cardigan around me protectively and hold my temples. This fucking headache had better go away. We have a wedding to go to on Saturday. Sean's sister is getting married and the girls are being Adrian's and Cam's dates. I'm looking forward to it. Joshua and I are staying on Sean's luxury boat because Maria doesn't want the girls to have to catch the small boat out to the big boat late at night after the wedding. It's just so Hollywood staying on a boat. Joshua and I are going to be alone at last and then I can give him my wedding present. I smile to myself. I can't wait to see his face when I give it to him.

The door opens and Joshua falls into the seat beside me. "What are you smiling at?" he asks as he hands over my coffee.

"I'm excited about staying on the boat." I smirk as I take a sip of my coffee.

He puts his hand on my leg. "Me too and we own another house now," he says casually as he starts the car.

I shake my head at this situation I find myself in. This is stupid rich at its best. *Oh, and we own another house now.*

We drive to Willowvale in silence and, admittedly, as soon as we hit that heavenly driveway lined with the beautiful trees, I can feel my worries slowly leaving me behind. This place is a sanctuary and although I was first scared that I would only ever relate it to bitch-vet...along with my reservations, her memories are starting to fade. She's not a threat to me anymore...was she ever? I'm such an idiot to think that she was. I close my eyes as the afternoon sun warms me through the windshield. I need these couple of days alone with my man.

"You ok, Presh?" Joshua asks me as he grabs my hand and kisses my fingertips.

I smile. "Yes, just got a bit of a headache, my Lamborghini. I feel better now that we are here," I reply softly.

He smiles warmly. "I love you," he whispers.

"I know you do." I smirk as he pulls the car into the parking space. Joshua gets out and comes around to my side of the car and opens the door for me as I gather my handbag and things.

"Come on, up to bed for the afternoon." He gestures to the house with his chin as the two cars of guards approach from up the driveway.

"Are you coming with me?" I ask a little too sweetly as I climb out of the car. I smile and bat my eyelashes to try and be cute.

"Yes, but we are sleeping. You have a headache and I have exhaustion," he says dryly.

I screw up my face at him in disgust. "Boring," I mouth.

He leads me through the house by the hand straight up to our bedroom and puts our bags on the end of the ottoman. He disappears, turns the shower on and undresses me. I smirk as he concentrates while undoing my buttons.

"What?" he asks, deep in thought. "Just you," I reply.

"What about me?" he asks.

"It's just a headache you know," I reply.

He nods and rolls his eyes as he pulls my shirt from my shoulders. "Yeah, well I've seen your 'just' headaches and they scare the shit out of me." He sighs.

"I'm okay, baby. I've got my tablets that will put me to sleep for a while and when I wake up, we can have dinner. What are you making us?"

He shrugs. "Toast."

"You're wrecking it," I murmur.

"Shut up and look pretty, Marx. Get into the shower before I put that mouth of yours to good use."

I kiss him gently on the lips and sink into my hot water therapy shower as he fusses around in the bedroom unpacking my bag and when I emerge fifteen minutes later and semi-conscious, I find my flannel pajamas laid out on the bed. He passes me a glass of water.

"Where are your tablets?" he asks.

"In my makeup bag." I sigh as I climb into bed.

He starts to rat through my bag and frowns as he pulls out a long skinny silver box with ribbon. "What's this?" he asks as his eyes meet mine and he sits down on the bed next to me.

Oh shit, I wanted to give him that on Saturday night before the wedding. Frigging hell. I'm hopeless at keeping secrets.

I lie back in bed against the high-top pillows.

"It's an early wedding present for you."

His eyes light up and he pops two tablets from their foil and hands them to me. I kiss him gently and take them.

He holds it in his hand and looks at it, deep in thought. "Open it," I say.

He frowns.

"Open it. I want you to open it." I smile.

He kisses me gently and slowly opens the wrapping. I hold my breath as I wait for his reaction.

Joshua frowns at the contents of the present and his eyes flick to me. "These are your contraceptive pills." He frowns.

"I know. I won't be needing them anymore," I reply nervously.

His eyes widen. "You won't?" he whispers.

I shake my head as I smile.

He sits still on the bed as he stares at the pill packet in his hand. I think he's in shock. "Are you sure?" he whispers.

I giggle. "I had better be. I haven't taken them for a week."

His eyes widen further when he reads the days of the week and does the math. He smiles broadly. "Really?" he gushes.

"Really," I repeat.

"Holy fuck!" he exclaims and then he seems to realize what is going on and he gently puts his hand on my stomach. "So, you could be..." His eyes drop to his open hand on me. "Right now?" he whispers.

"Josh, it takes a while. It won't happen straight away," I reply.

He shakes his head. "No, my boys are good swimmers. They are on the job."

I smirk. "Confident bastard."

His lips drop to my neck and he kisses it slowly. "I fucking adore you," he whispers.

I smile as I move my head to give him greater access.

"There's more." I smile.

"More what?" he whispers into my neck.

"More present," I reply.

He pulls back and picks the wrapping back up and rattles through it and frowns again.

I smile broadly. God I'm good. I am feeling oh so proud of myself at this very moment. *Fucking boom!*

"Your keys?" he replies, puzzled. I nod and smile. "I don't get it," he replies.

"They are my keys to the LA house."

"And?" he asks.

"I won't be needing those anymore either," I reply nonchalantly.

"Why not?" he asks.

"Because I'm going to be living here at Willowvale with my husband," I reply.

His eyes widen again.

"What?!" he shrieks.

"But there are conditions," I snap.

"Of course." He smiles.

"I want to go to LA two weekends a month." He smiles broadly. "And you are going to take care of the baby two days a week so I can go back to work."

He bursts out laughing and grabs me in an embrace. "Oh my God, Natasha, I fucking love you." He jumps up and then sits back down as he looks at the pills and the keys in his hand, then he stands again.

I smile broadly. "Do you like your wedding presents, Mr. Stanton?" I ask.

"Don't ask stupid questions, precious girl. What do you think?" He laughs out loud and bounces onto the bed, spilling the water from my glass.

CHAPTER 19

Natasha

Joshua's lips dust my neck as we scramble for air. His body still inside mine, he is on top of me and my hands are in his above my head. I smile into his kiss as once again his lips possess mine.

"I fucking love you," he whispers into my lips.

I smile mischievously. "If I knew I was going to get fucked this well and this often as you try to impregnate me, I may have stopped taking my pills sooner."

He pulls out and kisses me on the lips. "Oh, because you're so hard done by and you never get sex, right," he replies sarcastically as he sits up in bed.

"Now I get even more," I purr as I widen my eyes. "Mission accomplished."

He shakes his head. "You're a sex maniac, Marx," he mutters.

I smile. "I'm making up for lost time."

His face falls.

I frown. "Come here, that came out wrong." I pull him back to lie down with me.

"If I was a better person, I would tell you I'm sorry that you missed out for so long. But I'm not. I'm glad you did," he murmurs into my shoulder.

I smile. "You know, Joshua, that's one thing that I am proud of. You have no idea how proud I am of the fact I waited for you."

I can feel his smile. "Me too."

He rolls onto his back and looks around the space we are in. "Some boat, hey?"

I nod as my eyes shoot around the room in amazement. "Isn't it heavenly?" I say as I nod—this is ridiculous wealth. We are on Sean's boat for his sister's wedding tonight. The guards are moored on their own little luxury boat closer to shore. The gang and their guards are staying in a hotel closer to the reception.

"Do we have to go to the wedding? I just want to stay here." Joshua sighs.

"Yeah, me too," I reply. "This is our third wedding together."

Joshua smiles as he holds his arm out for me and I lie back down next to him. "Next one is ours."

I kiss his chest as excitement fills me. "I wish it was ours that was the third wedding."

He frowns. "What does that mean?"

I widen my eyes at his stupidity. "You know—three weddings and a funeral?"

He frowns.

"It means the next thing we are going to is a funeral." I smile. "God, don't you watch the movies, Joshua? You are so uncultured." I sigh sarcastically.

"You do know you're an idiot, right?" He smirks as he wraps me tightly in his arms.

"It comes naturally," I whisper. "I don't even have to try."

"I noticed," he murmurs.

We lie relaxed and peaceful for another twenty minutes until our precious time is up and we need to get ready. "Josh, we need to get up, baby."

"Hmm." He sighs sleepily. "Don't make me go. I want to stay here with you."

I smile softly. "We have the rest of our lives together. We can go to the wedding today." I gently kiss his lips

"Hmm," he murmurs.

"And besides you can get some ideas as what to write in your wedding speech." I smile.

"Shut up or you're going to cop it again," he purrs as he rolls on top of me and puts my hands over my head.

"Cause your wedding speech will be totally shit, I just know it." I squeal with laughter. Joshua narrows his eyes and then rips into my neck with his open mouth.

"That's it," he growls. "All aboard for Pound Town."

Three hours later, we are at the wedding and I think I have been introduced to everyone on the planet who has a huge bank balance. I will never in a million years remember any of their names. A lot of people are from horse-related activities and Laura and her now husband are merchant bankers, so the banking world are here too. Ben, Max and our security are lingering outside. They ate the same meals as us but in another room—they seem to be having their own party.

We are seated at the table with Cam, Murph, the girls and six other people that the boys all know well. Joshua's arm is slung over the back of my chair, and he runs his fingers back-wards and forwards over my shoulders as he listens. The speeches start and Laura's father is first to speak.

"I would like to thank you all for coming here tonight."

Joshua's phone beeps a message and he retrieves it from his pocket. He opens the message, his body straightens and he pulls his arm off the back of my chair.

My eyes flick to him and he glares at me. Huh? I frown in question. He blows out a deep breath and shakes his head angrily as he keeps reading the message. He starts to scroll through the message.

Jeez, it must be big.

I frown again. What now?

His tongue runs over his top teeth and I know he's angry. I lean into him. "What's wrong?" I whisper.

He passes me his phone as the crowd all bursts into applause. We both clap for the sake of good manners. I take his phone and look at the screen. Oh dear God, the blood drains from my face. The headline reads:

Natasha Marx caught having an affair with her bodyguard.

My horrified eyes meet his and he glares at me. Photo after photo of me and Max, arm in arm. One where we are holding hands— *When the fuck was this?* —and one where it looks as though we are kissing. What the hell?

"I don't understand," I whisper nervously. "These photos are not true, Joshua."

His cold eyes hold mine and he angrily pushes his chair back in a rush and stands and storms from the ballroom. Oh crap, my nervous eyes flick to Abbie and Bridget who are frowning at me. I stand and quietly follow him. Where is he going? I run into the foyer to find an absolutely furious Joshua.

I shake my head nervously. "Joshua, it's not how it looks," I whisper as my eyes fly around to the people surrounding us.

"I fucking warned him," he yells.

Everybody around us starts to stare and Ben immediately walks over to us. "What's the problem?" he whispers.

"Him," Joshua yells, too angry to articulate himself. "I have warned him time and again to keep his mother-fucking hands off of her," he yells.

I stand frozen on the spot. Shit, this is bad. This looks really bad… and it had to be Max, didn't it?

Ben's eyes immediately flick to the horrified guests around us and, trying to diffuse the situation, he grabs Joshua by the arm and pulls him outside. "What are you talking about?" he whispers angrily.

"Natasha and fucking Max," he sneers.

Ben screws up his face as his eyes flick to me. Max follows, unaware of what is going on. Joshua's furious eyes meet his and he lunges for Max. Max steps aside and misses Joshua's hit.

"What the hell are you doing?" I whisper angrily.

Joshua grabs Max by the shirt and pushes him up against the car. "Are you fucking happy now?" He slams him again. "Are you?" he screams.

"What are you talking about?" Max yells as Ben steps in and pulls Joshua off of Max.

My eyes flick around to the few people outside and my head hangs in shame. This is embarrassing, not to mention degrading. It looks as though I have been having an affair with my bodyguard. Poor Josh, no wonder he's furious.

"What are you talking about?" Max screams.

Joshua has red steam shooting from both ears and pushes Max again.

"Josh, stop it!" I scream

The security from the party comes down the steps towards us. "Is there a problem here?" they ask Ben.

"No," Ben snaps. "Get in the car, Stan," he yells.

"Shut up!" Joshua yells as he turns his attention to Max. "Is this what you have been planning all along?" He pushes Max again. I frown in horror. *What?! He thinks this is true?!* Oh my God, this is getting out of control.

"Joshua, it's not true," I whisper in a hushed voice to avoid attention, although it's way too late for that. We have a small audience watching us.

"Get in the fucking car, Natasha!" he screams.

"Don't speak to her like that!" yells Max and the bodyguards all exchange worried looks.

My face drops. Oh God, just shut up, Max. Joshua turns and with renewed vigor pushes Max again.

"I'll speak to her any way I want." He grabs me by the upper arm and pulls me toward the car.

"Oww," I yelp. "Joshua, stop it. You're acting crazy."

Ben steps in. "Stan, stop it."

Joshua pushes him too while having my arm in a pincer grip. "I'll kill him. Get him away from me before I fucking kill him." Joshua yells about Max.

He opens the door furiously and pushes me into the car and slams it hard behind me.

"Take Natasha home," he yells to the driver. "To LA." He turns and then starts to storm after Max who has disappeared around the side of the building.

My face drops. What the hell? I jump out of the car. "Joshua, get in the car now."

People are staring but this is getting seriously out of control. "Ben, do something," I scream. Ben runs his hands through his hair in frustration.

"Stan, get in the car!" he yells.

"That's it!" I scream. I start to storm toward the road and hold my arm up for a cab. I'm not putting up with this shit. He hasn't even given me a chance to look at the photos properly and make sense of them. Two of the guards run after me.

Joshua turns. "Natasha. Get in the fucking car," he yells.

"No," I scream. "I'm not putting up with this." My angry eyes flick around to the guards who are all following me out to the road, unsure what to do.

"Don't make me come and get you!" Joshua furiously yells across the carpark. The people who are standing around all gasp. Oh God, this is embarrassing but I'm too mad to care.

"Come and get me, asshole. I'm not putting up with this shit," I yell as I continue to storm out toward the road.

"You fucking guards are hopeless. Control her!" he yells. He turns and starts to sprint after me and I run.

"Get the car," I snap at Ben and he nods, realizing I have just run to get Joshua's mind off following Max and onto chasing me.

I continue to hotfoot it and Joshua catches up to me. "Where do you think you're going?" He staggers as if dizzy and I frown.

"Away from you, asshole," I snap. He must be drunker than I thought.

"Get in the car. I'm taking you home," he snaps

"To LA?" I scream, hurt that our lovely night has been ruined once again by the twisting paparazzi and their lying cameras.

He shakes his head. "No, to the boat." Ben pulls up in the

car and Joshua grabs my arm and pushes me inside and I fall into the seat and he climbs in next to me. He puts his head in his hands in anger. I drop to my knees in front of him.

"Joshua, this isn't true. They have just twisted the photographs."

"I told him not to touch you," he murmurs angrily.

"Joshua, he hasn't, I swear to you. Since you told me no touching, we have been completely unfriendly. They have twisted the photos. They could be photoshopped for all we know."

Joshua runs his hands though his hair.

"Joshua, you have just made a ridiculous scene over nothing. There is nothing to be suspicious of. You know how they twist photographs. They do it to you every day. Why do you think they wouldn't do it to me?"

He stays silent as he watches me and my heart aches for him. He actually thinks I would be romantically attracted to Max. I smile sadly. "Josh, I love you. You are the only drama queen around here." I sigh as I climb onto his lap.

He blows out a deep breath. "Fuck," he whispers as he seems to regain his composure.

"Josh, what the hell was that?" I whisper. "You just made us look like idiots," I whisper. "Everyone was watching us."

His eyes meet mine. "And you think I don't look like an idiot with those photos on every newsstand tomorrow?"

"Oh baby." I pull his head into my chest. "People are manipulating this situation to make it look bad."

He gently kisses my upper arm next to his face. "It makes me crazy thinking of you with someone else," he whispers.

I kiss his forehead. "I know but it's Max. He's my friend."

He shakes his head angrily. "He's going and I don't care what you say about it."

I nod sadly. I know that tonight the point of no return has been crossed with Max and our time together is over. Sadness brushes over me.

We sit silent as the driver makes his way to the boat ramp. Ben and the other two guards get the boat ready in silence and we get onto it and make our way out to the luxury liner. We didn't even say goodbye to the others. The situation went from zero to ten in about thirty seconds. Ben is furious. I can see the steam shooting from his ears and Joshua is still breathing heavily from the adrenaline in his system. We arrive safely at the yacht and Joshua stands quickly, then nearly falls over, and Ben grabs his arm for support and shakes his head at the other guards. He is so much drunker than any of us thought.

He helps me to stand and I gingerly climb up the stairs and the porters on the boat help me on board. "Thank you," I whisper. I don't even have my phone on me. It's on the table back at the wedding in my handbag. Joshua gets onto the boat behind me and Ben behind him. Ben starts to check the boat as Joshua goes directly to the bedroom, obviously embarrassed.

"Ben, can you call the girls and get them to take my bag and Joshua's jacket please?" I ask.

"Yeah. Are you okay?" he asks softly.

I nod as I blow out a deep breath. "What was that?" I sigh. He shakes his head. "Crazy bastard."

"Did you see the photos?" I ask.

He frowns. "No, what?"

I shake my head embarrassed. I don't want to go into this shit with him.

"We are just going to go to bed. Go back to the party and go out with the gang. The other guards are staying nearby in the next boat."

His eyes flick to the boat moored 200 meters from ours. "The porters don't stay on this boat overnight."

I smile. "It's okay, Ben. Go and guard my sister. We have enough guards out here."

He nods. "I'm just going to say goodbye to Joshua."

I smile softly. He wants to check on his friend. We walk down to the luxury bedroom, I open the door and Joshua is out cold, asleep on the bed. He frowns and looks at me. "I didn't realize he was so drunk." He sighs.

"Me either," I whisper.

I walk over and take his shoes off and he continues to sleep.

I smile at Ben and shake my head. "Not the night I had in mind, Ben."

He smiles. "I bet. Are you sure you don't want me to stay?" he asks.

My eyes flick to Joshua. "There is absolutely nothing going on around here," I mutter dryly. "Go and have fun."

Joshua

The sound of the water lapping on the side of the boat awakens me. It's still dark but the sun is just coming up. It's cold. I roll over and put my arm out for Presh... she's not in bed with me. She must be in the bathroom. I doze back off to sleep but wake again half an hour later, freezing. Fuck it's cold. Wind whistles through the room and I frown and sit up. "Tash," I call out. No answer, just the sound of the water gently hitting the side of the boat. It's dawn. She must have left the door open.

"Tash, baby, come back to bed. What are you doing?" I call again. Fuck, she's pissed at me. No wonder, I carried on like a lunatic last night. I don't even remember going to bed.

Christ, I didn't even drink much. I slowly get out of bed and look down at myself. I'm still in the clothes I wore to the wedding. I must have been wiped out. I never sleep with clothes on. I shake my head in disgust and head into the bathroom.

"Tash," I call.

Again, no answer. My eyes go through the kitchen and to the door that goes out onto the deck. It's open. That's why it's so fucking cold in here—she's really pissed and trying to freeze me alive. I rat through my bag and grab a sweater and head for the door. As I walk through the kitchen, I step in something, my feet slide from under me and luckily I catch my fall. My eyes go to the floor to see what I slipped in.

A huge puddle of blood is on the floor... what the fuck! "Natasha!" I scream as I run for the door. My eyes shoot around the cabin. "Natasha!" I call again.

Dear God, where is she? "Natasha!" I scream frantically as I run out onto the deck. My eyes widen and I gasp in shock. Blood is all over the deck and drag marks lead to the side of the boat and over the edge. A knife lies on the floor covered in blood.

"Ben!" I scream. "Help, somebody help!" I run to the side of the boat and look over the edge into the water... nothing.

"Natasha!" I scream. "Natasha, where are you?" I call frantically. My phone rings and my eyes dart around to look for it. It's on the cushion on the seat at the side of the boat. I scramble to answer it. It's Ben.

"What's wrong?" he asks. He obviously heard my calls for help.

"Where's Natasha?" I scream as I hold my breath.

"What do you mean? She's with you on the boat," he snaps.

"No, she's not." My heart rate feels like I am about to have a heart attack. "There's blood, Ben. Blood is everywhere," I cry.

"On my way."

I run to the side of the boat where the drag marks lead and dive overboard into the water. "Natasha," I call as I flap on the surface. I take a huge breath and go under the water to see if I can see her. My head frantically looks around. I can't see anything—the water is too dark. I can't breathe and my heart starts to thump in fear in my chest. I break to the surface and gasp for air as the rubber dinghy comes flying through the water towards me. Three of the guards dive into the water next to me.

"Ben, there's blood all over the deck," I gasp into the water as I half drown.

Ben's horrified eyes meet mine and he jumps off the dinghy and climbs the ladder onto the boat.

"Oh my God!" he screams. "She's in the water!" he yells frantically. "Find her," he yells to his men.

We all go back under the water frantically. Oh no, Tash, where are you, baby? What's happened? The water is too cold, and I am unable to move anymore and Ben drags me from the water and then dives in himself as I stand on the boat, frozen with fear.

"Natasha!" I yell. "Natasha, where are you?" I scream. I hold my head in my hands and start to hyperventilate. I can't breathe and I start to cough uncontrollably as my eyes dart around to the shore.

Where are you, Presh?

I'll call her. I race and climb the ladder onto the boat and fall as I miss the last two steps and I climb again and scramble to my phone. Oh my God... there's so much blood.

The tears start to run down my face, and I grab my phone and dial her number. It rings as my heart races. Please pick up, please pick up, please pick up.

"Hey Josh," Bridget's happy voice travels down the phone.

My heart drops. "Is Tash with you?" I stammer hopefully.

"No. Why? I have her phone because she left her bag at the reception last night after your tanty."

"Do you know where she is?" I snap.

"No, what's wrong, Josh?" she answers. "She should be on the boat with you."

The lump in my throat closes over and I can't speak... oh my god. "Josh. What's wrong? You're scaring me."

My eyes fill with tears and I shake my head. "I don't know, Didge," I whisper. "I woke up and she was gone from the boat."

"What?" she shrieks. "Were you still fighting?"

I clutch my head with my hand. "I don't know. I don't think so."

"What do you mean you don't think so? You were or you weren't," she yells.

I put my hand on top of my head. "No then."

"Didge, there's blood... there is a lot of blood on the boat," I sob. She stays silent on the other end of the phone.

"Josh. What happened?" she whispers.

"I don't know," I cry, suddenly panicked. How could I not know? "I don't remember anything. I was asleep and then I woke up and she was gone."

"Where were the guards? They must have seen something," she cries.

I shake my head in fear.

"What did the police say?" she stammers.

"Yes. I will call them. Get over here now!" I yell and hang up and I dial 911.

"Hello, fire, ambulance or police?" the lady's voice casually speaks.

"Police!" I yell.

"Hello, this is the police," the police officer's voice is calm. "This is Joshua Stanton. My fiancée, Natasha Marx, and I are staying on a boat. There's blood everywhere and I can't find her," I cry frantically.

"Whose blood is it, sir?" the officer asks calmly.

"I don't know," I cry as my eyes dart around at the men all combing the water. "I awoke and she was gone, and blood is everywhere," I sob. I put my hand over my mouth and dry-retch. I run to the side and vomit over the side of the boat. I put the phone down onto the table and hold onto the side of the boat to stop myself from fainting as I cry in fear.

Ben gets out of the water and climbs the stairs. "I need to call the police," he murmurs, devastated.

My face screws up as the tears run down my face. "They are on the phone," I whisper as I point to my phone. Ben picks up the phone and starts to tell them our coordinates. I start to shake as my body goes into shock and I continue to throw up.

"Natasha!" I cry as I lean over the side of the boat. "Natasha... dear God, no!" My voice is hoarse. "Naaattt-taaassshhhhaaa! Noooooooo!" I cry as I fall to the floor on my knees. "No, baby. Come back to me. You can't die. I need you!" I scream as I burst into full-blown sobs.

Ben drops onto the floor beside me and grabs me in an embrace as I scream. "Natasha, no. We need to find her. Please don't stop looking. Please keep searching."

Ben's body heaves as he holds in tears and the men all

pull themselves onto the boat too exhausted and freezing to carry on.

"Ben, no!" I cry. "They've got her. They've got her," I sob as I start to hyperventilate once again and begin to choke. The guards are all visibly upset, and I lie on the deck next to my love's blood.

"No. This can't be happening."

Ben cradles my head in his lap as he tries to console me, and I sob into his chest. Dear God, this can't be happening.

Beep...beep...beep, a machine sounds and a nurse quietly comes into the room.

She smiles warmly. "You're awake, Mr. Stanton. Welcome back."

I frown and my eyes dart around the room. "You are in the hospital, sir. You have been sedated for the last two days," she tells me sadly.

I frown. It's real. It wasn't a nightmare. "Natasha?" I whisper. She stands still and puts her hand on top of mine.

"I'm sorry." She drops her head. "They haven't found her."

Bile rises from my stomach and burns my esophagus. I shake my head as tears threaten. "Unhook me, please. I need to find her." I start to struggle to get the tubes out of the back of my hand. "Please," I whisper.

The nurse opens the door out to the corridor. "Dr. Stanton," she calls. "He's awake."

Cameron walks in and his haunted eyes meet mine. He has an air of resignation about him.

"Josh," he whispers as he cradles my head up against his chest.

"Where is she, Cam?" I whisper, distraught.

He continues to hold me as I try desperately to make sense of this.

"We need to find her," I whisper.

"We are doing everything that we can," he whispers. "Josh, the police are here. They need to ask you some questions," he says quietly.

I pull out of his embrace. "Of course." I wipe the tears from my face with my hospital gown and nod. Cameron goes out of the room for a moment and returns with two policemen.

The two officers shake my hand. "I'm Detective Miller and this is Detective Stevenson."

I nod nervously. "Have you found her?" I stammer.

They exchange looks. "No, I'm sorry we haven't." My face screws up in pain. "We need to ask you some questions about what happened on Saturday night."

I nod. "What day is it?" I frown.

"It's Monday afternoon, sir. You were so distraught that you were admitted and sedated against your will. You were starting to endanger your own life when you wouldn't stay out of the water in the freezing conditions."

I drop my head as my foggy brain brings forth the horrific memory.

"Tell us about the evening." One of the officers gets out his pen and notepad ready to take notes.

I frown. "We were at a wedding."

"Yes."

"And I got a text." I frown again as I remember what was sent to me. "Max," I whisper. "Have you tried Max? He might know where she is," I say hopefully and my eyes flick to Cameron.

"Yes, we have questioned Max at length, sir," the officer replies. "He says he doesn't know where she is."

My face falls again, and Cameron puts his hand reassuringly on my foot.

"Go on," the officer continues.

"I was sent a message that the story had just broken that Natasha was having an affair with Max."

The detectives exchange looks.

I raise an eyebrow. "You knew that?" I reply flatly.

"Yes." the detective mutters without lifting his eyes from his notepad.

I shake my head and close my eyes in regret. "I was angry and caused a scene, so we went back to the boat."

"Go on." He keeps writing.

I look at the ceiling as I try to remember. "I don't know. I fell asleep." I frown as I try to piece the puzzle together.

"And then what happened?"

"I woke and it was cold." I get goosebumps as I remember the quiet and cold of the morning. My eyes look straight ahead as I visualize the blood on the floor and a lump forms in my throat. "Natasha wasn't in bed with me," I whisper.

"Where was she?" he asks.

I shrug. "I thought she was in the bathroom and I went back to sleep," I whisper, mortified. "She could have been hurt then and I went back to sleep." I hold my hand over my mouth in disgust at myself.

They stay silent as they wait for me to speak. "Cameron, where is she?" I whisper and he puts his hand in mine and squeezes it.

"I walked out to look for her," I continue and then I frown

and tears fill my eyes as I remember the blood... so much blood. "Are they hurting her?" I cry. "What if they are torturing her?" I scream. "It's me...it's me... it's me." I shake my head frantically. "It's me they want. Tell them they can kill me." I shake my head frantically as I imagine what they could be doing to her, and I start to rip the drip from my arm. "I need to find her. Let me out of here."

I keep shaking my head frantically. "Yes, Cameron, come on," I stammer.

"He is no state to be questioned," Cameron snaps. "Look at him."

I shake my head. "No, Cameron, I'm going to find her." I stand to get out of the bed and Cameron pushes me back down.

"Stay there," Cameron snaps.

"Mr. Stanton, can you tell us why you have Rohypnol in your system?" the officer asks.

I frown and my eyes shoot to Cameron. "What do you mean?" I ask.

"You had Rohypnol in your system that showed up in a drug test. You fell asleep on Saturday night because you were drugged."

CHAPTER 20

Adrian

I SIT in the police station as we endure our tenth hour of
questioning in two days. I am with Bridget who has come to
supply a DNA sample to the police.

"So, what have you brought us?" the nice female officer asks
gently.

Bridget looks down and with shaky hands and produces
Natasha's hairbrush from her bag. Her haunted eyes meet mine
and I grab her hand for comfort.

The male officer immediately picks it up in gloved hands,
puts it into a plastic bag and then seals it. He writes the name
Natasha Marx and the date in pen on the name plate.

"I also have her toothbrush," Bridget whispers.

The female officer's eyes hold Bridget's and she smiles
softly. "Are you two close?" she asks.

Bridget nods and drops her head. "She's my best friend,"
she murmurs. I squeeze her hand just that little bit tighter.

Here we sit in a quiet office and yet my insides have never been so noisy... so confused. How did this happen? I had made sure that security was doubled... how did they get her? And what are they doing to her right now? My stomach has been sick since the moment Bridget got off the phone from Joshua and started to run around frantically screaming. How do you deal with this?

Please, Natasha, be okay.

"We are doing everything that we can to find her." The kind officer smiles sympathetically at Bridget.

Bridget nods through her tears. "I know," she whispers as her leg starts to bounce in nerves.

"What's your relationship with Joshua Stanton like?" the male officer asks.

"Very good," Bridget says softly. "I live with him and my sister."

His eyes turn to me. "I understand that you are the head of Mr. Stanton's company?"

I nod. I don't even have it in me to play nice and act polite anymore.

"Is there anyone else from his work environment who you can think of that would have a vendetta against your boss?" he asks.

"Only the ones I have told you," I reply flatly. "Are you chasing any of those leads or are you just wasting time interviewing the same people over and over again?" I glare at the officer, furious that they can't find her.

He nods. "We are very interested in the link to Coby Allender although there are a number of leads to be investigated."

Bridget sobs softly and I remember that I am here with her and need to shut my angry mouth.

I nod and drop my head.

Bridget retrieves a small black toothbrush holder from her bag and looks at it in her shaking hands.

A lump in my throat forms as I watch her and my eyes close in pain.

"Here is her toothbrush," Bridget whispers, unwilling to hand it over.

The female officer smiles sadly. "Thank you." She sits still, waiting for Bridget to pass it across the desk.

"We can buy her another one when she gets back, Didge," I whisper.

Bridget nods through her tears and shakily hands it over. "We need a DNA sample from you too, Bridget. Can you swipe this swab over the inside of your mouth please? You will have the closest DNA to Natasha," the policewoman gently says.

Bridget takes the swab, her eyes meet mine and I nod softly. "Go on. This will help them find her," I whisper.

She takes the swab and hands it over to the male officer who immediately bags and labels it.

"Are you still at the Jameson Hotel?" the female officer asks.

I nod.

"How long will you be there before returning to LA?" she asks.

I drop my head. "I don't know. Until we find Natasha and bring her home, I guess," I reply.

Bridget squeezes my hand in hers. "You will find her, won't you?" she whispers.

The policewoman nods sadly. "We are doing everything we can. We have a chopper searching the ocean and the currents, and ground teams combing the water's edge. You just concentrate on trying to think of any leads, no matter how small you think they may be. There are always clues in these things. You just have to join the dots together."

Bridget and I nod with a renewed purpose. "You're right," I whisper. "We will find her—we have to."

Joshua

I lie in the hospital bed as I await the doctor. "Cameron, get me the fuck out of here!" I snap.

"Listen, be calm and they will release you. You are in here because you have been losing your shit and they are worried about your sanity," he blurts.

I screw up my face. "Sanity, I will show you fucking insanity if you don't get me out of here. I need to find her. Natasha will be waiting for me to come and get her."

His face drops. "Josh," he whispers. Then he sits on the side of the bed and takes my hand in his. "This situation is out of our control. The police are doing everything they can to find her. You need to stay calm and you need to stay sane."

I drop my head back onto the pillow.

The door opens slowly and Ben walks in. His eyes are downcast, and my fury ignites.

"Where were you?" I snap.

He stays silent at the end of the bed.

"Answer me! Where were you when Natasha needed you?" I try my hardest to control my anger. I know the doctor will be here any minute to hopefully discharge me.

Cameron folds his arms in contempt. "Tell Joshua where you were Ben."

Ben drops his head. "I stayed on the mainland with Bridget," he murmurs.

"What!" I yell.

He shakes his head as he looks at the ground.

"You knew Max wasn't on that boat of guards and you left anyway?" I growl.

"Natasha told me to go. She said you two were just going to go to bed," he pushes out through tears as he holds his head in anguish.

"Why would you listen to her? You are the head of my security. Why would you go and leave us open to this?"

He screws up his face as the tears fill his eyes and he shakes his head. "I don't know. I don't know."

"I will tell you why," Cameron snaps. "You're incompetent, that's why."

Ben drops to the chair in the corner and holds his head in his hands as he weeps tears of guilt. "What did the guards hear?" I ask him.

He shakes his head. "Nothing," he replies, muffled through his hands.

"What, they heard nothing?" I snap.

He shakes his head. "From where they were, they heard nothing. No screams, no boat, nothing. Not a fucking thing. I called them three times through the night and they were unaware of anything until we heard your screams for help in the morning."

I frown and my eyes flick to Cameron. "What's the drug they were talking about I had in my system?"

"Rohypnol," he replies. "It showed up in the toxicology report."

"What's that?" I ask.

"It's a date rape drug. It knocks you out with no memory."

I frown. "Do you think Natasha was given it too?"

Cameron nods. "I think so, otherwise she would have screamed."

Ben stands. "You were asleep before I even left the boat."

I frown. "I don't remember going to bed," I murmur as I try to remember through the hazy fog.

Ben shakes his head. "You lost your shit at the wedding and then when you were getting into the boat you appeared drunk." He pauses while he thinks of something. "Natasha and I thought you were drunk."

"Where is Max? Did he do this?" I snap.

"No!" Ben snaps. "The photos weren't even real—you were set up."

I put my hand on my forehead in shame. The doctor walks in with three of his attendings.

"Hello Mr. Stanton." He smiles sympathetically. I nod.

"We understand you are under a lot of stress, sir. How are you feeling today?" he asks.

"A lot better, thanks."

He takes out his stethoscope and listens to my chest. "How are you emotionally?"

I drop my head. "I'm okay."

"We will be discharging you today, but we are putting you into the care of your brother and if any time he feels you are becoming unstable we would like to see you again."

I nod again. Just shut the fuck up and let me out of here. The doctor's eyes meet Cameron's. "I think that perhaps

Mr. Stanton may need to go on some anti-anxiety medication for a while."

Cameron's eyes flick to me and he nods. "Okay," he replies as he opens the door. He then follows the doctor out of the room, obviously so they can talk about me without me hearing them.

Ben stands. "I will find her, Stan. If it's the last fucking thing I do. I will find her."

I nod as my eyesight becomes blurry through the tears. "Who do you think did this?" he asks.

"The sick fuck from Australia," I whisper as my eyes close in pain. If he has her, she's probably being tortured right now.

Ben shakes his head. "It's not him. He doesn't have her." I frown. "What makes you so sure?"

"Serial killers have a pattern and I have studied his. This is too elaborate, too easy to get caught. They drugged you both. Got out to a boat. We don't even know if that blood is Natasha's. It wouldn't surprise me if we don't get a ransom note sometime over the next week. This isn't the pattern of a sex offender."

I stare straight ahead.

"Stan, I take full responsibility for this and as soon as we find her, I will be handing in my resignation," Ben replies quietly.

I nod again, unable to speak.

"Just find her, Ben," I murmur as I stare straight ahead. He nods and exits the room. Cameron walks back into the room with an overnight bag of clothes. "Get dressed. We are going," he murmurs.

My eyes glance at the bag on the bed. "Where are the clothes I was brought in here in?" I ask.

He bites his bottom lip. "You don't remember anything about that?"

I frown and shake my head.

"The ambulance crew cut them off you because you were so freezing from being in the water so long that your body had gone into shock."

I swallow the lump in my throat and drop my head as I

remember diving deep into the dark cold water in search of my love. I have never been so frightened.

Cameron puts his arm around my shoulders and pulls me into an embrace. "We'll get through this, mate. You are not alone. We are going to find her," he whispers.

I drop my head to his shoulder, and he holds me for a moment. "I... Cameron, I don't know how to deal with this. Who has her?" My heart rate picks up at the thought of her suffering. "I can't fucking handle this," I murmur as he holds me tighter. "What if they are hurting her?" I scream. "She needs medical treatment—she's cut." I pull out of his embrace and Ben comes back into the room.

"You need to quiet down or they will not let you leave. We need you at home to help us figure this mess out," he snaps.

I nod. Yes, he's right. I can't help her from here. I need to get out of here. I slowly pick up my clothes and put them on in silence.

I walk from the hospital forever a different man. My life will never be the same. Scarred. They have succeeded in doing what they have always wanted to do. The ultimate goal has always been to bring me to my knees, and they haven't done just that, they have cut off half of me. I'm a shell without Natasha by my side and they knew the only way to hurt me was to hurt her.

Where are you, Tash? Are you safe, baby?

Flanked by security I walk out the front doors of the hospital to hear my name screamed by photographers and the blinding flashes start. I drop my head and walk toward my waiting car.

"Joshua Stanton, where is your wife?" "Are you okay, Mr. Stanton?"

"Is it true your wife has been found dead?" another yells. I stop mid-step and make eye contact with the cockroach who has just said that.

"Get in the car," Ben snaps as he grabs my elbow and pushes me into the car.

"Get out of my way!" I hear Cameron yell as he falls into the car and closes the door behind him. I stare out the window as the car speeds away. A zombie-like calm sweeps over me. I cannot speak, "It's okay, Josh," Cameron whispers. "It's okay."

The ride in the car is silent. Ben is driving and another guard is in the front seat. There is a car behind and another in front of us.

Too little, too late.

It starts to rain and my heart drops. What if she's out in the rain? Does she have protection? My elbow rests on the door as I stare at the scenery rushing past us in a world where everything seems normal, everything seems fine. Finally, we arrive at our destination, the hotel, and I am ushered up the lift and along the corridor to a room. Ben slowly opens the door and I see Bridget in Adrian's arms. She turns and sees me and her face screws up in pain.

"Joshua," she whispers.

Tears instantly fill my eyes. "I'm so sorry," I whisper.

She rushes and grabs me in an embrace and holds me as I drop my head onto her shoulder. "I couldn't keep her safe. I couldn't keep her safe," I whisper.

"Joshua, stop. This isn't your fault," she sobs as she pulls back and holds my cheeks. "Joshua, do not dare blame your-self for this!"

"How can all of us love her so much and not one of us know where she is?" I whisper.

"This is totally fucked," Abbie yells. "Who would do this?" she shrieks.

"Quiet," Cameron yells as he turns the television up to hear the news.

More on the Stanton story, Natasha Stanton, wife of billionaire celebrity Joshua Stanton, has gone missing in what are very suspicious circumstances on the luxury yacht of a friend at some time in the early hours of Sunday morning. Witnesses say that the night before, the pair were involved in a very public heated domestic dispute that had Joshua Stanton forcing Natasha into his limousine against her will.

The camera goes to footage from someone's phone of the night before and I see myself acting like a lunatic and screaming at Natasha.

"Natasha, get in the fucking car!" I yell.

My eyes widen in horror at what is unfolding before me. What the hell was I thinking? I don't even remember this. I watch myself grab Natasha by the arm and throw her into the car and then start yelling that I am going to kill Max.

Cameron points the remote at the television and it goes dead.

I drop to a seat on the lounge in shock. I sit still as I stare into space. This can't be happening.

"The police are doing everything that they can, Josh," Adrian says softly. "There have been foot patrols and choppers. Everyone has been looking everywhere. A clue is going to turn up and then we will be able to piece together what happened."

"Check the emails again," Cameron says to Adrian and he nods and rises to check the computers.

The vision of Natasha smiling and laughing fills my thoughts and I drop my head into my hands.

"I'm going to find her." I stand with renewed vigor.

"Sit down," Cameron snaps. "It's not safe out there and photographers are everywhere waiting to get a shot of you. You need to be here and contactable in case someone produces a ransom note."

I drop to my seat, defeated. "I can't just sit here and wait like a stale bottle of piss. Natasha needs me," I yell.

Bridget stands and heads over to the window and stares out at the view. "Please be safe, Tash," she says in a monotone.

The room falls silent.

Please, Natasha, come back to me.

It's 3 am and everyone is in their beds trying to sleep. I can't lie down. I have been pacing back and forth in my room for four hours. It's raining outside. She may be in the cold. What if she has a headache? She has no medication on her. I dry-retch in the toilet for the tenth time in an hour. I need to stay strong. I look out the window at the street below. The police cars have all gone... everyone is gone. The reporters, the news channels... Natasha.

My beautiful Natasha, where is she? Where are you, baby?

Who has you? I can't stay here. I can't just sit here and wait.

I'm going crazy. I pull on my runners and a tracksuit and pull my hoodie over my head.

I'm coming, my love. I'm coming to find you.

Adrian

I am just dozing off when my phone rings. It's 4 am. I pick it up. It's Ben.

"Is Stan with you?" he snaps.

"No, why?" My eyes widen in fear.

"He's not in his room."

"Shit." I jump up immediately and turn the light on as someone pounds on the door.

"Who is it?" I yell, half-frightened.

"Me, you fucking idiot, who do you think?" Cameron snaps.

I open the door in a rush.

Cameron screws up his face. "Put your junk away."

I shake my head as I quickly pull up my pants. "Where is he?" I ask.

"I don't know but we have to find him. He's not fucking thinking straight. God knows what he will do," Cameron mutters.

"Fuck," I sigh as I grab my shoes. We run out into the corridor and toward the lift where Ben is waiting.

. . .

"My God, I'm getting worried," I whisper as we drive down the one-way street. Cameron, Ben and I have been driving around for two hours looking for Joshua. Our eyes all scan the pavement. He's not answering his phone.

"Where are you, fucker?" Cameron snaps. "I can't handle this shit. I can't handle not knowing where the fuck anyone is!" Cameron yells.

Ben pulls his hands through his hair in frustration. "Why would he go out in the middle of the night by himself?"

I drop my head. We all know the answer. "He's looking for her," I whisper.

As we go past each streetlight my eyes search the lit-up space. "Where could he be?" I whisper through my worry. "What if they have him, too?"

Ben narrows his eyes as he stares at the road. "I don't know how he got past security," he murmurs.

"Oh, what you mean is for the second time? Your security team is fucking shit. Natasha would still be here if they did their job correctly," Cameron snaps. "I have never seen such incompetence in my life."

Ben shakes his head in annoyance. "Yeah, well nobody went in, so he has snuck out, but definitely nobody went in."

"Same fucking shit," Cam snaps. "If you can get out you can get in. Tell me the difference."

I frown into the darkness as I keep my eyes peeled on the pavement. "Where are you, Joshua?" I whisper as we turn the corner to the bay where Natasha was taken from and Ben pulls the car into a carpark facing the water below. It's dawn and the sun is just starting to put a dim light on everything in its path. The rain is still falling softly onto the windscreen, and then I see it. A lone figure standing down on the rocks on the water's edge in the darkness and rain.

"There he is," I whisper.

We all sit still and watch him. His head is down, and he stands on the rocks on the shoreline. "He's looking for her," Cameron whispers. "I don't know what to say to him. How do I help him?" he murmurs.

Ben rests his elbows on the steering wheel as he watches his friend troll the rocks below. "This is all my fault," he whispers through tears.

Cameron stays silent as he watches his traumatized brother.

I shake my head as my tears break the dam. "This isn't how it's supposed to go, bad things aren't supposed to happen to good people," I ground out. "Tash, come back...please, come back." Cameron and Ben both drop their heads in the front seat. We have no idea what to do... what to say to him. No words can make anyone feel better and, because we feel so powerless to help him, the three of us sit in the car as we watch Joshua slowly walk around the water's edge for an extended time.

"Let's go," Ben whispers as he gets out of the car.

We all get out of the car and slowly make our way to the water's edge through the wind and the rain. Joshua's eyes stay focused on the boat still moored out to sea, the crime scene. Cameron slowly puts his arm around his broken brother and the four of us all stare out to the boat in silence.

"I can't find her," Joshua grinds out through the rain hitting his face.

I drop my head.

"What if she is hurt?" He screws up his face in pain. "Her nightmare, this is what she feared would happen and I promised her it wouldn't," he sobs.

We all stay silent, unsure what to say.

Joshua shakes his head. "This is my fault. I should have protected her. It was my job to keep her safe." He screws up his face as his tears fall with the rain. "I should have protected her. It was my job!" he cries out into the rain. "Natasha!" he calls out. "Where are you, baby?"

I drop my head, unable to swallow though my tears. This is too much. Cameron pulls his brother into an embrace and Joshua howls onto his shoulder. Ben slumps to sit on the wet sand with his head in his hands and I fall to the sand beside him.

What's going on in this world? I have lost all faith. Never have I felt so lost and disillusioned in my life.

Joshua

Her dark eyes smile up at me from our bed. "Put them on," she urges.

I shake my head in disgust at the flannel pajamas she has laid out on the bed for me.

"I'm not wearing those," I mutter. "Forget it." She smiles. "Then we can be snuggly."

My eyes meet hers. "The only thing I'm wearing in my bed tonight is you." I sit on the side of the bed next to her and slide my hand up under her pajama top, and my hand cups her breast.

Leaning up on her elbow she kisses me gently. "I can't wait to marry you, Joshua," she whispers into my lips as she runs her hand through my stubble.

"So you can turn me into a geriatric in pajamas?" I smirk as I lie her down under me and drop my lips to her neck.

"That's the only reason," she whispers as she kisses me again. "Tough shit," I whisper. "You can't make me wear those fuckers." She laughs out loud. "Give me time, big boy. We'll see."

I come back to the present—my mind is constantly jumping between memories and stupid conversations that we had. I can remember every damn detail about us but not

342

the most important thing. What happened last Saturday night—that's what I need to remember. I'm trolling deep through my mind for a clue but all I keep coming up with is more memories of my beautiful girl.

I look at the wall and see the clock turn over another hour and my heart sinks again. Time...how do you stop it...or better still turn it back? With every hour that passes I know the chance drops further of us finding her. It's been six days since Natasha was taken. Police are streaming in and out of our hotel room, photographers and journalists are camped outside. We have the whole top floor of the hotel to ourselves. My parents and Natasha's mother are all here. I am surrounded by people who love me and yet I am entirely and utterly alone. I have no way out of this. Natasha is gone.

I can't eat, speak...function. The only thing on my mind is my beautiful fiancée and how deeply I let her down. Bridget walks into my room with a protein shake.

"Josh, you need to eat." She passes me the shake. "Or drink." "Thanks," I murmur as I take it.

"Did you sleep last night?" she whispers.

I nod as I look at the floor. I can't lie to Bridget. I have hardly slept in six days.

"Are you still throwing up?" she whispers. I shake my head while still looking down.

"That means yes," she whispers as she runs her hand down my arm.

"Josh, Natasha would want me to look after you. Tell me how to help you," Bridget murmurs.

I smile sadly and walk over to the window to look out to sea, and she walks over and embraces me from behind. "Josh, please don't fall apart. We need you to be strong."

I drop my head. "I'm trying," I whisper. "

Try harder," she murmurs.

I turn and take her in my arms. "Are you okay?" I whisper into her hair.

She nods into my chest. "I'm so sad," she whispers in a muffled voice. "How do we do this?"

Cameron walks to the door. "The police want to have a meeting with the family," he says in a monotone. I pull from Bridget's embrace and my eyes meet his.

"Why? Have they found something?" I ask.

"I'm not sure," he replies.

With a heavy heart Bridget and I follow Cameron down the hall to a common meeting room that the police have been using as a base to coordinate with our security guards and search teams. There are three policemen in the room along with Natasha's mother, my parents, Cameron, Bridget and me.

The police all shake my hand. "Mr. Stanton." They nod.

My heart starts to race. This is the first time they have requested to speak to us together.

"What's happening?" I ask impatiently.

The policemen exchange looks. "We have a few reports that have come back from the crime scene."

"Any prints?" I blurt.

"No," the tall one answers. "Not that we can find." I shake my head in disgust, of course not.

"The DNA we got from Natasha's hairbrush and tooth-brush confirm that it was her blood on the boat."

I drop my head as Bridget and her mother gasp and embrace.

"Oh no," Bridget whispers.

"We can also confirm that she had Rohypnol in her

system too and that she would not have been awake during the ordeal," the officer says flatly, running on autopilot.

I start to hear my pulse in my ears.

The officers hesitate and exchange looks again. Don't say it. Don't say it. Please don't say it.

The policeman directs his conversation directly at me. "The coroner's report has come back from the crime scene, Mr. Stanton."

I lift my chin as I prepare myself.

"The search has been changed from one for a missing person to a body retrieval."

I stand still, unable to react.

"There were over three and a half liters of blood on the boat and it has been ruled that nobody could survive that amount of blood loss."

I close my eyes as my world comes to an end.

"I'm sorry, Mr. Stanton, but your fiancée has been ruled deceased." I grip the back of the chair to stop myself from falling. I start to sway as my soul is ripped from my body and distantly from somewhere in the room, I hear the howling of our families.

CHAPTER 21

JOSHUA

DARKNESS. Is it something ingrained in your psyche or is it a consequence of circumstance? With every hour I am away from my angel I feel the demons taking just that little bit more of my soul, pulling me into a darker place.

Revenge.

I can almost taste the blood of the person who did this to Natasha. I'm going to kill them with my bare hands when I find out who it is. And every last person involved is going to suffer and die a slow painful death along with them.

I sit in the back of my car on our way to LA. It has been sixteen days since Natasha died. Up until now I haven't been able to bear the thought of going home without her and if I had my choice I would never go back, but Bridget is distraught. She thinks I'm going to do something stupid and won't leave my side. It's killing me. I just need to be alone.

She is in the car behind us, a convoy. The united family

346

unit. What a joke. My mother and father are hardly speaking, and I can't even look at my mother. Cameron is not talking to Ben, Ben is blaming himself and hasn't spoken to Bridget since it was discovered Tash was missing. Brock is here, but we haven't spoken directly. I know he is blaming me. I blame me. Bridget and her mother are fussing around me protectively and I just want to be left the fuck alone. Adrian is trying to be strong for all of us, but I know he can't handle this either. He loved Tash, too.

We are falling apart and the glue that kept me sane is no longer here.

Finally, we pull into my driveway and I close my eyes as the car stops. I can't go into the house without her. This is her house, and she is meant to be here.

I stay seated in the car as I try to pull myself together enough to get out.

Bridget gets slowly out of the car behind and comes up to the door and opens it. "Come on, Josh," she whispers.

I sit still, unable to move.

She grabs my hand. "It's okay. I'll come with you," she says quietly.

I rip my hand from hers. "No!" I scream. "You are not Natasha! You will not come with me!" I yell.

I jump out of the car enraged. "All of you go!" I shake my head as the tears start. "I don't want you here. Any of you. Go."

"Calm down," Cameron whispers.

"Fuck off!" I yell. I turn to the security guards. "You're all fired, you are totally fucked. Get away from me!" I scream.

Everyone stands around defiantly as if expecting this and I storm into the house alone, slamming the door behind me.

I look around at the huge clean space and my chest starts

to contract. I feel like I can't breathe. I run to the stairs and take them two at a time until I get to our bedroom.

Instantly, a calmness comes over me and I sit quietly on the bed with my heart beating heavily in my chest. I can feel her presence here. For the first time in two weeks, I can feel her with me and it's strangely comforting. I look over to the side table and through bleary eyes I see her diary with her opened glasses sitting on top of it. I pick them up and hold them to my chest and, as if on autopilot, I open the diary and start to read.

Dear Diary

Today I bought my wedding dress. The dress I have wanted to wear for eight years.

I'm so excited, I'm so happy, I'm so in love.

Mum will be here soon, and I can't wait to see her and show her Willowvale. Joshua said we can build her a house there. I desperately hope she wants to live there with us. I can't wait to see Josh's face when I tell him I want to move to his dream house and live his dream life. I love it there too.

I close the diary and hold it to my chest and somehow feel comforted and grateful knowing that she was happy and loved in the last five months of her life.

She showed me a love like nothing I have ever known... and now, I am facing a loss like I have never known and I don't know if I can go on.

I curl up into a ball on our bed clutching her diary and glasses.

Help me, Tash. Help me get through this.

Adrian

My phone rings and I glance down at the caller. Nicholas.

My heart drops. I haven't thought of him since Natasha died a month ago.

"Hello," I answer.

"Hey... you okay?" his velvety voice whispers down the phone.

My eyes close and I feel a lump in my throat form and shake my head.

"Has there been any word?" he replies quietly.

"No," I push out. "How did you hear?"

"It's world news, Adrian. Are you okay?" he repeats.

My heart drops. Of course it's world news. "Yes," I whisper, but in all honesty I'm just not. I don't know how to help Joshua or handle the press on this situation. I'm getting swamped by both clients and investors. It's a nightmare on all fronts.

"How is Joshua?" he asks.

I shake my head and walk to the window. "Bad."

"Is he talking?"

"No," I murmur.

"And Cameron and everyone else?"

I close my eyes again. "It's bad, Nick. Everyone's fucked up."

He stays silent as he thinks. "I'm coming over to look after you for a while."

I stay silent. God, I want that.

"I can spend some time with Joshua and give him some treatment without him knowing," he replies.

I frown. That actually makes sense. "Are you busy at the moment?" I ask.

"Never too busy for you," he replies quietly. "And I can help you go through a few things at work and write some press releases for you and stuff."

"Could you?" I whisper. "That... would be really helpful."

"I will tie up things today and come tomorrow."

I smile my first real smile in a month. "I will send the plane for you."

"No, it's okay. Can you pick me up from the airport though?" he asks.

"Of course." And for some strange reason I am filled with relief.

"Thank you, Nicholas. It means a lot," I whisper.

I feel him smile down the phone line. "What are friends for if they can't support each other through tough times?"

I feel the lump in my throat again and I nod. "See you soon," I whisper before hanging up.

I sit at my desk and put my head in my hands. Nicholas will be here soon, and he can help me with the press. I'm so out of my depth here. The staff morale is at an all-time low and I don't know how to pick everyone up because I am struggling as much as they are. Joshua has insisted on coming to work today... I don't know why. He has hardly left his bedroom for the last two weeks since they got back. I'm so worried about him... everyone is worried about him.

I just need to keep him busy.

Joshua

With a heavy heart I put the last of Natasha's diaries into my duffle bag. I have wrapped them all in brown paper and then stacked them in leather shoeboxes. I need to get them out of the house without being detected.

For the last two weeks I have sat on our bed and read

every word written by my beloved and there is absolutely no way in hell I am going to let them become public property in an investigation. She has put her heart and soul onto the paper of these diaries and the level of intimacy that she writes about is nobody's business but hers and mine. There is absolutely no evidence in them of who did this to her and I will not let them tarnish her in any way with her most intimate thoughts released to the press. I throw my gym clothes on top of the boxed diaries and take a deep breath. Just let me get them out of the house without being intercepted. I have arranged a safety deposit box in another name across town and have a courier picking them up from the office mailroom, but I need to get them there first.

I throw the bag over my shoulder and head downstairs. "Good morning," I smile at everyone sitting around in the kitchen. They all look around at me in shock. I have hardly left my bedroom and now I'm shaved and in a suit ready for work. Unbeknownst to them I have a mission.

Bridget smiles warmly at me and jumps off her chair in excitement. "Are you going to work?"

I smile sympathetically. "Yes, Didge, I'm going to work."

She holds her hands as if in prayer. "That's good." she whispers hopefully.

I nod and smile again. Bridget really does want to see me through this. I don't think I have ever been so grateful for having her in my life.

"Joshua, it's too soon." My mother frowns.

"No, it's not," I snap. She better not even think about telling me what to do. My contempt for my mother and the way she previously treated Natasha is a huge hurdle for me at the moment, one I don't know how to get over.

I pick up the protein shake that Brigetta has made for me

from the kitchen counter and I head to the door. "See you all tonight," I call.

"Bye, bye," everyone replies, and I can hear the relief in their voices at my sudden turnaround.

I walk to the door with my duffle bag over my shoulder and Ben's eyes scan the bag when I reach the car.

"What's in the bag?" he asks.

"Gym gear," I reply flatly as I throw it into the back seat and slide in behind it.

He narrows his eyes at me. "You hate the work gym."

"I need a change," I snap, annoyed that I can get nothing past him.

"At the work gym," he repeats sarcastically.

"Will you just shut the fuck up and drive me to work? What's it to you where I work out?" I snap.

He shakes his head and raises his eyebrows questioningly and from the back seat I can almost hear his brain ticking.

After a very long and silent drive through the city we finally arrive at our destination and are buzzed through security. I head up to my office, Ben walking behind me and not letting me out of his sight, and I know if I try to get rid of him, he will only get more suspicious. I nod in greeting to all the staff I see on my way to my office. Nobody is game enough to actually speak to me. We get to the office and I smile.

"Thanks, Ben. I will call you if I need to go anywhere."

His eyes hold mine for a moment. "You okay?" He frowns.

I nod and readjust my suit coat. "Fine," I reply without looking at him—he's so onto me.

I wait for ten minutes until I am sure he has gone to see

his security staff down the hall and I slip out of my office and, carrying my duffle bag, disappear into the emergency stairwell. I need to get this package to the mailroom on level three. I run down the steps until I reach level three and take the package out of my bag and leave my overnight bag in the staircase. I exit the staircase and try to look as casual as I can carrying my precious packages. The address of the safety deposit is written on a label on the front, along with the delivery receipt for the courier. I even hacked a visa of a stranger last night to pay for the delivery.

I walk into the mailroom and see a young man I have never met before. "Hello," I smile casually.

"Hello," he replies as he keeps sorting the mail. Thank God, he doesn't know who I am.

"The courier is coming to pick up this package," I reply nonchalantly.

"Yeah, cool. Just put it with the other packages on the trolley at the end of the bay. The guy normally gets here in around half an hour," he replies without looking up again.

I nod and walk to the trolley at the end of the bay and hold my most precious possessions in my hand. God, this is risky. What if they get lost? I will never forgive myself. I drop my head as I reconsider my decision. No, Natasha wouldn't want anyone else to read these. She deserves respect in death, and they need to be somewhere safe. I put them into the basket and close my eyes in pain and then with renewed purpose and with my heart trying to beat out of my chest I walk out of the mailroom and back to my hell in the stairwell.

. . .

It's two o'clock and I shake my head as my email pings for what seems like the hundredth time today. I have just finished downloading all the videos and text messages from Tash off my phone into my cloud for lifetime protection. I can never lose those. I click open the email in annoyance, it's from Adrian.

Joshua Stanton/ Cc.Tiffany Nelson

As a matter of urgency please supply me with the training schedule for the next four weeks for the interns. Training schedules and timetables will be printed up tomorrow morning by Tiffany to be distributed tomorrow afternoon.

Tiffany, please block yourself tomorrow morning to have these completed by 12 pm for my perusal.

Adrian Murphy

I roll my eyes, fucker.

I storm into his office. "I know what you are doing," I snap.

Adrian is standing and looking through a file. His eyes don't leave his folder. "And what's that?" he replies sarcastically.

"Trying to overload me with work so I don't have time to think," I stammer, infuriated. "I can't have those schedules done today. I have put no thought into what I am doing."

His eyes look up from his folder. "Looks like you're working back then. Start thinking," he replies.

I narrow my eyes at him, and he looks at me blankly. "Go back into your office and start working on them. You know, finger on keyboard," he replies flatly.

"Fuck you," I murmur under my breath as I turn to walk out in annoyance and he smiles warmly, the door opens in front of me and Cameron walks in.

"Can we go to a bar?" he blurts out.

I smirk. "Why?"

He shakes his head angrily and drops into a seat at Adrian's desk. "So, the police have just turned up at both of your houses with search warrants," he replies.

I sit on the corner of the desk, and relief fills me that I got the diaries out just in time. I nod.

"What the hell for?" Adrian snaps.

Cameron shakes his head in frustration. "Evidence. Clues. I don't fucking know."

I stare straight ahead. I knew this was coming. I don't know why it's taken this long

"Where are the girls?" I ask.

"Abbie's dumbfuck cop root is one of the policemen doing the search, so she is following him around. Bridget is chucking a tantrum and not letting them touch any of Natasha's things."

I smile at the thought of Bridget telling them off—she's more like Natasha than we all know.

"Mum is crying and telling them to find the killer and stop wasting time searching the house," Cameron snaps.

"Seriously, I want to go to a bar and get fucking maggot drunk." He shakes his head. "I can't take one more day of this shit," he stammers

I smirk again. "I can't. I've got things to do," I reply. I think this is the most normal conversation I have had in a month.

Adrian buzzes Tiffany. "Tiffany, Joshua and I are leaving

for the afternoon and please ignore that last email I sent you. I have the dates wrong." My eyes meet his.

"Of course, Adrian," she replies.

"Maggot drunk sounds really good right now," Adrian snaps as he takes his jacket from the back of his chair and puts it on.

"Come on, Stan, we are out, and we are on it."

It's 8 pm and we are in a Mexican bar eating nachos as we drink margaritas in homage to my girl.

Cameron puts his hand up for another round.

"These suckers have a punch." Adrian frowns as he looks at his glass.

I nod. I'm feeling quite inebriated. "Yep," I stammer. "What do you reckon they were looking for?" Cameron

narrows his eyes as he goes over his conspiracy theory.

"I think they just want to see the surroundings that she lived in and stuff," Adrian replies.

"Willowvale though?" Cameron scoffs.

I scroll through my phone and notice I have an email I have been waiting for. My heart drops and I open it.

It's from the county council.

Dear Mr. Stanton

We are very sorry to hear of your loss and would like to extend to you our sincere condolences.

In regard to your application; your application has been successful and aligned with a class CVB license.

You have permission to bury your late wife on the property of Willowvale.

All preparations will need to be in accordance with regulations and carried out by a certified practitioner.

If you have any questions in regard to this matter, please contact our office during office hours.

Ray Cunningham

County District Court House

I drop my head.

"What are you reading?" Cameron asks.

I pick up my glass and drain it. "I have permission to bury Tash at Willowvale."

Their faces both drop.

"Too bad I don't have her body to bury," I sneer.

Cameron drains his glass and puts his hand up for another as I drop my head in my hands as my elbows rest on the table.

Adrian frowns as he thinks out loud. "Do you think they left her in the water?"

I shake my head as I think, and my eyes flick outside to the guards all waiting near the door.

"Yeah, I think so," Cameron answers. "She was asleep and wouldn't have felt anything. The level of Rohypnol found in her blood was much higher than in yours, although you were given it earlier than her."

I stare into space as I think and the feeling of overwhelming loss starts to register again. A sad silence falls over the table.

"At least she didn't suffer," Adrian whispers sadly.

"Do you think I should have a funeral for her now? I was hoping they would find her so I could do it properly." I frown.

Adrian shrugs. "Probably...I don't know."

"I think it would be good for her mother and Bridget if they had a funeral service," I mutter. "Might bring them some closure." The table falls silent again and the waitress brings us another round of margaritas and we take them thankfully. I wait until she leaves, and I raise my glass.

"I would like to make a toast." My thoughts go to the toast I was supposed to be making at our wedding and I blow out a deep breath. "My darling Natasha, today could have been a monumental day in our lives but instead I am sitting in a bar drinking your favorite drink and discussing your burial status." My eyes tear up. "I desperately wish we were drinking tea and celebrating our news," I whisper.

The boys both frown. "What news?" Cameron asks.

"Natasha's period was due today. We were trying for a baby," I reply on autopilot.

"Fuck," Cameron whispers as he runs his hands through his hair.

Adrian's eyes instantly tear up and he grabs my hand over the table. I sit still, unable to show any emotion. I have no tears left, nothing more I can give up. I am dead inside.

Cameron puts his elbow on the table and pinches the bridge of his nose as his tears form. "Do you think she was pregnant?" he whispers.

I shake my head. "I doubt it. We had only been trying for a week."

They both sit still, their sad eyes fixed on my face.

"She wrapped up her pill packet and the keys to the LA house and gave them to me for a wedding present. She wanted to move to Willowvale," I mutter flatly.

Cameron's haunted eyes watch me. "Joshua, I swear to you, if it's the last thing I do, I am going to find who did this."

Adrian nods.

The darkness overwhelms me. "And when you do, Cameron, it is going to be my hands that kill them," I whisper.

"Two wrongs don't make a right, Joshua," Adrian whispers, mortified.

I hold his eyes with mine. "No, they don't, but they can make me able to live with myself. She didn't deserve this. She wouldn't hurt a fly."

"Except you." Cameron smirks. "She loved fucking you up."

I smile broadly and nod. "Yes. Yes, she did."

"Yeah, you do look a bit like a fly." Cameron frowns. "A maggot even." Adrian smirks.

"Wasn't that the plan of the evening?" I smirk.

Cameron raises his glass. "To maggotism." He smiles.

I smirk and my dear friends and I raise our glasses:

"To maggotism."

It's 11 pm when we walk in the door. Bridget comes down the stairs on a mission.

"Are you for real?" she whispers angrily. "You couldn't come home? We have been here dealing with the police all day and you go to a fucking bar?"

Cameron shakes his head. "Fuck off, Didge. Not in the mood," he replies as we walk to the kitchen.

I sit at the kitchen counter as my head starts to slowly spin and Cameron makes himself some breakfast cereal.

"Where is everyone?" I ask.

"Abbie is out with the dick of a cop. Who I hate," she snaps.

Cameron holds his spoon of cornflakes in the air. "Me too," he chimes in drunkenly. "Hate him, hate him," he slurs.

"Our parents have gone to bed traumatized. Where's Ben?" she snaps.

Cameron and I exchange looks. "Why?" Cameron snaps. "Because I'm going to break his fucking neck, that's why." Cameron laughs and chokes on his cereal.

"Why now?" He laughs.

She narrows her eyes. "Because tonight when I texted you and you said you were at a bar, I thought it was a bad idea and so, I called Ben and he wouldn't pick up my call. Who in the hell does that guy think he is?"

Cameron points his spoon at the door and smiles stupidly. "You should go tell him off, in front of the other guards. Right now. Do it."

I drop my head and smile. Fuck Cameron is a troublemaker.

Bridget puts her hands on her hips angrily. "You just want to get rid of me, Dr. Dickhead."

Cameron points his spoon at her. "Bingo." He smiles as he shovels in his food.

"God, you're so fucking annoying," she snaps as she storms out the front to find Ben.

Cameron shakes his head and with a mouthful of food mumbles, "Poor prick, she'd be a bitch I reckon."

I smile and shake my head and then hear some male voices I don't know outside the front door.

"No, you cannot come in," I hear Bridget's raised voice reply.

Cameron and I frown at each other and I stand and make my way to the front door where I see four policemen talking to Ben and the security guards on the driveway. One of them catches my eye and immediately stops his conversation.

"Mr. Stanton." He nods.

"Hello, can I help you?" I ask.

"Yes, we would like to speak to you," the officer replies.

I frown. "Have you found her?" I ask hopefully.

The policeman hesitates. "No, I'm sorry we haven't." My heart drops.

"We would like to ask you some questions," he replies.

I roll my eyes. "This can wait till tomorrow," I reply. I'm half pissed and furious with these idiots. They are just going round in circles.

The men exchange looks, and I storm inside. For four weeks I have seen them dance around and tell me they have this investigation under control. What a joke. Nothing is under control.

They follow me into the house.

"Excuse me," Bridget snaps. "You were here all day and you are not coming in now. Come back tomorrow at a decent hour," she snaps.

They exchange looks again.

"Mr. Joshua Stanton, you are under arrest for the murder of Natasha Marx," the officer announces as he takes his hand-cuffs from his back pocket.

The room falls silent.

"You can't be serious!" Cameron yells.

"Anything you say can and will be used against you," he continues.

The two police officers walk over to me and I push one of them away from me in shock. "What?" I yell.

"He didn't do it, you idiots!" Bridget yells hysterically.

"Bridget, calm down," Ben whispers.

My father walks down the stairs.

"What's going on?" he asks.

"They are arresting Joshua," Bridget yells.

His face drops in horror and his eyes find me across the crowded room.

One of the policemen tries to grab my arm and I rip it from his grip. "Get away from me," I yell.

The policeman shakes his head. "Don't make this harder than it already is, Joshua."

I screw up my face. "Get the fuck out of my house," I yell.

Two of the policemen jump me and I struggle, and my mother starts to scream as she runs down the stairs.

"I didn't do anything," I yell.

"He's innocent!" Ben yells. "This is absurd."

I struggle to break free and I see the gun come from someone's belt.

"No!" Bridget screams as I fight.

"Mr. Stanton, come quietly or we will have to taser you." The policeman holding the taser gun yells.

"Get out!" Cameron starts to yell. "You are not taking him anywhere." He starts to struggle with the policeman holding the gun and one of the policemen pulls out his radio.

"Back up required," he snaps. The policeman tries to grab my hand again and I push him so hard he falls onto the floor.

From behind I am hit with an electric current so strong I fall to my knees as I hear the screams of my family. I am paralyzed.

"Stop it! Stop it!" Bridget screams. "You will kill him." She pushes the policeman in the back.

"No, no," Victoria, Tash's mum, yells as she runs down the stairs in her pajamas. "Bridget, stop it," she yells.

Next thing I know I am in handcuffs being dragged into the back of the police car to the sounds of screaming.

Electricity is running through my body like fire... burning me from within.

The door slams with a thud...and I am alone in the darkness.

CHAPTER 22

Adrian

I AM JUST DRIFTING off into sleep when my phone rings. "Hmm, go away," I murmur into my pillow. I'm frigging exhausted.

"Hello," I answer groggily.

"Get over here!" Cameron yells.

I sit up instantly. "What's happened?" I stammer. "What's he done?"

"Joshua got arrested for Natasha's murder," he yells.

With my heartbeat racing through my chest, I feel relief at that news—it could be worse. I'm half scared he's got something else in mind. Then the knowledge sinks in.

"What?" I frown. "Joshua?" I repeat.

"Who is our fucking lawyer?" Cameron screams.

Oh shit, I jump out of bed while rubbing my eyes. What now? "Um." I shake my head as I try to remember his name. "I'm on my way."

I hang up and get dressed as quickly as I can and call the

lawyer. Luckily, he has seen the news and is on his way to the police station now. How much more shit can we take?

Half an hour later, I arrive at Joshua's house and walk into the lounge room to find Bridget distraught and the mothers crying as they watch the news on the television.

Now on breaking news, Joshua Stanton, billionaire software developer has been arrested and charged with the murder of his wife, Natasha Stanton. Natasha went missing from their luxury yacht 26 days ago in what can only be described as bizarre circumstances. Many are likening this to the Robert Wagner and Natalie Wood case thirty years ago. In explosive allegations a love triangle had emerged between Natasha, her husband and Natasha's bodyguard only hours before her death. Police are yet to disclose the evidence they have found.

"Turn that shit off," Cameron snaps. I look around the room full of people, but there's no sign of Ben.

"Where's Ben?" I ask Bridget.

She shrugs. "I don't know."

I walk through the house in search of him. He's taking this hard and blaming himself for Natasha's death. It's not his fault; it's nobody's fault. I walk up the hall and the only light on in the corridor is coming from Joshua's garage. With a heavy heart I open the door and between the two cars I see Ben, his back to me and his head down.

"Ben," I call as I walk toward him.

He drops his head and doesn't answer me.

I walk around to face him, and he has tears streaming down his face.

Empathy fills me. "Ben," I whisper. He shakes his head, unable to speak.

I grab him in an embrace. "Ben, it's okay. This is not your fault."

"It is," he grinds out.

I pull back to look at his face. "Ben, pull your shit together. More than anytime in Joshua's life he needs you now to be strong and lead his security team."

He screws his face up as he tries to hold in the tears. "I don't know what to do," he whispers.

I run my hand down my face as I think—we are all so out of our depth.

He shakes his head. "I can't figure this out. I don't know how to figure this out, Adrian."

"Nicholas is a psychologist and may have an opinion on the suspects. He will be here tomorrow. We can work this out, Ben, but I need you with me."

His head stays down.

"Joshua and I, even Cameron, have full faith in you and the longer you sit around blaming yourself the longer the killer is walking free."

His haunted eyes meet mine.

"Get your fucking shit together and help us," I urge.

He nods.

"I mean it." He nods again.

"And talk to Bridget, she needs you more than ever and you're just being a prick."

He wipes his eyes. "I can't handle Bridget at the moment."

He shakes his head. "She's just screaming at me all the time and crying."

"Her sister was just murdered, Ben. What do you expect? You can't be that naïve as to think that she would take this well," I snap.

God, this guy is clueless when it comes to women.

He swallows as he listens and pulls his hands through his hair. "Man up, get out there and do what Joshua is paying you to do," I snap.

He nods with renewed purpose.

"We can do it, Ben, I know we can. We can find this person." He gives me a sad nod and walks toward the houseguests.

I blow out a deep breath. Now I just have to figure out what the hell I'm supposed to do next.

Joshua

I walk through the police station with my hands behind me in handcuffs. The officers all stop what they are doing and stare and I drop my head in shame. How could they think I did this to Natasha? I adored her. I wish it was me dead instead of her. I am ushered into a cell and a pair of orange overalls lie folded on the bed.

"Get changed, Mr. Stanton," the female officer says as she undoes the handcuffs behind my back. I hold my wrists in my hands as I stare at her. I don't think I have ever been so close to the edge. I'm about to lose it.

Stay calm, stay calm.

"I said get dressed," she snaps.

I frown. "What? Here?" I snap as I gesture to the twenty something people who can see into the cell through the glass wall.

She fakes a smile. "Get used to it. We save the privacy for non-murderers down the hall," she sneers sarcastically. The male guard snickers under his breath.

"We need to do a full body search," he replies.

"You are not touching me," I snap.

She rolls her eyes. "Just take all of your clothes off and put them onto the bed, pretty boy. Remove your underwear and socks and when we are satisfied you may put those two items back on."

I frown as my eyes flick to the bed. "I'm innocent," I state.

"Yeah, and I'm fucking Brittany Spears, asshole," she replies.

"Get out!" I yell.

She fakes a smile. "If you want, I can get the boys to hold you down while we do a cavity search. It's your choice," she sneers.

I am humiliated and drop my head again in shame. The male officer gives me a breath test and I blow into the tube. I'm going to fail. I've had a lot to drink.

The female officer takes a look at the reading on the machine and shakes her head. "Out celebrating that you got away with murder, were you?"

My eyes hold hers. I have never wanted to hit a woman so much in my life.

"Sorry to break up the party," she sneers. I step toward her.

"Get fucking dressed, asshole, before I taser your ass once more. If there's one thing I love to do is taser motherfucking wife beaters like you."

I narrow my eyes and undress in silence as their beady eyes watch me and they take my clothes and put them into a plastic bag.

"Watch?" she demands as she holds her hand out.

I remove my watch and pass it to her, and they look at it together. "How much did this watch cost?" she asks.

I glare at her. "More than your fucking house," I sneer. She narrows her eyes in disgust.

"You won't be questioned tonight because you are over the legal limit," the male officer replies. "Sleep it off. See you tomorrow." He throws a blanket onto the plastic bedding and they both leave the room.

The door locks behind them with a deafening sound.

Natasha

Four weeks earlier

The distant sound of a buzzer bounces off the walls around me and I struggle to open my eyes. Shit, my head hurts. My hands instinctively clutch my temples as I fight my heavy eyelids. My vision is blurred, and I continually blink to try and bring them into focus in the darkness. What the hell is going on? In my peripheral vision I see someone enter the room and attend to the thing making the buzzing noise. From what I can see it looks like a drip or something. I squint my eyes to try and see. Where the hell am I?

"Joshua," I whisper through a gravelly throat. "Baby, what are you doing?"

No answer.

I frown. "Joshua."

"Sshhh," a male voice whispers.

My heart rate picks up—that's not Joshua's voice.

"Joshua?" I call, more desperate. I blink my eyes frantically as I try to see. "Who are you? Where am I?" I stammer.

I feel my arm being lifted and something being injected into the drip. "Oww," I snap as I pull my arm from the grip.

"You are in the hospital, Natasha. Go back to sleep. Joshua is here," the gentle voice coos.

Oh, relief fills me, and I smile as I slip back into unconsciousness, my love is here. All is ok.

I wake to the dusting of sunlight kissing my face. It's early morning and my eyes search the space I am in. Where am I? Distant foggy memories of the night before and a man in the room make me sit up instantly.

Was that a dream?

My eyes dart around nervously. What the fuck? The carpeted room is huge and luxurious, with a king bed and bedside tables. On the far wall opposite the beds are six televisions hanging mounted from the ceiling and under that a small table for two and two high back chairs. I bring my hand up to wipe my hair from my face and see that my right wrist has a large bandage around it. What happened?

"Joshua?" I call.

I stand and slowly walk to the doorway to the right of the room and open it: a large bathroom complete with marble bath and shower. Where am I?

More urgently I walk to the large black door on the other side of the room and turn the knob.

It's locked. I jiggle the handle as I try to open the door. Panic sets in and I bang on the door.

"Hello," I call. "What's happening? The door is locked," I yell. "Joshua," I yell. "Ben."

No reply. Silence.

I walk back to the bathroom with my heart pumping hard. What's going on? Where am I? Where the hell is Joshua?

I look around the room nervously for my handbag. That's right, I left it at the wedding. Huh? I was on the boat. I sit on the edge of the bed while I go over the last thing I remember. We went to the wedding. The text. Max. My eyes widen and then we went to the boat and went to sleep. I frown. I don't understand. I stand and walk to the bathroom and look at myself in the mirror. I look like shit and what am I wearing? I look down at the black nightgown I am in. I don't own this. What the hell is going on?

I start to bang on the door frantically. "Hello. Is anybody there?" I scream. I start to panic. Where am I? Where is Joshua? "Ben," I yell. "Where are you?" I listen for an answer.

"Cameron," I scream.

Silence.

The televisions all come on at once. No sound. Just vision. I drop to the bed at what is unfolding in front of me. News channels, every one of them has a different channel. I frown as I try to make sense of this. I walk around the room once more and notice on one of the bedside tables a basket with six television remotes in it.

Huh? This is bizarre. I pick up one of the remotes and point it at the televisions to change the sound and the volume on one of the televisions goes up slowly. I try to change the channel but it doesn't work, just the volume.

I'm lost. I have no frigging idea what is going on. With the news playing in the background, I go into the bathroom and look in the bathroom cabinets. Hair products, face creams, moisturizer, tampons and pads. I slam the door shut in shock and storm back into the bedroom and swing open the closet doors. Clothes, underwear, pajamas. Whose bedroom am I in?

The television sounds.

Now to breaking news. Joshua Stanton's wife, Natasha, has gone missing from his luxury liner moored in the bay overnight. Mr. Stanton awoke to find Natasha missing and the boat covered in blood. Just whose blood still remains a mystery.

My eyes widen in horror. What?

The footage goes to an aerial shot from a chopper, of divers searching the water around the boat. Ben, Max and the body-guards are on the shoreline talking to police. Television cameras and reporters are everywhere. *Oh my God, what the fuck is going on?*

Joshua Stanton is apparently so distraught he has been taken against his will to County Hospital where concerned family members are by his bedside. Police are still unsure exactly what unfolded here but eyewitnesses report that the Stantons were involved in what appears to be a very public domestic dispute over Natasha's affair with her bodyguard last night.

Oh no. My hand goes over my mouth. Oh my God. I stand and start to pace. Oh my God. Oh my fucking God. I hold my hands together as if to pray. Joshua, oh my darling. I'm ok. I'm ok. My fury ignites and I start to pound on the door.

"What do you want?" I scream.

"Name the price, asshole," I yell. I pound on the door with all my might. The vision goes to the news story of us on another channel and I quickly run for the remotes and start picking them all up and aiming them at the television showing that story to work out which remote works with it. I finally find the right one and I turn it up. It shows the aerial vision of the boat again and then it goes to vision from the night before and footage from someone's phone of Joshua and me fighting in the parking lot. My stomach drops.

Joshua—did they hurt Joshua and that's why he's in the hospital? I start to bang on the door and then I run to the window. I am on a farm, paddocks as far as I see. No neighbors. I try to open the window, but it won't budge. I start to cry in frustration as I struggle with the heavy window. Oww, my arm is hurting. What happened to my arm anyway? I slowly unwrap the bandage and gasp when I see the huge cut across my wrist with large black stitches. God, it's a bad job.

My tears of fear start to fall. Whoever cut my arm didn't care if I bled to death as that's a main artery. With shaking legs, I walk into the bathroom and close the door. I throw down the lid and sit on the toilet. What do I do? For fifteen minutes I sit, frozen with fear.

Break the window. Yes, break the window. I look in the bathroom cabinet for something strong enough to do it with. Nothing but plastic bottles. I walk back out and look through the room for something, anything. God, why didn't I pay attention when I watched MacGyver all those years ago? There is a plant in the corner in a ceramic pot. I remove the plastic pot from the ceramic one and pick up the heavy pottery piece. I go back to the bed and take a run up and throw it at the window, but my arm hampers my throw, and it hits the windowsill and bounces off. I pick it up again and the door opens.

"What are you doing?" a huge man growls as he grabs my arm. I cower away from him, unsure of his intentions.

"What do you want?" I cry.

"I want you to shut your stupid mouth," he sneers.

"Help!" I scream as loud as I can over his shoulder into the house. "Help me!"

He raises his hand and hits me hard across the face and I fall to the floor and then he kicks me in my stomach and I scream in pain. "Scream again and I will fucking kill you," he growls as he picks my head up by the hair and slams my head against the ground.

I see the side vision of the door shutting behind him and the sound of it locking.

Tears roll down my face sideways to the floor. "Help me," I whisper through my pain. "Joshua, help me."

Joshua

I sit at the table next to Arthur, my lawyer, and opposite two police officers.

One policeman places two vials in a zip-lock plastic bag onto the table in front of us.

"Can you explain this, Mr. Stanton? Can I call you Joshua?"

My eyes narrow at the vial. "What is it?" I ask.

"You tell me," he says flatly.

I shake my head. "I'm not playing fucking charades. What is it?" I snap.

"Rohypnol," he says matter-of-factly. I frown.

"We found eight vials of it at your property Willowvale," the policeman continues.

My eyes meet Arthur's and I shake my head. "I don't know how they got there," I reply.

"'Course you don't, that's why your fingerprints are all over them." He fakes a smile.

"This is preposterous," demands Arthur. "He was drugged himself."

"Did you murder Miss Marx and then take Rohypnol to cover your crime, Joshua?" the policeman sneers.

I screw up my face. "No, I did not."

"Tell me about the prostitute in Australia who was murdered," the policeman asks as he sits back in his chair.

Arthur frowns at me in question.

Fuck. I swallow the lump in my throat. "I was being blackmailed by a prostitute. She had footage of me and her having sex and was threatening to go public. She was blackmailing many men and apparently one of them got sick of it and she was murdered. I don't know much about it," I reply.

Arthur rubs his face in frustration. He didn't know that before now.

The policeman cocks his head to one side. "Like you know nothing about the Rohypnol in your house."

I screw up my face. "It's obviously been planted there. You can't be that stupid," I snap.

The policeman sits back on his chair and folds his arms in front of him. "We can do this the long and hard way, or you can just admit it to now and go for a more lenient sentence. Either way we will have you charged with murder." He sneers as his eyes hold mine.

"Enough," Arthur snaps. "Application for bail is pending. There will be no further questioning until then."

"We are not finished."

"Yes, you are!" Arthur snaps as he bangs a folder onto the table in anger. "My client is innocent and unless you are going to ask some genuine questions and not seek a guilty plea, we won't be a part of this conversation."

The policeman narrows his eyes at me.

Arthur stands. "Joshua, I will see you at the bail hearing soon, son." His eyes stare at the policeman. "Show Joshua back to his cell." His eyes turn to me. "And Joshua, don't answer anything they ask you without me being present."

I nod gratefully. Thank fuck someone around here knows what the hell is going on.

The policeman stands furiously as Arthur leaves the room and I sit in silence. One of them pushes a security button alerting someone to come and get me.

The taller policeman leans over the desk and sneers. "Just because you have money doesn't mean you can get away with murder twice. We got you Stanton, and the evidence is rock solid."

I glare at him.

"Make yourself comfortable because you are not going anywhere soon."

Five hours later I am led into a courtroom by my cuffs. My father, Cameron, Adrian and Ben are seated at the back of the room and I nod gratefully at them for coming.

"All rise." We stand as the judge enters the room. He nods and then sits down and starts to read the file notes. He looks over his glasses and studies me.

"We are after bail, yes?" he asks.

"Yes, Your Honor," Arthur replies. "The accused poses no risk, and a substantial bail will be met."

"I object, Your Honor," the police prosecutor demands. "The accused is a cocaine addict with a criminal record of assault, aggravated assault and a history of aggression including cage fighting. He is currently under investigation for the murder of a prostitute in Australia who he was having sex with while he was in a relationship with the victim, Ms. Natasha Marx. We have photographic evidence of the level of abuse she suffered at his hands and video footage of him threatening to kill her bodyguard only hours before she went missing. The drug found in her system was found at one of his properties with his fingerprints on the vials. He has unlimited funds, his own private plane and is a huge flight risk."

I start to hear my pulse in my ears and my eyes flick to

Cameron who drops his head. Adrian gives me a weak smile to try and calm me and my father and Ben stay stone-faced.

I can't stay in jail. "Objection, Your Honor. You cannot discriminate against him because he is a wealthy man," Arthur argues.

"And nor can we let him get away with murder for the same reason," the prosecutor argues. "His victim has lost her life. Who is going to argue for her if we don't?"

"Miss Marx's body has not been recovered. She may be alive and being held hostage. Natasha Marx's family themselves are staying with Mr. Stanton. He is not a risk. He wants justice brought to the criminal who did this," Arthur argues.

"The sharks have eaten the body," the prosecutor yells. "She was dead before she hit the water—nobody can live through that blood loss."

"Enough," I scream as I stand. "Don't you fucking talk about her like she's nothing!" The guards push me back down in my seat. "Don't you dare!" I scream across the room through my tears.

The room falls silent and the judge studies me over his glasses.

I drop my head as I inhale deeply to try and calm myself and my racing heart.

The hammer sounds on the desk. "Bail is denied," the judge orders.

"Your Honor, please," Arthur argues.

"Decision made," the judge announces.

"Your Honor, I ask that we be given a quick trial. My client can not be in jail for months before this is heard. All evidence is circumstantial. He is an innocent man."

"Very well," the judge answers. "Court dates to be set within a month." He slams his hammer again and stands and leaves the room.

I sit still, stunned to silence. I'm not going home. I'm in jail. Cameron and Adrian run to the front of the courtroom to see me. "It's going to be ok," Cameron whispers as he puts his hand on my arm reassuringly. "It's ok, stay calm."

"It's ok, Joshua, we will get you out. You just be strong, ok," Adrian whispers. "We will get you out."

My eyes flick to Ben as the guards pull me to a standing position. He's the only one who can help me now. "Find him," I mouth.

He nods. "I will. I promise."

I am dragged by my cuffs out of the room and into my own private hell.

Natasha

I sit on the floor in the semi-dark room lit only by the lamp. I have a black eye from being hit earlier today and I think my rib may be broken, but I'm not sure. I have turned the televisions back on silent. If only I could turn them off completely. I'm unable to watch my sister and best friends cry at the water's edge as the police look for my body. Joshua is in the hospital. Who is with him? Who is taking care of him? I can't stand the thought of him going through this.

The door slowly opens, and I cringe, expecting that huge mean man, but instead I see something unexpected. A young sandy blond man smiles gently at me while carrying a tray of food.

"Hello, Natasha," he says softly. "I brought you something to eat." He places it nervously on the table and lifts the lid to show me pasta and dessert.

I frown and stay silent as I try to sum up this situation. What the hell is this guy doing here being nice? Am I in the fucking twilight zone?

He wrings his hands in front of him nervously and produces some Advil from his pocket. "I brought you some pain medication."

I frown in response. I'm so confused.

He stands nervously as I sit on the floor. "Are you going to eat?" he asks as he gestures to the plate.

I bring my knees up to my chest in defense and shake my head. "Natasha, I have to stay in here until you eat and if you don't I have to call Carl back in," he replies gently. I frown.

"He will hurt you. Please eat," he urges.

I swallow my fear of the animal who was in here earlier. I

have no doubt that he is the one who has been assigned to kill me when they are ready.

"What am I doing here?" I whisper.

He looks down at the food and puts the lid back over it. "Don't ask me questions." He holds my arm up, undoes my bandage, looks at the stitches and then wraps it back up.

"Please, I beg you. Please help me. Let me use your phone to call the police," I whisper.

"Stop it," he snaps.

I shake my head nervously and stand quickly. "Please, please. My family are looking for me. They are frantic."

He shakes his head nervously and leaves the room and I hear the click of the lock.

I close my eyes in frustration and slowly sit at the table and look at the food in front of me. I can think of nothing worse than eating right now. I put my hand on my chest. Joshua would not be eating. What pain is he going through? I need to get out of here. I need to get to him. Who is doing this? I look back at the food. I am hungry. I need to stay strong. I slowly eat the food that has now gone cold and I take two of the painkillers with some water. This is a nightmare. I pace through the room for another hour as I wrack my brain for some answers. So, there are two men here and I am being looked after. Why?

Ransom, they want money. If Joshua is in hospital who will they send the ransom note to?

I have an hour-long shower as I wrack my brain, trying to work out who is behind this. I get out and look through the dresser for some pajamas. A pair are folded in the top drawer and I shake my head as I put them on and lie on the bed. I have no idea what the hell is going on. I can only hope the demands gets through to the right person. God, what a mess. I look back up at the television and see a different angle of the crime scene being filmed from the chopper and I frown at the screen as I sit forward. Is that Jesten standing near the water in the crowd?

The camera shot moves, and he moves out of focus. I flick to the other television that is ten minutes behind the first news and I wait for the story to come back on. I stand closer to the screen and the story comes on.

There. Right there by the water. Jesten. Jesten is at the crime scene. What the hell is he doing in America?

CHAPTER 23

ADRIAN

I STAND NERVOUSLY at the terminal waiting to see that face. It feels like a lifetime since I saw Nicholas last. My mind drifts to the last time he came to my office and I couldn't even look at him. I knew then that if I made eye contact with him it would be all over.

I frown as my eyes stay focused on the ground.

Everything happens for a reason and maybe the reason Nick came into my life was to help me work out who killed our beautiful Natasha and how to prove Joshua innocent. This is the biggest challenge I have ever faced. I'm so grateful that he has come to help me and that I won't be facing it alone.

A deep sadness sweeps through my body. I've never felt like this before. I can't believe Natasha's dead—how can she be dead?

I'm so gutted. I can't even imagine how my dear friend Joshua is feeling. He lost his soulmate and now the world thinks he killed her. The media coverage on this story is just crazy. If there was anyone in the world who didn't know who Joshua Stanton was before, they do now. Every channel on every platform has hourly reports about Joshua and his past. The stories they are digging up are scaring even me. My eyes flick back to the clock on the wall for what feels like the hundredth time. Nicholas's plane is delayed. For some reason the image of Joshua and Natasha dancing at that fancy dress ball we went to in Sydney keeps running through my mind. It has been for days. *Why that image?* The way they looked at each other, the way he held her. I keep remembering him swinging her around, her carefree laughter and the deep love apparent in their eyes. How will he ever recover from this? How do you ever fill a hole so deep?

I am pulled from my thoughts as the doors open and Nicholas comes walking through. His smile broadens when he sees me. He gently leans down and kisses me on the cheek before pulling me into an embrace and I hold onto him tightly and close my eyes. "Thank God," I murmur.

He pulls out of our embrace and kisses my forehead. "I'm here now," he whispers into my hair as he senses my inner turmoil.

I smile and nod, embarrassed that I have just revealed how much I need him at the moment, and I take his laptop from him and we walk toward the luggage terminal.

"Did you have a good flight?" I ask.

He smirks. "Not really. Fifteen hours on a plane is never good." I nod and smile nervously. He's still beautiful—nothing has changed since I saw him last. I feel like I have known him for years and yet we only spent that month together. It's weird the connection we have. Why do I feel like this?

His eyes linger on my face a little too long. "It's good to see you," he murmurs.

Emotion overwhelms me and I feel like bursting into tears. "It's good to see you too, Nicholas."

We wait for his luggage in silence and I can feel my nerves rising. "I've booked you into a hotel," I reply.

His eyes meet mine. "I'm not staying in a hotel," he responds. I frown in question.

"I'm staying with you, Adrian."

"Nick." I shake my head in frustration. I should have known he would do this.

"In the spare room. There is nothing sexual about this visit. I am here to help you find who did this and to handle the press. That is all. I am a man supporting my dear friend through one of the toughest times of his life. My mind is far from sex, Adrian."

I smile softly. "Thank you," I whisper and after a moment of holding his eyes I add, "So is mine."

Joshua

I get out of the car with chains on my hands and feet. It's just on dark and I have been transferred from the police station to the prison. I have never been so terrified. I know what goes on in these places and it is not fucking going on with me. God help the bastard who tries it. The adrenaline has already started to pump heavily through my veins. I'm angry, so angry I can't see straight. Not only has the person stolen my beautiful Natasha's life, they are now stealing mine as well. This was a planned set-up. Their aim all along was to frame me for their crime. I am going to rip the life from their bodies quicker than they can say the word die.

"This way." The guard ushers me toward the doors and into the office where I am fingerprinted again and inducted into the system. Eventually, after an hour of paperwork, I am led into a long corridor lined with cells.

"Oh yeah." A big bald man calls, "Looky, looky what we have here." He purrs.

I glare at him through the bars and keep walking down the hallway to the collective sound of wolf whistles. Oh my God, this place stinks of body odor, cleaning fluid and sex, and my stomach rolls at the thought. Eventually we get to the end of the corridor and the guard slides opens the barred door with a key and holds it open. My eyes search the space: a small single bed with a plastic mattress on one side and a stainless-steel toilet with no toilet seat and a sink next to it on the other. No windows, no doors. My eyes close in pain. I can't stand the thought of being locked up in here. I feel claustrophobic. I can't stand it. Don't leave me in here. No.

"In," the guard grunts.

I bite my bottom lip to try and stop myself from losing it. "In," the guard repeats.

I hang my head and slowly enter the small cell. He undoes my handcuffs and feet chains and gives me a small smile. "Keep to yourself," he whispers quietly. "Don't get into any trouble and you will be rewarded."

I nod and drop my head.

"I will bring you some blankets. Have you eaten?" he asks. I shake my head with my eyes cast down. Food is the absolute last thing on my mind.

"I will bring you back some food," he replies, but hesitates before he leaves the cell, and my scared eyes rise to meet his.

"You will be okay," he says reassuringly. "Keep to yourself," he repeats as if trying to warn me about something.

I nod and drop my head again. Another guard comes up the aisle pushing a trolley and takes off some blankets and passes them to the guard and he puts them on the end of the bed in a folded pile. He then takes a tray of food and puts it on the bed.

I stand at the doorway and look down the hall. I need to run. I need to get so far away from this horrible place and have it wiped from my memory forever. My heart starts to race at the thought of being locked in here. I can't handle it. I'm going to go crazy.

The guard's eyes watch me closely as if he's seen this many times before. He must know when a man is close to the edge.

"Just eat your dinner and go to sleep," he says. I drop my head again.

"Just eat your dinner and go to sleep," he repeats, somehow knowing that those words will calm me.

I nod reluctantly.

"Just eat your dinner and go to sleep," he says softly as he closes the door behind me. I swallow the lump of fear in my throat as I hear the key turn in the lock. His eyes hold mine for a moment through the bars and I want to beg him to let me out. I'm innocent. I didn't do this.

He gives me a sympathetic smile. "Joshua, just eat your dinner and go to sleep," he repeats again as he gestures to the bed.

I nod and find those words more comforting than he will ever know as I watch his back disappear down the long corridor.

I turn toward the bed and see the silver tray on the end

and repeat the words in my head. Just eat your dinner and go to sleep. My heart is racing, and I feel like I am about to have a heart attack. I keep repeating those words again and again in my head as I cling onto them for a lifeline and as if on autopilot I do just that. I eat the cold dinner and make the bed with the linen they have supplied, and I lay down knowing that the only relief I will ever have in my life again is when I dream of my precious girl and her unwavering love. She is with me. I can do this.

I wake cold and shivering as I listen to the sound of skin slapping as two people have sex somewhere down the hall. They are both groaning in pleasure and I somehow find comfort in knowing that it is consensual. How has this happened? From the bed I look around at my surroundings. This place is a fucking shithole and my eyes glance across the hall to see a young man standing with his arms through the bars, staring at me. God, how is he eighteen? He looks fifteen at a pinch. I frown. How do people fall into this life?

"What's up?" he says.

I nod in response but don't reply. "I'm Jarvis," he calls.

I nod again. I'm not in the fucking mood to talk shit. Just go away. An alarm sounds and the doors all slide open in tandem and everyone starts to walk down the hallway to the right. I lie still, frozen. What the hell is going on?

"Breakfast," the kid calls.

I don't want to go anywhere. I stay lying in bed. The kid walks into my cell. "What's your name?" he asks.

"Fuck off," I snap.

He smiles. "Come on, fuck off. Your breakfast is ready." My eyes flick to him.

"Shouldn't you be in juvie?" I mutter.

He smirks. "Been there, done that." He waits for me to get out of bed and when I don't, he shakes his head. "First time?" he asks.

I turn my face away from him.

"If you don't eat now, that's it," he replies.

I continue looking at the wall to escape his gaze.

"Starve then." He sighs and walks down the hall. I lie alone in the evacuated cells and for the first time since arriving I feel like I can breathe. Personal space—I never knew I needed it so badly. I can't be in here. I can't fucking stay here. I feel my anxiety rise as fear grips me. I sit up and throw my legs over the side of the bed and put my head into my hands as my elbows rest on my knees. I take deep breaths to try and slow my heartbeat down.

"You have a visitor," the guard calls from my door. "Who? Me?" I frown as I look up.

"Yes, you. Hurry up and I will take you down," he replies.

I nod and pull on my overalls and follow him down the hall and through a security door and into a series of offices. He opens one of the doors and I am led to a desk next to a glass security screen. A phone is attached to the counter.

"Sit," the guard murmurs.

I fall into the seat and he exits through the door behind me. I watch the door in the office on the other side of the glass. Hopefully Ben has found something and is here to get me out of here. The door opens and instead of seeing one of my friends I see the face of the asshole I hate. My fury instantly ignites, and I stand so fast my chair falls back and hits the ground and I punch the glass. He spits at my face and it hits the glass. It's the guy Natasha nearly slept with, the cage fighter. He picks up the phone and I just glare at him.

"Pick up the fucking phone!" he yells.

I stand still, furious. I feel like a caged animal.

"Pick it up!" he screams and slaps the glass with an open hand.

I stand and go to walk out the door behind me and it dawns on me, what's he doing in America? Did he do this to Natasha?

I turn back to him and narrow my eyes. Was it him? Hate fills my every pore and I pick up the phone and hold it to my ear.

"What did you fucking do?" he sneers.

"What did you fucking do?" I reply. Fuck, I hate this asshole. I punch the glass in front of his face again and he doesn't flinch.

"Me? Are you kidding? I'm here to find her," he shakes his head in disgust at me.

I fake a smile. "Convenient you are in the country when she goes missing. Where is she?" I yell.

The guard comes in the door behind me. "What's going on in here?" he asks. "Keep it down."

I turn to look at him and shake my head angrily as I try to control myself.

"You make me sick. She didn't want you, so you fucking killed her. You gutless prick!" he sneers.

"I didn't touch her. I would never hurt her," I murmur as my eyes fill with tears. I can't take any more. I'm at my breaking point.

He stays silent as he watches me, and he frowns as he processes my words.

My eyes hold his as I hold the phone to my ear and a tear runs down the length of my face and I swipe it angrily away.

"She should have stayed with you. She would be still alive now if it wasn't for me," I whisper through my hurt.

His face falls as he watches me. "I know," he replies.

I let her down. I led Natasha into a lifestyle where I knew she would be in danger if she stayed with me and yet I was too selfish to let her go. What have I done? He is right —this is all my fault. I put my head in my hands and start to weep uncontrollably. I don't want him to see me like this. I stand and go to the back of the room and bang on the door.

"Guard," I yell hysterically.

The door opens and the guard's eyes flick between me and my visitor and he frowns in question. "I'm ready to go," I murmur, almost panicked.

He nods and leads me out of the room.

Adrian

I walk into the jail reception area with Ben and Cameron. We are trailed by three guards. Cameron walks up to the glass window at the office. "I would like to see Joshua Stanton, please," he announces.

"Sure, just a minute," the receptionist replies flatly. She types and reads something on her computer monitor.

"He has a visitor with him now," she informs us.

Cameron's eyes flick back to us. Who would be visiting him? Holy mother, someone after a ransom. "Can I go in?" Cameron mutters as he gestures to the door.

"No, only one visitor at a time. You will have to wait," she replies in a monotone.

Cameron nods and takes a seat next to us. "Who would be visiting him?" he whispers.

"I don't know," Ben whispers furiously.

I sit back in my chair nervously, oh shit. This is like a movie, but worse.

"Do we know what this maniac from Australia looks like?" I whisper to Ben.

Ben looks at the door stone-faced and clenches his jaw. "Off by heart," he murmurs.

Oh God, perspiration starts to form on my brow. I could never be a cop. I would be hopeless at this stuff. We sit for ten minutes in silence as we wait for someone to walk out.

"Cameron, did you ask her who it was?" I whisper.

He frowns in question. "Did you ask her who the visitor was?" I repeat.

He shakes his head.

"Why don't you go and ask her," I whisper.

"Shut the fuck up," Cameron snaps. "You go ask."

Oh shit, I look at the door in anticipation. "What happens if it's him? What do we do?" I whisper to Ben.

"I'm going to shoot him," he whispers angrily.

I frown and swallow the lump in my throat. "That's what I thought," I whisper, horrified, in reply.

Cameron's eyes meet mine and we wince at each other. This is going to end badly, I just know it. Finally, the door opens and the face I am seeing is not the one I ever imagined. It's Natasha's friend, the one who Joshua fights with. They hate each other. Cameron and I sit still, dumbfounded.

Ben rises immediately from his chair. "We need to talk," he snaps at the guy.

"What's his name again?" I whisper.

"Fuckwit," Cameron whispers angrily.

"That's right," I reply as my eyes stayed glued on him.

The arrogant bastard walks right past us and out the front door, and Ben follows him out.

"Oh God," I mutter to Cameron as he storms out after them. I stand in the foyer for a moment and watch them through the window. God. Fine—I storm outside to see what's going on.

"What are you doing here?" Ben snaps.

"Visiting a murderer," he sneers.

"Fuck you," Cameron spits. "You've got a hide." He steps forward in anger and I grab his suit jacket from behind. This guy would kill Cameron in one punch.

"What are you doing in America?" Ben snaps.

"I came to try and stop Natasha from marrying this wanker but I was a day too late. The bastard murdered her before I could get to her."

We all watch him. Is he telling the truth?

He smiles. "How cute of you all to wait outside for him. Too bad his asshole is being tag teamed right now."

Oh no, pain runs through me. He won't cope with that, he could never cope with that.

"How would you know?" Cameron snaps,

"I'm a fucking prison guard, you imbecile. I know what happens in these places," he replies.

Ben's eyes widen as realization sets in. "That's right, you worked at the prison where Natasha met Coby Allender, didn't you?" he asks.

"Yeah, so?" he replies arrogantly.

"They have made a definite link to Coby Allender and the break-ins at Natasha's apartment. We think he may have done this. The person who broke into Tash's apartment visited Coby in jail. There is a warrant out for his arrest."

The guy frowns as he thinks.

"But Allender's still in jail?" he asks confused.

Ben nods. "Yes, they think this is the accomplice they have been searching for."

He frowns again. "So why is cockhead in jail then?"

"He's been set up and things have been planted in his house. He didn't do anything."

He shakes his head angrily. "I don't believe that," he snaps.

"Can you come back to my office and fill me in on what you know about this Allender?" Ben asks.

"No. Fuck off. Why should I?" he snaps.

"For Natasha, that's why," Cameron replies softly. "We need to find her body so we can bury her. She deserves to come home and rest in peace."

My eyes tear up and I drop my head.

The four of us all stay silent as our thoughts go to our beautiful Natasha.

"Where is your office from here?" he sighs, defeated.

"In LA," Ben replies. "I will drive you and then drop you back here to get your car."

He thinks for a moment and hesitates. "I will just follow you. I am staying in LA tonight anyway," he murmurs.

Ben looks back at us. "You two go and see Joshua and I will go with..." he frowns, and his eyes flick back to the man. "What's your name again?" he asks.

"Jesten," the guy replies. "Jesten Miller."

Cameron and I go back inside to see Joshua and go back up to the counter. "Can we go in and see him again now?" Cameron asks.

The receptionist looks up from her computer. "What was the name again?" she asks.

"Joshua Stanton," Cameron snaps, annoyed that she doesn't remember.

"Take a seat." She gestures to the waiting lounge and we both sit down.

· · ·

Fifteen minutes later we hear her voice. "Excuse me, gentlemen," she calls. We both stand and immediately go to the desk.

"I'm sorry. He has declined your visit," she says flatly.

"But I didn't tell you who we are. I didn't give you my name." Cameron frowns.

"He is not accepting any visitors."

We both frown at her in horror. What does that mean?

"He doesn't want any visitors," she repeats.

"He would want to see me," Cameron says softly. "He's not thinking right. I'm worried about his safety in here," he mutters.

She rolls her eyes. "Sorry." Her eyes go to the man standing waiting in the line behind us. "Can I help you?" she calls.

The drive back to LA is made in complete silence. Both Cameron and I are filled with fear for Joshua. Why wouldn't he see us? Has something happened overnight? The weight of our thoughts are apparent but neither of us want to say anything out loud for fear of making it come true. He's on the edge, we know that. How much can a man take before he hits breaking point? We pull into the underground parking garage of our offices and head up to level 33, the new headquarters for our security team as we try to unravel this conundrum. Who killed Natasha and why has Joshua been framed?

Joshua's large office now has chairs and tables scattered throughout and there are five whiteboards at the front with notes scribbled on them. Each board is for a different suspect, and each board is filled with evidence. Why can't we work this out? We walk in to find Ben standing in front of the boards and Jesten, Max, Nicholas and six of the security team seated as they listen to Ben speak. He nods as we enter the room and sit.

"You weren't long." Ben frowns.

Cameron's angry eyes flick to Jesten. "He wouldn't see us. What did you fucking say to him?" he sneers.

Jesten screws up his face. "Don't speak to me like that or you will be eating through a straw."

"Will somebody please explain to me why this fuckwit is sitting in my brother's office?" Cameron yells, outraged.

Max shakes his head and Ben pulls his hands through his hair in frustration.

"Fine," Jesten snaps. "I will go." He stands angrily. "I don't want to be here anyway."

"Sit down," Nicholas yells. "You are not going anywhere until I question you about Allender. Do not dare start this shit now. All of you!"

The room falls silent and my heart does a double beat.

Nicholas is taking charge. Finally, someone is taking charge.

Jesten sits down angrily.

"Go on," Nicholas says calmly to Ben.

"Okay." Ben nods and pulls himself back into concentration mode. "Here are the suspects that we know of. Suspect one: Coby Allender. Natasha met him at the prison, and he took a liking to her." He gestures to Jesten. "Hopefully Jesten Miller who was a prison guard at the prison he is in can shed some light on this situation. Allender has an accomplice on the outside and Natasha had her apartment broken into before we left Sydney and some very personal things were taken. Allender told her he had them, and it was brushed off as scare tactics, however the items were returned months later, and we now know that this man..." He puts a picture from the security vision up on the screen of the dark-haired man leaving Natasha's apartment. "Has gone to see Allender in jail and a definite link was made for the first time. When police went to arrest him, he wasn't there but they found photographs of Natasha and the other victims strewn all over his apartment. These men raped, tortured and killed twelve young women." Ben points to the photos of the dead young women along the bottom of the whiteboard; their bodies were mutilated.

My eyes flick to Nicholas as he frowns in horror at this news. Jesten shakes his head in disgust.

He runs his finger over the photographs of the dead women. "The other women in the photographs have all been murdered along with Natasha but..." He hesitates as he takes a drink of water. "Natasha's disappearance does not fit the murders of the other young girls and, to be honest, I am having a hard time believing that this murder was carried out by the same men." He shakes his head. "It was a different country and we know that this particular man is not wealthy and hasn't left the country on his own visa. However, he could be travelling under an alias."

Jesten rubs his hand over his face.

"Natasha's murder involved drugging, a boat and getting around security guards. I think it was out of their league."

We all nod.

"Suspect two," Ben continues. "James Brennan. Joshua recently found out that his father is not his biological father, and that his biological father has been blackmailing his mother and beating her for many years."

"Bloody hell," Jesten whispers and I bite my bottom lip to stifle my smile.

"He has extorted millions of dollars from her and Joshua had recently demanded the money back or he was going to the police. This man stands to lose everything and with Joshua in jail for murder, he is a free man. He hasn't been seen for five weeks by his family as he is on a business trip. He has the money and motive to carry something like this out. We have just this morning traced his visa to London and have consequently hired intelligence to try and find him over there. They will be trailing him until we find out more."

We all nod. I think it's him.

"Suspect three," Ben continues. "Joshua was mugged in a suspected hit just over twelve months ago." He plays the security tape from the garage and we all sit and watch it. God, it's violent. Jesten rearranges himself uncomfortably in his seat as he watches. The three men attack Joshua, he fights back and then one of them pulls a gun, but the police siren sounds, and they jump in his Aston Martin and speed away. "We don't know who ordered that hit."

"How do you know it was a hit?" Jesten asks.

Ben replays the tape and points to the man at the back of the screen. "See, he has a gun."

Jesten frowns. "He was just pissed that Joshua was whipping their asses. If it was a hit they would have just shot him straight up."

Nicholas nods as he thinks.

"True," Ben replies. "But then when Joshua was in the hospital four days later, they showed up—the same three men showed up there." He produces photos of the three men in the hospital. "If it was random why were they at the same hospital unless they were looking for him? It could just be a coincidence, but we have no way of knowing."

We all nod.

"Suspect four. Four years ago, Joshua's company developed an app and sold it to a company for millions. Unbeknownst to him another man had made a similar program and the company was in talks with him first. They bought Joshua's instead of his. His name is Julian O'Reilly. He has tried to kill

Joshua on three occasions and Adrian on one. This is why bodyguards follow the two of them everywhere they go."

Nicholas's horrified eyes meet mine.

"Each time it has been by a shooting in a public area. Adrian was coming out of a restaurant when he was shot at and Joshua the same the other three times. Luckily, Julian's a hopeless shot. He has not been seen for eighteen months and is mentally unstable. He has paranoid schizophrenia and as far as the pharmaceutical records go, he is not taking any medication. His estranged wife and children have no idea of his whereabouts."

"Suspect five," Ben carries on.

"Oh, for fuck's sake," Jesten snaps. "You can't be serious." He runs his hands over his head. "How many people hate this prick?"

Cameron glares at him and I drop my head to hide my smile. "Joshua hooked up with a woman in Sydney a few times before he got back with Natasha. She came to his house a few times. Then months later when he was in a relationship with Natasha, she contacted him and demanded money. She had filmed them together and was going to take it to the press."

Jesten laughs. "Dumbcock."

"It was revealed that she was a high-end prostitute and was blackmailing many men for money. Before it came to a head she was found murdered, hogtied and shot in the back of the head."

"Bloody hell." Nicholas sighs. "This is ridiculous." I nod and raise my brow. It sure is.

"Why is she a suspect?" Cameron frowns.

Ben shakes his head. "We don't think that—she's dead." He raises an eyebrow at Cameron and the room snickers at Cameron's stupid comment.

"Oh right," Cameron answers, embarrassed.

"But we don't know who murdered her and if someone else is under investigation maybe they are throwing off the scent by setting Joshua up?" He shrugs. "It's a long shot, but we are clutching at anything."

"We are also currently screening security footage of one of Adrian's ex-boyfriends, Ross," Ben adds.

I frown, huh? What the hell? I didn't know this.

"Joshua and he hated each other so we are just going through old videos of his house to try and piece together any more information available. He mentioned in passing conversation the attempted hit on Joshua but there was no way he could have known that. I want to know how he does."

CHAPTER 24

Natasha

I PACE backwards and forwards in my room as I try to work out who has me captive and what the motive is. It's been twenty-four hours and nothing has been said to me other than don't make Carl angry or he will hurt me. They gave me a blood transfusion.

Why? Why are they keeping me alive? They must be going to ask for money but according to the television reports Joshua is still in the hospital. Maybe Adrian is organizing the money? I have seen Cameron on television at the hospital, and he looks frantic. It's seriously not worth having money to go through this. I hear the key in the door and stand back in fear over near the bathroom door.

The young man puts his head around the door and gives me a stifled smile and then picks the tray up off the ground and brings it in. "Lunchtime," he says gently.

I stand still watching him. What the hell is he doing here?

He's a nice guy, I can tell.

"Can I look at your arm, please?" he asks.

I swallow my fear and walk over to him and he unwraps the bandage slowly.

"Are you a doctor?" I ask.

He shakes his head. "I'm a medical student," he replies.

"Did I have a blood transfusion?" I ask.

He nods with his head down, unable to make eye contact with me, and produces something from his pocket. "I have some antibiotics. You need to take some tablets so that you don't get an infection."

My eyes search his. "Is your job here to keep me alive?" I ask. He swallows nervously.

"Because they cut my main artery. I could have died," I whisper. He frowns as he wraps my arm back up. "I know and I'm sorry. I don't know why they did that, but it's my blood we gave you. You don't need to worry."

"Do you know who I am?" I whisper.

He keeps his head down and turns to attend to my food. "Yes," he murmurs.

"Can you help me?" I whisper.

His eyes flick to the window and he looks at something above the windowsill. I frown. Fuck, I'm being filmed. I nod softly to acknowledge what he has just told me. Okay. Shit.

He takes the lid off my meal and with shaky hands gets out some salt and pepper.

"Can I get you anything else?" he asks softly.

"Diet coke," I ask hopefully.

He smiles. "You want some diet coke?" he asks, surprised.

I nod and give him a stifled smile. If I'm going to get out of here alive he is my only chance. I need to make friends with him.

"I don't have any here now but when Carl takes over, I will get you some and bring it back."

I nod. "Are you staying in the house here?" I ask.

He shakes his head. "No, we are doing shifts watching you."

I nod and bite my bottom lip as I think. I gesture to the camera with my head. "Is the monitor in this house?" I whisper with my head down away from the camera.

"Yes," he replies.

"Are there others elsewhere?" I whisper with my face away from the camera again.

His eyes meet mine and he shrugs. "Not sure," he mumbles.

God, like me he has no idea what's going on!

"I will be back with the diet coke," he says as he moves toward the door.

"Can you stay with me for a while?" I whisper. "I'm scared." My eyes search his for compassion. "Please tell me who you are working for."

"I can't, Natasha. I'm sorry." He sighs.

"I have money. I can give you more money than what they are paying you. Please," I beg.

His eyes flick nervously to the windowsill again and he shakes his head. "Stop talking to me or they will punish you," he whispers angrily.

My heart rate picks up. "How?" I whisper. "How are they going to punish me?"

"Carl has permission to do what he wants with you if you give us a hard time."

I step back from him in fear.

"And you know what he wants," he replies flatly.

Tears fill my eyes. Oh God, I'm going to be raped by that animal.

"Do you understand what I'm telling you?" he asks.

I drop my head and nod and I hear him quietly leave the room. I sit at the table someplace between life and death, evil and hell. They are going to rape me and film it to torture Joshua with the footage. That's why I'm being kept alive. My nightmare is real. What if it's more than one man like in my dream? Nine. Oh fuck, I close my eyes in fear. I have to get out of here. Adrenaline starts to pump the fear through my blood. I walk into the bathroom and close the door behind me and start to pace back and forth. Cameras, cameras, I need to check for cameras. I start to search the ceiling and walls, what does a camera even fucking look like? I get up and stand on the vanity, so I am closer to the ceiling. I can't see anything. I run my hand around the inside edge of the mirror, and I walk into the shower and check out all the tapware, nothing. I have to check out the one he told me about in the other room, so I know what I'm looking for. I walk back into the other room and glance at my dinner sitting on the table. I need to act normal, so they don't get suspicious. I sit down slowly at the table and start to eat my lunch while my brain is running at a million miles per hour. What do these idiots want? They want to torture Joshua... so they are going to torture me and make him watch.

Well, I've got news for them. Like hell they are.

My knee bounces nervously as I think. I need a plan. My eyes widen as a new idea comes to my brain. What if they lure Joshua here with the pretense of rescuing me and then kill him? Am I the bait?

Fuck. Think, Natasha. Think.

Two of the televisions that were not on before start to roll and I pick up my lunch and move to the bed to see what is coming on. These assholes are trying to fuck with my head.

Fury ignites deep inside me. If anyone is going to be fucking with anyone's head around here it's going to be me.

I watch as the two screens light up and I frown at them. What is this? I can't make out where they are. I watch the one on the left and then I see Brigetta walk past carrying a basket of laundry. My eyes widen in horror. This camera is from inside Joshua's house and that's his lounge room. My eyes instantly flick to the other screen. Oh my God. My stomach drops. That's our bedroom. These people have been in our house. My heart starts to pump heavily and just when I think it can't possibly get any worse, I see myself walk into the room. I watch myself slowly get undressed. Oh my God, how long has this camera been in our room? Joshua walks in and starts to talk to me, and I laugh out loud. I run to the remote-control box and start to scramble through, looking for the right remote. I point them all frantically at the screen as I try to turn up the volume, and I finally find it.

Joshua comes up behind me and wraps his arms around my chest. "Tell me how you want to be fucked tonight, my precious girl?" he whispers darkly as he pulls my hair to one side of my neck to give his mouth greater access. He cracks his neck hard.

I hold my hand over my mouth in horror, oh God, no.

With my mortified heart thumping though my chest I watch as I drop to my knees and pull his pants down and start to take him in my mouth as he holds onto the back of my head tenderly.

"You're the one who's getting fucked tonight, Stanton," I purr. I start to deep-throat him double time and his head throws back in pleasure as he starts to ride my mouth hard, his hands gripping my hair at the back of my head.

I drop to the bed in shock. How long? How long have they been watching us having sex? This is horrifying.

"On your knees," Joshua's voice purrs. "I need to slide my

cock into the beautiful tight cunt of mine." His fingers go to between my legs as he prepares me for his onslaught.

Oh my God, I put my hands on top of my head as I watch Joshua stand behind me as I kneel on the bed and with both of his hands on my shoulders slowly slide into me.

"You're so hot," he growls. "I'm going to blow inside you so damn hard tonight, my precious girl."

"Give it to me," I whimper. "Every last drop," I breathe. He bends over the top of me and kisses me aggressively.

For some sick reason I feel my arousal start to lift. God. I drop my head in dismay at this situation. What the hell is going on here? This is messed-up mind-games shit. My eyes flick back to the screen and we are hard at it, Joshua's beautiful body riding mine hard. God, so hard. I never realized how rough we are.

"I can feel you contracting around me, Presh. Can you feel how deep I am, baby?" he purrs as he continually slams into me. One of his feet is now up on the bed to give himself better leverage, his jaw is hanging slack and his body has a shimmer of perspiration all over it. I have never seen anything quite so erotic or more beautiful.

"Oh God, Josh. Harder," I whimper as he pushes my shoulders to the mattress to get deeper. He is slamming into me so hard that I find I am holding my breath watching and my insides are starting to liquefy just watching us. With one, two, three hard pumps he holds himself deep inside me and I scream into the mattress in orgasm. I hold my breath as I watch him lie tenderly next to me and swipe the hair back from my face and kiss me gently. We lie close, kissing passionately for a long time, and I can't look away.

"I fucking adore you, my precious girl," he whispers as he holds my face between his two hands.

I smile and kiss his chest. "That's good because I love you, Joshua Stanton," I reply.

I drop my head as I gasp for air. I feel like I can't breathe. Oh my God.

I stand furious. How dare they violate us like this? How long have they been filming us? What have they seen? I pick up my water jug and throw it at the back of the door in rage and it smashes to pieces.

"You assholes!" I scream. "I hate you! I fucking hate you!"

Just when I think the situation can't get any worse the door opens in a rush. Oh no, it's Carl. My eyes widen and I run to get away from him, but he grabs me by the hair and drags me over to the glass on the floor.

"Pick it up," he yells.

"Go to hell," I snap. He slams my head hard three times against the wall and I scream in pain.

"Stop it," the young medic calls from the door.

Carl puts his face right into mine as he rips my hair. "Get on the floor and pick up the glass before I cut your throat with it."

Fear fills my every cell and through my tears I drop to my knees and slowly pick up the glass. When I have handed him the last of it, he kicks me hard in the stomach on the way out the door and I fall to the floor in a ball as the air is pushed from my lungs.

Help me, someone please help me.

Adrian

My eyes flick to Nicholas in the front seat as Cameron drives us to Corcoran Penitentiary. We are worried sick. Joshua has been in prison for nine days and has refused to see us. We have driven the hour and a half each day to the prison only to be turned away. What's going on with him? Why won't he see us?

The boys are going through the case notes and following up every lead that we can but without knowing if Joshua is ok, we are all struggling. I have offered Jesten a role to stay on and help us. He was due to go back to Australia yesterday but his input and insight into Allender has been helpful. And, besides, I hate to admit it, but I actually like the guy. He's uncultured and rough and raw and brutally honest, qualities that we so desperately need at this delicate time when we don't know who to trust. Cameron refuses to even look at Jesten but Nicholas thinks we need him. If it comes down to giving evidence against Joshua, we will need him on our side. Joshua's court case is next week. We haven't even been able to see him to try and prepare him for the trial. Today we are pulling the psychologist card and Nicholas is demanding to see him. He can't refuse a psychologist and half an hour later the three of us sit in a private room as we wait for him to be brought to us by a guard.

"Why is it taking so long?" Cameron asks quietly.

"He would be refusing to come out of his cell," Nicholas replies calmly.

I rest my elbows on the table and put my head in my hands. "Oh God, my heart is breaking for him. They won't hurt him, will they?" I ask.

"Shut the fuck up," Cameron snaps, annoyed at my suggestion. Nicholas smiles broadly at our interaction and I smirk in return.

"What?" I ask.

"You two are like an old married couple." He smirks.

"Oh God." I wince. "I'm hoping my husband is hotter than him."

Cameron screws up his face. "Don't even go there. Are you trying to make me sick?"

The door opens with a clang and we all sit speechless. Joshua is led in in foot chains and handcuffs, his eyes cast down. Oh no. Cameron stands so quickly that his chair falls back and hits the ground. I gasp when I see his face. Joshua is black and blue. He has a large cut over his right eye with stitches in it and a cut cheekbone and lip. He has grazing on his forehead.

"Dear God," Cameron whispers as he grabs his brother in an embrace.

I hold my hand over my mouth in shock, I don't know what I was expecting, but it was never this. Nicholas turns his anger immediately onto the guard. "This prisoner needs to be moved to protective custody."

"No." Joshua snaps.

"Yes!" Cameron demands.

The guard's eyes flick between us. "I will make you an appointment with the office to prepare the application," he replies to Nicholas.

Joshua falls into the seat. "Joshua," I whisper as I grab his hand across the table.

"Are you okay, mate?" Cameron asks gently as he puts his hand on his brother's forearm.

Joshua nods. "I'm fine," he replies in a monotone.

"Why won't you see us? We have been out of our minds in worry. Who hit you?" I ask.

"It's okay, just a fight in the gym," he murmurs.

But it isn't okay. For him to be this messed up he was fighting more than one person. Are they holding him down to beat him?

"We are going to get you out of here, I promise," Cameron whispers, terrified.

He nods and gives us a sad smile.

"Joshua, you need to accept your visitors. It's unfair to put them through this without speaking to them," Nicholas scolds.

Joshua just stares straight through Nicholas. "Is Bridget okay?" he asks.

I shake my head. "No, Joshua, she is not. We haven't let her come down here to see you, but she is coming tomorrow and you will see her. She can't take much more," I snap.

He nods, as if ashamed that he has put us through this. "We have some leads," Cameron says gently. "We are going through all of the security footage now and things are progressing. We will have some answers this week. Won't we?" Cameron says nervously as his eyes flick to us.

I nod. "Yes, and your court case is next week." I smile hopefully. "And then you will be out of here and we can try and..." I pause, I was going to say get over this nightmare, but I know Joshua is never going to get over this.

"Try and what?" Joshua snaps.

"Try and find who did this," I murmur. His eyes find the floor.

Nicholas, who has remained silent, sits and watches Joshua. I can almost hear the diagnosis his brain is making.

"I would like to speak to Joshua alone, please," Nicholas asks.

Cameron's eyes and mine meet. "Of course," Cameron replies. He gets up and goes around to the other side of the desk and embraces his brother. I can see Joshua's resistance melt and he drops his head to Cameron's shoulder and relief fills me.

I give him a quick hug. "We will be back tomorrow, okay," I say hopefully.

Joshua nods.

"You will see us, won't you?" Cameron asks.

"Yes." Joshua nods.

"Promise me," Cameron pleads.

"Yes. Fuck," Joshua whispers and I smile. There he is. He's with us again. "You're a pair of nagging bitches," he snaps

"We are missing your cranky ass." I smile hopefully.

He drops his head and smirks. "You're so gay, Murph," he mutters, and I smile broadly.

"That's why you love me," I reply.

Joshua's eyes flick to Nicholas as he raises his chin defiantly. "This is your first and final warning. You hurt him again and I hurt you." My eyes widen. *Oh my God, he did not just say that.*

Nicholas clenches his jaw, and his eyes hold Joshua's. "They are just friends, Stan," Cameron mutters, embarrassed. Joshua nods seemingly appeased by the answer.

"I need to talk to Joshua alone please," Nicholas reminds us.

"Yes, of course." We both stand and leave the room and for the first time in nine days I feel relief.

Natasha

Days have turned into weeks, sixteen days that I have counted, although I don't know how long I was unconscious for in the beginning. I'm in hell, I have literally been beaten into submission and have no doubt that he is the one who will kill me when given the word. I have never been so petrified of anyone in my life and as if my subconscious knows that this was my fear all along, I haven't been having nightmares at all. I don't need to dream about terror anymore. I'm living it.

The six televisions are haunting me, four of news and the excessive reporting on this story, one of our bedroom playing reruns of our sex and lovemaking and one that flicks through to different rooms in the house. I've even watched Bridget and Ben have sex. He's smoking hot just quietly... not that I was looking.

Somebody wants me to know that they are watching us. It's a powerplay. They have control of my house and they have me hostage. Someone wants me to know that they are controlling this situation. They needn't bother. I am fucking well aware of that. I can't get out of here; I've tried everything I can think of. I'm trying to find a tool to cut through the plaster in the ceiling of the bathroom. I thought if I could get into the roof, I could escape but I can't even punch through it. I don't know what's behind it, but it seems unbreakable. I sit and stare out of the window as my mind searches for an escape plan. How do I get out of here? I look at the ceiling and watch the air conditioning vents above. Why are they so small? This never happens to Bruce Willis—he can always fit into air conditioning vents. I'm trying to think of all the movies I have watched where people are taken hostage and break free to try and get an idea of what to do, but I've got nothing. Bruce Willis and huge air conditioning vents are the only ones I can remember. One good thing is that I'm starting to work out when Carl and the other boy are working. I hear a car pull up every twelve hours. Carl's car is noisy and has a rattle thing going on and the other car must be a new one, with hardly a sound at all. And I also have found that whatever I ask for is delivered so I am trying to think of foods that have packaging which may come in handy in an escape. If only I could order a gun pizza.

What am I going to do?

My mind goes to my mum and Bridget. Poor Mum. She's lost so much and now she thinks she's lost me too. If only I could get a message out to them... think Natasha, think. What if I seduce Carl and break down his defenses? Would he let me go? What about the kid? Maybe I could seduce him, but then. I close my eyes in pain, I couldn't do it. I would rather kill them than sleep with them. My eyes go to the paddocks out the window as I concentrate.

Now there's an idea. Kill them, but how do you kill someone?

Neck, eyes, what body part do you go for if you have no weapon? How could I kill them, and would I be able to live with myself if I did? The thing is, if it backfires and I don't succeed I know for certain that they will kill me. What a mess.

A weapon, I need to make a weapon. If I wasn't such an idiot, I wouldn't have thrown that planter pot at the window and missed. I could have thrown it at their head, but now they've taken it. Why the hell did I do that? What if I pretend to kill myself by hanging using the bedsheet and then when they think I am dead I jump up and run? Hmm, no. They will probably stab me a few times to make sure I'm dead and then have sex with my corpse.

I stand and walk to the bathroom to check the cabinets for the ten thousandth time since I have been here, and I notice something different on the television of our house. I run to the basket to get the remote and turn up the volume. It's Joshua. Oh God, my hand goes to my mouth and tears instantly fill my eyes, I haven't seen him on camera at all. He looks terrible. They have arrived back at the house. He is looking around the house in a panic and then he runs up the stairs two at a time. The other television from our bedroom flicks onto present time and I see him sit on the bed and pick up my diary and glasses. He reads it as he wipes his eyes. "Oh baby, I'm okay, I'm okay." I jump up and down on the spot. "Joshua, I'm here, I'm alive." But he can't hear me. I drop to the bed as I watch my love curl up into a fetal position and lie on the bed clutching my glasses and diary as his tears run onto his pillow.

Goosebumps cover my skin and fury starts to drip from my every pore. Oh, I'm going to fucking kill someone alright. If they think for one minute, they have the last word they can think again. I'm not taking this shit. You are going to regret the day you messed with me, assholes. And as my love's heart breaks on the screen I turn and walk into the bathroom with a cool renewed purpose. I need a fucking weapon and I need to find one now. I'm getting the hell out of here.

It's day 26 and I go over the plan I have in my head for the hundredth time today. I have unscrewed the shower screen and have it placed it strategically in the bathroom, waiting for my attack. For the last seven days I have woken up every morning determined that today is the day, today I'm going to escape, but then I'm so scared I'm going to mess it up and end up dead and my love will really lose me that I chicken out. I have to be positive my plan will work before I do it or else it's just a death wish. I just wish I knew if the coverage of me in here is going back to base somewhere else or if this is the only outlet, because if this is the only outlet, I have a much bigger chance of getting away before anyone knows I'm gone. I know what shift Carl is on and I have to do it when the young boy is here, as I have a much greater chance of surviving against him. He won't even talk to me because he knows I'm trying to break down his defenses. I have strategically started to call myself Cinderella and asked the two men to call me Joshua's nickname Cinderella on the off chance that the person doing this is someone we know and that they may refer to me as Cinderella to Adrian. He knows that he and I are the only two people who know about that. It's a long shot, but I'm trying anything.

I got my period this morning, and I cried. Both tears of sadness and tears of relief. I had been holding off my escape, half thinking that I may have been pregnant, and I didn't want to endanger Joshua's and my child, but I needn't have worried. I'm not pregnant and that makes me just plain sad. I just pray I survive this, and we get the chance to try again. More and more I know that as time goes on my chances of getting out of here alive are diminishing. I will wait now until my period finishes because if it works and I do get away, who knows how long I will be in the forest. My eyes flick down to my feet. I don't even have shoes. How do you escape through the forest without shoes?

Adrian

"Are you ready?" Nicholas asks me.

I nod and swallow my fear. We are in the foyer of our building and I am doing the first press release since this nightmare began. With the court case coming up I need to make a statement on behalf of Joshua. There must be at least fifty reporters and cameramen here. Bridget sits in the front row with Abbie and Cameron. Ben and the security line the walls, and I'm as nervous as all hell.

I walk to the small podium at the center of the room and with shaking hands retrieve my notes that Nicholas has written for me.

Hmm, hmm. I clear my throat.

"Thank you for coming." The cameras start to click.

"Thirty-eight days ago, off the coast of Portofino, Joshua Stanton and his beloved fiancée Natasha Marx were staying on the luxury liner of a friend. They attended a wedding and during the course of that wedding, unbeknownst to them, their drinks were spiked with the drug Rohypnol. Joshua Stanton awoke in the morning to find Natasha missing and a large..." I stop as I struggle to read the next words. *You can do this.* "Amount of blood on the deck. Natasha had been attacked overnight when Joshua was unconscious." The cameras all click double time and my eyes flick to Nicholas who stands silently against the wall next to Ben. He nods reassuringly. I take a deep breath and continue. "The coroner ruled Natasha Marx's death as a result of massive blood loss and was a direct result of the premeditated attack on her.

We, Natasha's family, are devastated at the loss of her life and Joshua Stanton is in deep mourning. After an anonymous tip off, police searched Joshua Stanton's properties to uncover eight vials of Rohypnol that had been planted there by the perpetrator with the intention of framing Joshua Stanton for the murder."

I swallow the lump in my throat as the cameras click and the reporters start to buzz at the impending story. "Joshua Stanton does not know who put the Rohypnol at his country estate, nor does he know where his beloved fiancée's body is. He is deeply in mourning and currently being held in Corcoran Penitentiary for a murder he did not commit." I stare down the barrel of the camera with renewed purpose. "These allegations against him are false in every regard. Joshua Stanton is innocent and has been framed. We will be fighting these allegations on all fronts and are confident that justice will prove to be the victor and the true criminal brought to justice. It is our greatest wish that Natasha's body can be recovered so that she may be laid to rest in peace."

The cameras go crazy and reporters start to scream questions. "Mr. Murphy, Mr. Murphy." They call. I bend back to the microphone. "No further questions will be answered. Thank you."

CHAPTER 25

Adrian

WITH JOSHUA I stand outside an office in the courthouse. Joshua has been freed from his cuffs and has two security guards following him. Today is the court case, and we need to get him out of here. We are waiting for his lawyer and, like clockwork, he walks up the stairs towards us with his three PAs trailing behind him.

He smiles warmly. "Hello, I'm Vincenzo Di Luca." Wearing a dark grey suit, he is flawless. We have hired a new hot shot lawyer who doesn't lose.

Joshua and I shake his hand. Joshua could have only one person with him in this meeting and he chose me. I am as nervous as hell.

"Joshua Stanton," Joshua replies "Adrian Murphy." I nod.

We follow him into the designated office, and I feel myself become a little awestruck at being in Vincenzo's presence. The rock star of the legal world, he represents murderers, Mafia, hitmen and politicians to name a few. He is a large Italian man with model-like good looks and the personality of an asshole...or so I hear. He has a cult following on social media, and he's a bit like Joshua in that his outsides don't match his insides. Too good looking to be this successful and intelligent, the puzzle doesn't add up.

We sit down at the table and he sits calmly and clasps his hands in front of him on the desk. His eyes bore into Joshua's. "I have been studying the case for the last week and I have a few questions I need answered," he replies.

"Yes," Joshua answers.

Joshua is very nervous, and empathy fills me.

"The prostitute you had sex with in Sydney?" Vincenzo continues. Joshua drops his head in shame; he would never normally talk about something like this in front of these secretaries.

"Yes," he replies.

"How did you first meet her?" Vincenzo asks.

Joshua hesitates. "Um." His eyes flick to me sitting next to him and I nod to him to go on. "She arrived at my door as a housewarming present," he replies.

Vincenzo nods and scribbles down notes. He doesn't even flinch—what must he hear doing this job?

"Who ordered that present?" he asks.

Joshua hesitates. Joshua won't tattle on his friend, I know him too well, so I cut in. "Um Vincenzo, if I may."

His eyes snap to me. "Call me Vin," he replies.

I nod thankfully. "Okay, Vin. It was Joshua's friend, Carson Milane," I reply.

Vin's eyes flick back to Joshua. "With friends like him who needs enemies." He raises his eyebrows as he flicks the page of the notepad.

Joshua drops his eyes to the floor.

"I will be calling him to the stand," Vin replies without further thought.

Joshua frowns. "I would prefer him to be left out of it."

Vin's cold eyes snap to Joshua. "Are you aware of the seriousness of your plight, Joshua?"

Joshua's eyes hold his. "Yes," he murmurs.

"Are you aware that I am the only person who can get you off this charge, and what I say goes?"

"I didn't do it," Joshua snaps.

"I don't give a flying fuck if you did," Vin sneers in reply. "I don't lose cases and I don't play nice. I will degrade everyone in your circle if it makes you an innocent man and if you have a problem with that I will go now."

Joshua glares at Vincenzo and I feel my uncomfortable gauge hit ten. Oh shit, this guy is full on.

"Fine," Joshua snaps, annoyed.

He starts to flick through his pad and notes he has made. "I read on a statement from Natasha's mother that Natasha kept diaries." His eyes rise up to Joshua. "But there has been no mention of them. Where are those diaries now?" he asks.

I frown. Oh shit, I forgot Tash kept a diary. My eyes flick to Joshua in question.

Joshua runs his tongue over his top teeth in contempt. "I don't know anything about diaries," he replies.

I frown. What?

Vin's eyes hold Joshua's. "You need to work on your lying skills—you're atrocious. You lie very poorly," he says dryly.

Joshua sits back in his seat annoyed. "Listen if you are going to be a cock..." he replies.

Vin cuts him off. "That's exactly what I'm paid to do. I

am paid to be an in-your-face cock and I do it very well for a very high price. Send someone to get the diaries," he sneers.

"I don't know where they are," Joshua snaps. "I think they were taken by the perpetrator to cover the evidence. I'm not sure."

Vin's eyes meet his. "What did you tell the police about their whereabouts?" he asks.

"They didn't ask me," Joshua replies.

Vin shakes his head. "Fucking useless," he mutters under his breath. His eyes meet Joshua's across the table. "Okay, so here is the story. The prosecutor they are using used to work for me and he's brilliant. He is going to rattle you like you have never known. Keep your mouth shut. Do not elaborate on anything. Do not give him ammunition to twist your words."

Joshua nods and swallows.

His eyes hold Joshua's across the table, and I can hear his brain ticking. "I'm going to request a closed hearing. I understand how much you hate the press."

Joshua's gaze holds his. "Thank you," he mutters.

"Can you give us a minute alone, please?" Vin asks me and his assistants who are sitting behind him silently.

We nod, stand and leave the room as my heart starts to beat hard in my chest.

"All rise," the bailiff calls as the judge enters the room, and everyone stands silently. The gallery is full of reporters with notepads. Joshua, dressed in a navy suit, stands in front next to Vincenzo and two of his assistants. Then in the front row are Victoria, Bridget, Abbie, me, Cameron and his parents, and Ben and Nicholas. I feel like I am going to have a heart attack.

The judge walks in silently, sits down and flicks through the notes in front of him.

Vin is the first to speak. "Your Honor, I request that this hearing be held in a private court room," he calls.

The judge looks up from his papers, seemingly surprised. "Denied, this is a matter of public interest."

Joshua's head drops, oh God. Everything is going to be dragged through the press—this is Joshua's worst nightmare.

The prosecution lawyer stands. He is about forty, nerdy looking and grey. He also appears very confident which only escalates my trepidation.

"We are here today to bring to justice the man who has taken his innocent fiancée's life. To bring the truth out in the open. Natasha Marx did not die in vain and her case will prevail. I call to the stand Joshua Stanton," he calls across the room.

My heart sinks and Cameron drops his head. "Fuck," he whispers.

The room sits in silence as Joshua swears on the bible and goes through the motions.

"Is your name Joshua Stanton?" the lawyer asks.

Joshua nods. "Yes," he replies.

"I'm going to go back to the beginning, shall I?" He pauses and looks around at the room for effect. Oh, this jerk should have been an actor. "Natasha Marx is your first cousin, is she not?" he purrs.

Joshua swallows the lump in his throat. "Yes," he replies. The reporters gasp and start to scribble on their pads fervently.

"And when she was just a seventeen-year-old child you

snuck into her tent one night on a camping trip with the sole purpose to seduce her?"

Joshua hesitates as he thinks about his answer. "No, we had started a relationship that was consensual," he replies.

"But you did have sex with her when she was just seventeen in a tent," he replies.

"Yes," Joshua replies.

"And did Natasha's parents know about this?"

"No," Joshua replies

"You didn't tell them because you knew that they would not approve, is that right?" he asks innocently.

"Yes," Joshua murmurs.

"You left her then and moved to America and made your fortune in app development and became a household name," he asks.

"Yes," Joshua replies.

"But then you went back to Australia to see Natasha?" he questions, seemingly puzzled.

"I went back for my brother's wedding," Joshua replies.

The jerk-off raises his eyebrows in humor. "Oh yes, you mean Natasha's cousin," he replies.

Joshua glares at the prosecutor.

"It was at this wedding that you reconnected?" he asks.

"Yes," Joshua replies.

"But you didn't reconnect at all, did you? You decided on that very day that Natasha Marx was going to belong to you and nobody else." He sneers.

"No," Joshua replies cold-faced.

"Joshua, have you ever used prostitutes?"

Joshua drops his head shamefully. "Yes," he murmurs.

"Oh, that's right, because you were sleeping with one in

Sydney while you were..." He holds up his fingers to accentuate his point. "Dating Natasha."

"No," Joshua replies. "I was never unfaithful to Natasha."

"Did Natasha not satisfy you in bed?" he sneers.

I can feel the anger radiating from Joshua. "You will pay
her more respect," he sneers.

Vin jumps to his feet. "Objection," he yells.

"Move on, Mr. Grieves," the judge calls.

The prosecutor fakes a smile and holds up a series of
photographs to the audience. "Can you tell me what these
photos are of, Mr. Stanton?" He passes them to Joshua.

Joshua looks at the photos and hesitates.

"Let me tell the jury what these photos are of. Mr.
Stanton leaving a strip club with a stripper and kissing her as
he got into his car." He smiles broadly.

Oh no, it's from when Joshua was trying to make Natasha
leave him, back in the very beginning. Cameron shakes his
head and drops it softly. This is a fucking nightmare. I
thought they would at least ease into it.

Joshua stays silent and his eyes flick to Vincenzo.

"Was Natasha heartbroken when this story hit the head-
lines, Mr. Stanton?" the prosecutor snaps.

Joshua stays silent.

"Objection," Vincenzo yells. "Mr. Stanton cannot be
asked how another feels."

The judge nods. "Carry on," he replies to the prosecutor.
"Are you a cocaine addict, Mr. Stanton?" he purrs conceitedly.

"No," Joshua answers quickly in return.

"But you have been hospitalized in the past for a cocaine
overdose, have you not?"

"Yes," Joshua answers.

"What are your fitness pursuits, Mr. Stanton?" he demands.

Joshua swallows. "Boxing and kickboxing," he replies.

The prosecutor smiles. "Please tell the court what other extreme sport you do?"

Joshua rolls his lips. "Cage fighting," he murmurs.

"So, you like to beat the hell out of people," he asks.

Joshua looks at him deadpan. "Some more than others," he replies, and the gallery all break into chuckles knowing that Joshua would love to beat the hell out of this guy right now.

The prosecutor narrows his eyes at Joshua. "Am I right in saying you are a self-absorbed, womanizing drug addict who uses his power and wealth to control the people around him?"

"Objection!" Vincenzo calls.

"Overruled," the judge responds.

Everybody looks back to Joshua alone on the stand. "No," he whispers.

"Did Natasha Marx love you in the beginning?" the prosecutor asks.

"Natasha loved me till the end," Joshua replies angrily. "But she didn't—she fell in love with her bodyguard," the

Prosecutor sneers. "No," Joshua snaps.

The prosecutor smiles. "That is all, Mr. Stanton, for the moment." He turns to the audience. "I call to the witness stand Simon Wells."

Joshua frowns, stands slowly and returns to his seat next to Vincenzo at the front and the door opens and Simon, Natasha's friend from Sydney, appears. Fuck.

"Hello, may I call you Simon?" the prosecutor asks.

"Yes," he replies.

"You worked with Natasha Marx at the Sexual Health Clinic, did you not?"

"Yes," he replies nervously.

"And you know Mr. Stanton?"

"Only what Natasha had told me," he replies as his eyes flick nervously to Joshua.

"What did she tell you?"

"She told me that he was playing her and that he drove her crazy. She never knew where she stood with him."

"When Natasha started seeing him, did she change at all?" the prosecutor asks.

"Yes."

"How so?"

"She was crying all the time, nervous, unsettled at work," Simon replies.

"Did this bother you?" the prosecutor asks.

"Yes."

"How long did this go on for?"

He hesitates as his eyes flick to Bridget.

"For a few months, during which time he was caught with a stripper and Natasha believed it was for her own good."

The prosecutor frowns. "So, he began to brainwash her in effect?"

"Yes, I believe so."

"Then what happened?" the prosecutor asks.

"Um, they told Natasha's parents about their relationship and her father died of a heart attack."

"Objection," Vincenzo calls. "He had an existing heart problem."

"Overruled," the judge calls.

"Natasha slipped into a deep depression and was on

heavy medication. She didn't get out of bed for months," Simon replies.

"And where was Joshua Stanton at this time?" the prosecutor asks.

"I believe he was in LA sleeping with one of his staff and taking cocaine," Simon replies.

The gallery gasp and Cameron inhales deeply as his stress levels hit a crescendo.

"Did Miss Marx find out about this other woman?" the prosecutor asks.

"Yes."

"Did Mr. Stanton tell her of his infidelities?"

"No."

"Who told her?"

"Amelie Richards, the other woman," Simon replies.

"I see. Tell me how Natasha handled this?" the prosecutor asks.

"She was devastated and became reclusive."

Joshua's head drops in shame. God, what must be going through his head right now?

"But Joshua came back, didn't he?" the prosecutor asks.

"Yes."

"And what happened?"

"He started to pursue her again," Simon replies.

"That's right, in fact you saw him out one night, didn't you?"

"Yes," Simon replies.

"Tell us about that night."

"Natasha and I had been out for dinner and then went onto the Ivy, a nightclub in Sydney. Joshua turned up and was watching and frightening her, so we went to the dance floor to escape him." He swallows nervously, his eyes flicking to Joshua. "Natasha was very drunk, and we were dancing, and he stormed out onto the dance floor and grabbed her aggressively by the arm and started screaming at her."

"What did you do?" the prosecutor frowns.

"I told him to back off."

"And what did he say?"

"He asked me if I was trying to get myself murdered," Simon replies.

The gallery gasp.

"And what happened then?" the prosecutor asks.

"He carried her kicking and screaming out of the night-club over his shoulder."

"How frightening," the prosecutor replies. "How was Natasha after that attack?

"Reserved, she never mentioned him again in fear of what I would say to her."

"Mr. Wells, you are a psychologist, are you not?"

"Yes."

"In your opinion, was Miss Marx a domestic violence victim of Mr. Stanton?"

"Yes," he replies. "Without a doubt in my mind."

Ben receives a text, reads it and frowns, and then he hands his phone over to me.

Ben, this is Detective Smith. I am just calling to let you know that we have found Mr. Julian O'Reilly. He is deceased and it appears he has been dead for a long period of time by suicide. Maybe over twelve months. Call me and I will let you know what we have found.

Julian is the man who has tried to kill both Joshua and me —the software geek. He's dead? The bastard is dead. I close my eyes in relief and up until now I didn't realize how scared of the man I actually was. He couldn't have killed Tash if he's been dead that long, so this narrows the suspects down. This is good. This is progress.

My eyes flick back to the court proceedings as I hand the phone onto Nicholas so he can read it.

"That is all, Mr. Wells. I call to the stand Mr. Todd Smithson."

Joshua drops his head and Vincenzo whispers something in the ear of his secretary and she nods and scribbles something down on a pad. I turn to see who is coming out and my stomach drops. It's that fucking idiot that Joshua is on the assault charge for. This just gets worse.

"Hello Todd," the prosecutor purrs.

"Hello," Todd replies.

He points to Joshua. "Do you know this man?"

"Yes," he replies.

"How do you know him?"

"I lodged an assault charge against him in Australia."

"Why would you do that?"

"Because he attacked me one night in Australia when I was dancing with Natasha Marx."

The prosecutor frowns. "Please explain what your injuries were."

"I had a broken nose and three broken ribs," he replies.

"All because you were dancing with Miss Marx?"

"Yes."

"Why is that?"

"He was insanely jealous. He just ran at me on the dance floor and attacked me right there and then, and then when we were taken to the security office he attacked me again. He was arrested and spent the night in jail."

The questioning goes on, but I have stopped listening—

they are twisting everything. For hours I sit still, traumatized by the evidence they are supplying. Witness after witness attesting to Joshua's cocaine usage, his cage fighting, his dominance and his past womanizing. Finally, when I don't think any of us can take any more, I hear the words "Court adjourned, resuming 9 am tomorrow." And the sound of the hammer rings through the room. Joshua drops his head into his hands as the journalists go into overdrive.

It's about twelve at night and I am tossing and turning in my bed. What's going through Joshua's mind right now? Is he okay? I have never felt so out of control—Natasha, Joshua, work... Nicholas. He is staying in the bedroom next to mine and it's comforting. What does that mean?

He walks past the door in pajama pants. "Are you still awake?" he whispers.

I roll onto my back and my eyes drop to his muscular naked torso and the scattering of dark hair on his chest.

"Yes," I reply.

He walks in and sits on the side of my bed and takes my hand in his. "Are you okay?" he asks.

I smile sadly as I look at his face in the darkness. "I don't know to be honest," I reply.

He tenderly swipes the hair back from my forehead and his eyes hold mine. "It will work out, sweetheart. I don't want you scared in here alone," he whispers gently.

For some reason those words bring a lump to my throat.

"Let me sleep in here tonight. Nothing sexual. Just sleep," he whispers as his eyes hold mine.

I bite my bottom lip and nod. "Okay," I whisper nervously.

He smiles and walks around to the other side of the bed and climbs in behind me and pulls my body close to his and wraps me in his strong arms. I feel myself instantly relax as he kisses my temple from behind.

"I'm here, babe. I'm here," he whispers. "I'm not going anywhere."

I smile sadly into the darkness. Oh Nicholas, I love you. I wish desperately that I was your first and only love... like you are mine.

Natasha

I lie in bed as I watch Joshua and me making love. I could watch it all day. In fact, I have been doing just that. We are making slow gentle love. He is on his widespread knees, one forearm is holding his bodyweight off me and the other hand is on my behind as he holds me how his body wants me. God, I miss him, I miss his smell, his touch, his love. I can't live like this, without him. I'm like a plant starved of the sun. I'm suffocating even though I have air because the air that I'm breathing is polluted with hate. *Help me. Somebody, please help me.*

On the other screen I see Joshua walk into our bedroom and I grab the remote and point it to the television. I smile a sad smile as I watch him. He lies down on the bed and starts scrolling through his phone. He smiles softly when he gets to an image. I can't see the image, but I know it's of me. He has been reading my diaries word for word and I have seen that smile many times over the last two weeks. He sits up slowly and frowns— what's he doing? He stands and goes to the wardrobe and from the back of the door takes off my wedding dress in its black velvet bag and holds it up to look at it. Tears instantly overflow from my eyes. I'm supposed to be planning our wedding right now. He hangs the hanger back over the door and slowly unzips the bag as my heart breaks. *This isn't how he is supposed to be seeing this dress.* He takes it out and holds it out for his gaze and then turns it and looks at the back. The lump in my throat is big and hurts so much as I try and deal with watching him do this. He then lays it up against his body and puts his cheek down to rest on it as it drapes over his shoulder. Dear God. He starts to sway as if dancing, oh no. He is dancing our wedding dance alone. He thinks I'm dead. I watch a tear roll down his cheek. The full extent of the horror we are living overwhelms me and the scariest thing of all is soon I might be dead — there is every possibility that death is just around the corner for me. I will be a distant memory in the lives of the ones I love. How do I turn this around?

Dad, please help me. Help me think of a plan to get out of here.

I need to get out of here.

I flop back to lie on the bed and then something comes up on the news channel that I haven't seen before, so I flick the remote to turn up the volume.

In breaking news, Joshua Stanton has just been arrested for the murder of his wife Natasha Marx. Evidence has been found in his place of residence that is a direct link to her murder.

I screw up my face, what? He didn't do this. Why would they think he would do this? Oh my God, oh my God. My heart starts to race and I am instantly filled with fear. The door opens and Carl walks in carrying a tray of food.

My furious eyes turn to him. "Who are you working for, Carl?" I snap.

"Why do you think I'm working for someone?" he asks.

"Because I can pay you ten million dollars tonight if you let me go."

His eyes hold mine.

"Twenty," I reply as I up the ante.

"You're lying," he sneers.

"No, I'm not. I can pay you more money than you ever dreamt of."

The television story continues about the evidence they found in Willowvale and my eyes flick to the screen.

Carl smiles broadly and I glare at him in disgust. "Not long now." He smiles.

I frown. "What does that mean?" I ask. "Not long now till what?" I ask panicked. Oh shit, are they going to kill me tonight?

"He will be dead very soon," he sneers sadistically.

I frown. "Who, who will be dead?" I ask.

"Your pretty boy. He won't last in prison. I give it a week and he will get himself killed."

Horror dawns.

That is totally true—Joshua won't last in prison. He will get himself killed.

"Is that what this is about? You want Joshua to get himself killed?" I whisper, mortified.

"You can't be punished for a crime you didn't commit. Nobody has to kill Joshua Stanton. He will do it for us," he whispers. "There are no bodyguards in prison, Natasha." He laughs sadistically and my blood runs cold.

My eyes widen. "Please name your price. Carl, I beg of you, we will pay you everything we have to let me go," I beg.

"Liar!" he screams as he backhands me hard across the face and I fall to the floor. I curl into a ball instinctively as I know the kick is following and sure enough it does, but in my hip and I close my eyes against the pain.

"Keep your lying mouth shut!" he yells before disappearing out the door.

I lie on the floor, broken and hurt. They are going to kill him. My eyes close in pain at the thought of what they might do to him before they kill him. Is he being beaten right now? I sit up and put my head in my hands. What do I do? My eyes flick back up to the television and I notice a date on one of the reports and I frown. That's the wrong date. I count on my fingers the number of days I have been in here and that doesn't add up. I stand and frown. What the hell is going on? Shit. They are manipulating the news in here, they are repeating old news. Why? I walk into the bathroom and throw up. I can't deal with this shit any longer. This is too much!

Twenty minutes later I walk back out and sit next to the window deep in thought. They are trying to mess with my head. You know what, I'm not buying into it. No fucking way. I grab a blanket from the bed and stand on the chair and drape it over the televisions.

I stand furious in front of the camera. "I'm not watching—do you see this?" I scream. "I'm not watching. I don't care what you do." I throw an apple at the wall that the camera is attached to. "Go to hell, you sick bastard." I am so enraged that the veins are standing out of my neck and my breathing is labored.

The door opens, Carl appears and I instantly cower. He pulls the blanket off the televisions and leaves the room without a word. No hit, no kick. I slump to the floor and fall deeply into self-pity and sob.

It's about midnight, I think. I am sitting at the window in a chair looking at the paddocks below lit by moonlight. I feel sick to my stomach, I don't know if this plan is going to work and if it does how far away civilization is from here. I could run for days and not see anyone. What if this is in fact a property and there are guards on the gates surrounding it? I don't think that's the case though because I can see the forest just over the hill. I wish the bushland came right up to the house because then it would be easier for me to run without being seen. I think it's about 500 meters to the forest from the house but that is only on this side of the house. What's the other side like?

What will I do, Dad? Tell me what to do? Which way do I run?

I have no shoes, so I have to try and make some, but from what? How do you make fucking shoes? I asked them for some bed socks tonight, and said my feet were cold. Bed socks are thick and hopefully will protect me a little. If only I had something hard to strap to my feet. I've got nothing... like my brain. I can't sit still and start to pace my ten thousandth pace for today. I'm so nervous I'm going to get myself killed. Strategically, I think I have about a thirty percent chance of making it out alive. First, I have to attack, then I have to run, then I have to find a phone and call the police. What's the frigging number for the police in America again? I frown as I try to remember it; is it 555 or 551?

I am pulled from my thought by the sound of a strange car pulling up on the other side of the house. I can see the headlights out the window but not the car. Fuck, who is here? Is the boss here? Have they come to kill me? I run to the door and hold my head up against the back of it to try and listen but I'm upstairs so I can only hear the front door opening. I strain my ears...nothing. Oh my God, the boss is here. They would only come here in the middle of the night if they were going to do something.

What are they going to do?

CHAPTER 26

Joshua

"CAN you tell me what this photograph is of, Mr. Stanton?"

I narrow my eyes to look at the picture. I am on the stand and have been getting interrogated for three hours. I can't take much more.

The photograph is of bruising on hipbones and arms and I frown in confusion. I have seen these images before, but I can't place them. Where have I seen these? Black fingerprints on the insides of someone's arms—I don't get it.

"No," I reply.

The prick of a prosecutor shakes his head. "These are images from Natasha Marx's phone saved under the title 'Joshua's handiwork'."

I frown. What?

"She was trying to leave us a trail to convict you." He turns to the jury box. "Images from the very phone of the victim, stating Joshua Stanton had done this. Do you need more proof, jury, that this man is evil?"

They all stay straight-faced. My eyes flick to Cameron who is putting his hands up in a gesture and I frown. Huh? He holds his hands up again as if water skiing. Oh shit, the penny drops.

"Those are photos that I took when we went water skiing in Thailand. I put the heading 'Joshua's handiwork' because Natasha wanted to send it to her mother as a joke," I stammer. "The bruises are from being pulled from the water onto the boat. Ask anyone," I stammer. "There were ten other people with us."

The prosecutor fakes a laugh. "Yes, of course they are," he replies sarcastically.

"Mr. Stanton, where are Natasha Marx's diaries?" he asks.

My stomach drops and I stay silent.

"Miss Marx has kept diaries for years and years but they have not been recovered. Where are they?"

I swallow. This is the first outright lie I have told, and I know I can't do it for shit. "I don't know," I reply.

"Yes, you do. You have disposed of these diaries because you don't want anyone to know what Natasha really thought of you and how she was falling in love with Max, her bodyguard," he yells.

I shake my head. "No," I answer.

The prosecutor turns to the jury. "Joshua Stanton's house is under constant guard twenty-four hours a day. Nobody could have gotten to those diaries except Mr. Stanton himself. He is hiding the evidence of his murder," he yells.

"No," I reply and my eyes flick to Vincenzo and he shakes his head in frustration.

"That is all for today, Mr. Stanton." He takes a seat as he smiles smugly at his assistants.

I stand and go back and sit next to Vincenzo and he gives me a reassuring smile as he stands. "I call to the stand Bridget Marx."

I hold my breath as I watch Bridget nervously walk up and take a seat and swear on the bible. She smiles softly at me and I drop my head. This is bullshit. Why are we going through this?

"Miss Marx, you are Natasha's sister?"

"Yes," she replies.

"How would you explain your relationship with her?" Vincenzo asks.

"We are..." Her eyes drop to the ground. "We were best friends," she replies softly.

My heart sinks. Were. Natasha and I were in love. We were planning a future. Were will never be are. It's all gone. Natasha is dead and she is never coming back, and neither is my happiness. I feel emotion start to take over me and my eyes frost over. I drop my head to shield my face from the photographers.

"When did you find out about Natasha's and Joshua's relationship?" he asks.

"The morning after they first kissed eight years ago," she says confidently as her eyes flick to me.

I lift my head and frown—that's a lie. What are you doing, Bridget?

"How did you find out?" he asks.

"Natasha called me excited to share the news," she replies with a determination in her voice.

"Did you tell anyone else?"

"No."

"Why not?" he asks.

"Sisters keep each other's secrets, Vincenzo," Bridget replies coldly. God, this is rehearsed.

"Do you spend a lot of time with them together?" he asks.

"I live with them," she replies.

"How would you describe their relationship?" he asks.

Bridget smiles warmly at me and I feel my tears rise again. "They are madly in love. I don't know a couple who are so in love." The lump in my throat breaks and I drop my head, unable to hide the tears again. I hear the clicks of the cameras as they capture my tears. Fucking get me out of here.

"Have you ever seen Mr. Stanton be abusive to Natasha?"

"Never once. He adores her and worships the ground she walks on. There is no way he would ever raise a hand to her," Bridget replies, annoyed at the question.

"Would Natasha have told you if there had been abuse?" he asks.

"Definitely, we tell each other everything," she replies.

"Do you think Joshua Stanton killed your sister, Miss Marx?"

She shakes her head. "No, definitely not. He didn't do this. He has been framed for a murder he didn't commit." Her eyes go to the jury. "He is suffering enough. Please don't make him suffer anymore," she pleads. She starts to cry and nervously retrieves a tissue from her pocket.

"Are you still living with Mr. Stanton?" Vincenzo asks.

"Yes," she sniffles. "His parents, my mother and Natasha's, my friend and Cameron, Joshua's brother, are all staying there at the moment. We are trying to support each other through this terrible time," she replies.

"But Joshua is not there, is he?" Vin asks. She shakes her head.

"No, he is in prison for another person's crime," she replies in a loud clear voice.

"That is all, Miss Marx. I call to the stand Max Carter." My head drops. Fuck this is it. He's going to crucify me. Max goes through the motions and takes a seat.

"You are the bodyguard that so much speculation is surrounding," Vincenzo announces.

"Yes," Max replies.

"What was your relationship with Miss Marx?"

"I was her bodyguard and had become her friend," Max replies.

"For how long?" Vin asks.

"Just over twelve months." Max stares straight ahead, not once making eye contact with anyone.

"What was your relationship with Mr. Stanton like?" he asks.

"Normal."

Vincenzo frowns. "Normal, what does that mean? Did you fight?"

"No," he replies, and I swallow the lead ball in my stomach.

He's doing this for Natasha, not me.

"But I saw vision of you being abused by Mr. Stanton on the night of Natasha's disappearance on the television."

"Mr. Stanton had been drugged. Doctored images had just been sent to him in regard to the two of us," he replies.

"But he went over the top, don't you think?" Vincenzo frowns.

"No, any man would have been the same if he had been sent those images," Max replies.

"Did you ever see any evidence of Miss Marx being abused by Mr. Stanton?"

I swallow the lump in my throat.

"No, he loved her. He would never have hurt her."

I drop my head thankfully as the gallery starts to whisper and the cameras start to click.

"That is all, Mr. Carter. I call to the stand Victoria Marx."

My stomach drops, Natasha's mother. I close my eyes as the torture continues and slip back into my darkness.

"You have a visitor," the guard says as he opens the door of my cell.

I frown from my position lying on the bed. Visitors are the last thing that I want. It's Saturday and I have been in court all week. Two more days to go. I will know my fate by Wednesday. I slowly walk down to the receiving rooms and take a seat, the door opens and my mother walks in. I instantly drop my eyes. We have hardly spoken a word since I found out my true paternity.

She smiles nervously and takes a seat, then she lifts up the telephone. "Hello Joshua," she whispers.

"Hello," I reply. My eyes hold hers. I'm so angry at her I can't even articulate how I feel.

She twists the cord around her finger as her haunted eyes hold mine. "I miss you," she whispers as her eyes tear up.

I swallow the lump in my throat. I miss her too. I nod sadly. "Joshua, can you yell at me? Can you scream at me? Show me some kind of emotion. I can't stand that you have just cut me off. Can we talk about it, please?" she whispers.

I shake my head. "Just leave it, Mum," I reply.

"Joshua, please, my biggest fear was that I would lose you.

And it's come true, you're gone." She screws up her face as she tries to hold in her tears.

With my elbow on the desk, I lean on my hand, and my eyes don't leave her face.

"Joshua, I love you so much," she whispers.

"People who love each other don't tell lies," I reply flatly.

She nods. "They do if they are scared for their life."

My eyes stay fixed on her face.

Her tears run freely down her face. "Was it really that bad?" I ask.

She nods and wipes a tear away. "It was worse than I can ever explain." She frowns as she thinks. "The physical abuse was horrific... but the mental abuse and threats were much worse," she whispers.

I don't understand this woman at all. I shake my head. "I don't understand. I will never understand why you wouldn't tell your own husband about this. He loves you, he would have believed you."

She shakes her head. "No, Joshua, he wouldn't have believed me. My own sons didn't believe me."

My eyes hold hers.

"Joshua, my life has been hard, and I have made stupid, stupid choices." She tears up again. "I have never known a love like the one you give to Natasha. Your father and I were different. He has always been distant." She pauses before she speaks. "I was not his first love, Joshua, and he has never recovered from her." She rolls her lips as she thinks. "I could never measure up," she whispers.

I frown, huh? "What are you talking about?" I snap.

She smiles. "I don't blame your father. It was never his intention to make me feel insecure. The relationship with the other woman was before we met. His heart could never be mine because it was already taken."

I look at the ceiling in frustration.

"Joshua, imagine if you and Natasha didn't get back together and through circumstances you got another woman pregnant."

My eyes hold hers.

"He did the right thing, he married me, and he's been miserable ever since."

Pity fills me. "That's not true," I sigh.

She fakes a smile. "Isn't it? He would only be home when you boys were awake. He would go out at night."

I swallow as I think—that's true. I remember it myself. "And I don't blame him, he was a good husband. He cared

for me and our boys, we never wanted for anything. We made love once a week." She hesitates and frowns. "But he was never really with me and I knew that and if I told him that his best friend was blackmailing me with sexual favors and beatings, I knew he would leave me and he would take you boys with him. I have no family, Joshua. I have close friends that know nothing about me. I've been living a lie for twenty- nine years, hiding the truth from even myself." Her tear-filled eyes hold mine.

"Mum," I whisper. "I would have stayed with you. If you had given me the chance to help you, I would have helped you."

The tears drop onto her cheeks.

"Joshua, stay with me now, I need you now." She puts her open hand onto the glass wall and I look at it. "I need you to forgive me. It's the only thing in this world that matters to me." She shakes her head as she cries. "I can't contemplate a future without you in it."

"What about Dad?" I ask.

"I love your father, I have always loved your father. He's too good for me." She shakes her head sadly.

I frown. "He's not too good for you. This is the abused woman mentality that has you thinking like this. He is not too good for you. You deserve happiness." I put my hand onto hers on the glass and she screws up her face in tears.

"I love you, Joshua," she whispers.

My tear-filled eyes meet hers. "I love you too. It's okay. I don't want you to hurt anymore," I whisper.

"But I am, because my son is in prison for a crime he didn't commit. He has lost his love at the hands of another. How can I help you, Joshua. Tell me what you need," she sobs.

My eyes hold hers and the tears break the dam and run down my face. "Find me Natasha's body—that's all I want. I need to bring her home to bury her."

Her tears match mine as they run down our faces. "Joshua, where are Natasha's diaries?" she asks.

I shake my head. "No, I'm not handing them over. Don't ask me to."

Her face drops. "So, you do have them then? This will prove you're innocent," she whispers. "Natasha would not want you in prison like this. You need to be with your family. Please Joshua."

I shake my head. "Her words die with me," I whisper. "Her words die with me."

Today's verdict will be tomorrow's headline and the look of anguish on Cameron's face is unbearable. He has been with me blow by blow since Natasha went missing— they all have.

Every member of our family has been behind me 100% and I couldn't have asked for more. I'm so grateful for their unwavering support but I can't put my family through this any longer. I just need this to be over.

The details that they have brought up publicly about my past life have been unsavory to say the least, my worst nightmare. Natasha's mother and sister should never have had to listen to any of it let alone have to deal with it splashed all over the world news. The paparazzi presence in this courtroom today is overwhelming and I keep my eyes cast down so that they can't get the shot of my face that they all so desperately want. Why is it that the perfect days in my life like the ones in Natasha's arms flew by in the blink of an eye but the horrific final day of my court case is the slowest day in history? My mind goes back to the last interrogation I received at the hands of the prosecutor.

"So, Mr. Stanton, I understand that the prostitute was blackmailing you with movie footage of you and her having sex?"

I drop my eyes in shame. "Yes," I murmur.

"And you didn't want Natasha to ever know about this movie, did you?" he yells.

"No," I reply in a monotone.

"But she found out, didn't she?" he yells.

"Yes," I reply.

"But then the prostitute kept going, didn't she, and she wanted more money and she threatened to go to the press with it and shame your fiancée and her family," he yells.

"Yes," I reply.

"So, you had her murdered," he screams.

"No," I reply.

"Yes, you did!" He walks over to the jury members.

"Because that's how this controlling, rich, self-absorbed man thinks. He can control every situation. Every person he comes into contact with must do as he demands or there will be hell to pay. So, you can imagine the rage he felt when the love of his life fell in love with her bodyguard." His eyes come back to me.

I shake my head. "No," I reply. "That's not true."

"The outrage and furious state you would have been in," he yells.

I shake my head. "No."

"We have the footage. You were threatening to kill the bodyguard. You pushed her into the car against her will. You drugged her and cut her throat and murdered her in silence and then drugged yourself to cover your crime," he yells. "Didn't you?" he screams.

I shake my head. "No!" I yell. "I did not."

"Your fingerprints were on the Rohypnol which was found in your house." He yells across the crowded hushed room. "Your fingerprints were on the knife that killed Natasha Marx."

"I don't know how they got there," I reply.

"Do not insult my intelligence!" he yells. "We are not stupid, Joshua Stanton. You have full-time guards on every property. Nobody could have gotten that drug onto your premises without being seen! You are a control freak! You have murdered a prostitute because she wasn't playing by your rules and got away with it and now you have murdered your own fiancée because she dared to fall out of love with you. Money can't save you this time, Joshua Stanton." His eyes go back to the jury and he paces in front of them. "I beg the jury to not let Natasha Marx's death be in vain. Joshua Stanton will do this again, he is aggressive and violent, he is a drug addict and dangerous to this community. Can you have another death on your conscience?" he yells. "Because that is exactly what is going to happen if this man walks free today."

The jury all stay silent and I drop my head. I really would like to kill him right now—maybe he's right. I am a danger. I am going to kill the person who did this—without a doubt. I have no fear anymore. I could die tomorrow and not feel any pain. I have crossed over to the other side, a zombie in this life without my love. My heart and soul have been ripped from the very body that sits here and the only thing that is keeping me alive is the internal image of me killing the person who has done this. What's happened to me? The darkness has taken me over and I am scared of what I am going to do. I don't know what I am capable of anymore. am I?

My cold eyes rise to meet the prosecutor's and I glare at him.

I've had enough.

I am brought back to the present moment. "All rise." The court official calls as the jury enters the room in single file as we all stand and watch. I look back to Bridget behind me and she gives me a soft smile; my eyes flick to Cameron and Adrian and they both nod to acknowledge me. This is it.

"The jury finds Joshua Stanton guilty of murder in the first degree."

There are cheers in the gallery and the cameras start to flash. "No," I hear Bridget and my mother cry out. "No, he's innocent." The cries come from behind me from my supporters.

I stand still, frozen in time, and stare straight ahead.

Guilty.

Guilty.

Vincenzo glares at me and drops his head. "It was the diaries," he whispers angrily. "I told you we needed the fucking diaries." My heart drops.

"He is sentenced to thirty-one years without parole," the judge calls out.

The crowd gasps and my face flickers under the flashes of the photographers—thirty-one years without parole, thirty-one years without parole. I will be sixty years old when I am released. My eyes stay focused straight ahead—what's happening?

Cameron grabs me in an embrace. "We will fight this injustice," he cries. My mother and all of the family embrace me as they cry, and the guard comes over with the handcuffs and I drop my head. I can't have those fucking things on. My eyes cloud over.

"Please no," I whisper.

The guard looks at me sympathetically and opens them up.

"Get away from him," Cameron yells as he pushes the guard away from me. "He didn't do this," he yells. "You have the wrong man!" he screams to the courtroom.

Two other guards walk over and physically restrain Cameron who is close to hysterical.

I feel the cold hard snap of the handcuff around my wrist and I close my eyes to try and block out the hysteria of my family as they lose control.

"Come on," the guard snaps. And just like that, my life is over.

Adrian

I sit in my office with my elbows on my desk and my head in my hands. That's the fourth resignation from the board this morning. How in the hell am I supposed to keep this company afloat when the brains of the operation is in jail for murder? Never have I felt the pressure I am under today. Joshua's company is entirely in my hands and to be honest I don't have a clue what I'm doing. I need to get a professional in to help me. Who handles this kind of stuff?

My mind goes to Natasha and how she made everything easy simply by being around. That beautiful smile and those dimples. *I miss her.*

My buzzer sounds.

"Mr. Murphy?" Ella asks. I buzz her back.

"Yes, Ella," I reply.

"Bridget is here for your lunch meeting," she replies.

"Send her in," I buzz back.

I'm taking Didge out for lunch. She's flatter than flat and I am desperately trying to pick her up. She's being strong for Joshua and I am being strong for her. Let me rephrase that. I'm acting strong for a lot of people, but I am crumbling on the inside like a flake.

The door opens and her gorgeous face comes into view. "Hi." She smiles sadly.

"Hey, Marx girl." I smile.

She smiles and kisses my cheek. "Where are you taking me for lunch?" she asks.

I smirk. "Anywhere you want," I reply.

She bites her lip as she thinks. "Can we go to McDonald's?" she asks hopefully.

I smile sadly. "We can," I answer as I inhale deeply. Oh, I so don't want to go there.

"I'm eating a salad," I reply.

"Oh please." She rolls her eyes. "Eating a salad in McDonald's is like going to a hooker for a hug. What's the damn point?"

I smirk and shake my head. "Just let me finish up here. I won't be long." I start to shut down my computer and she sits at the desk and starts to scroll through her phone.

"Is Ben here?" she asks.

My eyes rise to meet hers. "No. What's going on with you two anyway?" I ask.

She shrugs sadly. "Nothing. We have hardly talked since Tash went missing. He blames himself. I blame myself. It's a vicious circle."

I frown. "Have you tried to talk to him?"

She shakes her head again. "The thing is, I am just so sad." She blows out a breath. "I can't even focus on anything, let alone think about a relationship." She shakes her head again. "I don't have the energy. It's all too hard." She sighs.

I nod as I continue to shut down the computer. "I know what you mean. Nicholas has been staying with me and yet he is the last thing on my mind," I reply.

"Shit," she whispers. "We are a messed-up bunch, aren't we?"

I raise my eyebrows. "Unfortunately, yes."

My phone rings. It's Ben. "Hi," I answer.

"Clear Joshua's office," he snaps.

I frown. "Why?"

"Just do it!" he snaps and then hangs up.

I frown again as my eyes stay on the phone in my hand.

That was weird. "Um, Didge, just wait here for a minute. I have to do something."

"Yeah, sure thing," she replies as she goes back to her phone.

I walk into the office to find Nicholas and Jesten talking to Brock as they scribble down notes. The three of them are bouncing ideas off each other about Coby Allender a lot lately.

Okay, this is uncomfortable. "Guys, Ben just called and asked me to clear the office," I announce.

They all look at each other. "Why?" Jesten asks.

I shake my head. "I don't know to be honest. Ben just called." I am cut off by the door banging open and Ross coming flying through the air onto the floor. What the hell?

Ben storms in and picks up Ross and punches him hard in the face. "Ben!" I yell. "What are you doing?"

He drags Ross up by the shirt and sits him in the chair and punches him again as hard as he can in the stomach. Ross gasps for breath and doubles over in pain.

My hands go to my head. "Oh my God. What the hell do you think you're doing, Ben?" I whisper angrily.

"Get out, Murph and Nicholas," Ben yells.

Nicholas immediately stands and the other two, Jesten and Brock, who obviously know what's going on, fold their arms ready for the show.

"Start talking, fucker, or I will kill you," Ben sneers.

Ross starts shaking his head nervously. "It was just meant to scare him. It was never a hit." He shakes his head. "I swear to you. It went too far—it was never meant to go that far," he whimpers.

I frown and my horrified eyes flick to Nicholas's. "I don't even know these fucking guys!" Ross yells.

"Oh, so *you* ordered the hit on him." Jesten smiles. "I can't wait to watch this." He smiles sarcastically.

"What?" I stammer.

Ben punches him again three times in succession. "Stop it!" I yell.

"Adrian, let's leave them to it," Nicholas says nervously as he grabs my hand to drag me out of the room.

"Somebody tell me what the hell is going on!" I snap.

"Old mate here has had the red dreadlock dude at his house. I watched him on his driveway through his security footage pay him $1000," Ben sneers. "What did you pay him for?" he yells again.

My eyes glare at Ross. "Are you kidding?" I scream. "Are you kidding me? They could have killed him!"

Ross shakes his head. "I swear to you, Adrian. I never meant it to go that far. They were just supposed to rough him up a bit. I'm sorry. I'm sorry," he pleads.

I don't believe this. Ross the weasel is behind the attempted hit. I don't know whether to laugh or cry.

Ben grabs Ross by his hair and pulls his head back.

"You are going to pay, pretty boy," he sneers.

"Ben, stop!" Bridget's voice snaps out.

Ben's mortified eyes meet Bridget's. "Who the hell are you?" she screams at him.

The room falls silent and time seemingly stands still. Ben's chest rises and falls with deep regretful breaths.

"Who are you?" she whispers through tears. "Is this the real you? Is this who you are, Ben?"

I shake my head and hold my hand out for her as sympathy fills me. "Let's go, baby," I murmur. This is abysmal. I lead Bridget out of the room as I myself try to reconcile a side to Ben that I have never seen before.

I don't even know where to start with this one.

Joshua

I lie in the bed in the cell as I think of my beautiful Natasha. Even the memory of her lifts me from my darkened place. Her soft hair, her beautiful smile and dimples, the way she loved me and how much she hated horses. I smile at her hate of horses and then my face falls—my horses. I need to let Jasper go to a person who will love him as much as I do. It's not fair that he be forgotten in all of this. My eyes flick around the depressing small cell, my new home. How do you adjust to this? I can't. I can't live here for the next thirty-one years. I'm supposed to be in Willowvale with Natasha and our children and my horses. It's not meant to be like this— this was never how it was meant to end.

"Hey, are you awake, Fuck Off?" I hear the young kid across the hall call out.

"No," I reply flatly.

"Are you going to get out of bed today?" he asks.

"No," I reply. Why bother?

"Come on. Why don't you come to the gym?"

My eyes flick to him. "You saw what happened last time I went to the gym," I reply. I got into a fight with three other men over nothing. I don't even know how it started.

"Come on. It's nearly the end of May. It's been a week since your court case, and you need to start leaving your cell."

I frown as I sit up in realization. I was supposed to be getting married in three days. A deep sadness overtakes me as I remember Natasha's wedding dress. She would have been such a beautiful bride. All I have ever wanted for as long as I can remember is to be with Natasha on our wedding day. I sit on the side of the bed and put my elbows on my knees and my head into my hands deep in thought. I want to see you again, baby. How can I see you again? My dark eyes flick around the empty cement room I am in; this isn't living. I would rather be in hell than here...or in heaven with my beautiful girl. My mind drifts off into a dark place where I imagine myself meeting up with Natasha. I need to be with her and there is only one way to do that.

I will be completely yours, Natasha, on our wedding day, in death as I was in life. I won't let you be alone anymore... see you soon, Presh... I'm coming, my love.

I stand and move to the bars of my cell. "Hey," I call.

The young kid looks up surprised, smiles broadly and walks over to my cell.

My eyes meet his. "You know everyone in here. Can you get me something?" I ask.

"Like what?" he asks.

"Heroin," I reply.

He frowns. "What do you want that shit for?" he frowns. "You're not a junkie."

I bite my lip as I think of the appropriate answer.

"I can transfer a million dollars today for you," I reply.

His face drops. "You will transfer me a million dollars to get you some heroin?" he repeats. "How much do you want?"

I lift my chin defiantly. "A lot."

I sit at the window of the visitation room as I wait for Cameron and the door opens and his smiling face comes into view. A sense of calm sweeps over me and I smile in return.

"Hey mate," he says softly into the phone.

"Hi," I smile in return.

"You okay? What's wrong?" Cameron asks.

I shake my head. "Nothing, why?"

He frowns. "You have never called and asked me to come down here to see you, so I thought something may have been wrong. I was coming down on Saturday." He hesitates as his eyes hold mine.

"To visit me on my wedding day," I reply. He nods as he bites his bottom lip.

"Can you do something for me?" I ask.

He nods. "Sure."

"Can you go and pick up my suit from the tailors, please?"

He frowns. "Which one?"

"My wedding suit," I reply.

His questioning eyes hold mine. "What do you need that for?" he asks as his mind ticks over.

I shrug. "I just want it." I pause before I ask him the next question. "Can you pick up my wedding ring also?"

"Yeah, okay. I will swing by next week," he replies casually.

"No, now. Today," I answer without thinking.

He frowns. "Josh, why do you need your wedding suit and your ring now?"

I bite my bottom lip as I think of the appropriate answer. "I just want them in the house before the wedding date, that's all," I reply. "If we don't pick them up now I may never get them."

He nods sadly as his eyes stay glued on mine.

Tears fills my eyes as I realize this is the last time I will see my beloved brother. We have glass between us, and I can't even hold him.

"Josh, we are going to get you out of here. You just need

to hold on, okay? I promise you we are working as hard as we can and we have leads, new leads," he pushes out in a panic.

I nod calmly.

"Can you look after our mother?" I ask. "And Adrian, can you watch over Adrian?"

He frowns. "Joshua, you can look after them. They need you. We all need you," he whispers as his eyes glass over.

"I love you, Cam," I whisper through the lump in my throat. "I want you to know that."

He puts his hand on the glass. "Josh, what are you thinking? You're scaring me. Please don't do anything stupid. You are down. It's okay to be down. It's just a very hard time. But hold on. We are going to get you out of here and then we can move to Willowvale and..." he pauses.

"What Cameron? What can we do? Carry on like none of this happened? Return to normalcy?" I sneer.

His tear-filled eyes hold mine.

"Natasha is dead and alone because of me. I failed to protect her when she needed me the most," I reply in a whisper.

He shakes his head. "No, Natasha is with her father and she is watching what you do. She is still with you and I need you, Joshua. We all need you," he pushes out in a rush.

I put my hand up against the glass to rest on his and smile sadly. I need to get out of here before I lose my shit. "Just pick the stuff up for me today, please." I stand abruptly.

"Sit back down. I want to talk to you some more," he pleads.

I shake my head. "I've got to go," I whisper through my hurt.

"Got to go where?" he snaps.

"Cam, don't," I whisper.

"Do you want to see Amelie?" he asks hopefully. "She called yesterday. She's desperate to see you."

I turn back to him and frown. I would like to see Am one last time. I need to make peace with her. I nod. "Yes, please. I would like to see her," I whisper.

He smiles as he nods. "Okay, that sounds good. I will bring her down with Adrian on Friday."

I frown and then nod. "Okay," I reply

Natasha

I sit scrunched up in the bottom of the closet in the darkness. In my hands I have two hooks that I have unscrewed from the tops of coat hangers, my pitiful weapons. A strange car pulled up four hours ago. Somebody else is here in the house but nobody has come to my room yet. They are probably outside digging my grave. The taste of bile fills my mouth—I have never been so scared. I don't know what they're doing. I haven't a frigging clue.

The televisions are all showing different dates, Joshua has been arrested and now someone has turned up here. They must be going to get rid of me. I am no longer of any use. I put my hands over my face, oh God. Please let it be quick and pain- less. I re-clutch the hooks in my hand and practice swinging them at someone in the darkness. If I can just get their eye with the hook. Aim for the eyes. Why didn't I take self-defense classes? I'm such an idiot.

I hear the bedroom door open and the light switches on. I hold my breath in the darkness. No, no, no, oh my God.

"Natasha," the young boy calls.

I stay silent as my breath quivers in fear. He opens the

wardrobe door and turns on the light and frowns when he sees me. "What are you doing?" he asks.

I screw up my face. "I'm scared," I whisper.

"Nothing's happening," he replies softly.

My face drops.

"You need to come out in the room, so they can see you on camera. They haven't seen you before. Nobody is going to come into the room."

I stay seated as I frown. Nobody's seen me before so that means that here is the only monitor. I start to hear my heartbeat in my ears and I subtly put my hooks onto the carpet and stand slowly and walk out into the room. The young boy leaves the room and shuts the door behind him. Refusing to look at the camera, I sit on the bed and wring my hands nervously in front of me. What are they looking at? Are they checking that I'm going insane? Because I fucking am, and their plan is working perfectly. Act normal, act normal, I remind myself. I get into bed, turn my back to the camera and hold my breath as I try to calm myself down and after what seems like about an hour, I hear the other car leave and the light in my room turns off.

I get up and put my hands and forehead on the back of the door as I think in the darkness. I need to be home before my wedding in three days. Think. How am I getting out of here?

"Listen, Dad, I don't know what the fuck you are doing up there. But I need help," I whisper angrily.

I shake my head in anger. Is there even a Heaven? Is that a load of shit too? If he could help me, I know he would. He would have gotten me out of here by now, and he would have told me what to do. I turn around and lean my back on the door and slide down into a sitting position against the door. I'm going to get home to Joshua and I'm going to wear my wedding dress on Saturday. But how? The moonlight shines through the window and under the bottom of the curtain I see something glimmer in the light. I frown. What's that?

I crawl over on my hands and knees and pull back the curtain to reveal a large sliver of the thick glass from the water jug I threw at the back of the door. I must have missed it when I picked it up. It is about four or five centimeters wide and about twenty centimeters long. I run my finger along the edge of it in the darkness... razor sharp.

I sit in the darkness as my mind goes into overdrive. I have my weapon.

CHAPTER 27

Natasha

I STAND in the bathroom with the glass in my hand as I wrap a sock around the base of it, so I don't cut myself. I've thrown up three times this morning already with nerves and my leg is bouncing uncontrollably. Breakfast will be here in fifteen minutes and I'm going to do it. I don't know what I'm going to do... but I'm going to do something violent and someone is probably going to die... hopefully not me. They have pushed me to the point of no return.

"I'm sorry but you have forced me to hurt you," I whisper to my reflection in the mirror to try and justify what I am about to do. I'm going for Carl. I don't care if I kill him, but I know I couldn't live with myself if I hurt the boy. He's just a kid trying to get himself through med school. But the downside of my plan is that Carl is bigger and more dangerous and way more fucking scary. Oh my God, oh my God. I put the glass knife on the sink and put my hands over my face. Am I really going to stab someone with that? I walk back to the closet and put on another sweater. I am wearing sweatpants, three pairs of bed socks, a T-shirt and three sweaters. It's going to be cold if I do get away. Shit. I start to pace. Should I stay in the bedroom? No, I need to run out from the bathroom and take him by surprise. I look at my reflection in the mirror. "You can do this," I whisper. "You can do this." I slowly pick up the glass knife and wrap my hand around the base and I swing it through the air as I practice. No, it needs to be harder. Shit. I bring it up over my head and with all my strength I stab it down through the air. Fuck, this is a nightmare. With my heart beating hard in my chest I open the bathroom door with the knife in my hand and I wait.

On cue the bedroom door opens and Carl walks in carrying the tray of food and I screw up my face in tears and run at him with my hand over my head. I bring the knife down hard into his neck and he screams in pain. Oh my God, I scream as blood starts to spurt from his wound and I put my hand over my mouth. He staggers back and falls, and his head hits the bedpost, and he is knocked unconscious. I put my hands over my mouth in shock. He lies still and silent with blood coming from the wound. I need to tie him up. I run back to the closet and grab a belt from one of the robes and pull his hands behind his back and tie them together. Is he dead? I screw up my face as nervous energy runs through me. Run. Run. Run. With my heart racing I jump over his slumped body, out the door and lock it behind me. I race down the stairs two at a time to the front door and I grab the handle and frantically rattle it. Fuck, it's locked. My eyes dart around, and I run to the back door, which thankfully is open. I run out onto the deck and into the sunshine.

My eyes fly around my surroundings. Forest on one side and paddocks on the other. Which way, which way? The forest.

I sprint as fast as I can towards the forest. Oh my God, I killed him, he's dying. He is dying. My mind flicks to Joshua and the fact that it's going to be him dying or Carl and I screw up my face and run faster. I need to get out of here. I get to a barbed wire fence and bend to get through it and keep running towards the trees. I am desperately out of breath. Keep going I chastise myself, keep going. The landscape is rugged, and I am treading on rocks and my feet are hurting but I keep pushing. Get to the trees, get to the trees. I cry to myself as I run and finally, after what seems forever, I make it. I run into the shrubbery and under the veil of protection and I fall to the ground in exhaustion as I gasp for air.

Which way? My eyes search my surroundings. On one side of me a hill inclines up and it seems to be bushland and the other way goes down a hill but seems much more rugged terrain. Up, I will go up the hill. I look down at my feet. Fuck, I wish I had some shoes. On getting my breath back I stand and start to run, and the sticks break under my feet. Oww, my feet. Shit, I'm an idiot. I should have grabbed Carl's shoes. Who am I kidding? I wouldn't steal a person's shoes that I had just stabbed. I put my hands on my head in disbelief. I just stabbed someone in the neck. What the fucking hell has my life turned into? If Carl hasn't died, he is either calling for backup right now or bleeding to death but if he has died it's going to be eleven and a half hours until the boy gets back. I need to get the hell out of here and with renewed purpose I pick up the pace. I keep running through the bush as I try to negotiate the terrain with my feet looking for the best places to stand. Why didn't I run on that damn treadmill? I should be fit but no I have the aerobic fitness level of a ninety-year-old. This gasping for breath is not helping my escape at all.

Exhaustion doesn't come close to what I'm feeling. It's late afternoon and I've been walking for hours. I can't physically run anymore. It will be dark in about two hours judging by the sun and I am staying on the edge of the forest that follows the road as I don't want to get lost. I turn and look back the way I have come. God, am I even going the right way? I do seem to have come a long distance but what happens if the closest house is like eighty miles from anywhere. Shit. Just keep going, or the mind will hold you back. Stop thinking I remind myself. I won't be able to see when night falls so I will have to find somewhere safe to sleep. Where is it safe to sleep here? My eyes search the forest. Now, in Australia most of the scary things don't come out at night, all the nocturnal animals are relatively harmless, but in America I have no frigging idea. My face drops. Oh shit, bears. Are there bears in these woods? My eyes widen. Do they eat people? What about wolves... I'm so screwed.

Shit, I need a fire. How do you light a fire without a match? I shake my head at my stupidity. *Survivor...* I hate that fucking show and now I know why. This is totally shit. I hate surviving. At least if I had watched it, I would have a faint idea what to do now, but no... I had to watch *Dating Naked*. What the hell am I ever going to learn from a show like *Dating Naked* other than that people are surprisingly stupid? I'm such an idiot. I keep walking and looking up into the trees as I walk. Maybe I should climb a tree? Hmm, no. I will fall out and break my neck as soon as I go to sleep, but I should sleep under a tree so that I can climb it if a bear comes to eat me. Why didn't I bring the knife, oh God. I had to think of that, didn't I? It was lodged in Carl's neck, Natasha, you idiot.

I carry on up a steep hill and when I finally get to the top I hear the rushing sound of water in the valley below. Omg, water. I start to run with renewed purpose down the embankment towards the sound of the stream. Shit, it's away from the road. I stand and look at the road and then back into the forest where I hear the water coming from. It could be a long way away—I'm not risking it. I get lost in a shopping mall parking lot, no way am I getting lost out here. I have drunk nine liters of water over the last three days in preparation for this so I should be okay. I really would love a drink though. Tough shit as Joshua would say and I trudge back up the hill towards the road as I smile. I'm going to see my man soon and I picture his face when he finds out I'm still alive. My eyes tear up. After tonight it's only two days until our wedding. I look down at myself covered in dirt, filthy with ripped track pants on. This isn't the preparation I had planned. Oh well, suck it up princess and get moving.

After another hour of walking, I am too exhausted to carry on and I sit on a large rock just in the bushland. The road looks to be about 500 meters away and I see a car come out of a road up ahead that I hadn't noticed before and turn onto the one I have been following. I dip down to go unnoticed. Shit, they are going towards the house I have just run from—have I been busted? I look back in the direction the car came from. I'm going the right way. That car came from somewhere and I stand with renewed purpose and start walking again. I was going to stop and sleep somewhere for the night but forget it. I'm getting home to my family tonight, even if I have to walk all night. I stay just inside the line of trees and finally come to the turn-off in the road that the car came from and I look down it tentatively. What do I do? Which way do I go? Here I stand on the corner of two roads, not a clue in Hell which way to go, and I know my and Joshua's whole entire future rests on this decision. I look down the road that I just followed that goes to the house of Hell and then down the road to the left. I'm going this way because that car came from somewhere.

I continue to keep walking, but I keep tripping as sunlight turns to darkness and I can't see where I'm going. This is getting dangerous. I have to stop, or I am going to break my leg. I find a large tree that has a big flat rock under it, and I curl up into a ball on top of the rock. My eyes look around at the dark, cold and scary surroundings and for the first time today I let my fear sink in and the tears start to flow. "Please let me get home," I whisper into the darkness. I know nobody is looking for me. Everyone already thinks I'm dead and if I die out here nobody will be any the wiser. "Please let me get home, please let me get home," I repeat as a mantra. The darker it gets, the noisier the forest becomes with insects and animals and I lie still as I listen to them. What's my beautiful Joshua doing now in prison? Is he ok? I smile. I did it. I broke out. I'm tougher than I think I am.

Hold on, Joshua my darling. I'm coming.

I wake freezing and slightly damp. It's dawn and I survived the night... just. I stand and pain rips through my muscles and I smile stupidly. Funnily enough rocks are uncomfortable to sleep on, fancy that. I stretch to try and relieve some of the tightness in my muscles. I'm so frigging sore from my sprinting yesterday. That's it, if I make it out of here alive, I'm getting fit. Hell, I might start cage fighting too, why not? I just stabbed a guy in the frigging neck. I frown in disgust at my alarming thoughts. Oh God. I look back at the bushland following the road and I start walking. It's overcast and cold, and I need to keep moving.

After walking for hours, it's late afternoon. I'm starving hungry and thirsty, and I need to find some water to drink. For the last hour I have been running. It's raining and although I need the water, I know I will be freezing overnight out here with no protection. I keep stopping and opening my mouth to the sky, trying to get some fluids into my system. Where's that honey Bear Grylls when you need him to make you a tent and a water bottle? I keep going and up ahead I see a driveway go off the main road and up into a mountain. Oh, a house. I start to run through the forest in the direction of the house until I reach the driveway. It's on the opposite side of the road to the forest I am in and I have to go across a paddock and then the road to get to it. It's risky. If the car comes looking for me at that same time I will be found as I will be totally out in the clear with nowhere to hide. They would probably be looking for me by now. Actually, why hasn't anyone driven down this road? I frown. That's strange. He's dead, Carl's dead, so he hasn't called for help at all. But then sometimes he would stay with me for twenty-four hours so maybe that was a long shift and so nobody's found out yet.

I look both ways, scooch down and start to go out into the open paddock towards the road. I continually check the road to make sure nobody is coming and continue up the hill towards the road. My feet are cut up and the socks have spots of blood on them, but I haven't taken my socks off to look because I don't want to see the damage. I don't need another barrier in my head.

I finally get to the side of the road and bend down and look both ways. This is risky. The road is dirt with big rocks on it and I have to sprint which means my feet are going to be ripped apart even more. The rain starts pouring down and my heart starts to pump heavily. I take some deep breaths and then I sprint for my life across the road and up the winding driveway. My feet are hurting so much that my tears start to fall as I run up the driveway in the torrential rain. I keep running and running as I cry until finally I am out of sight of the main road and I slump on a rock and cry into my hands. This is a nightmare. "You're nearly there," I scream out into the raindrops. "Keep fucking going," I yell at myself. I stand and keep hobbling up the hill. What if this isn't even a house? What if it's just a road that goes to nowhere? "Why are you raining on me?" I scream. "This is hard enough!" I yell. "Pull yourself together, fruitcake," I mutter under my breath.

The driveway has gone over a hill and down a few bends and darkness has fallen. I am deep in the forest and scared as hell. I can't even walk properly now. I'm hobbling like an old woman. I need to rest my feet, so I will just walk over this next hill and then I will sit down for a while and rest. Yes, keep going, keep going, I keep repeating to myself.

I get to the top of the hill and look down into the valley below and see a sight that makes me burst into tears. A house, there is a house down there on the cleared land, an oasis in my hell. "Thank God," I whisper as the tears roll down my face. "Thank you, thank you."

I walk for another half an hour until I finally get to the house. It looked so close but it's so far away. The house is in total darkness and I walk tentatively up the creaky front steps. It's a large house with a big wrap-around verandah and there are rooms in the attic by the look of the windows jutting out of the tin roof. I open the heavy screen door and knock loudly. My heart is in my throat with fear, but I have to knock. I desperately need help. I can't get out of here alone. I knock again and wait but an answer doesn't come. "Please be home," I whisper.

I follow the verandah around the side of the house and go

to the back door and knock loudly on the door and wait. No answer again. What do I do? I sit on the back step and think for a moment. No one is home but I bet there is a telephone inside so I could call the police. I stand and walk back around the verandah, peering in the windows. I just need to get into this house. I pick up a pot plant next to the front door and smash it through the glass. Then I put my hand through and unlatch the lock, jiggle the handle and it opens. Shit, I did it. I walk in and feel around for a light switch on the wall to the right but nothing. I then feel around on the wall to my left and finally find some switches and turn them on and the house lights up. I smile broadly for the first time in two days.

"Hello," I call out. "Is anyone home?" Silence is the reply.

"Hello, I need your help. Please help me," I call again as I look up the stairwell.

I wait for a reply. The last thing I need is to be mistaken for someone breaking in and shot on the spot.

"I have been kidnapped. Is anyone home? I just need to call the police," I call again.

Nobody's home. Right, I need to find the phone. I walk through the house and make my way into the kitchen and I immediately open the fridge. Shit, no food. Nobody lives here —it must be a weekend cabin. I turn on the tap and thankfully water appears. I bend and drink straight from the tap. My eyes close in gratitude. Thank God, water—it tastes so good. Phone, I need to find the phone.

My eyes search the kitchen and then I walk into the living area and I see the phone on the sideboard, and I run and pick it up. No sound, oh no. I push on the receiver repeatedly as I try to get a dial tone...nothing. Shit, the phone has been disconnected. My eyes search the room for a computer or something, internet. There must be internet in this damn house somewhere. Nobody could stay out here in the sticks without inter-net, surely. There are three rooms off the hallway and I make my way down to them and check each of them. The first is a weird little room with a high-back wing chair and an ottoman but no internet. The next room has nothing but bookshelves. I open the last room and I screw up my face in disgust. Animal heads are all mounted on the walls—he's a hunter. The man who stays here is a hunter. My mind goes back to my fear of being eaten alive overnight, so I wasn't frigging imagining it, and it could have easily happened. There are definitely huge wild animals around here.

I walk up the stairs and I find two large bedrooms and a bathroom and no damn computer. Oh my God. I stand in the hallway—what am I going to do? Shit, I walk back down, pick up the phone again and repeatedly bang on the receiver. "Why is there no fucking phone?" I yell to myself. "Seriously, can I get one break? This is bullshit." I walk back into the kitchen with my hands on my head. What am I going to do? The rain is really coming down now and I look out the back window into the cold wet darkness. I can't stay out there unprotected overnight but what if they come here looking for me?

This is a nightmare and I feel my heart rate pick back up. I thought I was saved... obviously not. I sit down at the dining table and pinch the bridge of my nose as I try to think. "Is there anything to eat?" I whisper to myself. I open the pantry and am blessed with the sight of several cans of various foods. I open the drawer, find a tin opener and open a can of baked beans. I eat them cold from the can as I walk through the house.

I'm uncomfortable being here. If they come looking for me I'm screwed. I walk to the front door and look at the smashed glass in the windowpane and the rain pouring heavily outside. God, I'm such an idiot. Why would I smash the window next to the front door? It's a dead giveaway that I'm here. My fear starts to reignite again, and I start to eat my baked beans at double speed. I need to get out of here. I will be found here, and the smashed glass will let them know from what direction I have come. Fuck. My heart starts beating fast as I realize I have sabotaged myself with my stupidity. I walk back into the kitchen and open another can of beans and eat them as I walk upstairs to check to see if there are any shoes I can wear. I open the closet in the bedrooms. Nothing but men's clothes. They will have to do—at least they are dry. I take off my cold wet clothes and my eyes go to the bathroom. I would kill for a hot shower right now. No. If they come when I'm in the shower I will have no chance. Who am I kidding? If they come here at all I'm dead meat. I hate this. I walk into the bathroom, get a towel from the cabinet, then I quickly undress and dry myself. I dress again into a large pair of men's sweatpants, a white cotton shirt and a large woolen knitted sweater. There is a dark green beanie and I grab that too for when my hair dries. I run back down the stairs with renewed purpose.

I need to find some weapons to defend myself and I walk into the kitchen and open the second drawer. I have never been so glad to see the large collection of carving knives in my life. I slowly pick one out and grip my hand around the handle. The memory of stabbing Carl fills my mind and I close my eyes in disgust at myself. I will never as long as I live forget how a knife feels as it slices through flesh or forget seeing blood spurt from a wound. I shake my head in disgust at myself. "Stop it," I snap out loud. "He deserved it—he was going to kill you," I mutter to try and justify my brutality.

Carrying the knife, I walk back through the living room to look out the front door at the torrential rain. Maybe I should stay here, cut the power and then if they turn up, I will have more of a chance to defend myself. Yes, and then I will be out of the weather and I can rest my feet while I wait. Ok, where's the power box then? I walk up the hall and peer into the room with all of the hunting stuff and I see a metal cabinet at the back. What's in there I wonder? I walk over and jiggle the handles— it's locked. Why would there be a locked metal cabinet in a room like this. I frown as I think, and my eyes widen. Guns, there are hunting guns in this cabinet. I start to rattle the handle violently. I need to get into this cabinet. Shit. I run back into the kitchen in search of a tool to break open the cabinet and I get three big knives I can hopefully use as a jimmy. I start to desperately try to fit them through the crack in the door to try and break the lock. I bang repeatedly on the door as I try as hard as I can to open it. "Open," I scream. "Open!"

I bang on the door and run back out into the kitchen in search of other tools. I look around desperately and for some reason I feel panicked as if any moment they are going to drive up the driveway and I need to turn the lights off immediately. My heart starts to pump adrenaline heavily through my system. Shit, shit, shit. What will I use? What will I use? I look under the kitchen sink and find a hammer and I run back up the hall and start to hit the lock as hard as I can. The noise is deafening on the metal, but I keep hitting as hard as I can. "Open, please open," I cry as I frantically bang on the cabinet door. I am in such a panic that I can hardly breathe, and I start to bang on the door with both my hands in frustration. I kick the door with such force that I dent it and I stop to think for a moment. Hang on, if I tip it over perhaps there is a weakness at the back of the cabinet. I narrow my eyes. Yes, tip it over. I move to the back of it and I start to rock it backwards and forwards and eventually I move it out from the wall enough that I can get my feet under it. I push with all my strength and I get it away from the wall. It rocks forward a little bit and just when I am about to tip it to the ground, I hear a metal ping hit the ground and I look to see what it was. Keys. A set of silver keys have fallen off the top of the cabinet and I grab them desperately as a lifeline. I fumble to try and find the right key and eventually I do. I open the door and am blessed with the sight of two shotguns and ammunition. From sheer relief I fall to the floor breathless. "Thank you, thank you." I whisper as I am momentarily paralyzed. I grab the two guns and the bullets and run to the backdoor and out into the rain. Hang on. I need a flashlight or something. I run back into the kitchen and look under the sink and find a flashlight first thing. God, that was too easy. I run back out into the rain and around to the power box and I cut the power to the house. I return back inside, lock the doors and slowly make my way upstairs into the darkness. I walk into the main bedroom, sit on the bed and stare out the window at the driveway coming up to the house and I slowly load the gun. I then turn the flashlight off and stare out into the darkness.

I'm ready. Come and get me.

CHAPTER 28

Joshua

I sit at the desk in the consultation room as I wait for Nicholas. I know why he's here. The door opens and he appears and smiles warmly.

"Hello Joshua." He frowns when he notices my handcuffs and his eyes flick to the guard who has just brought him into the room. "Remove the cuffs immediately, please," he snaps.

"Hello," I reply as my eyes flick to the guards. One of them fumbles for his keys and then undoes the tight steel band around my wrist.

"Thank you. Now leave us alone," Nicholas says.

The guards both nod and leave the room in silence. Nicholas then comes around to my side of the desk and holds his hand out, and I frown as I look at it. "I would like a hug, please," he asks.

I shake my head. "Just sit down." I sigh.

"No," he replies. "Stand and give me a hug."

"Fuck, man," I whisper.

"I'm not going any further until you hug me," he repeats.

I shake my head and stand, and he grabs me into a tight embrace. He holds me still and close and for some reason my emotions immediately rise, and I feel the dam about to break. I haven't been physically touched since I was arrested. As if sensing my inner turmoil, he stands still, and I drop my head to his shoulder as he holds me.

"These are dark days, yes," he whispers into my hair.

I nod because the lump in my throat leaves me unable to speak and he holds me tighter.

"It's okay to be dark," he whispers.

I briefly escape my emotional cloud, pull back from his grip and wipe my eyes with the heels of my hands.

"Is Adrian okay?" I mumble as I angrily wipe my face.

Nicholas smiles and takes a seat opposite me. "Adrian is doing okay although he is struggling with the company," he replies as his eyes hold mine.

I shake my head in disgust. "What a mess," I whisper.

"Joshua, you had your lawyer here yesterday?" he asks.

My eyes rise to meet his. "Yes," I reply.

"Were you changing your will?" he asks. "Is that why he was here?"

I drop my eyes immediately to evade his truth-serum glare. I don't answer him.

"Do you have a plan, Joshua?"

My eyes once again rise to meet his and I stay silent. He sits back knowingly on his chair and watches me.

"Tell me about your plan," he asks. "How would you kill yourself?"

I frown and drop my head again. "Stay out of my head, Nicholas," I whisper.

"Tomorrow was to be your wedding day," he replies. I nod as my eyes search the floor to escape his gaze.

"You should have been in Kamala today with Natasha arranging things for tomorrow," he says quietly.

My heart drops and I nod. "Thanks for reminding me," I whisper.

"You hadn't forgotten. Don't bother pretending you had," he replies.

I smirk knowingly at the floor.

"What do you think Natasha is doing now?" he asks.

My eyes tear up and I shrug. "Don't know," I whisper as I run my hand over my stubble.

"Tell me something." He sits back on his seat again and folds his arms. "If it was you who had been murdered and Natasha had been left alone and then convicted of your murder, what would you want her to do?" he asks.

I roll my lips. "I know what you are doing, and you can forget it. Natasha is gone and she is not coming back," I stammer.

"It will get easier," he whispers. "I promise you it gets easier."

"How would you know?" I snap through my tears. "Living without her will never be fucking easy. I will never be happy again."

He sits forward. "Joshua, I lost my husband. I know first-hand the depth of your grief. I could have happily killed myself a thousand times."

I sit back shocked. I didn't expect him to say that.

He stares into space as his thoughts go to another time. "Olivier was intelligent and funny." He pauses as he remembers. "We met in a café in Paris." He smiles softly. "It was like a movie. We fell madly in love. I had released my first three books and he was a lawyer so I moved to France and we became inseparable." His eyes meet mine. "He loved me so deeply—I was his only one," he whispers.

My eyes tear up—like my Natasha.

He shakes his head as he becomes visibly upset. "The years we were married were the happiest days of my life. And it's my fault he's dead," he replies through haunted eyes.

I frown.

He shakes his head in disgust at himself. "We had a skiing trip organized for months but I was trying to become this hotshot author." He pauses as he thinks. "And then three days before we were due to leave for our trip, I got a call from my publicist saying that I had been asked to appear on a morning show and it would be great for my career. I wanted to go, but Olivier wanted to go skiing and he went on the ski trip alone." He shakes his head in disgust at himself and his eyes meet mine. "I wasn't worried at the time. I was excited about my great opportunity and I thought I would just fly down and surprise him when I finished the promo stuff."

I drop my head in sadness. I know how this story ends.

Nicholas's eyes glaze over as he stares into space. "He had a bad fall on the slopes but instead of going to the hospital he just went back to the hotel alone."

I blow out a deep breath as the room falls silent and we both become engulfed by our grief.

"He had a brain aneurysm in the bath two hours later and drowned. He was alone and he would have been frightened and in pain." Nicholas wipes his tears away angrily. "I know about being so distraught that you would rather die than face another day alone," he whispers.

My bottom lip quivers and I drop my head.

"I know how it feels to just want the pain to stop. You would do anything to just not feel anymore," he whispers.

I nod as I focus my eyes on the table leg.

Nicholas shakes his head to himself. "And then it gets worse...you die while you are still alive. You don't feel anything anymore. No joy, no happiness. The only thing that seems to be present is a massive hole in your life, one that can never be filled. An emptiness that won't go away."

"Yes," I whisper through bleary eyes.

"I wanted to die too, Joshua. I know how it feels to want to join the person you love." He grabs my hand over the table.

My tears drop onto my cheeks. I can't hold them in anymore. "Why didn't you?" I whisper.

"I had the plan, I had the medication, I had it all worked out. But every time I would go to do it, I would think of Olivier and how disappointed he would be. He was strong and if every day I could just try and be strong like him." He pauses as he wipes a tear, and our eyes meet again. "One day at a time," he whispers. "I just survived one day at a time."

I nod and close my eyes in pain.

"For seven years I ambled through grief trying to find myself. Trying to find happiness in the arms of others, only to wake disgusted with myself, and then I would dive deeper into despair."

I nod. I can relate. I did that for the whole of my early twenties when I was trying to get over Natasha the first time.

Nicholas smiles broadly through his tears. "And then one day in a crowded restaurant I saw this..." He pauses again as he remembers and smiles. "Blond American."

I smirk—Adrian.

"He didn't want anything to do with me and for some reason that's exactly what I needed."

He stands and walks over to the fake glass pane and looks into it. "You know the morning I left Adrian?"

My eyes look at his back. "Yes," I answer.

He bites his bottom lip as he contemplates telling me. "Adrian and I had been inseparable for a month and had been intimate for the first time all weekend, as you probably already know. He was different to anyone I had ever met: smart, strong and yet gentle. Pure, he was so pure. I remember waking that morning and feeling so..." He shakes his head as he remembers. "So unbelievably happy and Adrian was asleep next to me and then I looked at my phone and I realized the date."

I frown.

"The day before had been my anniversary and I hadn't even realized. I had missed Olivier's and my wedding anniversary because I was making love to another man all day without a care in the world. I had never been so disgusted with myself in my life."

"Lots of men miss anniversaries," I murmur to try and make him feel better.

He nods, "I know. I missed three when we were married, and Olivier had to remind me. But this was different. I realized that moment that I had fallen in love with someone else and I wasn't mentally prepared to do that."

He sits back down opposite me and folds his hands in front of him. "And I have been miserable again every day since. I have lost two men that I love, one through death and one through punishing myself for living."

I frown. "I thought you and Adrian were working it out?" I reply.

He shakes his head. "I'm in love with Adrian but he won't let me in again... and I don't blame him."

I nod and drop my head—stubborn shit of a man.

"And besides, Olivier would not want me to move on," he continues sarcastically.

I shake my head. "That's wrong. It's not your fault that he died. Olivier was a good man, and he would want you with someone who can make you happy and who loves you. You deserve happiness, Nicholas."

Nicholas's eyes meet mine. "And so do you, Joshua, and Natasha would want you to live for her."

I swallow the lump in my throat.

"Don't let her death be in vain," he whispers.

He grabs my hand over the table. "Just take it one day at a time. I beg you don't do this to your family and friends," he whispers. "It's so dark now. I know this darkness."

I nod as I squeeze his hand.

"Just one day. Just worry about getting through today and let us out there work on getting you out."

I nod.

The door opens and the guard walks in. "Time's up."

Adrian

Cameron and I wait outside for Nicholas who is in with Joshua. Cameron is pacing back and forth nervously. He is beside himself. He thinks Joshua is on the edge and we are trying everything we can to move him to protective custody with no access to other prisoners. Once it's done, it's done. You can't undo death.

The door opens and I hear the click of the heels on the cement floor. I turn and my eyes find Amelie.

She lifts her chin defiantly as she glares at me. "Adrian," she mutters.

"Hello," I reply cold-faced. God, I can't believe Cameron actually called and asked her to come and see Joshua. He would try anything to keep his brother safe. Even do a deal with the devil.

"I'm going in now," she mutters as she looks at her watch.

"He has someone with him," I reply.

"Who?" she snaps.

I frown at her venom. "A psychologist," I reply.

Cameron turns and sees Amelie and his eyes light up. "Am, thank you for coming."

"What's the problem?" she asks.

Cameron runs his hands through his hair in frustration. "We are worried about Joshua's frame of mind. He asked to see you." He smiles hopefully.

Amelie smiles triumphantly. "I knew he would wake up to himself eventually," she mutters.

My blood runs cold. Fuck, I hate this bitch.

Cameron bites his bottom lip as he holds his tongue and his eyes flick to me as I blow out a deep breath.

"He was never suited to Cinderella anyway," she replies. I narrow my eyes at her. What?

Cameron frowns. "Why do you call her that?" he asks.

She smiles knowingly. "That's a pet name that Joshua called her." She shakes her head and does an exaggerated eye roll. "Pathetic really," she mutters.

My world spins and I drop my head as I think. How would she know that? Not even Joshua knows that. My heart starts to thump heavily in my chest and my eyes flick to Ben and Max who are waiting over on the lounge. Ben frowns in question. I shake my head subtly as I try to reconcile what she has just told me. She called Natasha Cinderella. It's her. It's Amelie. She would only know that if Natasha had told her, and I know that

Natasha had not spoken to her before she went missing. My eyes flick back to Amelie and her phone rings. I walk calmly over to Ben and Max.

"It's Amelie. Amelie killed Natasha," I blurt out in a whisper.

"What?" Max frowns.

Amelie is having trouble with her coverage and the line drops out. She walks out toward the doors to get better coverage and leaves her handbag on the seat next to me.

"What do you mean?" Ben snaps.

I shake my head nervously as goosebumps run up my spine. "She just called Natasha Cinderella," I whisper. Oh my God, I put my hand over my mouth.

Ben screws up his face. "What do you mean?"

"I am the only one who called her that. It was a code between us. Natasha is sending me a message."

Max stands immediately as if on autopilot, takes his phone from his pocket, switches it to silent and then unzips the outside zipper on her handbag and drops his phone inside and zips it back up.

Ben frowns and Cameron walks over. "What's going on?" he asks, oblivious.

"It's Amelie," I whisper.

He frowns. "What's Amelie?" he asks.

"She killed Natasha."

"What?" he snaps.

Amelie comes running back inside and our eyes all flick to her guiltily. "I have to go. I have an emergency I have to attend to." She picks up her bag and throws it over her shoulder.

"But you haven't seen Joshua." Cameron frowns.

She shakes her head. "I'm sorry," she calls as she makes a dash for the doors.

Ben stands and signals to Max to meet him outside and Cameron starts to look between the three of us. "What's happening?" he whispers.

"Get in the car," Ben snaps.

Cameron frowns.

"What?" he whispers. "Can't be."

I shake my head as I try and make sense of this.

"How do you know Natasha hadn't told anyone this?" Cameron asks.

"It was a code that she wanted me to use if there was someone around, she didn't trust," I murmur. My eyes flick to Ben. "Natasha is sending me a message. It's her, I swear to you it's Amelie."

Ben stands with his legs wide and his hands in his pockets as he thinks. His jaw ticks in concentration. "Let's go," he snaps as he heads toward the door and Max follows him. My eyes dart to Cameron who is still in shock.

"Where are we going?" he asks, horrified.

"Following her. She must know something." I shrug as I start toward the door after Ben and Max.

Cameron stands still on the spot, defiantly. "What about Nick?" he calls. "How is he going to get home?"

I turn and frown at him. "I will call him," I snap, annoyed at his procrastination.

He shakes his head and follows us out to the car. Ben and Max get into the front seat and Cam and I get into the back.

Cameron shakes his head. "I swear to God, Murph, if this is a wild goose chase, I'm going to bash you. Joshua needs us today. I don't want him alone today and tonight. Tomorrow is supposed to be his damn wedding day. He's on the fucking verge," he snaps.

"Joshua needs us to prove him innocent, you dead shit, and

we are trying our best! Now shut the fuck up or get out of the fucking car!" Ben snaps and he slams on the brakes and we all lurch forward.

Cameron looks at the roof of the car in frustration. "Fine. Drive," he replies flatly.

Max starts to type something into Ben's phone and Ben's eyes flick to him as he drives. "Where is she?" Ben asks.

"Fifteen kilometers in front." He holds the phone out for us all to see the little red dot driving along the road.

The car falls silent and Cameron scratches his head in frustration as he thinks. "Explain to me why we are following Amelie again. I don't get it."

"Okay, so when Natasha came to LA with us the first time, remember when she had the fight with Carson?" I reply as my eyes flick between the three of them.

Max turns around in his seat to listen. "Yes," replies Cameron. "Natasha wanted to make up a code word for snake," I continue.

Cameron frowns. "For snake... as in cock?"

I widen my eyes and shake my head. "You are such an imbecile. No, not cock—a snake as in someone she couldn't trust."

"Oh right," Cameron mutters. Max laughs and Ben smirks into the rear-vision mirror and shakes his head.

"She said that if I saw someone, I didn't think she could trust I could say the word Cinderella to her as a warning."

"Yes," replies Max from the front seat.

I nod. "So, whenever we have been alone, I have called Natasha Cinderella as a pet name."

Cameron frowns. "And nobody knows this but you two?" he asks.

I shake my head. "No, because if anyone knew, including Joshua, we couldn't use the code anymore."

Ben rubs his fingers over his lips, deep in thought as he drives, and Cameron rubs his hand over his stubble as he processes the information.

"Today, when Amelie was talking, she said that Joshua had lost his Cinderella. Nobody knows that but Natasha," I murmur. "It has to be her. She has to know what happened to Natasha."

Cameron frowns. "Amelie is a bitch but she's not capable of this. It's not her," he snaps. "No way."

"She's turning off," Max replies from the front seat. "Slow down so she doesn't see us," he adds and Ben slows the car down.

I shake my head. "I know it's a long shot, but I know Natasha would not have told Amelie our code word. I think Natasha is trying to send me a message."

Max smiles with renewed purpose.

"Don't get your hopes up," Ben snaps and once again we fall into silence. For four hours we follow as we vent. Nicholas has had to stay at the prison and Bridget and Abbie have gone to visit Joshua and pick him up. Joshua is low and Cameron just wants to get back to his brother's side. We are all very worried about him and out in the countryside hours from anywhere, this could be stupidity.

It's eight at night and dark, the roads have gone to dirt and we are well off any highway.

"What the hell is she doing out here anyway?" Cameron frowns as he cranes his neck to look ahead.

"Hiding a body," I murmur.

Cameron puts his hands up and drags them down his face. "You know what. Just stop talking. You're stressing me the fuck out," he snaps.

Ben smirks into the rear-view mirror as his eyes flick to us. "What are we going to do when we get to her anyway?"

Cameron holds his hands up in question.

"Just watch what she is doing," Ben replies calmly.

"She's probably here to see a sick horse. Did anyone think of that?" Cameron scoffs, disgusted. "She's a fucking veterinarian you know. This is where horses live, you know, in the countryside." He gestures to the paddocks surrounding the car with his hands.

"Pull the car over. I'm going to fucking bury *you* in a minute," I snap, annoyed.

"The car has stopped," Max replies as he looks at the screen.

Ben pulls over. "How far away are we?" he asks.

"Ten kilometers," Max replies. "Get closer and we will ditch the car and go by foot."

Cameron and I exchange horrified looks. "By foot?" Cameron frowns.

"Just shut up," Ben replies.

We amble up the road slowly and Ben turns the car headlights off.

"Oh my God, this isn't James Bond," Cameron whispers. I nod as I frown. It does seem very dramatic.

"Why are you whispering then?" Ben asks, amused.

"I don't know," Cameron whispers back. "But if you crash the car into a tree 'cause we can't see I am taking your gun and shooting you in the head."

Max smiles from his seat in the front.

We keep ambling up the road until we get to a little laneway and Ben pulls the car off the road. "Leave the car here and we will walk up," Ben says to Max who nods.

Cameron and I exchange looks again. "What will we do?" I ask.

"You two can stay in the car," Max replies.

My eyes dart out into the silent darkness. "I'm not waiting

here. Anything could happen here—this doesn't feel safe," I whisper mortified.

Cameron shakes his head. "The only thing that is going to happen to you is that I am going to run you over, you idiot!" Cameron snaps as he points at me.

I open the car door. "I'm coming," I reply.

Cameron frowns. "Well, I'm not staying here by myself," he replies as he gets out of the car.

"No, you two stay here in case we need you to pick us up," Ben replies.

Cameron shakes his head as he looks out into the dark forest. "This is fucking sketchy, man. I don't like it. This place gives me the creeps," he mutters.

I nod as I look around at our dark surroundings. "Me too," I reply. "Shit, this is heavy."

We get back into the car and Cameron sits in the front seat and I sit in the back. His phone rings.

He looks at the screen and screws up his face. "Oh, fuck it," he whispers. "It's Callie, I forgot to call her. Shit." He drags his hand over his face and answers the phone. "Hey babe," he answers casually as he screws up his face.

He listens for a moment. "Um." He pauses as he listens. "Yeah, about that, I can't come tonight."

He holds the phone out from his ear as the girl on the other end explodes. "Look, I'm at the prison. Some shit has come up that I didn't know about," he replies.

I smile and sit back on the seat with my hands behind my head. This new girl Cameron is seeing has a lot of demands for someone who is supposed to be casual.

He listens and shakes his head as he rolls his eyes at me. "I will see you tomorrow night. It's only a work party—just go alone." He frowns. "Stop being a fucking drama queen," he snaps.

She says something and he narrows his eyes.

"Fine, don't see me tomorrow night then!" he snaps. She says something and he shakes his head.

"See you, Cal," he snaps. "Have a nice night now that you've ruined mine." He hangs up and throws the phone onto the seat as he shakes his head angrily. "Demanding little bitch," he snaps. "I'm not taking her shit. Who does she think she is?"

"Funnily enough she sounded like she thinks she's your girlfriend," I reply sarcastically.

He fakes a smile. "Shut up," he murmurs. "She knows the score."

"Where were you supposed to be going?" I ask.

"A work party thing." He sighs.

I raise my eyebrows. "Meeting the work friends, very domesticated, Cam."

He looks at me deadpan in the rear-view mirror. "It's a work party, not a wedding, you cock," he replies.

I smile as I throw my head back against the seat. It's now about ten at night and the rain is hammering down. They have been gone for what seems like hours. The car windows are all fogged up and I'm starving.

"Do you think she did this? Amelie I mean, do you think she is really capable of this?" Cameron sighs.

I shrug. "I wouldn't have thought so," I reply.

"How would she know that, the Cinderella thing?" he asks.

I shake my head. "I don't know, did she even say it, or did I imagine it?" I ask.

"She said it, I heard her. She knows that name but maybe she has just heard you call Tash that."

I nod. "Maybe." My mind goes to Tash and whether I have

ever been with her and Amelie in the same room. I really don't think I have.

Max bangs on the door in the darkness and Cameron nearly jumps through the roof in fright. "Scared the shit out of me," he whispers as he opens the door.

Max jumps into the car out of the rain. He's out of breath and panting heavily.

"What's wrong?" I frown. "Did you see anything?"

Max shakes his head. "Something's going down, I don't know what. They are at a huge house at the end of the road and Amelie and a young man are searching the forest around the house with floodlights and Amelie is screaming at the kid."

"Screaming what?" Cameron whispers.

"I don't know. We can't hear what they are saying over the rain, but Amelie has a gun."

"A gun," Cameron shrieks. "Why the hell does she have a gun?"

"Call the police," I snap. "This bitch is tapped."

"No. We have no proof of anything. All that will do is alert Amelie that we are onto something. You two go and find a hotel close by, we can't let her see the car and it's only a matter of time before they find you both," he replies.

"You can't stay out here in the rain all night. You will freeze to death," I murmur, horrified.

"We're okay. This is what we are trained to do. But we need you close in case we need the car. Give me a charged phone in case ours runs out," he replies.

I fumble the code off my phone and hand it over.

"We are just going to follow them and see what they do. Is the phone on silent?" he asks as he passes it back to me.

I switch the sound off and hand it back.

"Stay close but out of sight," he replies. "Find a hotel and then tomorrow start checking the neighbors to see if we can find out who owns that house at the end of the street."

He leaves the car and runs off into the darkness and into the rain. Cameron jumps into the driver's seat and starts the car and I jump out and into the front seat. "Where to?" Cameron asks.

I shake my head. "I don't know," I whisper.

We pull out onto the dirt road with the windshield wipers going full speed and head off in the direction we came from. After about another five kilometers in the darkness we see a driveway off the main road disappearing up the hill. "What do you reckon is up there?" I ask.

Cameron slows down in the torrential rain and we both crane our necks to see up the hill. "I don't know, a house it looks like," he replies.

"Shall we go up there and ask if we can lodge for the night?" I frown.

Cameron thinks for a moment. "No, we had better not. We don't know who lives there. Let's try and find a hotel for the night and if we can't find one, we will camp in the car away from here where the car is out of sight."

I nod. "Okay, good plan."

Natasha

It's 4 pm on my wedding day and distraught doesn't even come close to how I'm feeling. I wanted so badly to be home for my beautiful Joshua today. I know he would be suffering, today worse than any other. I am sitting on the floor and freezing in the back garden shed of the house I have found, my two shotguns and ammunition by my side. It's still raining so heavily that I can't leave the protection of the house, but I know if I stay in there and someone comes... I'm a dead woman. At least if I stay out here, I can see a car if it approaches and run into the forest behind me without being seen. The garden shed I am in is really only a shack of a building. A tin roof and three falling down walls, the opening is at the back facing the forest, ready for my escape.

My mind goes to what I'm supposed to be doing now.

As long you love me,
We could be starving,
We could be homeless,
We could be broke.

I softly sing the words of the song I wanted as my wedding song. *As long as you love me.*

My mind is on autopilot and I'm singing to distract the negative scared thoughts from entering my psyche. I keep repeating the words again and again as I sit alone on the floor. And then I hear the crunch of tires on the pebble driveway and slowly pick up the gun and clutch it in my hand. Oh my God, oh my God. I squeeze the gun in my hands as fear starts to make my bottom lip tremble. I slowly stand and peer through a gap in the metal wall.

I gasp. Oh my God. No.

CHAPTER 29

Natasha

I DIP MY HEAD, shit. What am I going to do? Like clockwork the damn rain speeds up and hits torrential. I watch as a person in a large black hooded raincoat gets out of a car and walks up to the front steps of the house. Damn it, why did I smash that window next to the front door? I'm such a fucking idiot. Now they know for sure I'm here or at least have been here. My eyes flick to the forest behind me—should I just run? My eyes look at the skies, rain. Where is all this fucking rain coming from anyway? I would have been miles from here if it wasn't so damn wet. With my heart pumping adrenaline heavily through my body I start to do an internal risk assessment as I look between the forest and the house. If I run, my back is a target. I can't get away and watch them at the same time. I will most likely get shot in the back. If I stay here, they can't see me, but I have a gun. I only hope I loaded the bloody thing right and it works. What will I do, what will I do? I look back at the house through the crack in the metal. Maybe it's the owner of the house and he will call the police to report a robbery and they will come to the house. That's a best-case scenario—yes, please, let that happen. Think, Natasha, think. I look down at the gun and put my finger on the trigger. You just pull it right? Yes, you just pull it. I practice pulling the trigger and I hold it up as if I am going to shoot something out in the forest to try and get the feel for it. Oh my God, I'm so out of my depth here. Shit.

For fifteen minutes I watch the house with my heart hammering. What in the hell is going on in there? Who is it? My eyes flick to the car in the front yard. It hasn't moved so they are still here. My eyes widen—shit, can they see me and are sneaking around in the forest behind me to catch me unawares? My eyes dart around the dense trees behind me. I look up at the sky and realize it will be dark in an hour or so. If I'm still here I'm going to run when it gets dark but maybe I should just go inside and knock and ask for help? Shit.

The back screen-door slams and I duck away from the hole in the tin so they can't see me as I hold my breath. The rain is so loud on the tin roof it's deafening. Oh god, just fuck off rain. Shit, shit, shit.

"Natasha," I hear a woman's voice call out. I frown. What? "Natasha, I've come to save you. The police are looking everywhere. We have caught them," the voice calls.

Really, oh my God? My heart starts to race as I try to place the voice. I've heard it before... I know I have.

I hold my breath with my back to the tin, oh God. Who is it? Can I trust them?

"Natasha, you killed him. He's dead, you did a good thing," the voice echoes over the hammering rain.

I screw up my face as my tears come. I killed him—Carl's dead. Oh God, what have I done?

"Natasha," the voice calls and I hear a trace of an English accent.

My eyes widen and my face drops. Is that Amelie?

"Natasha, please come out so I can take you back to Joshua," her voice calls over the rain.

I shake my head as anger starts to pump through my veins. Don't tell me that fucking bitch vet has done all this. Why? Why would she do this?

"Natasha!" the voice screams angrily.

Shit, she's close, oh my God. I have to move so I can see her. I turn back to look out through the small crack in the tin. It is Amelie and she is looking on the other side of the yard out into the forest and has a gun in her hands.

I swallow the lump of fear in my throat. Bitch. How dare she? What do I do? I have no choice but to stay here and fight. My eyes close and I picture my beautiful Joshua in prison on our wedding day. Please be okay, baby, please be okay. It will be dark soon. I have to step out of the shed, or she is going to have me cornered. My heart is racing out of control and I grip my chest. I don't have to worry about her killing me because I'm going to have a damn heart attack before she gets the chance.

I hear the crunch of tires again on the pebble driveway and my face screws up. Shit, there's more of them. I will be outnumbered. "Joshua, baby, I love you," I whisper as my eyes fill with tears and I grip the gun with white-knuckled force. This is it—it will all be over soon.

I keep looking, through the gap in the tin, towards the car that has just pulled up around the front of the house. I frown as my eyes flick to Amelie who is now hiding behind a tree. They are not with her. She doesn't know who it is either. I grip my gun with renewed purpose and then I hear a familiar voice.

"Hey, look, the glass has been broken," Cameron calls out.

Oh no, it's Cameron. Cameron, she has a gun. Get out of here. Where's Ben and Max?

I watch in horror as Adrian walks around the car. I put my hand over my mouth. It's Cameron and Adrian. A phone rings and I hear Cameron's voice. "Hey," he answers. "Shit. They lost her," he calls out to Adrian. "Yeah, okay. We will be there in a minute," he replies.

What the hell are they doing here? My eyes flick back to Amelie who is now sneaking toward the other side of the house to take them by surprise. She's going to kill them but it's me you want. No.

I step out into the rain with my gun. "I'm over here," I call.

She stops, turns and smiles a sadistic smile when her eyes find me. I'm sopping wet in men's clothing and I'm holding a rifle. This is just like a fucking horror movie.

She lets out a sickening laugh and my blood runs cold as I raise the rifle and point it towards her. Her face drops and she raises her gun.

"Drop it," she yells.

Fury drips from my every pore and I keep the gun aimed at her head. The rain is running into my eyes and I try to blink it away.

"I said drop it," she yells again over the sound of the rain on the tin.

I keep the gun still and try to focus. Pull the trigger, pull the trigger. What are you waiting for? Pull the trigger, Natasha.

The back screen slams shut and her eyes flick to the verandah but I keep my eyes firmly on her.

"Amelie, what are you doing?" Cameron yells.

"Go, Cameron," she yells in reply.

My eyes go to Cameron and his terrified face as his eyes flick to me with the gun.

"Amelie, you don't want to do this," he calls. "We can get you some help... it's okay," he calls as he walks out into the rain and toward the stairs.

Cameron, stop. Stop where you are, I whisper to myself. My eyes flick to the side of the house where I see Adrian sneaking down toward me and I grip the gun tighter.

Amelie points the gun at Cameron. "I will kill you too. Get in the house," she yells at him.

"Amelie, calm down," he replies as he keeps slowly walking down the steps towards her. She seemingly loses control and fires the gun, and he runs up the stairs. She sprays bullets at him as he runs back into the house and Adrian lies on the ground. The sound is deafening.

"Stop it!" I scream and her attention comes back to me and she points the gun toward me and fires. It clicks—she's out of bullets.

My heart stops completely.

"Oh, you idiot," she sneers with the gun pointed at me as she walks closer.

I keep the gun pointed at her head as I grip the trigger. Does she have another gun under her jacket? Why is she still coming toward me?

"What are you going to do?" she screams. "What are you going to do? You haven't got the guts!"

I stay still as the rain comes down.

"You make me sick, Natasha Marx." She sneers and something inside me snaps,

I close my eyes and pull the trigger three times. She falls to the ground as she starts to bleed.

"My name is Natasha Stanton, bitch," I whisper. I stand over her and gasp for breath, the gun drops from my hand to the ground with a thud and I fall to my knees next to her body. I raise my face to the rain as the dam of tears breaks.

It's over... it's finally over...I did it...I did it.

I lie in the hospital bed late at night and the last of the police officers takes his final notes. Adrian and Cameron are at the end of my bed and haven't left my side since they found me this afternoon. Thank God they found me. I'm so grateful they were there with me when it ended. I won't let them out of my sight because I'm worried if I take eyes off them for even a second they are going to disappear and none of this will be real.

"Is there anything else you can think of, dear?" the officer asks.

I shake my head. "No," I reply, and my eyes flick back up to him. "Actually yes," I reply. "Are you sure he's okay?" I ask.

The officer smiles sympathetically. "Yes, like I told you the last three times. The only person who died today was Amelie Richards and she had another gun under her jacket and without a doubt was going to kill you. It was self-defense, Natasha. You did the right thing. The other offender, Carl, is under police guard in hospital but he will make a full recovery. There is another young man in police custody, and we have arrested a guard that used to work for Joshua Stanton,"

I frown. "What do you mean? Who?" I ask.

"The house was leased in his name and we think that he is the person who planted the cameras inside your house and the one who rowed on a boat out to your yacht that night and took you. The other two men involved were working as waiters at the wedding and spiked your drinks.

I hear Cameron tut to himself.

My mind flicks back to when Joshua's cars got stolen by the

guard. That was a decoy all along. They didn't want the cars; they wanted to put the cameras in. Shit.

The police officer smiles warmly. "You're very brave, Miss Marx."

I smile softly. "Not really," I whisper. "I've never been so scared in my life."

"Your family are on their way. Enjoy your time with them." He smiles and walks out the door.

Cameron immediately stands and comes to my bedside where he picks up my hand and holds it.

My eyes search his. "I didn't mean to kill her, Cam," I whisper.

"I know," he replies as he swipes the hair back from my forehead gently.

I shake my head as my confusion hits crescendo. "I should have picked this up. How did I not pick up that she was so unstable?" I question. "Cameron, I'm a psychologist. I should have known."

He shakes his head. "Me and you both, Tash. She wasn't even on our radar. We had no idea she was involved in any of this," he replies.

"Why?" Adrian sighs. "I just don't understand why she would do this?"

Cameron's eyes flick to Adrian. "She wanted Joshua to feel the same loss that she felt when he went away and then she wanted him to suffer," he replies. "Revenge at its worst. She spent all of the money that Joshua gave her on the ultimate revenge. The cameras were a power play to make Natasha pay, too."

"She didn't hurt me," I whisper, mortified at what I have done.

He nods. "She was going to, Tash. Deep down you know that. It was never going to end well," he replies.

My eyes drop to the bed and then back up between the two of them. "Thank you so much for finding me," I stammer.

Adrian smiles warmly and stands and comes over to the bed and cuddles me. "No, thank you for being alive," he whispers into my hair. "Thank you, thank you, thank you."

Adrian

We wait in the office at the jail as Vincenzo goes through the relevant paperwork. It is 1 am in the morning, Natasha is still in the hospital and we are waiting to be led in to tell Joshua the news.

"It will be twelve hours," the duty officer states flatly. "You will need to get an injunction in the courts tomorrow morning."

"I want him released immediately," Vincenzo replies.

"Get in line. Lots of prisoners want to be released but we don't have the authority so take it up in court," he snaps.

"This man is in here for murder, but the supposed victim is alive and in the hospital. He will not be going back into his cell and will have full use of telephone and internet," Vincenzo asserts.

The guard's eyes hold his. "He can wait out his time as a free man inside the prison. There is a lounge area that he may use until the paperwork is complete," he replies.

Vincenzo nods and continues to fill out the paperwork and my eyes flick to Cameron. He can't get the smile off his face... we all can't. The intense feeling of relief is immeasurable.

The guard knocks on the door of the office. "This way," he gestures.

We all stand, and Vincenzo immediately embraces Cameron and me.

"You did good." He smiles warmly.

"Natasha did good," Cameron replies as he slaps Vincenzo on the back. We leave the room and follow the guard through a maze of corridors and finally into an office where Joshua is seated at a desk. His face falls when he sees us. "What's wrong? Is it Mum?" he asks, panicked.

The guard closes the door on the way out and Joshua frowns at the back of the door. "Cameron, what is it?" he asks again.

"Joshua, we have her," Cameron whispers.

Joshua frowns. "Who?"

"Natasha, she's alive and we have her," Cameron stammers. Joshua frowns.

"It's true." I nod as I smile—I still can't believe it.

"Can't be," Joshua whispers as his eyes flick to me. I nod as my eyes well up with tears.

"She's alive?" he whispers.

Cameron laughs. "Very much so. She's in the hospital for observation but she is unharmed. She was given a blood transfusion and survived."

Joshua stands. "What!" he whispers.

Cameron grabs his brother in an embrace. "We found her, we found her," he whispers into his hair. "It's over, everything is over. You can come home."

"She's alive," Joshua whispers again as his eyes flick between the two of us in disbelief. "She's okay?" he gasps. He holds out his arm for me to join them and the three of us stand in an embrace as we let our emotions overload together for the first time since this tragedy began.

Natasha

I sit in the back of the car with a huge smile on my face which I can't control. I'm going to see him. For the first time in seven weeks, I'm going to see my love. We are waiting in the car outside the prison exit door located at the side of the prison entrance. There are cars lined up and news reporters tele-casting from everywhere and for once I don't begrudge them being here. I want the world to see the footage of the moment he is set free. Ben and Max are in the front seat and we have brought a limousine at my request. I want to be alone with him on the hour-and- a-half drive home. This is it—I look at my watch again—1.55 pm. He is being released at 2 pm. I clasp my hands nervously on my lap as I wait. Yesterday, after the police came I was transferred by ambulance to the hospital but thank-fully was released this morning. My eyes flick out the window as I think of Amelie and what she went through. I feel nothing but deep pity for her. The level of grief she must have felt when Joshua pushed her aside sent her over the edge. She was hell-bent on revenge and making him feel the loss that she had felt when he left. But she was good to me and I was essentially looked after. She could have just killed me on that night, but she didn't. Instead, she gave me a blood transfusion and kept me in a luxury house. I wish I could have helped her... instead I killed her. Regret twists my stomach and I close my eyes as I remember firing the three bullets. At that moment I had snapped; I had passed my point of rational thinking. She pushed me past the point of no return but I'm relieved Carl survived.

I'm so grateful for this family that we have. A broad smile covers my face when I remember my mum, Bridget and Abbie's tears of joy at the hospital. Adrian and Cameron were so proud of themselves for finding me that they kept cuddling each other while the police were questioning me at the house. What a bunch of crybabies we all are...even Margaret. I have never been so glad to see her in my life. I was worried that she may have ended her own life by now. Thank God she hasn't.

The gates open. "Here he comes," Ben says. "Just stay in the car."

My heart jumps through my chest as I see him come through the gates and I can't stop myself. I fling open the car door and run through the parking lot toward him. He sees me, drops his bag and I jump into his waiting arms.

And he holds me, and finally my tears break the dam and I sob into his neck.

I feel like I am having an out-of-body experience as I hear the reporter's cameras click in the distance from every angle.

"I'm here, baby," I whisper into his neck and he pulls me tighter into him. "I'm here."

For some reason the beautiful memory returns to my mind of that very first night when we danced to 'Diamonds' and started this journey, and I smile into his strong neck.

We stand still... lost in the moment... A moment I have waited so long for and he's here, he's here with me. He feels it too.

He kisses me gently on the lips and pulls out of the embrace and smiles and the reporters all clap and cheer. In a very spontaneous un-Joshua moment he raises our linked hands in the air, much to their delight, and the cameras go wild. I laugh and he smiles warmly at me. We walk hand in hand to the car where Ben and Max are standing. Joshua embraces Ben and then Max and the cameras go wild again as I get into the backseat.

I have him back, my man is here, and all is well in the world. The security screen is up, and Joshua gets in behind me and closes the door. He grabs my face between his hands and stares at me as if not believing this is true. "I'm here, babe," I whisper.

His eyes fill with tears and he pulls me onto his lap and buries his head in my shoulder with his arms so tightly around me that I can hardly breathe and without a word he breaks into full-blown sobs.

Joshua

My heart hammers in my chest as I hold her. Is this really happening? I pull back to look at her face, unable to hide my emotion.

Natasha smiles at me through her tears. "I'm here, baby. We made it. We made it," she whispers. "It's okay. Everything is going to be okay."

My heart rips open, and I sob loudly as I grab her face with both hands and kiss her lips with my eyes closed. I bury my head in her chest again to try and pull myself together enough to speak. She starts to cover my face in gentle kisses and I smile into her breast at the familiarity of the gesture.

"Are you okay?" I whisper.

She nods and smiles as she brings her leg over to straddle me in my seat.

"I am, are you? Oh Joshua, you have been through so much," she whispers as she wipes her hand tenderly down my face.

I smile broadly through my tears. "I am okay now that you're here," I reply.

She bends and kisses me as she holds my face, her tongue gently swipes through my open lips and my hands run up and down her bare thighs under her skirt.

My girl is back. I'm saved.

Unable to help ourselves, we keep kissing... and kissing... and kissing. I can't believe this is happening—it's like we have never been apart.

"Oh Joshua, I love you. I love you." She smiles into my lips and I laugh out loud.

"I love you too." I smile.

As our kisses deepen, I try to hold off the raging hard-on in my pants. Fuck, this isn't the time. Natasha, who is straddled over me, starts to slowly rock herself backwards and forwards over my cock and I close my eyes to hold off my arousal. She starts to really ride me as her kiss continues.

I shake my head. "Tash, you have just been through so much. I'm not taking you like this in the back of a car," I whisper as I kiss her again.

"This is our car. This is our life. And I need you inside me more than I need air," she whispers defiantly as she rolls her hips again onto my cock. Her eyes darken as her eyes watch my lips.

"I need this, Josh. I need you," she whispers into my mouth and my eyes close in reverence. I lean back and undo my fly and release myself and she smiles broadly as her eyes glaze over again. She starts to really kiss me as she rises to her knees. I pull her underpants to the side and swipe the back of my fingers through her flesh. Fuck. Dripping wet. Oh, I've missed this woman. My eyes close with need and as I hold her pants to the side, bring her body down onto mine and slide home in one movement, we both groan in pleasure. We don't move, we stay perfectly still and the only thing that can be heard is the sound of our hearts reconnecting. I love this woman so much and once again my tears start to fall.

Natasha

We sit at the dinner table after the meal with our family. Everyone is here and the atmosphere in the house is electric with celebrations, and laughter is floating throughout the space. My eyes stay locked on Joshua. If I didn't know it before, I definitely know it now.

We have both recovered from our combined meltdown in the car this afternoon on the way home from the prison, although somehow I think our trauma is far from over. I'm not sure it ever will be.

Wearing dark denim jeans and a white T-shirt that is stretched over his broad shoulders, Joshua is the epitome of male perfection. My oasis in the desert of life. His dark eyes and beautiful large red lips call to me, and I think it's the only thing on this Earth that I do understand. One is not supposed to look this orgasmic when they have been in prison, but it's as if every one of his senses has blossomed today. He has hit his peak and is alive with electricity and it is coming loud and clear my way. If I touched him with my finger, I would feel the zap of the electric current running through him.

I want this party over—I want to be naked with my man. "So, what are the plans for the next week?" my mother asks.

Joshua's eyes lock on mine. "Tomorrow we are flying to Kamala and Natasha and I are getting married," he replies.

"But I need to get my hair done," shrieks Abbie. "Can't we

leave the day after tomorrow?" she asks as everyone breaks into excited chatter.

He shakes his head as he gives me that look. Fuck me, it screams, and God, it's smoking hot.

"Nope, the plane leaves at ten. And I don't care who's on it except for my bride," he replies as his gaze burns a hole in my underwear.

I smile broadly as my cheeks heat. God, he makes me feel like a giddy schoolgirl.

Everyone groans at his soppiness. "Yeah, thanks a lot," the chorus of sighs sings. "Good to know we are needed," Adrian groans.

"Now if you don't mind us being rude, Natasha is tired, I'm sure. We're going to go to bed." He stands and puts his hand out for me, and I take it as my nerves start to pulse through me.

"Yeah, because you are going to let her get so much sleep." Cameron smirks and everyone giggles.

Mum blows me a kiss and Bridget smiles through teary eyes as she gives me a little wave.

"See you in the morning." I smile, slightly embarrassed. Oh jeez, it's so obvious what we are going upstairs for.

I follow silently as Joshua leads me up the stairs by the hand. My heart has picked up speed and I feel nervous. Why do I feel so nervous? As if sensing my inner turmoil Joshua turns and looks at me as we hit the top step.

"You okay, Presh?" he whispers.

I nod and smile softly. I'm much more than ok. I'm perfect. I have never been better. He leads me into the bedroom and straight into the bathroom and turns the hot water on in the shower. I stand like a nervous child waiting for my next instruction.

He turns and takes my jaw in his hands and runs his tongue

through my lips. "What's wrong, baby?" he whispers as he pulls back to look at my face.

My eyes well up and I shake my head as I try to stop myself from having a full-on breakdown and sobbing like a baby.

His eyes hold mine as he grabs the bottom of my shirt and lifts it over my head and slides my jeans down. His lips drop to kiss me gently on the neck and my arms go around his neck. He's being so gentle with me as if I might break and the tenderness between us has never been stronger. His eyes go to the marks on me, the faded bruising on my body from Carl's beatings, and I look down at them shamefully. Very slowly he places his hand tenderly on my stomach and his eyes meet mine in a silent question. I shake my head as tears fill my eyes. "There's no baby," I whisper, and he kisses me gently, sensing that I desperately need him to tell me it's okay.

His eyes meet mine again and he picks up my hand and turns it over and looks at the deep dark purple scar on my wrist. "I'm so sorry," he whispers. "I'm so, so sorry that you have had to go through this nightmare."

I shake my head. "Don't," I murmur. "I don't want you to remind me of what has happened, Joshua." I brush my lips over his.

"You don't," he breathes as his tongue gently swipes through my lips.

I shake my head and bring my hands up to his face. "I want you to make me forget," I whisper.

He smiles softly.

"It's just us now," I whisper.

He smiles into my kiss. "It will always just be us—it has always just been us." He breathes into my kiss. He grabs the back of his T-shirt at the nape and pulls it over his head and takes off his shoes and jeans. My eyes drop down the magnificent beast in front of me, my name etched in ink down his side. He is thinner than before but somehow more muscular if possible. There is a distinct V of muscles that runs down his lower abdomen, his six-pack is exposed, as are the wide shoulders and cut arms. I follow his stomach down to his dark pubic hair and then his thick penis that hangs heavily between his legs. I smile as my eyes rise to meet his, and he smirks darkly.

"Yes." He smirks.

I smile as I shake my head. "You are just so fucking hot," I whisper. I will never get used to this.

His dark eyes hold mine and he cracks his neck hard... there it is. He rips my underpants down to the floor as he kisses me deeply. "I need to be fucked hard tonight, Mr. Stanton," I whisper into his kiss. He steps back, his dark eyes hold mine and I feel the burn of his gaze. He needs it hard too—I can feel it. As if taking that as a green light to be himself he rips me into the shower and under the hot water where I find myself up against the back wall. He is on me, and his hands roam up and down my body as if he doesn't know where to touch me first. Our kiss turns frantic as I grab the back of his head to bring him closer.

"I've missed you," he growls into my neck.

And I throw my head back in ecstasy as I get the visual of what we must look like.

The thing is, I've watched porn of the two of us for six weeks without a release, not even a touch, because I knew I was being filmed. I know what my man is capable of, and I now know just how orgasmic he looks as he does it. Joshua Stanton having sex in his animalistic way is without a doubt the best viewing I have ever witnessed.

God, I need him now. I need to taste him. I drop to my knees and take him in my mouth and his dark eyes drop to my lips.

"Fuck, yeah," he whispers as he cups my jaw. "Oh baby, yeessss," he purrs as I am gifted with my first taste of pre-ejaculate in so damn long. I can feel every vein, every ridge and, as if my body is running on autopilot, my hand goes around to his behind to push him deeper into my mouth.

I'm too aroused to use technique and I start to take his full length into my mouth while I fist him deeply. He growls in acceptance, lurches forward and puts his hand out on the tiled wall to hold himself up.

"Fuck. Tash, baby. Stop. I'm going to come already," he murmurs through his arousal as his body racks with shivers.

I smile around him and bare my teeth and work him harder. When I tell you you're copping it tonight, big boy... I meant every damn word.

"Fuck," he yells as he lurches forward again and comes in a rush into my mouth. His hands gently come to my head as I gently clean him up with my tongue. His eyes are closed, and he is breathing heavily. I lick my lips and smile triumphantly as I stand and when he opens his eyes, Mr. Stanton is here and I know who's going to cop it now.

He kisses me and slams me up against the wall and brings one of my legs up around his waist. My heartrate escalates out of control and slowly he pulls back and watches my face as he swipes his fingers through my wet flesh, his eyes closing in reverence. "You feel so good, so tight. So ready for my cock," he whispers into my mouth. "Are you hungry for some cock, baby?"

My eyes close, oh God, yes. Give it to me now.

"How do you taste? I need you on my tongue," he whispers as he pulls me out of the shower and kisses me deeply. All the while kissing me, I am slowly walked into our bedroom and he lies me down on the bed. My body is quivering with need and then he is on top of me as he holds his weight off me with his elbows. One of his knees comes up and rests next to my hipbone and he starts to slide his thick length through my waiting flesh as his dark eyes watch me. This is the best kind of porno.

"You're going to feel so good around my cock, baby girl," he whispers.

I close my eyes, I know, just do it already. I need this. His soft lips go to my neck and he starts to kiss down to my breasts and one by one he brings them into his mouth and gently bites them, my back arching off the bed in anticipation. With his eyes focused on mine he drops down to my stomach and slowly starts to lick me.

I can't lie still, and my body is writhing in excitement under him. Slowly, ever so slowly, his tongue finds the flesh between my legs and he groans into me as he closes his eyes in reverence.

Oh hell... my eyes roll back in my head and my hand goes to his face. He starts to suck me. I can feel his cheeks dip as his suction gets deeper and my legs start to fall to the bed by themselves. "So perfect," he whispers. "You are so perfect, my precious girl."

My eyes close and I drop my head back to the mattress. No, I need to watch him. My eyes meet his again and he slides a finger into me, hisses in pleasure and pulses it in and out slowly. I watch him slowly take his cock in his other hand, unable to control it, and stroke himself as his eyes stay focused on my pulsing open flesh. His mouth hangs slack with arousal and he cracks his neck hard. He adds another finger and starts to pulse them in and out of me slowly, my body starts to instinctively ride his hand and he drops his head and takes my clitoris between his teeth while his tongue flicks violently. I can't help it, I lurch forward in orgasm and cry out in ecstasy. Oh, what this man does to me, and then he is on me again, deep licks from front to back. The stubble on his face is burning me and I don't give a damn if it's a third-degree burn and I need to go to the hospital. At this moment, I need this man to do exactly this to me. There isn't anything else I need more. He swipes his tongue through my flesh again and adds three of his fingers and I jump at the pleasurable sting.

"Sshh," he whispers. "It's okay, baby," he comforts.

He leans up and kisses me passionately again and my body starts to relax and then he starts to ride me with his hand, deep hard strokes that move my body up and down the bed and which rock the bed so hard it hits the wall. My back is arching off the bed with need. His eyes are locked on mine as my hands find his forearm to feel his muscles clench with the movement.

"Open your legs wider," he whispers as his jaw hangs slack in arousal. I drop my legs to the bed and my eyes flick to his shoulders where I can see every muscle flex with his movement.

He cracks his neck hard and that's it, I can't take anymore. I convulse forward in orgasm as I feel him slide into my body.

We lie still, our hearts racing out of control. Our faces are millimeters away from each other. The intense feeling of his possession brings me undone.

"I love you," he whispers through his tear-filled eyes. "I love you too, baby... so much," I reply.

He kisses me and it's a different kiss. It's a kiss of hope. The tenderness behind it cuts my heart wide open as he pulls out slowly and slides back in.

"Are you okay?" he murmurs.

I kiss him deeply again. "I'm more than okay. I'm perfect. Go, give it to me. I need this," I whisper.

He lets out a groan as he pulls back and slams into me and I cry out.

"Fuck," he murmurs into my shoulder as he kisses it.

And then he starts to drive deeper and deeper, each thrust harder than the last until I don't think I can take it anymore. He lifts my knees up to his chest as he holds himself up on straightened arms and really lets me have it. His dark eyes are watching my face as his jaw hangs slack. Oh my God, what this man can do. I lurch forward as he holds himself deep and we both scream out as an orgasm the size of a freight train rips through our bodies in tandem. He drops his body over mine and kisses me gently and I laugh out loud.

"What's funny?" he purrs.

I smile as I pant. "Well, I thought maybe you would have forgotten what to do," I whisper breathlessly.

He smirks. "You think I could ever forget what to do?" he repeats, affronted.

I nod with wide innocent eyes and a stupid grin on my face.

As if Joshua Stanton could ever forget how to fuck... he was born to do it.

"You and your smart mouth just got yourself a ticket," he growls. "Pound Town, here we come." He bends and rips into my neck with his teeth and I squeal in laughter.

Oh, it's so very good to be home.

CHAPTER 30

Joshua

THE SOUND of laughter and chatter fill the cabin—we are finally on a plane to Kamala. I didn't think this day would ever come. I walk back from the bathroom up the aisle. As I hold onto the seats my eyes flick to my beautiful girl who is up the front. She is laughing while sitting with Adrian, her mum and the girls and they are deep in conversation. Gratitude sweeps over me. Three days ago, my life could have been so different—I may not have even been here.

"How's Tash doing?" Nicholas asks as his eyes go to her as he walks up the aisle towards me.

"She seems okay," I reply.

Nicholas nods and his eyes come back to me. "Prepare yourself—she's in for a tough time."

I nod. "Yeah, I know," I sigh as my eyes move to my love again. She's been through hell, the mental ramifications are going to show eventually and when they do, she will fall into a heap.

I look back at Nicholas and I shake his hand. "Thank you," I whisper. "You saved my life. I don't know what I would have done if you hadn't come and seen me that day in prison."

He smiles sympathetically and pulls me into an embrace. "You're welcome," he whispers. "I'm just ecstatic that it turned out how it did. Imagine if she went through all of that to come home to find you dead?"

I shake my head at the disturbing realization of just how close that scenario came. Adrian and Natasha burst into laughter and both of our eyes flick to them.

"What's happening with you and Adrian?" I ask.

He shrugs sadly. "I'm trying my hardest, but he won't let me in."

I shake my head, stubborn bastard. "Don't give up." I smile.

He smiles warmly as he shakes his head. "That, my friend, is a whole other story." He smiles.

My eyes hold his. "I'd like to hear it one day," I reply.

He hugs me and slaps me on the back. "One day," he repeats.

I keep walking up toward my seat and I pass my mother and father. I bend and kiss my mum on the forehead as I hug her. She smiles warmly as she puts her hand over mine on her shoulder. "Thank God, you're home, Joshua," she whispers.

"You okay?" I ask her.

"Yes, darling, I'm okay." She smiles. One thing this whole nightmare has taught me is that life's too short to hold grudges about what you were or weren't told. Things that happen in the past should stay in the past. Suffering or making other people suffer does not make you happy. My mother has suffered enough. Natasha has taught me how to love and more importantly the power of compassion. She holds no grudges and takes everyone on how they treat her that day... something I am striving to achieve with my beautiful mum. James Brennan, on the other hand, is a whole different story and my eyes flick to my father. "Have you made that call yet?" I ask him

He shakes his head.

"What call?" my mother asks.

"I need someone to do a job for me and Dad has the contact," I reply.

"Do it or I will," I say to him as I kiss my mother again on the forehead. Nobody treats my mother like that and lives to tell the tale. Dad nods knowingly and I keep walking back to my seat and sit down. Cameron falls into the seat next to me and smirks as his eyes scan my face. I look at him deadpan. "What?" I ask.

"You look like shit, man," he frowns.

"Nothing a seminal fluid transfusion couldn't help," I mutter as I yawn and put my hands behind my head.

Cameron rolls his lips. "Big night?" he asks.

I widen my eyes. "Huge. I've created a monster." I smirk as I rub my face.

Cameron shakes his head. "You're a lucky prick."

I smile at him. "I know."

Natasha walks back up the aisle and Cameron stands so she can sit down. "I'm going to take a nap," she says softly as she takes her blanket from the overhead carriage.

I pat my lap, and she smiles as she sits like a child across my knee and puts her head on my shoulder. I shake the blanket and spread it over us, and she nestles into me.

"I love you," she whispers as she kisses my neck.

"I love you too." I smile softly. "Go to sleep." I kiss her forehead and before I know it, we are both snuggled and content and sleeping like babies.

This is the meaning of my life.

Natasha

I sit and look in the direction of Bridget who is putting my lip gloss on. She kisses me gently on the cheek.

"It's here, Tash. You're going to marry him," she looks at the clock, "in approximately ten minutes."

A knock sounds on the door. "Come in," I call.

A Thai girl bows her head and enters with a white gift box and I smile broadly. "For you, Miss Natasha," she says softly.

I smile and bow. "Thank you," I reply as I take it from her. I inhale deeply as I open the card attached.

Today I marry my best friend
Always, Joshua

CHAPTER 31

Natasha

I SMILE BROADLY as my heart flutters with nerves. I open the box and find a single red rose and a package wrapped in white paper. I frown and open the wrapping to find my diaries bound in a bundle. My heart stops. He was going to rot in prison rather than have my diaries read out in an open court. My eyes overflow with tears at the amount of love I have for this man. It's overwhelming.

"What does it say?" Bridget asks and I hand over the card. "Oh God, he's beautiful, Tash." She sighs.

"I know." I smile as I turn and look at myself in the mirror. I'm wearing my white wedding dress which has a low back and shoestring straps. It's very simple but uber-sexy. My hair is out and full and pulled back on one side with a large white flower pinned behind one ear. I have a veil but I'm not wearing it because it makes me feel like a beekeeper.

Brock walks into the room with Mum behind him and he smiles softly. "You look beautiful, babe."

My eyes well up with tears. "Thanks," I whisper. That means a lot coming from him.

I grab his and Mum's hand. "Bridget, hold hands with us. I want to talk to Dad," I ask. She grabs Brock's and Mum's hands, and we stand in a circle and bow our heads.

"Dad," I whisper and instantly the tears block my voice. "I wish you could be here today, Dad...and I know you would be if you could." Bridget's bottom lip starts to tremble, and I pause again. "I just wanted to thank you...for everything. For bringing me into this world...for showing me what true love was by the way you loved Mum...and for saving my life. For never leaving me in that room alone. I know it was you who saved me." The lump gets really big in my throat and I hesitate. Mum sobs out loud, unable to hold it in any longer. "My dream has come true, Dad. He loves me and today I am marrying him." I sob as I start to ugly-cry. "Your empty seat will be at the table next to Mum's," I whisper. and Brock drops his head as a tear rolls down his face. "I promise to make you proud, Dad. I'm going to be such a good wife." It gets too much, and the room falls silent as we cry, all lost in our own grief.

"I love you, Dad," I sob.

"I love you, Dad," Bridget repeats.

"I love you, Dad," Brock whispers.

We all stay silent as we wait for Mum and after a silence that seems to go on forever, she whispers, "I love you, my darling. Meet me at the gates when my day comes."

I drop my head as the sound of broken hearts sob. Brock breaks the moment and wraps his arms around us, and we all embrace.

"Enough sadness." He smiles as he wipes his face, and we all shake our heads as we pull ourselves together.

Abbie sticks her head around the door. "It's time." She is smiling but her face falls when she sees we are all in tears. "Those better be fucking happy tears." She smiles and we all laugh.

Brock holds his arm out for me, I take it and we follow Bridget and Abbie as we walk out over the pool and around to the metal gates. I stand at the top of the stairs as the wind catches my face and I smile when I see Joshua, Cameron and Adrian standing at the flower-adorned altar. The violinist starts to play a traditional wedding song and slowly, as goosebumps cover my skin, we make our way down the steps. Joshua looks up and sees me and instantly his eyes cloud over in emotion and I see him swallow the lump in his throat. I break into a full-beam smile and I want to run and jump into his arms but instead I somehow hold it together and we walk up the aisle between our closest family and friends. This walk seems never-ending. When finally we get to Joshua, he shakes Brock's hand and he then takes mine. Unable to help it I lean up to gently kiss him.

"Hello," I whisper.

"Hello, my beautiful bride," he whispers back. He kisses me again and then again, and then our kiss turns passionate and we forget where we are, and our family all laugh and clap. Realization hits and I giggle into his kiss and pull back. We turn around to everyone and they all laugh and shake their heads.

Embarrassed, we turn back to face the minister.

And then I am lost. I watch in slow motion as the beautiful man in front of me declares his love and I declare mine.

"Do you, Joshua Stanton, take Natasha Marx to be your wife, to have and to hold from this day forward, for better or for worse, for

richer, for poorer, in sickness and in health, to love and to cherish; from this day forward until death do you part?"

His eyes hold mine and my heart stops. "I do," he replies.

And then it's my turn

"Do you, Natasha Marx, take Joshua Stanton to be your husband, to have and to hold from this day forward, for better or for worse, for richer, for poorer, in sickness and in health, to love and to cherish; from this day forward until death do you part?"

I smile broadly. "I do," I reply.

Joshua places the gold band on my finger, and I place one on his and we both laugh out loud and our family claps and cheers.

"I now pronounce you husband and wife. You may kiss the bride."

Joshua's eyes meet mine and I smile through my tears. To the sounds of our friends and family cheering, he tenderly kisses me and as my eyes close, I melt into a new kind of wonderful.

As long as he loves me, there will always be magic.

To continue reading Natasha & Joshua's story in the epilogue, Stanton Bliss, it is available on Amazon now

Read on for an excerpt of Marx Girl, Ben & Bridget's story...

MARX GIRL EXCERPT

AVAILABLE NOW

Bridget

"Don't look at me like you want me... not if you don't," I murmur into the silence.

He sits back and readjusts himself in his pants. His dark eyes hold mine, yet he doesn't answer me.

The water laps around me as I lie on the inflatable mattress, floating around the pool in my white string bikini. The sun is just setting, and everyone has disappeared to get ready for dinner.

We're alone.

His eyes are locked on me from his poolside deckchair position.

He has no right to look at me, to watch me with wanting eyes.

But he does.

And I still like it.

Ben is my sister's family's bodyguard and the head of their security.

Things are difficult between us, to say the least.

The attraction between us wasn't supposed to happen, but forbidden had never felt so good.

Six-foot-three-inches tall with sandy hair, honey-brown eyes, and a large, muscular physique, he's a by-product of being ex-military.

Ben Statham is one hell of a man.

From the lingering looks, the clenching deep in my sex when he looks at me, the smouldering fire whenever he would sneak into my room late at night...

It led to our story beginning six months ago, when my sister Natasha became involved with her then-boyfriend, Joshua Stanton.

I was always with Tash, and Ben was always with Josh. We came together through circumstance. Acquaintances and nothing more.

He was the strong man at the back of the crowd, watching over everyone.

I was busy watching him.

The rest of the world was concentrating on my beloved sister and Joshua's blossoming relationship.

I was concentrating on fighting the attraction, but the pull to him only grew day by day.

Laughter turned to conversation, conversation introduced lingering looks, and lingering looks turned to goose bumps, until one day in the kitchen pantry it happened.

Ben kissed me.

It was the most perfect kiss I've ever had.

It was sweet, sexy, and it opened a world of passion I never even knew existed.

For three weeks we snuck a kiss in where we could until, in a moment of foggy passion, I asked him to come to my room after everyone went to sleep that night. He did.

We made love. Storybook love.

The perfection we'd created carried on for six weeks, until tragedy struck our family. As the head of security Ben blamed himself, and pulled away from me.

When I needed him the most, he was nowhere around to offer support.

We've hardly spoken since.

And now we're here on a family vacation in Kamala, Thailand.

My feelings for him haven't changed.

He's still the head of security.

I'm still his boss' sister-in-law.

But he left me when I needed him the most, and I won't forget that anytime soon.

Our eyes are locked.

"Why would you think I don't want you?" he whispers in his heavy South African accent.

I frown, unsure how to answer. Eventually, I reply, "Do you?"

He sips his beer, contemplating the right way to answer.

I run my fingers through the water beneath me as I try to articulate my thoughts.

I don't know what's going on with us, but I do know I can't stand feeling the way I feel.

I can't go on without him giving me the answers I need. He's a strong man who doesn't show his true feelings, but what happened to us? How do you go from passionate lovers to being nothing, without even a conversation?

There was no fight, no discussion. Just silence.

He doesn't answer my question. His jaw clenches as his gaze holds mine. My eyes search his.

What the fuck is going on with him?

Does he want me to beg?

Answer me, damn it.

I climb off the inflatable mattress and make my way to the pool steps. I want to be the one who ends the conversation, not the other way around.

Who am I kidding?

I'm the only one in this conversation. I slowly walk out of the pool, and his hungry gaze drops down my body. I bend and pick up my towel to wrap it around my waist, and with one last lingering look I walk inside.

His refusal to address our issues infuriates me.

It hurts me, and it makes me wonder if everything we shared was an illusion.

I know he's strong. I know he's not a talker. But those nights in his arms were filled with tenderness and love.

Where is *that* man?

Because I want him back.

I lie in the darkness at 1:00 a.m. The sound of the ocean drifts through the room, and a soft breeze rolls over my body. As usual, I'm torturing myself with thoughts of Ben Statham and his beautiful body. *Where is he now? Is he asleep?*

The last time we were together I told him I loved him. I never meant to, but I couldn't help it. I was all soft and emotional from my orgasm high, and the words just slipped out.

Is that why he ran?

I blow out a deep breath and stare at the ceiling as I go over that last night we spent together for the ten-thousandth time.

If I knew it was to be our last night together I would have done more, said more, done anything to make him stay.

The door opens, and I roll over. My heart catches in my chest.

"Ben," I whisper.

He walks in and closes the door behind him, his hands clenching at his sides. He seems nervous.

I frown into the diluted light as I watch him.

"I wanted to see you," he whispers.

I lie still. He can do the talking this time.

"I look at you like I want you..." He pauses and clenches his hands at his sides. "...because I do," he whispers.

I frown.

"You have no idea how badly I want you, Bridget, or how hard it is for me to stay away."

"Then why? Why are you doing this to us?" I whisper.

He sits on the side of the bed and cups my face in his hands, his eyes searching mine in the moonlit room as his thumb gently dusts over my bottom lip. He hesitates, and frowns as if pained. "I'm not who you think I am."

I sit up, resting on my elbow, and I frown as I watch him. "Are you married?" I whisper. Oh, no. My heart starts to hammer. He has a whole other life in South Africa, doesn't he? I have no idea what's going on at home for him.

He shakes his head, and a soft smile crosses his face. "No, I'm not married." He frowns harder, and leans in to kiss me softly. "But I'm not able to give you my heart." Tears fill my eyes.

He shakes his head. "Please..." He pauses. "Know that I love you,

Bridget."

"Ben," I whisper. "What's going on? Talk to me."

He leans in and sweeps his tongue gently between my lips, and I scrunch my face up to fight the tears.

It's there again, the urge to tell him that I love him.

This man makes me so weak.

I sit up and wrap my arms around his broad shoulders. We kiss slowly, and I feel my arousal start to rise.

"I've come to say goodbye," he whispers against my lips.

"What?" My eyes search his again. "But you said—"

He cuts me off. "I can't be who you want me to be, Bridget."

"Yes, you can, Ben. You're who I want," I whisper angrily. Damn it, I hate this sneaking around shit. I can't even raise my voice the way I want to.

He runs his thumb over my cheekbone as he studies my face. "I have a past, Didge, one that I don't want to ever catch up with you. I won't bring that into your life."

I shake my head. "What are you talking about? We all have a past. We can work it out together, Ben."

"Goodbye, Bridget," he whispers sadly before he tries to stand, but I grab his wrist.

"No. Don't go," I beg as I lose control. "Don't leave me. I love you."

He bends and kisses me gently. "Remember me with love, angel." I stare at him through my tears.

"I love you," he whispers.

I suddenly become panicked. "Don't go," I beg.

He stares at me in the darkness.

I shake my head, unable to stand it. I need more time. I need more time to try and make him stay. "One more time," I whisper. "Say goodbye to me properly."

"Bridget," he breathes.

"Ben, it's just the two of us here." I pull him down to kiss his lips softly. "If you want to say goodbye to me, do it when you have to. I can't bear to let you go tonight." My voice cracks in pain.

"Baby, *shh*." He calms me as he sweeps the hair back from my forehead and studies my face. "It will be all right."

"How can it be all right if you're leaving me?" I whisper through tears.

He takes me in his arms and we cling to each other tightly; so tight that it feels like I might break if I let him go. Maybe I will.

"I need you," I murmur against his lips as he kisses me. His tongue dances with mine as his hand roams over my hip and he squeezes it with force.

"Bridget," he murmurs, and I know that he's having an internal battle with himself.

He wants me, but he thinks this is the wrong thing to do.

But making love to Ben could never be wrong, and I'll face those consequences tomorrow. I slowly sit up and slide my white silk nightdress over my shoulders and throw it onto the floor. His eyes drop hungrily to my breasts. I lay back and spread my legs as a silent invitation. His eyes drop to the crotch of my pale pink panties.

His eyes darken and his tongue darts out to swipe over his bottom lip.

Oh... he wants me all right.

I run my hand up over my breast and squeeze it. "It's been six weeks since you've been inside me, Ben." I arch my back off the bed. "I can't stand another moment without you."

He frowns, and I see the last of his resistance teetering on the edge. "Fill me up, big boy. Make sure I never forget you."

His jaw clenches as his eyes flicker with arousal, and he stands in one quick movement to take his T-shirt off over his head.

My eyes roam over his thick, broad chest that's covered with a scattering of dark hair. His arms are huge, and I can see every muscle in his stomach. The distinct V of muscles that disappear into his jeans holds me captive. I drag my eyes to his perfect face, and my heart somersaults in my chest. He has the most beautiful body in the world... but it's his soul that I love. The dominant alpha man who has shown me what it's like to really love someone.

What it feels like to be adored and loved by someone so deeply that nothing else matters.

He knows what my body needs more than I do, and I wriggle on the bed as he slides his jeans down his legs. My mouth goes dry.

Holy fucking hell. He's a god.

His thick, hard cock hangs heavily between his legs, and he takes it in his hand to stroke it three times as his eyes hold mine.

"You want this, Bridget?" he whispers as he strokes himself.

I nod as my mouth goes dry, my eyes fixed on the pre-ejaculate that drips from the end. *Fuck, yeah.*

"You get over here and suck me. Make sure I never forget you."

Our eyes lock, and he gives me the best 'come fuck me' look I've ever seen.

Suddenly, I'm desperate. Desperate to please him.

Desperate to make him stay.

I scramble towards him on my knees and take him deep in my mouth. He inhales sharply.

"Good girl," he breathes as his hands fall to the back of my head.

My insides begin to melt, and I moan around him. He

pushes himself deep—so deep—and his eyes close in pleasure. I have to concentrate to block my gag reflex.

Fucking hell. Bringing him to his undoing is my favourite thing in the whole damn world.

He hisses as he builds a rhythm, my hair gripped tightly in his hands.

"Fuck, fuck, fuck," he murmurs under his breath.

"You like that, baby?" I whisper around him.

His eyes flicker with arousal. "I fucking... love that," he pants. A sheen of perspiration covers his skin and it revs me up even more.

He loses control and throws me onto the bed. I bounce high and then he's on me as he slides my panties down and throws them in the air, off the bed.

His lips trail down over my breasts, and he takes them into his mouth to suck them one at a time. His suction is so hard that my face scrunches up in pain and my back arches off the bed.

This is what he does to me.

He gets me so hot for him that I beg him to be rough, like I'm some kind of crazy animal beneath him that needs to be tamed.

Controlled.

His lips drop lower... and lower... and I hold my breath and close my eyes.

Oh, dear God, he's amazing at this.

The king.

His tongue sweeps through my flesh, and he grabs my legs and forces them back to the mattress. "Open up," he growls as his dark eyes hold mine. He tenderly kisses my inner thigh.

This is too much, too intense, too intimate. I look away.

"Watch me, Bridget," he commands.

I drag my eyes back to his.

"You watch my tongue lick up your cream and make this pretty little cunt dance." He licks his lips and sucks me again. The look of sheer pleasure on his face makes me blush.

I begin to convulse. For fuck's sake. How is one man so hot?

He bites my clitoris and I throw my head back and come in a rush.

Fuck's sake, I lasted two minutes.

He smiles as he licks me up, and then lifts one of my legs and then the other over his shoulders. In one sharp movement, Ben slams home deep.

"Ben!" I cry out.

"I got you, babe," he murmurs against my lips, and lies down on me.

Then he kisses me, and it's soft and tender and caring and... God.

This can't end. What we have is too good to ever end.

As if sensing my feelings, his face creases with pain against mine and he holds me that bit closer.

His body starts to ride mine. Long, slow, and deep. Our eyes are locked, and damn, this is the best sex I've ever had in my entire life.

Who am I kidding?

Every time with Ben is the best time of my life. The man is one hell of a lover.

Perspiration covers us as we drink each other in.

"Now..." he whispers, sensing his fast-approaching climax. "You need to come *now*." He picks up the pace and I clench around him.

He moans a guttural sound and buries his head deep into my neck, while I smile at the ceiling.

You won't forget this in a hurry, big boy.

His pumping gets harder and deeper, faster and faster, and I clench around him before I fall.

"Ahh..." I breathe.

I scrunch my eyes shut to stop the tears. He moans as he comes deep inside me.

We kiss, for a long time. It's soft and tender, and his body is still in mine, slowly emptying itself with slow pumps.

"I love you, Ben," I whisper.

"I love you, too," he breathes as he rests his head against my cheek. He pauses for a moment. "That's why I have to leave you." He pulls out of my body in one quick rush.

What? I sit up. *No.* "What are you talking about?" I whisper. "We can work it out."

His eyes search mine. "This is goodbye, Bridget; don't make this any harder than it already is."

"Ben..." I whisper. My body is still throbbing from the beating he just gave it.

He pulls on his clothes and I watch on in silence.

Don't go. Please, don't go.

With one last, lingering kiss, he stands and leaves my room without looking back.

I stare at the door after it closes behind him.

No. Please, God.

That didn't just happen.

Despair fills me.

I curl into a ball. My heart physically hurts in my chest, and I weep.

To continue reading this story it is available on Amazon now.

AFTERWORD

Thank you so much for reading and
for your ongoing support
I have the most beautiful readers in the whole world!

Keep up to date with all the latest news
and online discussions by joining the Swan Squad VIP
Facebook group and discuss your favourite
books with other readers.
@tlswanauthor

Visit my website for updates and new release information.
www.tlswanauthor.com

ABOUT THE AUTHOR

T L Swan is a Wall Street Journal, USA Today, and #1 Amazon Best Selling author. With millions of books sold, her titles are currently translated in twenty languages and have hit #1 on Amazon in the USA, UK, Canada, Australia and Germany. She is currently writing the screenplays for a number of her titles. Tee resides on the South Coast of NSW, Australia with her husband and their three children where she is living her own happy ever after with her first true love.